Praise for the novels of
ELIZABETH
LOWELL

"Romantic suspense is her true forte."
Minneapolis Star-Tribune

"Lowell manages to balance
the right amount of intrigue [and] romance. . . .
[Her] characters come alive."
Columbia State (MD)

"Lowell is adept . . . at writing gripping suspense."
Stuart News (FL)

"I've read at least a dozen books by Lowell,
and I can say with confidence that I would crawl
on hands and knees across carpet tacks
if I thought it would get me a few hours
with almost any one of her heroes."
Akron Beacon Journal

"Lowell's keen ear for dialogue and
intuitive characterizations consistently set her
a cut above most writers in this genre."
Charlotte News & Observer

"I'll buy any book with
Elizabeth Lowell's name on it."
Jayne Ann Krentz

By Elizabeth Lowell

WHIRLPOOL • ALWAYS TIME TO DIE
THE SECRET SISTER • DEATH IS FOREVER
THE COLOR OF DEATH • DIE IN PLAIN SIGHT
RUNNING SCARED • MOVING TARGET
MIDNIGHT IN RUBY BAYOU • PEARL COVE
JADE ISLAND • AMBER BEACH

WINTER FIRE • AUTUMN LOVER
ENCHANTED • FORBIDDEN • UNTAMED
ONLY LOVE • ONLY YOU
ONLY MINE • ONLY HIS

EDEN BURNING • THIS TIME LOVE
BEAUTIFUL DREAMER • REMEMBER SUMMER
DESERT RAIN • WHERE THE HEART IS
TO THE ENDS OF THE EARTH • LOVER IN THE ROUGH
A WOMAN WITHOUT LIES • FORGET ME NOT

And in Hardcover

THE WRONG HOSTAGE

ELIZABETH
LOWELL

WHIRLPOOL

(Originally published as *The Ruby*)

AVON BOOKS
An Imprint of HarperCollins*Publishers*

This book was originally published, with the author writing under the name Ann Maxwell, as *The Ruby* by HarperCollins in January 1995 and reissued May 1999.

This is a work of fiction. Names, characters, places, and incidents are products of the author's imagination or are used fictitiously and are not to be construed as real. Any resemblance to actual events, locales, organizations, or persons, living or dead, is entirely coincidental.

AVON BOOKS
An Imprint of HarperCollins*Publishers*
10 East 53rd Street
New York, New York 10022-5299

Copyright © 1995, 2006 by Two of a Kind, Inc.
Excerpt from *The Wrong Hostage* copyright © 2006 by Two of a Kind, Inc.
ISBN-13: 978-0-06-051113-5
ISBN-10: 0-06-051113-3
www.avonbooks.com

First Avon Books paperback printing: November 2006
First HarperCollins special printing: May 1999
First HarperCollins paperback printing: January 1995

Avon Trademark Reg. U.S. Pat. Off. and in Other Countries, Marca Registrada, Hecho en U.S.A.
HarperCollins® is a registered trademark of HarperCollins Publishers Inc.

Printed in the U.S.A.

10 9 8 7 6 5 4 3 2 1

Prologue

Jamie Swann really didn't want to put his daughter on the firing line. He just didn't have any other choice. Reluctantly he handed over a package and special label to the freight agent. A hundred-dollar bill went with the label.

The money vanished into the man's pocket. The label went on the box. Before Swann could change his mind, the package was on a conveyer belt, headed for an airplane. Without a word he turned and hurried toward the part of the airport which handled human cargo. He had to beat the package to California.

If he didn't . . .

Swann didn't want to think about it.

I'm sorry, baby.

But don't worry. I'll get there before they do.

The contents of the package were priceless. Yet in Swann's world, everything had a price.

Even his daughter's life.

1

When the pager on Cruz Rowan's belt went off, he was waist deep in a hole the size of a grave, hacking away at debris in front of a rock wall, trying to find order at the edge of chaos.

The pager wasn't impressed by his search. It kept on beeping.

With a grunted curse Cruz stabbed at the pager button and went right on digging. Only his boss had the pager number. At the moment, he wasn't interested in talking to Cassandra Redpath. He had more important things on his mind.

He wielded the twelve-pound pickax as easily as other men would swing a hammer. Each time the pick smashed rhythmically into rock, loose soil and chips of stone flew up and stung his face like birdshot. He ignored it. When he was chasing a ground fault, trying to discover if the earth had opened up a year ago or a century or an eon, he didn't care about personal comfort. Human years and human fears meant nothing to geological time.

Cruz liked that as much as he did the workout the rock

was giving him. His short dark brown hair was nearly black with sweat. His naked back dripped like he'd just come from a shower.

After a time he set aside the pick, stretched, wiped sweat from his eyes, and grabbed a nearby shovel. With the easy movements of a man who was naturally coordinated and unusually fit, he attacked the rubble, clearing it away one shovelful at a time. At just under six feet, he wasn't a particularly big man, but he was solidly built. The sun was a heat lamp on his hardworking body.

While Cruz pursued the tantalizing fault, he didn't notice the heat, the clouds of grit, or the increasing fatigue of his body. He was used to ignoring comfort in favor of the hunt, whether he was chasing scientific facts or international crooks.

Despite the sun, despite the ache across his back and arms, despite the stubborn rock, he kept digging, chasing a strand of geological truth that had been ancient long before he was born. To him the fault lines in the earth were as fascinating as the flaws in human souls.

The fault that had piqued his curiosity revealed itself for just a few feet in a wall of rock before diving underground beneath a cape of debris. Though small, the fault fascinated him.

It was in the wrong place.

There were dozens of faults over on the other side of the nameless flat-floored rift valley southwest of the Salton Sea. All those faults were offshoots of the famous San Andreas. But the fault Cruz was sweating over was all alone, located in a sun-baked slot canyon that cut into the base of the Santa Rosa Mountains. The slot canyon was several miles away from any other fault lines.

Though modest to the point of invisibility, the isolated

crack suggested new activity beneath the seamed surface of the land. He'd been all over the crack like a wolf on a lamb chop. His hobby and passion was to find signs of new seismic activity, tracks of weakness or stress. He believed that fault lines—unlike people in general and women in particular—could be understood by anyone willing to spend enough time, sweat, and logic on the matter.

He was more than willing.

When he was out in the desert, reality changed. There were no clocks. No desperation. No split seconds to decide whether to kill and live or hold fire and die. No willfully naive media types to sell ad space with bloody pictures on the front page and antiviolence editorials on the back.

The desert didn't have any newspaper except anonymous tracks quickly scattered by the wind. The desert had no ads to sell and no editorial judgments to make. It didn't need any. The survivors left tracks and the losers left bones.

End of story.

Time in the desert wasn't a clock ticking seconds, minutes, hours. Desert time was the slow shrinking of shadows as noon approached, followed by an equally slow expansion of shadows until darkness flowed from every crack and crease to reclaim the land in a cool black tide.

Cruz loved the night as much as he loved the blazing sun itself. He loved standing in the desert, absorbing its silence into his soul, feeling peace well up inside him like a transparent spring. The desert was what had kept him sane when every institution and person he'd ever believed in had turned on him and demanded that he hate himself as much as they did. They had almost succeeded.

He'd been a long time pulling himself back from the brink.

Even now there were moments when he wondered how

close that brink still was. And if any of it was worth the cost. Those were the times he headed out into the desert. There he listened to the silence until there was no past, no present, no future, nothing but the desert around him like a benediction whispered by a generous god.

The beeper on Cruz's belt went off again.

With a muttered curse he jammed the shovel up to its rim in the rubble pile and stabbed the button on the pager, silencing it. Then he levered himself up out of the hole and got ready to head back to Risk Limited's headquarters in Karroo.

Cassandra Redpath beeped once if something was important enough to disturb Cruz even if he'd made it clear that he didn't want to be disturbed. If he chose to ignore the summons, fine. Redpath would look elsewhere.

Two beeps meant it was raining shit.

2

Laurel Swann touched the agate with the tip of her index finger. The translucent stone was smooth, cool, and had a single band of pale amber the exact color of her eyes. And her father's eyes. Seeing the color made her wonder where Jamie Swann was, if he was healthy or sick, thin or well fed, free or captive in some country whose name changed with every headline.

"Don't think about it," Laurel told herself aloud. Living alone as she did, without even a pet, made the house pretty quiet. Sometimes she broke the quiet by talking with herself. "There's nothing you can do about your father. He's old enough to know better. Hell, he's old enough to retire, get a cat, and write his memoirs."

The thought of it made her smile. Like her mother, Laurel couldn't stop caring about the man whose open smile and guarded eyes had shaped her life. Now that her mother was dead, there was only Laurel to care.

Slowly she turned the agate in the light from the north

window of her weathered A-frame cottage. Sunlight spilled over her workbench, making the stone glow like it held all the sunshine it had gathered during countless years of being tumbled by surf on a beach.

As a professional jewelry designer, Laurel had much more valuable gems in the safe in her workshop. That just made her appreciate the agate more. This stone was different, a small treasure discovered on the beach in front of her house. A clear agate like this was a slice of time, a memento of the forces that shaped the earth, the mingling of enduring rock and restless ocean.

There were tiny specks scattered through the agate, dark bits of the stone's history preserved in a crystalline frame. The flaws made the agate more interesting to Laurel than perfection would have been. As she turned the stone in the light, she began creating a design in her mind. A simple setting of flowing gold would bring out the best in the agate. A geometrical silver setting would kill the stone's beauty.

That was the endless fascination of making jewelry. Each stone challenged her to create a setting that was as unusual and enduring as the gemstone itself.

The rattle of a truck turning into Laurel's steep driveway broke her concentration. Frowning, she set aside the agate and looked out the ground-floor window of her small house. A delivery van was idling just outside. The driver had driven down to the garage level, saving her a trip upstairs to the street.

Even so, she wasn't happy to see the truck. She hadn't ordered anything, which meant that someone was sending something back to her. Not good news. Selling jewelry on consignment was a chancy way to make a living.

"Damn. There go the new tires for my car."

Mentally rebalancing her checkbook, Laurel headed from

her workroom and opened the small door that connected to the garage. The living area of the house was overhead, on the same level as the street. It was an odd, cramped arrangement common to Cambria houses that had begun life as weekend beach cabins but had been transformed into full-time residences when land prices soared.

Outside, the driver hopped down from the van and headed toward the open garage door. He carried a clipboard in his right hand. He'd stuffed a rectangular box under his left arm. The box was big enough to be awkward, but obviously it wasn't very heavy.

"Hi, Tom," Laurel said. She received and sent parcels often enough to be on a first-name basis with several delivery agents.

"Hello, Ms. Swann."

Tom tried to be casual, but he spent too long looking at her. He started at her cap of black hair, took in the loose man's shirt she wore knotted to one side, and lingered on jeans whose snug fit came from countless washings. Though she spent no time trying to catch a man's eye, there was an offhand sensuality to her that was more attractive than the overproduced blondes that California turned out with numbing regularity. Those blondes were spectacular, but not for the likes of a deliveryman. Laurel Swann, on the other hand, was a real woman.

Guiltily, Tom switched his attention back to his job. "Is it your birthday?" he asked.

"Nope."

"This week, maybe?"

"Nope." Though she smiled pleasantly enough, she didn't say anything more.

He sighed, accepting that this contact was going to be like all the rest had been. Business, plain and simple. He began flipping slowly through papers, finding the one for her to sign.

Laurel kept her professional manner in place. She was so accustomed to holding men well beyond arm's length that she hardly noticed any longer that she was doing it. Watching her parents cope with love, anger, regret, rage, despair, and finally divorce had taught her that diamonds might be forever, but a relationship wasn't.

And if it wasn't forever, it wasn't worth the pain.

"Well," Tom said, "this must be your lucky day. Somebody's sending you a big present."

She made a sound that could have meant anything. Like most jewelry makers, she shipped her work materials without fanfare. She hid gold and even parcels of precious stones in plain sight beneath brown wrapping paper and ordinary packing tape.

But she'd just gotten a shipment of gold from her Armenian metals broker on Hill Street in Los Angeles. She wasn't expecting anything interesting to come her way—unless finding new ways to stretch a dollar qualified as interesting.

"Here you go," Tom said.

Laurel took the box in both hands. Ten pounds. Perhaps more. Certainly not much less. She gave a mental sigh of relief.

I haven't mailed out pounds of jewelry to anyone, so they can't be returning it to me.

"Need any help?" Tom asked.

"No, thanks. I handle heavier stuff all the time." She looked at the label. There wasn't a return address on the waybill. "Well, I hope no one's made a mistake."

"What do you mean?"

"I'm not expecting anything and there's no return address on this. Can you tell me where it came from?"

Eagerly the man leaned forward, happy to have an excuse to prolong the contact with her. He inspected the waybill on the box, saw that she was right, and muttered beneath his breath about hiring part-time help for full-time jobs.

"Back in a sec," he said.

Laurel watched as he went to the van, grabbed a handheld scanner from the dashboard, and waved it across the barcode sticker that was attached to one corner of the box.

"Huh," he said.

"Something wrong?"

"The waybill is domestic, but the bar code gives me an international routing number, like the shipment originated overseas. Who do you know in Tokyo?"

"No one."

The response was automatic and probably untrue. Her father's last letter had come from Tokyo.

Laurel discussed Jamie Swann with no one.

Part of it was her natural sense of privacy. Most of it was because as a child she'd had it drilled into her that no one—and that included her mother—knew where Jamie Swann was or wasn't. All questions about Laurel's father were to be ducked, ignored, or answered with bland lies. If the questioner became too persistent, her mother called an unlisted number.

End of questions.

"It must have come through a customs broker," the driver said slowly. "It was shipped out of Los Angeles International Airport late yesterday."

Laurel searched her memory once more for an international shipment she might have coming.

There wasn't one.

Silently she wondered if her father was on his way to her home once more, turning her life upside down with his easy charm and bleak eyes. Sometimes she was curious about what Swann saw and did during his long absences.

Most of the time she was glad she didn't know.

"Thanks," Laurel said to the driver. "I'm sure there's a packing list inside."

"If not, give me a call."

"Mmm," was all she said.

With a final impersonal smile, she went back into her house and shouldered the door shut behind her. She glanced again at the package.

Nothing had changed. It was still a shipping label with no return address.

Suddenly the package's weight triggered a memory of her mother's funeral urn filled with cremated remains. A ripple of gooseflesh went down Laurel's arms.

Quickly she walked to what once had been the main room of the cottage and now was her studio. She'd been working on a large, elegant brooch of bent gold wire for a client's wife. Actually, Laurel suspected it was for the client's mistress.

Just one more reason not to put up with a man, Laurel thought with grim humor. *You can't trust them even when their work keeps them close to home.*

She cleared away the bending jig to make room for the unexpected package. Casually she cut the shipping tape with the wickedly curved knife she used for cutting paper templates. As she peeled away layers of reinforced cardboard and bubble paper, a wooden box slowly appeared. Her breath came in with a rushing sound.

This was no ordinary shipping container.

The box was a work of art. Heavily lacquered, unmarked, it had been created from a pale blond wood whose grain was finer than any furniture Laurel had ever seen.

"Can it be birch?" she asked softly. "Lord, it's nearly as

fine as ivory. It reminds me of something I saw once. Was it in a museum?"

She couldn't remember. With an impatient sound she examined the box's construction. The corners were mitered and reinforced. Though the box had a seam down the longer axis, the position of the latch told her that the box was meant to stand on end.

After setting the box upright, she undid the small brass latch. The front half of the box divided and swung open like the doors of a well-made cabinet.

"My. God."

She blinked, shook her head, and blinked again.

A jeweled egg winked back at her.

Even though she was shocked, she couldn't help smiling at the egg's sheer beauty. It was nested in pale, creamy satin that set off the intense scarlet of the egg's lacquer work. A net of gemstone-studded gold flowed over the egg in a pattern subtly enhanced by the shape of the egg itself.

The objet d'art was almost the size of an ostrich egg, yet it was so exquisitely made that Laurel had a hard time believing it was real. Wonderingly she touched the egg with her fingertip, as she had the beach agate. Like the agate, the egg was cool, solid, real.

For a time she simply stared at the unexpected piece of art. Then reason took over, prodding her out of her bemusement.

She looked critically at the box. There wasn't a maker's mark. Bending over the box, she inhaled deeply. There was no faint savor of wood or glue telling her that the box had been recently made in a nameless Third World sweatshop. In fact, the more closely she inspected the box, the more clear it became that the box was the result of a long tradition of craftsmanship that was as exacting as that of the egg itself.

And like the egg, the box did its job perfectly.

Laurel knew her first feelings of surprise and pleasure at the egg's beauty were exactly what the artist had intended. As a designer, she'd learned that a good piece of decorative art was much more than a handful of expensive metals and flashing gems. A good objet d'art should make viewers catch their breath and then smile with pleasure.

The egg was a spectacularly successful piece, as close to flawless on first sight as anything she'd ever seen. She wondered how many people had reacted to this egg in the way she had.

And how many years it had been hidden away in the private safe of a collector—or a Soviet commissar.

"But it can't be what I think it is," she said in a raw whisper. "He never made one like this."

She bent down to see what she could of the egg without touching it. The gold scrollwork was finely made. If there were flaws in the design or execution, she couldn't spot them without a magnifying glass. The red enamel of the shell was as perfect as a human hand could make it. The small gems set in colorful precision were clear and so clean she could hardly believe they were natural.

Automatically she reached for her jeweler's loupe. She examined stone after stone under the loupe's ten-power magnification. A few tiny feathers and dark specks, invisible to the naked eye, convinced her that the stones were imperfect enough to have been created by nature.

Under magnification the stones confirmed something else. The facets were just irregular enough to suggest that they had been cut before computers took over and created the monotonously regular, sterile gemstones that she so disliked.

"Fabergé. It has to be."

The scarlet egg had been created in the workshop of the most famous craftsman Europe had ever produced.

"But that can't be. It must be a fraud."

She frowned and examined the egg again. After a long time she straightened, sighed, and set aside the loupe. If the egg was a fraud, it was a fraud so meticulously created that it was a masterpiece in its own right.

Again Laurel looked at the label on the wrapper. Again she saw her own name and address.

A chill rippled down her spine.

In the past, Jamie Swann had sent her bright stones from various parts of the world, silent apologies from an absent father. Yet even taken all together, the stones he'd sent wouldn't come close to touching the worth of a Fabergé egg.

"A million bucks at least," she said in a low voice. "Probably a lot more, if it can be authenticated and sold openly."

But she wasn't naive enough to believe that a national treasure could be bought and sold on the open market like oil futures.

Her father wasn't that naive either.

"Daddy, where the hell are you when I need you?" she said loudly, then grimaced as her own words echoed in the empty room. "Dumb question. You're exactly where you always were when Mom or I needed you. Somewhere else."

Laurel began to think about all the unhappy reasons why her father might have sent her a million-dollar gift with no warning and no return address. The longer she thought, the more certain she became. Somewhere on the violent face of the earth, Jamie Swann was in trouble.

And now, so was she.

3

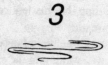

Southern California
Monday

A shiny Grumman Gulfstream executive jet flashed low over Cruz Rowan's head and turned onto final approach. There was only one runway within reach, the six-thousand-foot private landing strip owned and maintained by Risk Ltd., Cassandra Redpath's international security firm. The cryptic design on the Gulfstream's fuselage was the Risk Ltd. logo, which meant that a new client was on the way to Karroo.

A client who was the source of the two-beep summons.

After a last regretful look at the fascinating crack in the bedrock, Cruz picked up his day pack, climbed aboard a battered ATV, and kicked its engine to life. Once he left the jumbled rock floor of the slot canyon behind, he twisted the throttle hard and headed back across the slope toward Karroo at forty miles an hour.

And with every bump, he wondered what had blown up, and where.

The last time Redpath had beeped him twice, he'd ended up negotiating at gunpoint for the release of an Italian businessman's son. The boy had survived with no more than rope burns on his wrists to show for the experience.

Cruz hadn't been as lucky. He'd recovered enough to run and walk without a limp, but his left knee still ached with every change in the weather.

When he pulled up to the main house in a cloud of grit, Cassandra Redpath was waiting in the shade of the ramada she'd built with her own hands. The structure was open on all sides to the wind and thatched on top to provide shade. She'd been so intrigued by the native structure that she'd done a short monograph on the ramada's name. She postulated that the Soboba Indians had adopted the name from the Spanish *ramada,* which in turn sprang from Ramadan, Arabic for "the hot month." The Spanish had taken the name from the Moors and then traveled halfway around the world to give it to a prehistoric Native American invention that was both ceremonial and practical.

Redpath savored those kinds of unlikely historical linkages. They strengthened her conviction that mankind was connected by language and human need, even as it was separated by politics and greed.

"Where's the fire?" Cruz asked as he walked into the ramada's ragged shade.

Redpath squinted up at him. He was still a black shadow silhouetted against the burning light of day.

He had no such disadvantage in watching her. The subdued light beneath the ramada revealed a lean, sun-weathered woman in cotton slacks and shirt, short red hair shot through with gray, and green eyes. Redpath was in her fifties or early sixties. Cruz had never been sure which, and it hadn't ever mattered enough to ask.

He knew that Redpath had started out in life as an academic historian, specifically a student of everyday life in other eras. But she'd an unusual turn of mind that allowed her to see patterns in contemporary life that others missed. As a result, she'd spent thirty years as an analyst and then as a senior executive with the Central Intelligence Agency. She'd resigned from the CIA to become U.S. ambassador to the United Nations. She'd held that post for four years.

Then she'd resigned in disgust and formed Risk Ltd.

"You're blocking my view of the fire," she said.

He stepped aside, turned, and followed her glance. Heat shimmered up off the blacktop runway where the company Mercedes waited, distorting the shape of the Grumman until it looked like something from a horror show. The airplane's door opened. A staircase emerged like a rumpled steel tongue.

After a few moments, a figure appeared in the doorway of the aircraft. He seemed to hesitate.

Redpath smiled. "Some people are intimidated by the Mojave Desert."

"Good. Too many people out here as it is."

Redpath ignored Cruz.

A man descended the stairway to the hot tarmac. Two steps behind, like a well-trained hound, came another man. The second man was taller and dressed all in black. Even at this distance, he looked stooped but powerful, a strong man who had to lean down to fit into the ordinary world.

Cruz didn't identify Redpath's welcoming committee until he moved toward the plane. Sergeant-Major Ranulph Gillespie was a big man who didn't bend knee or neck for much on earth. He was also a former operator and instructor in the British Army's Twenty-second Special Air Services Regiment, a professional soldier, and one of the most deadly counterterrorists in the world.

The sergeant-major briskly stowed his passengers in the

backseat of the Mercedes, climbed aboard, and headed at a crawl down the shimmering runway toward Karroo's headquarters. The passengers would get a good long up-close look at the ageless crucible of the desert.

With a catlike sound of satisfaction, Redpath turned to Cruz. Her generous mouth turned down as she looked at him. In his dirty jeans and sweat-darkened, unbuttoned blue work shirt, he looked like a hard-rock miner at the end of his shift rather than the highly educated, thoroughly trained operative he was. His hair was streaked with grit, he hadn't shaved for several days, and he needed a bath.

The pale, glittering slits of blue that were his eyes warned that he was not a happy camper.

That made two of them.

Cruz noted the thinning of Redpath's mouth and the narrowing of her eyes. He didn't need a road map to know where she was going. She required a minimum level of personal cleanliness in her employees. At the moment, he was well below her standard.

"I'm off duty," he said. "Remember?"

"I could have called Bob Williams, I suppose," Redpath said.

"But you want your best, right? So you'll have to take me the way you find me. And so will our client."

She shrugged. "Even if you were willing—"

"I'm not."

"—to clean up, it's too late," she finished, ignoring the interruption.

Cruz glanced toward the Mercedes. It was still too far away to make out the sex, much less the faces, of the passengers. Gillespie still hadn't kicked up the speed, which told Cruz that Redpath wasn't thrilled with the client.

"Who is it this time?" he asked. "Not the government of the Philippines again?"

"They can afford us."

"I know the president is a powerful personage, and I know they're still trying to recover the fortune a previous first lady invested in Italian footwear, but the woman is a major pain in the ass."

"How do you think women get to be president?" Redpath retorted. "Or ambassador, for that matter. I made a lot of people unhappy along the way."

"You still do."

"Thank you." She bared her teeth in a smile. "But the specimen coming closer with each breath isn't a female politician. He's from the artistic side of the political spectrum."

"Bloody wonderful," Cruz said under his breath. "They're the worst. What is he, a ballerina?"

"Our potential client is a curator of art for Russia."

"Does he have a name?"

Though Redpath didn't move, Cruz sensed that she was bracing herself.

"Aleksy Novikov," she said with outward calm.

"*Christ.*"

She waited for the rest of the explosion.

Silence.

The kind of silence where you could hear yourself sweat.

Finally Cruz asked softly, "Are you aware that Novikov and I have what is politely called a history?"

"Your paths crossed while you were with the FBI," she said. Her tone said that it didn't matter.

"Paths crossed," he said as if tasting the words. "That's one way of putting it. I spent six months chasing Novikov's charismatic ass all over Silicon Valley."

"Your approach was very creative."

"Not enough to get the job done."

"I disagree. Novikov was sent back home."

"I'd rather have given him a permanent home in a federal pen," Cruz said grimly. "Novikov's passport said he was a cultural attaché with the consulate in San Francisco, but we caught him with all kinds of classified material, as well as a basket of trade secrets from a company that was working on laser information retrieval technology for the Pentagon."

"In other words," Redpath said, "Novikov was an intelligence operative. Quite a good one, actually. If I could trust him, I would hire him myself. But . . ." She shrugged. She was too smart to trust Novikov.

"As far as the FBI was concerned, every Soviet diplomat was an intelligence operative," Cruz said. "Novikov had a real appetite for it. He just loved getting in a closet with that Cal Tech engineer. Wonder if the poor fool was tested for AIDS before he killed himself."

Redpath shrugged. "Novikov's sexual preferences are well known."

"It came as news to the engineer Novikov seduced, especially when the flashbulbs went off."

"Ancient history. Novikov is no longer a Soviet diplomat. He's a Russian, and the Russians are our friends."

Cruz smiled thinly. "If I thought you believed that, I'd quit. Nobody has friends in this brave new world."

Redpath's smile was feline, predatory. "That's why Risk Limited is doing so well."

"What does Novikov want with us?"

"I don't know."

"Good. Keep it that way. There are some things that don't come off with soap and water. Novikov is one of them."

"Risk Limited is a private agency. We don't have to take clients if what they want offends us."

"I'm offended just knowing that bastard is alive."

"It's time for you to get past what happened and get on with the rest of your life."

At first Cruz couldn't believe he'd heard Redpath correctly. In the years he'd worked for her, she'd never once mentioned the incident that had stripped him of everything that mattered to him in the world. Now she was talking about his humiliation with the offhand manner of a woman ordering a salad with dressing on the side.

Before Cruz could say anything, the Mercedes braked to a halt in a small swirl of dust. With military precision Sergeant-Major Gillespie slid out from behind the wheel, popped open the back door smartly, and stood aside to allow the prospective clients to step out.

Aleksy Novikov had straw-colored hair and androgynous features that were both handsome and beautiful. He was small and very well made, like a gymnast or a professional dancer. He moved with a grace that was fascinating, for it was neither male nor female but simply animal. Every eye was drawn to him. Every eye followed him.

Cruz had often thought that standing next to Novikov would be as close to being invisible as it got in this life.

Behind Novikov, a thickset man emerged from the car. He had haunted dark eyes, pallid skin, and a ragged black beard. The black suit he wore was made of dense felt. It was the wrong choice for the desert.

Novikov's suit was made of pale gray silk, Italian cut, understated and elegant. If the heat bothered him, it didn't show in his movements. His clear skin was only faintly flushed. His widely spaced gray eyes took in the clever desert landscaping in front of the headquarters building before pausing on the Joshua tree supports and Washingtonia palm-frond roof of the ramada.

"Surely you haven't gone native, luv?" Novikov asked, looking at Redpath.

She laughed and stepped forward, offering her hand. "You haven't changed, Aleksy."

"Nor have you, Ambassador, except to grow even more formidable." Smiling, he raised her hand to his lips, keeping a fingertip on her pulse point. "But your fingers still are soft and scented with roses."

Sourly Cruz noted that Novikov pulled off the hand-kissing and the compliment with his usual flawless grace. A glance at Gillespie told Cruz that he wasn't alone in his irritation.

"Thank you for coming out to the desert," Redpath said. "I know it's not to your taste."

Novikov's shrug was as elegant as his clothes. "It was a small test, no? If the mountain will not come to Muhammad, then Muhammad must care enough to undertake the journey."

"I'm surprised you cared enough," she said.

The Russian smiled thinly. "In my government, Risk Limited has many fans in high places."

Redpath's arched eyebrows were as measured as Novikov's smile.

"How odd," she said. "We certainly haven't done much business with the new Russia."

"No," agreed Novikov, "but you made enemies under the old regime. They still speak of you with great, ah, fervor."

"How very flattering." Redpath made no move to withdraw her hand from Novikov's. He could pull a gun on her and her pulse wouldn't jump. He was a very attractive man who didn't appeal to her at all. "But we aren't interested in fighting old wars. Risk Limited is a private security firm. Nothing more. Nothing less."

This time Novikov's smile was full and apparently spontaneous. It transformed his face the way sunrise transformed night.

"Direct. Succinct. Delightfully American." Novikov's lips brushed over Redpath's fingers again. "Do you always greet your new clients with that speech?"

Cruz had had enough of the hand-kissing and lethal charisma. He stepped out of the shadows into the pitiless light. "No. We save the speech for *potential* clients who think they can hire us to do illegal work."

The incandescent smile vanished from Novikov's face. He stared at Cruz for several long seconds before he turned back to Redpath.

"With men like Cruz Rowan on your staff," Novikov said, "I understand why you think a warning might be necessary. Truly, Ambassador, would it not be easier simply to avoid employing known criminals?"

Redpath withdrew her hand from Novikov's and said calmly, "Cruz is one of my most valued operatives."

"A pity," the Russian said in a neutral tone. "He tried to embarrass the Soviet government by planting evidence on me several years ago in San Francisco. He did such an inferior job that nothing came of it. Surely you can hire more adept operatives?"

"All that saved your slick ass was a diplomatic passport," Cruz said.

Novikov's tall, thickset companion stepped forward in a way that was meant to intimidate.

Cruz looked at the second Russian with a complete lack of interest. He'd taken down bigger men. It was the small ones you had to watch.

"Gapan," Novikov said softly.

The man called Gapan stepped back.

"I see you're still hiring out your muscle jobs," Cruz said. "Be a man, Aleksy. Tell the ambassador the whole truth, just for the novelty of it. What can it hurt? The game has been over for years, the score totaled, and the dead buried."

"It always was a game for you, wasn't it?" Novikov asked gently. "What a shame your government decided not to let you play anymore. Do you miss your toys?"

Cruz's eyes narrowed in the instant before he controlled his reaction.

The curve of Novikov's mouth was too cold to be called a smile. "I was in London for two years after I left San Francisco. My dear boy, how those British tabloids loved to hate you."

"I'm a regular prince, but I'm not your dear boy, now or ever."

"I have a confession," Novikov said, turning to Redpath. "I took an almost orgasmic pleasure in watching the FBI snip off Cruz Rowan's buttons and drum him out of the service."

Redpath shook her head and said something that sounded like, "Testosterone." Then she looked at Novikov and said clearly, "Cruz quit the FBI because I made him a better offer. I suspect you know that as well as I do."

Novikov flicked a spot of dust off his coat, dismissing the subject. And Cruz. "I can understand why Rowan would leap at the chance to work with your organization. Risk Limited is widely regarded as the most effective private security firm in the world."

Redpath smiled politely.

"What surprises me, luv," the Russian added, "is that you would have him."

"Nearly everyone involved in Risk Limited was once part

of one government agency or other," she said. "But all of us, myself included, left government service because we ran up against something we couldn't accept."

Novikov sent a cool glance in Cruz's direction.

Cruz gave it back with interest. He knew that Novikov was baiting him. What he didn't know was why. In the past, before his own private world came crashing down, Cruz wouldn't have cared about an enemy's motivation. He would have thrashed it out with Novikov one-on-one, and to hell with what or why.

But the past was dead, and Cruz had nearly died with it. He'd learned to get answers before he acted.

Most of the time.

Redpath looked from Cruz to Novikov. Her green eyes were shrewd, penetrating, and missed nothing. Like Cruz, she wondered why Novikov would bait a man whose services he required.

"In my case," she said, "I left government work because of a set of policies that paid more attention to the interests of banks and multinational corporations than it did to human needs."

"Very American of you," Novikov said.

Redpath gave him a sweet, gentle Mona Lisa smile that would have melted the heart of a marble statue. "Cruz Rowan has my complete confidence."

Cruz hid his own smile. When Redpath wanted to, she could make a man feel ten feet tall and handsome as Michelangelo's *David*.

She was also good at making men feel lower than a snake's ass.

Novikov didn't say a word.

"Being in the private sector has some disadvantages," Redpath said calmly. "We can't act as policemen or operatives."

The Russian didn't look convinced.

"We've lost our access to the old boy network of government agents that some of our competitors utilize so cleverly," she said. "We're on our own. On the other hand, we can take cases or turn them down as we see fit. And we do."

"You are free to employ whom you wish, of course," Novikov said. "So, of course, am I. As you pointed out, you have competitors."

"You appear to require that I disqualify Cruz for this job even before I know what you need from Risk Limited," Redpath said. "If you insist on that, I will decline your retainer. I assign operators. The client does not."

A flush showed briefly on Novikov's pale skin. He started to reply, then bit back the words before they were spoken.

"Of course," he said softly. "You are the professional. I am not."

"There are other professionals," she said. "If we make you uncomfortable, go to them."

"You are the organization that tracked down Marcos's billions," Novikov said. "You orchestrated the rescue of three Anglican priests in East Beirut. You rescued a CNN correspondent from headhunters in Borneo. You are, unfortunately, the best there is."

Redpath nodded. She knew even better than Novikov just how capable her organization was.

"I need the best," the Russian said simply.

"Why?"

Novikov looked at Cruz one final time, shrugged, and gave in. "One of Russia's greatest art treasures has gone missing."

"Which one?" Redpath asked.

"The Ruby Surprise."

Redpath looked blank. "I'm not familiar with it."

"The Ruby Surprise is the most important artifact to survive the Bolshevik era," Novikov explained. "It was only recently recovered by true Russian patriots."

Cruz and Gillespie looked at each other. Neither of them knew what Novikov was talking about. Even though Russia was selling off assets right and left in order to survive, there hadn't been any rumors of a high-level art theft.

"What, precisely, is the Ruby Surprise?" Redpath asked.

Novikov hesitated, then said the easiest part of the truth. "It's the last imperial egg made by Peter Carl Fabergé."

4

Above Colorado
Monday

Flying gave Damon Hudson a sexual thrill. No matter how often he climbed aboard the *Hi-Flyer One,* Hudson International's executive flagship, he felt a tingle somewhere below his belt, like a beautiful woman had just given him a lazy, sultry smile.

Perhaps it was the phallic look of the plane itself. The long, tapering fuselage of the Boeing 757 had glistened in the hazy sunlight that fell on the La Guardia Airport tarmac. In his mind Hudson could see the plane taking off, then thrusting through the air to thirty-five thousand feet, heading back to Los Angeles.

Or perhaps the sexual thrill was in the ostentation, the sultanlike opulence of the aircraft itself. A plane this large usually carried one hundred and eighty passengers, which meant that maintenance and upkeep were much too expensive for normal executive service.

Hi-Flyer One was Hudson's private plane partly because he knew the importance of a grand public presence. But most of it was simply that he liked doing things in an imperial manner. He'd ordered the plane directly from Boeing. Then he'd furnished it with Middle Eastern carpets, Chinese silk wall coverings, and antiques from all over the world.

The aircraft's cost had been charged off against Hudson International, a public company with thousands of stockholders. Yet Damon Hudson regarded the plane as his personal property, regardless of what a few unhappy investors and narrow-minded busybodies from the Securities and Exchange Commission had to say.

There was plenty for small minds to complain about. *Hi-Flyer One* was among the most grandiose executive aircraft in the world. The forward portion of the plane was given over to staff and guests. They flew in comfort, but hardly in style. The back half of the plane was Hudson's very own pleasure dome. It was equipped with the latest in communications gear, a discriminating collection of erotic art, and often the most alluring sex workers in the world.

Though Hudson was a man of relentless sexual appetite, he was far too shrewd to seek release in circumstances where his control wasn't absolute. He hadn't become grossly rich by being stupid about his pleasures.

Hudson International was the third time up the ladder of success for him. Two of his previous business concerns had ballooned and then collapsed. Each time he'd escaped with his personal fortune intact. And each time he'd left behind wreckage that would have destroyed the reputation of a lesser man or a man with a lesser public relations staff. Now in his seventh decade and his third career, Hudson was a master of corporate and human manipulation.

The president and CEO of Hudson International drew a deep breath of the plane's carefully purified air. He breathed clean air as much as he could, and bottled oxygen when he had to. He also was extremely finicky about water and food. He intended to live to be at least one hundred.

More important, he was going to stay virile every minute of that life.

With crisp movements, he shed his coat, pulled off his tie, and rolled up the sleeves of his white broadcloth cotton shirt. Then he put on a loosely woven cotton sweater. It was tight enough to show the world that while his chest had thickened with the years, he had a flatter and harder belly than most men three decades younger.

For a moment he stood in front of the full-length mirror that hung on one bulkhead wall between original Vargas nudes. He inspected himself the same way he would have inspected a prospective whore—carefully, critically, almost clinically. He was still handsome, with a full head of steel-colored hair and a smooth, unwrinkled face that glowed with pink-cheeked English health. He looked forty. He'd achieved this effect as he had his other successes.

Pure illusion.

At the age of sixty-five, when most men began the descent to sickness and oblivion, he'd undergone a complete make-over by a famed French plastic surgeon. The treatment had involved nips, tucks, liposuction, and implants. The recuperation had taken three months, but the result was just short of miraculous. The photo his public relations staff had planted in *People* magazine showed a man whose appearance most men over forty would envy.

It had been almost eight years since that transformation. He'd gone through several tucks and lifts since then. The black eyes and the ugly bruising took weeks to heal, but they kept his face taut.

There were other therapies, too, ones that were less well known and far more intimate. These treatments were intensely painful, but they were effective, the equivalent of putting a new ink cartridge in a well-used yet still useful Mont Blanc.

Hudson was convinced that he'd mastered the process of physical aging. He'd locked himself in an expensive time capsule, remaining stationary while those around him got older or less virile, which in his mind was the same thing. He relished every moment of his surgical rejuvenation, especially when he came into contact with men of his own generation.

Satisfied by his daily ritual of inspection, he went to the burnished cherry Federal Period writing table at one end of the suite. He would rather have called for the two women who were waiting for him in the forward cabin, but he had business to take care of first. As much as he was driven by his own sexuality, he'd learned that delay only made the climax better.

With a throttled, impatient sound, he picked up the cell phone. He disliked using the cellular because it made eavesdropping easier for his enemies. Encoding the calls made it more difficult for spies to pick information out of the air, but nothing was wholly secure. An encoded conversation could be recorded and decoded at leisure. While he regularly recorded his own conversations, he hated having others record *him*. But when he was flying, he hadn't any choice except the cell phone or the even more public radio.

The first and most important call Hudson made was to his Los Angeles office.

"Hudson Museum," the woman at the other end of the line said. "How may I help you?"

"This is Hudson. Is Aleksy around?"

"Oh, Mr. Hudson, good afternoon."

The voice belonged to his personal secretary. Knowing his

habits with employees, she didn't wait for a polite greeting from him. Hudson had no patience for little social rituals.

"Mr. Novikov isn't here right now," she said quickly.

Hudson grunted. "Where is he?"

"He didn't say where he was going."

"When will he be back?"

"He didn't say."

"What *did* he say?" Hudson asked impatiently.

"Nothing, sir. He seemed rather upset about something, but he didn't say what it was."

Uneasiness slithered through Hudson. He'd invested an extravagant amount of money in the Hudson Museum's new building. He'd spent almost as much simply to bring "The Splendors of Russia" show to Los Angeles for his museum's first exhibit. That exhibit opened on Friday.

It had to be a success.

The money for building the museum and securing the exhibit had come from the operating funds of Hudson International. He must have a very good museum opening on Friday to offset complaints from stockholders who felt it was more important to pay dividends than to construct museums for Hudson International's extensive art collections. Hudson's collections, actually.

"Find the effete little bastard and find him fast," Hudson said.

"Yes, sir."

"We're paying his government a hell of a lot of money for this show, yet that catamite acts like he's in charge."

"Yes, sir."

Hudson had complained about Novikov to everyone from the Russian minister of culture to his closest allies in the president's office, but the complaints had been turned away with surprising coolness. Everyone said the same thing:

Mr. Novikov has our fullest support. You would do well to follow his aesthetic advice.

"He better be back in time for the press briefing," Hudson said harshly. "The media is the most important part of the show."

"Yes, sir."

"I'm not some dumb podiatrist from Wichita. I've been supporting Russian art and culture longer than that little faggot has been alive."

"Yes, sir."

"What about the displays? Are they in place?"

"Shall I check, sir?"

"No. Get me Novikov's assistant."

"I believe Mr. Gapan went with Mr. Novikov."

Hudson began cursing with complete disregard for federal regulations regarding profanity, obscenity, and the airwaves.

"I pay the Russians a fortune for the exhibit, and the only cocksucker the Russians will allow to touch their precious art is off buggering some steroid queen on Muscle Beach!"

"Er . . ."

"Call me the second he gets back."

"Yes, sir."

Hudson slammed the phone back in its cradle and glared at the Vargas nude. He knew he had an unreasonable phobia of homosexuals. He suspected that Novikov knew it and was taunting him. Without the Russian, there was no exhibit. And without the exhibit, Hudson was in trouble.

Big trouble.

With a muttered oath, he got up from behind his desk and paced. He'd already promised private previews of the Russian exhibit to the principal culture writers for the *Los Angeles Times* and the *Washington Post*. He'd even sent a private jet to bring the chief art critic for the *New York Times* to preview the event on Wednesday, two days before the public opening.

The right kind of coverage in those three papers was essential. Without it the American arts community might not acknowledge Hudson Museum's artistic coup. Then the stockholders would get restless about the cost of what had turned out to be just one more show, rather than the art exhibit of the decade.

Philanthropic work was as political as running for public office. It was entirely a matter of knowing which buttons to push. But Aleksy Novikov had his hand firmly in place above the power buttons, not Damon Hudson.

He doubted that the Russian knew enough to use the power wisely, much less profitably.

"Damn all fairies," he said loudly. "They're worse than women."

He paced a while longer, examining his options. Reluctantly he decided it was time to play his hole card, the interview he'd hoped he wouldn't need. He picked up the intercom phone.

"Tell Bill Cahill to update Toth's file one more time and bring it to me ASAP."

5

Cambria
Monday

"Sammy, are you sure?" Laurel asked. Her voice wasn't tense, but the hand holding the phone was.

"I couldn't be more sure if you asked me whether I can fly without drugs," Adams said.

"But—" she began.

"My dear child," Adams cut in impatiently. "The raw, unvarnished truth is that you couldn't buy an imperial Fabergé egg for one million or ten million American dollars. There simply aren't any eggs of that quality running around loose in the world to be bought."

"I see."

But what she saw was a red-and-gold lacquered masterwork on the workbench in front of her. The sunlight flooding through the glass wall of her work area gave the egg a brilliant, unearthly glow.

For a crazy instant she almost laughed out loud. Samuel Adams was chief curator of Eastern European and Central Asian art at the Metropolitan Museum of Art in New York.

He was an old family friend, a protégé of her mother, but he'd decided he was better at acquiring art than creating it.

Most of the time Laurel loved Adams like the elegant, carnivorous little flower he was. Most of the time. But not when he was condescending to her.

"How can you be so certain?" she asked.

"My darling baby girl," Adams said, sighing. "Hasn't anyone ever told you the facts of artistic life?"

"You have. Many times."

"Then you haven't listened very well, have you?" he retorted. "Your own work is beginning to attract attention from collectors. You'd better learn, really *learn,* how the acquisition game is played."

She wanted to groan out loud. He was right, and she knew it. Unfortunately, he knew it too.

"Private collectors and curators are like spiders," he said. "Each builds his web with great care, trying to catch all the good pieces that come along. My web happens to be the best in the world. Believe me, if a good Fabergé piece—much less an imperial egg—should become available, I would know."

"Yes, but—"

He talked right over her. "Eastern Europe is hot right now. In fact, there's a fabulous Russian show, just fabulous, opening in your part of the world."

"Really? Where?"

"Damon Hudson's horrid new museum. Everybody who was anybody wanted 'The Splendors of Russia.' We bid a pot of gold for it, but Damon bid more."

"Why?"

"We'd have made three pots of gold, that's why. People haven't seen good Russian art since their tedious little revolution. Patrons would have been fighting for a place in line at thirty bucks apiece."

Laurel made an unconvinced sound.

"Baby girl," Adams said, "you really should pull your head off your workbench and take a look at the business of museums and art. The crown jewels of England are damned mundane as art goes, but people line up to see them all day, every day, day after day. The same is true of the Mona Lisa. It's the hold on the popular imagination that brings in the crowds, not the intrinsic quality of the art itself."

"Does Fabergé have that kind of hold on the popular mind?" she asked.

"You can bet your last machine-cut diamond on it."

The long-distance line hummed with silence as Laurel thought quickly, trying to reconcile Adams's blunt truth with the equally blunt truth of the egg on the bench in front of her.

"Hello?" Adams said after a time. "Are you still there?"

"Yes. . . ."

At the other end of the line, Adams felt a tingle down his spine. The aggressive curator's mind shifted into high gear. When he spoke again, there was no more haughtiness in his voice. "Laurel, sweet baby child, do you know something you're not sharing with Uncle Sammy?"

When she heard his words, a faint flush spread across her face. She didn't know how she'd given the game away, but somehow she had. Probably because she was a lousy liar, especially when it came to friends and family. Though Adams wasn't a blood relation, he'd shared much of her childhood. He'd loved Ariel Swann as much as Laurel had.

But he'd hated Jamie Swann.

That was why Laurel was being cautious about the egg. Adams would enjoy skewering the man who had made Ariel cry. It was a familiar problem to Laurel, so familiar that she picked her way through the minefield of conflicting loyalties without even being conscious of what she was doing.

As always, Jamie Swann won.

Deep down inside, buried far beneath the sophisticated jewelry designer, lived a little girl who believed that if she was just good enough, long enough, Daddy would approve of her and come home to stay.

"What would I know about Fabergé that you don't?" Laurel asked. "I didn't even know there was a show coming. I'm stuck out here in the tules trying to make a living. I haven't been in the city for weeks."

"Spare me the shit-kicking hick act," Adams said. "You have a telephone, don't you? The one in your hand right now, for instance."

"I'll spare you my act if you'll spare me yours."

"What act?"

"Bitch queen, Manhattan-style."

He gave a hoot of delight. She was one of the few people in the world who could stand up to his sarcasm.

"Ah, baby girl," he said. "What a pity you weren't born a baby boy. We'd have been fabulous together."

Laughing, Laurel shook her head. Adams's razor intellect and equally slicing honesty were two of the reasons she loved him. The other reasons were more complex, linked with her childhood and her mother, the woman both Laurel and Adams had loved.

And lost.

"So tell Uncle Sammy what you've heard about a loose imperial egg," Adams coaxed.

"That's easy. Nothing."

"Think. Maybe it's something that somebody else picked up from the people around the Hudson show. Last year when

I toured the Hermitage, I met the curator, a truly fabulous beauty called Novikov. Now, *there* is a work of art. Nasty piece of business too, I understand."

"Never heard of him."

"Just as well. He's out of your league. But there's always the possibility that the Russians are willing to put art like that on the block."

"Sell Novikov?" she asked in disbelief.

"No. Fabergé eggs. Though I'd certainly bid my bank account if they did auction him off."

Laurel blinked, trying to follow the zigzag thread of Adams's conversation.

"Yessss," he said, dragging out the word. "It's quite possible. Quite, quite possible. The whole Eastern Bloc is absolutely desperate for cash. Everything is for sale. Even Siberia, if the price is right, though why anyone would want a freezer five times the size of Texas is beyond me."

She made a sound that said she was listening. She could sense his mind picking up speed as he speculated aloud.

"A few weeks ago there was a rumor that a Japanese collector had picked up a Fabergé of some sort," Adams said. "Of course, it was of very dubious provenance."

"An imperial egg?"

"Bite your tongue. If it was an imperial egg, I'd have known. It could have been one of the smaller ones, though. There are hundreds of them," he said almost dismissively.

Making small sounds from time to time, Laurel let Adams think aloud, grateful that he was no longer pursuing her for information she didn't want to give. Not until she knew what, if anything, her father had to do with the mysterious appearance of the egg on her doorstep.

As Laurel listened, she slid off the high work stool and stretched her back, trying to drive out the tension that had gathered in her shoulders. Lifting the long phone cord so it didn't knock over any of the jeweled, oversized chess pieces she'd been testing for loose stones, she went closer to the window and watched the brilliant western sky.

Yet when she closed her eyes, it was the mysterious scarlet egg she saw, not the sun.

She stretched again. She'd been on the phone too long, calling everyone she could think of, trying to discover if there was any buzz in the art and collecting world about a missing, previously unknown imperial Fabergé egg.

Adams had been her first call, but he hadn't been available right away. While she waited for him to call back, she'd talked to several dealers and to a cultural historian. Actually, they'd done the talking. She'd listened.

And she'd said not one word about the jeweled egg sitting on her worktable.

All the experts she'd talked to agreed that imperial Fabergé eggs were very, very valuable. They were also exceedingly rare.

The cultural historian from Laurel's alma mater, Pratt Institute, had been more precise. And more unsettling. It was his voice ringing in her ears right now, not Adams's.

Miss Swann, if someone is offering an imperial Fabergé egg for sale, the piece is counterfeit or stolen. Either way, I would keep my distance. Art is like every other human endeavor. It can be beautiful, but it can also be very, very dangerous.

Calling Adams had reinforced the warning. He'd come to quivering alert at the very mention of an imperial egg. The truth, much less the egg on the workbench, would bring out every bit of the predator in Adams.

Even so, Laurel wished she could tell him about the egg. But if knowledge was truly dangerous—and if her father was involved, so was danger—everyone would be better off if she didn't draw Adams into the mess.

Swann returned Adams's hatred, with interest.

In any case, Laurel felt she owed her father the silence he'd always expected and received from her.

"On the whole, any rumors of eggs must have come from 'The Splendors of Russia,' " Adams concluded.

"Mmm," she said.

"So is it something to do with the Hudson show?"

She turned her back on the worktable. The sight of the egg made it more difficult for her to lie, even by omission.

"I haven't had a single contact with the show," she said honestly. "I was just playing with a lacquer design in my head. I wanted a jeweled effect without the jewels. Everyone is trying to be less ostentatious—"

"Cheaper," Adams interrupted dryly.

"—now, so I'm trying to do a vanity case that looks completely jeweled but isn't."

That, at least, was the truth.

"The Chinese lacquers I saw weren't quite the effect I wanted," she added. "Then I remembered the Fabergé eggs. I thought maybe you knew where there was one I could examine firsthand. But if the Hudson Museum has one, I'll just trot on down to LA and have a look."

Adams's laughter had a cutting edge.

"Baby girl, you never were much of a liar," he said. "Remember when you tried to convince me that you didn't want to sleep with that actor? I knew right away you were lying, mainly because he really was fabulous. Sometimes switchhitters are the best."

Laurel's mouth flattened. "You always had a taste for the personal and poisonous. This is purely professional."

Adams sighed. "I'm sorry. I only seduced him because

I didn't want you to catch something fatal from him. You were far too green to protect yourself."

"Not anymore."

"I hope so. The world needs more people like you. People with integrity. Most of us have lost it along the way, and a lot of other things as well."

"Sammy . . ." Her voice died. She didn't know what to say. There was a sadness in his tone that made her throat ache.

"Yeah," Adams said. "I know. Life's a bitch and then you die. So call me if you have something you want to share. There would be a fabulous finder's fee for an imperial egg."

"Take care of yourself," she said softly.

"Too late for me, baby girl. But not for you."

6

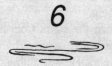

Cambria
Monday

Laurel hung up and turned back to the egg, halfway hoping
it had disappeared.

It hadn't.

The silence was so complete that she could hear seagulls
crying in the pauses between the waves rolling over and dis-
solving on the beach. Then she heard the sound of a car turning into her driveway and stopping. A door slammed.

Without realizing it, she held her breath.

Three firm raps, evenly spaced and delivered with strength.
The faint noise of the front door opening. A familiar voice
calling her name.

"Laurie?"

That solves the mystery of the egg, she thought with faint
bitterness. *Why am I not surprised?*

"Down here," was all she said aloud.

She settled onto her tall work stool to inspect the egg once
more. And to wait for an explanation of how the exquisite

objet d'art had come into Jamie Swann's hands. He was always good at explanations.

Even for her silver-tongued father, this explanation should be a real imperial gem.

Swann came down the stairs from the upper level in a well-coordinated rush that suggested a man much younger than his fifty-two years. He was a physical man who'd been genetically blessed with a strong body and had worked out regularly to keep fit. Vanity was part of it.

Survival was most of it.

He stood just under six feet one inch tall and weighed five pounds more than he had at the age of twenty-one. He still had a full head of dark hair that showed only a few streaks of gray. His dense, closely clipped beard was a good deal more silver. The beard, his tan, and his faint outdoorsman's squint gave him the look of a pirate.

Her father was the most physically confident man Laurel had ever known. He strode straight ahead without fear and seemingly without thought. Yet she knew that in many ways he was shrewd to the point of being scary, a handsome puppet master pulling everyone's strings.

In the seven years since her mother had died, Laurel had come to understand that her parents had parted not from lack of passion but from too much of it. Years after their divorce, they had still longed for each other.

Yet Swann had hungered for his own life and freedom even more.

The past seven years had taught Laurel that her father's visits made his absences all the more demoralizing. It wasn't like he was dead. Dead was finished. Dead could be confronted and accepted.

She'd learned that when her mother died.

But with Swann it was never finished. He was always

alive, always dropping by just when Laurel had given up hope of seeing him again. Her father's sudden, unexpected appearances—and disappearances—kept her subtly off balance, never able really to trust him, and never able to stop looking for him.

There were times when she wondered if her uneasy relationship with her father had ruined her ability to love any man. Certainly she hadn't found a man who was worth the anguish.

She loved her father, but the older she got, the less certain she was that she *liked* him.

Yet when she saw him striding toward her, grinning in his vivid, masculine way, her heart lifted. If she had many unhappy memories of being left behind, she also had happy memories of laughter and homecoming.

"How'd you know it was me, kid?" Swann asked.

"I just did. Good thing, too. When did you decide to grow a beard?"

"Your mother used to recognize me a mile away, but I didn't know the ability was inherited."

Laurel didn't ask again about her father's beard. She'd learned that a question he ignored was a signal that she was being too nosy.

"Come here and give the old man a hug," Swann said, holding his arms wide.

She hesitated.

Suddenly he looked hurt, like a little boy who had been scolded for having too much energy.

"A little hug isn't a problem, is it?" her father asked quietly.

"Of course not," she said, smiling despite their unresolved past.

She went across the room in a rush and hugged Swann

hard, holding on to his strength, feeling safe for just a moment in some small corner of her soul.

Swann hugged his daughter just as hard, but he was thinking even harder. He'd planned to arrive before the package did. It would have been so much easier that way.

But when Laurel moved away from her worktable and into his arms, he saw the egg.

Balls. This will bugger it up but good.

Laurel was like her mother had been, honest to the soles of her feet. The explanation he'd worked out for the package would be harder to sell now. Much harder.

Much more dangerous.

"You're taller than I remembered," was all he said.

"You always say that."

"Do I?"

"Uh-huh."

He laughed. "Guess you'll always be somewhere between twelve and fifteen in my mind until I see you. Then I know all over again how much water has gone under the bridge."

Like the beard, the bitterness in Swann's voice was new. She tilted her head back and studied her father's face. Wherever he'd come from, it had been a long way away. He must have been traveling hard to get home. He looked as tired as she could ever remember seeing him.

"Looking for new lines?" he asked.

She shook her head. "Just . . . looking."

Swann smiled sadly. "You remind me of your mother when you do that." He released Laurel and glanced at the workbench. "I see you got my package."

"It came about an hour ago."

Just one hour, he thought savagely. *Goddamn it. So close . . .*

But close only counted in horseshoes and hand grenades, and no one knew that better than Jamie Swann.

Laurel saw the subtle shift of her father's expression and knew that he wished she'd never unwrapped the box.

"It was addressed to me," she said evenly. "That's why I opened it."

Saying nothing, her father walked slowly toward the egg. It glowed with a light that was almost eerie.

"It's something, isn't it?" he asked softly.

"Yes. But what, exactly?"

Ignoring the question, Swann kept walking up to the worktable. When he was within arm's reach of the egg he bent down. His squint became more pronounced. With a muttered curse he straightened, snatched a pair of half-glasses out of his shirt pocket, and started to put them on. Then he looked at his daughter.

"I don't know why I even carry the damn things," he said. "Bad light is the only time I really need them."

Laurel felt a stab of sadness. Her father was stronger and more fit than any man she knew, however young, yet he felt he had to apologize for needing reading glasses.

What will it be like for him when he's truly old? she thought unhappily. *How on earth will he deal with the loss of his strength?*

How will I?

Impatiently Swann put on the glasses and bent down to the egg, inspecting it closely. He poked randomly at a jeweled fleur-de-lis. Nothing moved. He wiggled the gold wires that made the net around the egg. Nothing happened. He began picking at the net with his thumbnail.

"Dad, be careful! The gold is so malleable, so soft, that it would be easy to damage."

For an instant Swann looked up at her over the top of his glasses. Then he went back to worrying the jeweled egg.

Before she could think, Laurel was beside her father, protective of the egg.

"Are you looking for anything in particular?" she asked in a neutral voice.

"Just trying to figure out how it's put together. Can't see a seam anywhere."

"Let me look."

"You already had an hour and you didn't get it open." Swann paused and added softly, "Did you?"

"I was too busy admiring the egg to wonder how it opened."

Swann let out a hidden, relieved breath. "You and your mother," he said, shaking his head. "Ariel could look at the same thing for hours and never get bored."

"And you got bored after three minutes. Then you left."

Surprised by the bitterness in Laurel's voice, he looked up from the egg. She took advantage of his distraction to move between him and the delicate objet d'art.

"My guess is that the web of gold wire is designed to hide the seam in the egg," she said.

Swann grunted. "So peel off the froufrou and find out."

"Peel off the—" She took a breath and asked sharply, "Do you know what this is?"

"Do you?"

"It looks like one of Fabergé's imperial eggs."

"Yeah, it does, doesn't it?"

"Is it real?" she asked.

Surprised, Swann's glance shifted from the egg to his daughter. Usually she took her cue from his silence.

"It looks damned real to me," he said. "What about you?"

For an instant Laurel wanted to scream in frustration. If

her father knew anything about the egg, he wasn't going to tell her.

"It looks damned real to me," she said, her tone an exact imitation of his. "What about *you*?"

Swann shrugged.

"Do you have any idea what this is worth?" she pressed.

A cold, mysterious smile slashed across Swann's face.

"Millions," he said succinctly. "Enough to keep me the rest of my life. Enough to keep you in beans and bacon when I'm not around to send you gems from all the shitty little backwaters on earth."

"I don't want money. Not like this."

"Too late. It's the same kind of money you've been getting all along."

"But—"

"But nothing, Laurie," Swann cut in, fixing her with his bleak amber eyes. "It's time you learned how the world really works. Blood washes off gold, time only goes one way, and Jamie Swann takes care of his own."

As he watched the color drain from his daughter's face, he knew he'd made a bad mistake in sending the package here. Laurel was Ariel's daughter more than she was his. Laurel was too decent for her own good.

And for his.

He knew himself. He was an honorable if not always an honest man. He'd broken laws in more ways and countries than most people could name. Yet he hadn't done it for his own gain, but for a higher good: the rule of law.

Long ago he'd reconciled himself to the irony of breaking international laws in order to ensure an international rule of law. But other people didn't have to face that irony on a daily basis. He often forgot just how harsh the truth looked to outsiders. Especially the innocent ones.

"You okay, baby?" he asked, reaching for his daughter.

"I'm fine." She shook off the sensation of feeling the earth shift beneath her feet, tripping her. "Just fine."

Swann took his daughter by both shoulders and turned her, forcing her to look directly at him.

"Listen to me," he said. "Listen good. The package never came. You never opened it. I never was here. Got that?"

It was a voice Laurel had never heard from her father—cold, savage, ruthless. Like his yellow eyes.

Suddenly she knew why he left so often and came back so rarely. He hadn't wanted his wife and daughter to know just how dangerous a man he was.

"Laurel."

That was all Swann said, or needed to.

"I'll do the best I can," she told him in a thin voice. "But I'm not much good at your kind of games."

He let out a long breath, changing before her eyes, becoming again the man she knew. He touched her cheek with surprising tenderness.

"I know, baby," he said. "I never wanted you to be. So forget about tonight. Okay?"

The voice was familiar again, deep and warm, a little rough at the edges.

"Okay," Laurel whispered.

Releasing her shoulders, Swann turned away. He stared out at the restless ocean for a long, silent moment. Finally he turned back to his daughter.

"I think it's time we had a talk," he said calmly. "So sit down before you fall down."

As he spoke, he gestured toward the high work stool.

Laurel sat without protest. In truth, she was glad for the support. Her worktable was familiar, comfortable, predictable—all the things her father wasn't.

Swann shoved his hands into the hip pockets of his jeans and began to pace.

"You don't know much about my life," he said finally. "Neither did your mother. It was better that way. Safer. But not anymore."

Abruptly he turned and pinned Laurel with eyes that were like a wolf's, clear and tawny and untamed. Untamed most of all.

Poor Mother, Laurel thought distantly. *She never had a chance. Not really. Jamie Swann is wild all the way to his soul.*

"For the past thirty years," he said, "I've been employed, more or less continually, by the Central Intelligence Agency."

"I thought you were a mercenary."

"That's what I told your mother. And that's what I was, from time to time." Swann's teeth gleamed in a cold smile. "But never the times people thought I was. Even her."

"You were—*are*—a spy?"

"Nothing that fancy. I'm what the media pansies call a 'shadow warrior.' "

Laurel absorbed that for a moment before she asked, "What do you call yourself?"

"Once we called ourselves heroes."

"And now?"

"Now?" Swann laughed harshly. "Now we know what we were. Bloody fools. Bloody, bloody fools."

She winced at the bitterness in his voice.

"You see, baby," he said, "wars aren't fought in nice, honorable, standup ways like they were before Korea. Now wars are fought in alleys where sewage draws rats, secrets draw gold, and men get their throats slit, often by friends. I should know. I cut my share."

She closed her eyes for a moment, then opened them again. All her life she'd resented being kept away from the true Jamie Swann. Now she had what she had always wanted—the truth, however difficult.

"The name of the game I've played all my life is cross, double-cross, triple-cross, and keep on crossing until there's no one else left standing," he said.

"Why? If it was that bad, why didn't you quit?"

"I didn't believe it was that bad until it was too late to quit. Ariel was dead." Without warning he turned sharply, facing his daughter. "Ah, hell, who am I jobbing? I would have gone nuts being in one place all the time with nothing more exciting than dying to look forward to."

"But if mother had been alive . . . ?"

"Big 'if,' Laurie. Too big for this cowboy." He shrugged. "Anyway, I can't complain. I chose the life and I'd choose it again. But I didn't plan very well. I made good money when I worked, and I spent it all."

She thought of the rainbow of gemstones her father had given her over the years and felt guilty. "I know. Too much of it came to me."

A smile flickered over his lips. "Don't worry about that. The stones I gave you were real bargains. Way, way below wholesale. Cheaper than dirt. Like life."

Laurel hoped the shock she felt didn't show on her face. Part of her had assumed that her father's talk of cutting throats was an exaggeration. Now she knew it wasn't.

Swann looked at his daughter's face and swore beneath his breath. "Listen. If I'd gotten here before the package, you could have gone on being sweet and naive and kind and caring and all that horseshit. But there was a storm in Kowloon and a delay in Hong Kong and I got here late. So now you

have to grow up, and grow up fast, or you'll spill your guts—
and mine—to the first asshole with a smile and a badge who
comes knocking at the door."

Numbly Laurel watched her father and listened to all the
answers whose questions no longer mattered. He was getting
closer to the truth now. She sensed it.

And she knew she wouldn't like it.

7

Cruz watched Novikov like a rattlesnake watching a rat. After the Russian's slow, reluctant discussion of why he'd come to Risk Ltd., Redpath had relented and moved the meeting indoors. Cruz, Gillespie, and Redpath were used to the desert blast furnace at midday, but the Russians were getting beaten flat by the heat. Poor Gapan hadn't said a word the whole time, as if he'd been struck dumb by the weight and intensity of the sun.

Even Novikov had given up on half-truths and evasions in order to get out of the sun. He sank gratefully into a couch in Redpath's cool, subterranean office, which was in the half of the compound that had been carved into the side of a hill. The surrounding earth moderated the desert's extreme temperatures. Everything learned to accommodate the reality of the desert, even Cassandra Redpath.

The thought made Cruz smile faintly.

At an unseen signal from Redpath, Gillespie handled the

refreshments. To Cruz, there was something both charming and amusing about the sight of the six-foot four-inch black giant—dressed in cammie shorts and khaki singlet— serving lemonade with the delicacy of a maiden aunt.

Though Cruz was no stranger to the dark arts of mayhem, Gillespie could have taught him a new way to kill every day for a year. That was why Cruz was careful not to grin while Gillespie served everyone from a plate of ginger cookies he'd baked himself. The big sergeant-major was a complex man, proud of his Scots birth and Zulu grandparents, a deadly fighter, an excellent cook, and intelligent beyond the understanding of most men.

But not beyond Redpath's understanding. She savored the evenings of chess and conversation with Gillespie. So did he. Being Redpath's bodyguard, tactician, and confidant had brought out a gentle, almost sweet aspect of Gillespie's nature. He even managed to play houseboy with grace, although Cruz sensed that Gillie would like to serve Novikov cyanide with his cookies.

Elegantly at ease but for his shrewd eyes, Novikov finished his third glass of lemonade with too much enthusiasm for mere politeness. Though he'd been outside for less than half an hour, the overwhelming reality of the desert had created a thirst in him that was only partly physical.

What really irritated him was that Cruz knew it.

"More lemonade?" Cruz asked gently.

Except for a sideways glance, the Russian ignored Cruz. Novikov was beginning to enjoy the coolness of Redpath's office and the chance to decide for himself whether rumors of a sexual liaison between Redpath and Gillespie were true. Obviously there was respect between them, and probably affection. As for sex . . .

Novikov hadn't decided yet. If it became important, he'd find out. Until then, he'd just have more lemonade and be grateful to be out of that hellish sun.

"I don't mean to rush you, Aleksy," Redpath said, "but if the matter that brought you here is urgent, and I must assume it is, it should be addressed."

Novikov frowned.

Sourly Cruz noted that the lines in the Russian's forehead only increased his physical beauty. Maybe Novikov practiced the expression in front of a mirror. Several mirrors. He talked out of so many sides of his mouth that one mirror wouldn't be enough.

"I am forced by circumstances to reveal several important state secrets," Novikov said reluctantly. "Therefore, I would very much appreciate speaking to you alone."

Impatiently Cruz rattled the ice cubes in his glass of lemonade. They'd been around this track before, when Cassandra had been trying to melt Novikov under the desert heat.

"I'm here because Cassandra wants me to be and you know it," Cruz said. "Stop doing laps and get to the point."

For a time Novikov studied his former adversary. There was something different about Cruz now, something that the Russian couldn't quite name.

It made him more wary.

Cruz Rowan had been an operative with a peculiarly American sense of world politics as a grand adrenaline-filled game. Despite that exuberance, he'd trapped Novikov as neatly as a chess master traps a less-gifted opponent. It had galled Novikov.

It still galled him.

But he was too intelligent not to realize that while he'd won the final round by using his diplomatic credentials like a second queen added to his side of the chessboard, all the other rounds in the match had gone to the American.

Again, Novikov tried to put his finger on what had changed about Cruz. The operative had always been cheerfully ruthless and efficient. Now he was cold rather than cheerful. More Old World than New. The change made Cruz all the more dangerous.

At that moment Novikov decided that Cruz had to be removed from the game.

"When we last met," the Russian said to Cruz, "you thought I was merely a spy who used art and culture as a cover."

Cruz gestured abruptly with his glass. "Water under the bridge."

"For you, perhaps. You chose your work. I did not. My KGB assignment was forced upon me. I was, and still am, an art historian by training and by inclination."

"Yeah. Right. Whatever you say, darlin'."

"In fact," Novikov said, ignoring Cruz's sarcasm, "I am the chief curator for the most important traveling exhibit of Russian art ever assembled. Perhaps you have heard about it? 'The Splendors of Russia'?" Before Cruz could speak, the Russian answered his own question. "No, of course you haven't. Art means nothing to you."

Novikov turned to Redpath. "But surely you have heard of the exhibit. It is scheduled to open this Friday at the Damon Hudson Museum of Art in Los Angeles."

Redpath's neutral expression shifted to one of faint amusement. "I did hear that Hudson was christening his latest monument to narcissism with an exhibit of Russian works."

"The show just closed in Tokyo," Novikov said. "It was very successful there."

Cruz held out his glass for a refill.

Without a change in expression or position, Gillespie poured. The big man was never more than an arm's reach from Novikov or—more to the point—Gapan.

"The exhibit was packed up and moved as a single group," Novikov said. "One shipment, you understand?"

"The missing egg—" Cruz began.

"It is called the Ruby Surprise," Novikov interrupted, a pained look on his face.

"Whatever. It was there when you packed up in Tokyo?" Cruz asked.

"Yes. We used a commercial air freight company which specializes in such shipments. Terribly reliable."

"You're certain the egg you shipped was the right one? No substitutions?" Cruz asked almost idly.

"Quite certain. The entire exhibit arrived in Los Angeles yesterday. As soon as everything passed through your very efficient Customs personnel, we began checking for shipping damage."

"And you found the egg gone," Cruz said.

"Yes."

"How much is it worth?"

Novikov seemed unhappy at having to put a monetary value on the egg. He looked at Redpath.

She looked back at him.

"The egg is priceless, both as history and as art," the Russian said finally. "The House of Fabergé was the leading designer and manufacturer of art objects in imperial Russia. It created all manner of extraordinary trifles which have little intrinsic use."

"The kind of things that are more properly called objects of fantasy than art," Redpath said to Cruz.

"Precisely," Novikov said, his voice approving. "Although many art historians would be pleased to argue that in the imperial eggs, the House of Fabergé transcended craftsman-ship and became true art."

"Not a popular point of view in Russia for the past seventy years," Cruz said blandly.

"Fashions change with politics," Novikov said with an elegant shrug. "When the czar fell, Fabergé was doomed. The Ruby Surprise was the last imperial egg to be commissioned. In fact, no one even knew the Ruby Surprise had been completed until recent exhaustive inventories of state assets."

Redpath nodded. It was an open secret that Russia was scrambling for every possible source of cash, including selling off works of art that had been hidden away for generations.

"So some hero of the Revolution overcame his proletariat prejudices and stashed the Ruby Surprise in his concrete villa," Cruz summarized. "Then some other hero of the masses pried the egg out of him when the people rebelled again."

Novikov's jaw tightened. "I do not know how the egg came to be in the treasury. It was discovered during a thorough inventory of other state treasures."

Eyes half closed, Cruz absorbed information like a computer. When he reached for his lemonade glass, Novikov stared. Cruz knew exactly what had caught the Russian's eye. Cruz's left index finger had been severed about an inch from the palm.

Novikov realized he was staring at the stub and Cruz was watching him over the rim of his glass. Deliberately the Russian stared for a few moments more before he resumed his story.

"The exhibit is made up of a cross section of pre-Soviet art and artifacts, but its heart is the Fabergé objects," Novikov said. "There are crystal and lacquer flowers, exotic animals carved in crystal, twenty magnificent lacquered cigarette boxes, and gilt picture frames encrusted with diamonds."

"So what's the provenance on these goods?" Cruz asked. "Bills of sale from previous owners and such?"

Redpath shot him a sideways glance.

Cruz smiled. It wasn't a gesture of goodwill or humor.

"Hundreds of such objects were seized from the aristocracy by the Bolsheviks," Novikov said.

"Diamonds, too," Cruz added. "Buckets of them."

"The spoils of war," the Russian said, dismissing it with a wave of one beautifully manicured hand. "During the most difficult years, the Soviet state liquidated much of the treasure in order to raise hard currency."

"And the rest was looted by corrupt communist officials and cultural bureaucrats, right?" Cruz said.

"Possibly." Novikov smiled as coldly as Cruz had. "My exhibit represents the best of what remains in the state treasury. Some of the pieces are truly exceptional. The Ruby Surprise is one. The St. Petersburg egg is another."

"Easter eggs," Cruz said.

"Glorious ones," Redpath pointed out mildly. "Alexander the Third commissioned the first one for his wife. It was such a success that he made it a tradition."

"Indeed," Novikov said. "His son, the last czar, commissioned two a year, one for his mother and one for his wife. A number of others were made for Russian industrialists over the years."

"Why is it called the Ruby Surprise?" Gillespie asked.

Novikov glanced at the big man, startled that he'd dared to speak. A single look into those fierce, intelligent eyes made the Russian revise his estimate of Gillespie. Whatever the color of the man's skin, he wasn't simply a houseboy or a gigolo.

"Traditionally," Novikov said, "each of the eggs contains a secret inside."

"State secrets?" Gillespie asked immediately.

"No," Redpath said. "Some very clever baubles."

"Precisely," Novikov said. "Sometimes the surprise is a series of miniature portraits framed in diamonds and concealed behind jeweled panels. Sometimes the surprise is a single miniature landscape, which rises out of the center of the egg on exquisitely concealed watchworks. Sometimes the surprise is an animal with a windup mechanism which allows it to walk."

Gillespie's black eyebrows lifted. Without a word, he withdrew to refill the lemonade pitcher. The look he gave Cruz told him to keep an eye on Gapan.

It wasn't necessary. Cruz knew a thug when he saw one.

"How many eggs are there?" Cruz asked.

"One hundred and fifty eggs were made in the late nineteenth and early twentieth centuries," Novikov said, looking at Cruz.

"Who bought them?"

"Some were acquired by the British royal family," Novikov said. "Others disappeared during the Bolshevik Revolution. The rest have become the most expensive collectibles in the world."

"Who owns them outside of Russia?" Cruz asked.

Though he still looked relaxed, there was an intensity in Cruz that hadn't been there earlier. Whoever owned a Fabergé egg now would be a likely candidate to buy another one, no matter how suspect the egg's provenance might be.

"Damon Hudson, the industrialist, has several," Novikov said. "Malcolm Forbes, the American publisher, acquired a dozen in his lifetime."

"What did he pay for them?" Redpath asked.

"More than one and one half million dollars American for the last egg to become available," Novikov said. "That was some time ago. No one knows what such a piece would be worth in today's international art market."

"And you've managed to lose one," Cruz said. "No wonder you're sweating."

"I am not nearly as concerned about personal responsibility as I am about a great cultural loss, and the political ramifications of that loss."

Cruz wasn't impressed.

"As you have pointed out," Novikov said, "I work for a government which is balanced on the crumbling edge of disaster. Democracy is under siege from all sides. The Communist Party is still powerful."

Novikov switched his intent gray glance from Cruz to Redpath.

"The men you call hard-liners," the Russian said, "would destroy all the progress of the past several years in order to regain power."

"Don't forget the right," Cruz said, biting into a cookie with a flash of healthy white teeth. "The military and the former state bureaucrats have gotten in bed together."

"Never count out the lure of White Russian nationalism," Gillespie added, appearing in the doorway with another pitcher of lemonade in one big hand. "There are old families who got their money out before the Revolution was over. They would be delighted to go fishing in troubled Russian waters. More lemonade?"

Novikov blinked, then gave Gillespie the kind of look a woman gives a man she suddenly finds interesting.

"Thank you," Novikov murmured, holding out his glass. "You are correct. My country is a sad mixture of forces with the potential of exploding without warning."

"It happens," Cruz said.

Novikov glanced disdainfully at him and then at his left hand.

"A social and political disaster might amuse a cowboy such as you," Novikov said, "but men—and women—of intelligence understand how terribly serious the situation really is."

Cruz crunched into another cookie.

Novikov looked at Redpath. "Unless, Ambassador, you have lost interest in world stability since you left government service?"

"My colleagues and I aren't in the business of carrying out national policy anymore," she said. "But we're human beings. We do concern ourselves with the state of the world, just as any citizen should."

"Then you will help Russia?"

"I think Customs or LAPD might get the job done quicker," Cruz said to no one in particular.

"The loss has not been reported," Novikov said.

Cruz didn't bother to act surprised. He wasn't.

"Surely other people have noticed that the egg is not with the rest of the exhibit?" Redpath asked.

"Yes, but when I discovered that the egg had gone missing," Novikov said, "I took the liberty of signing it out to myself."

"So you're the only one who knows the Ruby Surprise is gone?" she asked.

"Mr. Gapan, who was in charge of security, knows. Now, of course, you three know."

"Don't get set to blame any leak on us," Cruz said. "At least one other person knows about the egg."

"What? Who?" Novikov demanded.

"The thief."

8

Damon Hudson glanced impatiently at his watch. Surely it couldn't take his chief security officer much longer to update Claire Toth's file. He paid enough to buy the best.

Or at least the most available.

Hudson stretched out on a red velvet chaise. Before he was comfortable, there was a smart knock on the door.

"Come in," Hudson said, knowing who it was.

Bill Cahill opened the door and stuck his head in. He was the image of a retired FBI special agent—good-looking in a generic, square-jawed, all-American-tackle sort of way. He was still at his playing weight, beefy enough to stop a bullet, but his real appeal for Hudson wasn't as a bodyguard. Cahill was Hudson International's liaison with the national law enforcement and intelligence apparatus. He could produce more information with two phone calls than most investigators could learn in a week of hard work.

"You rang, boss?"

Cahill still used the kind of gruff, shouldering, man-to-man style that the Bureau encouraged. Hudson found the familiarity irritating.

"I need a briefing on our guest," Hudson said.

Cahill smiled and pretended not to understand. "Which one? The redhead or the blonde?" he asked, referring to the gorgeous prostitutes who awaited Hudson's pleasure.

"The journalist," Hudson said impatiently. "Claire Toth."

"Oh. That one."

Carefully Cahill closed the door behind him and walked to the red chaise. He looked at home in his charcoal gray suit, white shirt, and burgundy tie. The only false fashion note was the bulge beneath his arm.

It wasn't an oversight. Cahill knew Hudson enjoyed having an armed man on his payroll.

"Do you want the long form or the short one?" Cahill asked. "There's a lot of ground to cover on this piece."

"She's just a freelance reporter. I'm not even sure why I agreed to see her."

"Her voice?" Cahill asked with a wink.

Hudson grimaced but didn't disagree. Claire Toth had the kind of voice that made a man aware of his prick.

"Short form," Hudson said. "If I need more, I'll tell you. Just be sure to give me the most recent information."

Cahill unbuttoned his tailored coat and stuffed his hands into the slit pockets of his trousers.

"Well, Ms. Toth is a freelancer," Cahill said, "but that's because she likes it, not because nobody would put her on staff."

"What makes you say that?"

"According to the IRS, she makes more than three hundred thousand bucks a year. Anybody who makes that much is good enough to work anywhere."

Hudson grunted. "I buy people for a good deal less than that."

And Bill Cahill was one of them.

"I've been meaning to speak to you about that, Mr. Hudson," Cahill said smoothly. "Prices are going up. My old group leader just got hired by American Airlines as head of security. With his stock options, he's making almost a half million. And all of his duties can be spelled out in his job description."

Hudson studied the former agent until even Cahill's FBI training in command presence gave way to unease.

"Is that a reference to the work you did in sabotaging the so-called 'public interest' law firm that was harassing us?" Hudson asked.

"They were a decent enough bunch of kids. I kind of hated to dry up their donations with that phony Bureau investigation."

"But you did it."

Cahill looked grim. The longer he worked for Damon Hudson, the less he liked the man. But the Bureau had taught Cahill that he didn't have to like his boss. All he had to do was shut up and obey orders.

"And you'll keep on doing things like that for me," Hudson said softly, "because you'd find it very difficult to land a job at American Airlines or anywhere else if word got back to the Bureau that you were the source of the false allegations which triggered their probe."

Cahill straightened up and took his hands from his pockets. He met his employer's cold, steady gaze with one of his own.

"I do what I have to do," Cahill said.

"You do what I *tell* you to do."

"I just want to make sure you understand what the

marketplace is like out there," Cahill said evenly. "A former federal agent with good ties to the Bureau and Customs and the Agency is worth a lot of money to corporate America. Particularly if the former agent is willing to use those ties."

Hudson smiled. "Of course. Do the job I've hired you for, and I'll see to it you're well paid. Now tell me more about this high-priced purveyor of journalistic truth."

Cahill thrust his hands back in his pockets. "Claire Toth has all the moves. Columbia Journalism, London School of Economics graduate degree, an internship with a senator on Capitol Hill, and then an apprenticeship at the *New York Times*."

Hudson nodded. It was a typical background for powerful journalists.

"She's been around Washington and New York for about ten years," Cahill said. "She was on the staff of the *Washington Post*'s investigative unit for a while and broke a couple of scandals involving international diplomats and the like."

Hudson's dark eyes narrowed, but he didn't say anything.

"The only real knock on Toth is that she had to give back a Pulitzer prize early in her career," Cahill said.

"Oh? Why?"

"Seems she wrote a story about thousand-dollar-a-night whores that didn't exist. They were composites rather than real people. According to the guardians of media ethics, that's a real no-no."

Hudson laughed coldly. "Getting caught is the no-no. The rest is window dressing for people who still believe in Santa Claus."

"Toth has been involved in a number of PBS documentaries on diplomatic stuff," Cahill continued.

"Any particular area of expertise?"

"Whatever makes the U.S. look bad."

"Examples."

"She uncovered the FBI's infiltration of Latin American refugee groups. She did an exposé on ties between the State Department and drug gangs in Panama and El Salvador."

"Perhaps she has sources on the left."

"Yeah. All the way to the Eastern Bloc," Cahill muttered.

"Proof?"

"Nothing that will stand up in court."

"How about enough to embarrass her?"

"No."

"Interesting."

Hudson sat up, selected an apple from the basket of fruit on a table beside the chaise, and buffed it on the sleeve of his sweater.

"She's a Bob Woodward wannabe," Cahill concluded.

Hudson bit into the apple with the strongest, whitest teeth that money could buy. He chewed thoroughly and swallowed, enjoying the knowledge that few men his age could bite into, chew, and digest a fresh apple with pleasure.

"What does she want from me?" Hudson asked.

"My guess is she's on a fishing expedition."

"What makes you think so?"

"Normally a freelancer has to submit a query to whoever is commissioning the piece," Cahill said. "Sort of an outline of the proposed article."

"What did Ms. Toth's query say?"

"Well, she has a letter of introduction from the editor of the *New York Times Sunday Magazine,* like she's working for them. But when I checked, I found out she hasn't submitted a query, a proposal, or anything else."

"Is the letter valid?"

"Yeah. She called the editor and told him she was thinking

about writing a profile of Damon Hudson. He took the piece, sight unseen."

Hudson shifted on the lounge, thinking quickly. In many ways, he knew more about how journalists worked than Cahill did. For one thing, they screamed like babies when you checked into *their* background.

"You have to be very careful when you start digging up stuff on reporters," Hudson said.

"Don't worry. I was real titty-fingered."

Saying nothing, Hudson bit savagely into the apple.

"I had your public relations department make the inquiry," Cahill said. "They hinted you might not cooperate if you thought the piece was going to be antagonistic."

Hudson decided that was harmless enough. Most truly newsworthy figures avoided the press, unless they had something to sell to the public.

"And?" Hudson asked around a mouthful of apple.

"The *Times* told them anything Claire Toth wanted to write was okay with them, with or without your permission."

Hudson's eyebrows rose like elegant silver wings. Whoever Toth was, she was highly valued by the *New York Times*. But as far as Hudson was concerned, journalists came in two varieties, fawners and muckrakers. He used the first and avoided the second.

Unfortunately, no one could be absolutely certain which journalists were which until after the piece came out.

"What does she look like?" Hudson asked.

"Half white, half Asian, half black, and two hundred percent high-test snatch."

Hudson looked up sharply. The expression on Cahill's face was sexual and predatory.

"Before you go off half cocked," Hudson said coolly, "show Ms. Toth in."

Less than a minute after Cahill left, someone knocked firmly on the cabin door.

"Come in," Hudson said clearly.

The door opened.

Hudson's first impression was that in a lifetime devoted to fornication, he had seen few women as beautifully built as Claire Toth. Never had he seen one who carried herself with such complete sexual assurance. He half expected the carpet to ignite beneath her elegantly arched feet.

Belatedly Hudson realized that Claire Toth was nearly six feet tall, lithe, and strong. She easily handled a heavy leather Coach bag that was big enough to conceal a minicam, an Uzi, or both at once. Proud, full breasts swelled beneath a dark silk shirt that was unbuttoned just enough to show cleavage above a small triangle of cream lace camisole. Taut, lushly curving buttocks were enhanced by a skirt that ended well above the knees. The broad leather belt she wore emphasized the classic hourglass of her figure.

Hudson discovered with a mixture of gratification and dismay that he was fully aroused. The woman wore her sexuality like a dark, primal perfume.

"Well, well," he murmured.

The opening salvo had been fired in a sexual war. He didn't want to be caught off guard again.

And, damn, but he felt like a man.

He came to his feet. It wasn't meant as a polite gesture. It was a way to show her what she was up against.

Ignoring him, Claire Toth glanced around at the unique furnishings of the cabin. Her eye fell on a Chinese painting that looked as though it had once graced the wall of an imperial pleasure house. With a faint smile she compared it to her own experience.

"It's better when you aren't *completely* tied up," she said.

Her voice was smoky, husky, ruffling primeval nerve endings.

"Most things are," Hudson agreed. "Sit down, Ms. Toth. Forgive me if it takes a moment for me to organize my thoughts. My staff failed to warn me."

"That I was black?"

Slowly Hudson shook his head. Quite openly he studied Toth like an objet d'art he was considering acquiring for his museum.

"You're black," he said. "You're Asian. You're Caucasian. You're what Eve must have been. You're one of the most stunningly sexual females I've ever seen."

"I'm flattered." Toth's smile was as cold as the silver buckle on her belt. "The two waiting for you in the commoners' cabin are dynamite, tits and ass to make a showgirl sweat with envy."

As Toth spoke, she let her clear black glance travel down Hudson's body until she was looking at his crotch. Her research on Hudson had told her that he was a virile, sexually aggressive man.

What it hadn't told her was that he could—or would—get hard just watching her walk toward him.

"We could delay the interview for a time," she said, "while the whores take care of your little problem. Actually, it's not so little, is it?"

The approval in Toth's smile made it difficult for Hudson to keep his mind on anything but his crotch.

"Whores?" he asked. "Do you mean the temporary members of my secretarial staff?"

"They're working girls, all right." She laughed low in her throat. "Your constant need of sex is understood by all who know you and a lot who don't. The clinical term for it is satyriasis."

"A term coined by jealous men."

"Yeah. I've often thought so. Must have been tough to get enough ass before you were rich, though."

"The world is full of willing women," he countered, "but most of them aren't attractive enough to fuck face-to-face."

Toth flashed him a smile that was part streetwalker and part coquette. "Maybe they're more attractive when they're less willing?"

"We'll probably find out, won't we?" Hudson said, smiling. "Would you care for a drink?"

"Some champagne would be nice, if you have it."

"Certainly."

He went to a sideboard and opened a small door, revealing a well-stocked refrigerator. He passed over a bottle of La Grande Dame—too expensive for the moment—selected a bottle of Moët, opened it expertly, and poured two glasses. He presented one to Toth and offered his own in a small toast.

She glanced at his glass and arched a single, perfectly shaped eyebrow. "I'm honored. I was told you seldom drink alcohol. Something about your age or your metabolism or your dick."

Hudson felt the flick of her claws and almost smiled at the pleasure-pain it brought. With every word she revealed herself more clearly to him.

"You're very well informed," he said.

"You have no idea how well informed I am."

Something in her smile sent a twinge down his spine that had nothing to do with sex.

"I have an extremely complete file on you," Toth added.

Then she clinked her glass lightly against Hudson's, curled her wrist around his, and drank from his glass. Looking him right in the eye, she rubbed her abdomen slowly against his erection.

"Do you?" he asked, rubbing back where it would do the most good.

"Oh, yes," she said huskily. "And unless you give me a spectacular reason not to, I'll publish every tawdry word of it."

9

Cambria
Monday afternoon

Swann looked at his daughter.

She wasn't looking at him.

Silently he cursed the circumstance that had brought him back into Laurel's life. He didn't know how much more of the truth she could take. But he knew there was a lot more she had to take.

It was a matter of survival.

His.

Hers.

Finally he sighed and continued talking. "At the underground level where I worked," he said, passing over things he couldn't tell her, "intelligence operators aren't nice clean folks with pressed trousers and computer printouts from Langley. The guys I worked with were smugglers or black marketeers or out-and-out thugs, the kind of men who bought and sold everything from missiles to little girls at two cents on the dollar."

Laurel wanted to look away from her father. She couldn't.

She could only face the answers she'd stupidly asked for all her life.

Swann winced inwardly at the change in his daughter's eyes, but he kept on talking, fast and hard, telling her things she didn't want to hear.

But she had to hear him or he would be up to his lips in shit the first time someone asked her about a flashy red egg, and had she seen her daddy lately?

"Not pretty, but that's the way it is in the trenches," he said. "The agency has to hire thugs because thugs are the last realists in the world. They're the ones who know how to work the system, any system, anywhere on earth."

As he talked he began pacing, his hands stuffed into the hip pockets of his jeans. He paused beside the workbench and stared out at the ocean.

"There's nothing new in the shadow alliance between the crooks and the good guys," Swann said. "It's been going on since the Second World War, when the OSS hired the Union Corse in France and the Mafia in Italy. When I started, I was running a network of Fukien Chinese gamblers and cutthroats who lived in Kowloon and did the government's dirty work in Saigon."

When her father leaned toward the window, Laurel saw the butt of a pistol outlined underneath his loose cotton shirt. The gun was stuffed behind his waistband, nestled in the small of his back. She stared at the outline of the weapon. Somehow it looked natural on him, like a wallet would in another man's pocket.

It was the first time Swann had worn a gun in her presence. She wondered why he thought he needed one now.

None of the explanations she thought of comforted her.

"Nothing much has changed in the business," he said in a clipped voice, watching the ocean. "The last job I had

involved ethnic Basque businessmen in a little town called
Medellín, Colombia. The Basques are as brutal as anyone
I've ever worked with. Sort of the Colombian equivalent of
La Cosa Nostra. In spades. Real assholes, but they sure knew
how to smuggle guns to the folks we wanted to see in power
in the interior of South America."

He glanced at his daughter and read her emotions in her
dilated pupils, pale skin, and compressed mouth.

"Jesus, kid," he said, "I wasn't a criminal, not in my own
mind and not in Uncle Sam's. But I wasn't a Boy Scout either.
Ask any undercover cop what it's like. If you're sitting around
arguing about perfect morality, somebody who doesn't know
moral from moron sticks a knife between your ribs."

Turning, Swann began to walk again, measuring the perimeter of the room like a captive wolf pacing out the limits
of his prison.

"I did things that would make your blood run cold," he
said bluntly. "That's why I've never talked to you like this
before. But I've never done anything bad to anybody who
wouldn't have done it to me first, and worse, if I'd given them
the chance."

He paused by the window again, drawn by something in
the afternoon ocean that only he could see.

"If I made a mistake," he said bitterly, "it was in not realizing until the end of the game that I was just a tool, an asset
like any other hired help. Expendable. I wasn't one of them,
an intelligence officer, a spy with a four-in-hand tie and a
college degree. I was a contract agent—cheap, anonymous
protection used for a single mission and then thrown away.
Like a condom."

Her father's laughter made Laurel's throat ache with tears
she couldn't shed.

"I never got on the federal gravy train," he said. "Lots of

guys did their time in the trenches and then retired with pay and went into private business. Real private. Most of them got rich buying and selling guns or airplanes or communications gear to friendly countries. Sometimes even to unfriendly ones." He shrugged.

"Did you?" Laurel asked before she could help herself.

"Hell, no. I was too dumb. I believed the bullshit about country, loyalty, and God. Thirty years in the trenches and I didn't get retirement. I didn't get medical benefits. Neither did the other people like me. All we got was fucked."

Abruptly Swann turned to face his daughter. "I can't file for Social Security for ten years, and let me tell you, I ain't gonna last another ten years out there in East Bumfart, South America."

She wanted to look away from her father's savage eyes, but couldn't. She'd never seen him like this, a dark power and an even darker bitterness that was almost tangible.

"But all that's over now," Swann said softly. "I'm coming back to live in a civilian world that loves splitting moral hairs. And I'm bringing my own brand of retirement with me. I sure as hell earned it."

Laurel looked at the crimson egg.

"Yeah," Swann said, following her glance. "I won't have to pump gas or flip burgers or sell pints of blood for the next ten years so that I can buy dog food because it's the only meat I can afford. And neither will you."

She swallowed against the emotions knotted in her throat. "The egg," she said huskily. "Where did it come from?"

"The less you know, the better off you'll be. I shouldn't have had it sent to you at all, but you were the only person in the world I could trust not to screw me over if I was late getting here."

She smiled sadly.

Swann blew out a harsh breath from between compressed lips. "Well, it's done now. Time only runs one way. I might as well put you to work finding the mechanism."

"What?"

"The mechanism inside," he said impatiently. "The egg was made to hold a ruby engraved with the likeness of Nicholas the Second. Then it all went from sugar to shit. He was executed before the gem could be engraved, and the rest is history."

Laurel closed her eyes, then opened them slowly. Nothing had changed. Her father was still looking at her with shuttered expectation.

"The surprise," she said.

"Yeah, I suppose all this is a bit surprising to you. Sorry, baby. But life is full of nasty little surprises."

"Not that. The egg. The engraved gem is the surprise. All the imperial eggs had one."

A hard, amused smile transformed Swann's face.

"A surprise," he said, turning back to the egg. "Yeah. It's that, all right. But how the hell do I open it? I'll slice it up if I have to, but I might damage something I can't repair."

Something very close to anger snaked through Laurel. Abruptly she slid off the stool and began pacing, trying to control the emotions that were tearing at her. Her father might have wanted to protect her, but she had the distinct feeling that he was manipulating her at the same time.

She wondered if he even knew what he was doing or if he had lived so long in a shadow world that he kept secrets even from himself.

Swann picked up the egg in both hands and inspected the bottom end.

"I can't see a bloody thing," he said, squinting at the golden latticework. "What about you?"

She didn't answer.

"Laurie?"

"I didn't see anything," she said through her teeth. "But then, I wasn't looking."

Yet even as anger grew in her, so did guilt.

She'd taken so many gifts from her father through the years, and never once had she asked what he'd sacrificed to send them. Now she felt sucked down into a whirlpool of loyalty and betrayal . . . and she no longer knew who was loyal and who was not, who was innocent and who was betrayed.

If you're sitting around arguing about perfect morality, somebody who doesn't know moral from moron sticks a knife between your ribs.

She shuddered and wondered how her father had lived for so many years with nothing but a whirlpool under his feet.

"Did you look?" he asked.

"For the mechanism?"

"No, for the King of Siam. Jesus, Laurie. Get it together. The sooner I get inside this egg, the sooner I'll be gone and the safer you'll be. That's what you want, isn't it? A return to the world of your nice, safe, moral choices?"

Guilt gnawed at her. She'd been wishing that none of this was happening, that she could go back to seeing her father through a child's rose-colored glasses rather than the bleak clarity of adult eyes.

Time only runs one way.

"Did you steal the egg?" she asked.

"It was stolen from crooks. That doesn't count."

"How do you know they were crooks?"

Impatiently Swann set the egg down in its cradle and turned toward her. The egg stayed upright only for an instant before it began to topple.

Laurel grabbed it by reflex. "Be careful! You could break it."

"I'm going to get into that thing one way or another." He glanced at the tools arrayed on a pegboard close to the workbench. "How about a chisel? You have one that's up to the job?"

"A *chisel*? Dad, that egg is a work of art."

"So is a dollar bill. Ask any counterfeiter."

Numbly Laurel shook her head. She finally understood what made her father good at what he did. He had a single-minded focus that blocked out everything but his goal. It was the kind of intense focus a pilot needed to bomb an enemy position in a cathedral or a radar emplacement next to a hospital. Pity, horror, sadness, guilt—those would come after the mission was over.

If they came at all.

When Swann reached for the egg once more, Laurel discovered that her choice was made.

As usual, her father had won.

10

Cruz was fed up with watching Novikov waltz around every fact that Redpath tried to pull out of him. The Russian could outdance Baryshnikov.

"Right," Cruz cut in. "What we have now is an egg you say is real but has been stolen by person or persons unimaginable to you, and you want to hire us, then pin the rose on us when word of the theft gets out. Have I missed anything?"

For an instant Novikov looked surprised. Cruz was indeed a more dangerous man now than he'd been before.

"I do not know what you mean," the Russian said evenly. "As I have said many times, I want the loss of the egg kept secret."

"Tell the thief," Cruz said.

"But he, or she, will want it kept quiet, is that not true?" Novikov pointed out.

That does it. Cruz leaned forward. "Assuming the thief wants to sell the egg—and you'd have to be butt-stupid not to assume it—the thief will have to put out the word to potential buyers. Once it's out, it's out. You know it. I know it. So let's just cut to the chase, whatever it is."

"I have told you many times, word must not get out," Novikov said instantly.

Cruz shrugged and said what he'd been saying. "Talk to the thief."

Novikov turned to Redpath.

"The situation in Russia is exquisitely delicate," Novikov said carefully. "There are people in power who did not want any of these treasures to leave the country."

Finally, Cruz thought as he crunched into an ice cube. *Progress on the political front.*

"Why?" she asked.

"They are what you call superpatriots. They feel that these objects are the soul of Russia and as such must be sheltered from impure eyes."

"Superpatriots?" Cruz said under his breath. "How about plain nuts?"

Novikov didn't look away from Redpath. His eyes were luminous with emotion. "Cassandra, please, you must track down the thieves before the loss of the Ruby Surprise becomes known."

"Why come to us?" Cruz said before his boss could speak. "If the idea of LA cops makes you unhappy, call up the FBI. They'll be falling all over their wingtips to help you."

Novikov looked stricken. "The police? The FBI? All are bureaucrats! Either agency would turn the whole matter into a publicity opportunity."

Cruz didn't argue. It was the truth.

"In addition," Novikov continued urgently, "your federal authorities report to Washington. Your government would attempt to turn the theft and the investigation to its own advantage. That is the nature of governments, is it not? They have no friends. They have only interests, as the ambassador once wrote."

Redpath glanced from Novikov's handsome, intent face to a crystal globe on the table in front of her. The solid sphere was delicately engraved with the continents and major islands, making it a cross between a fortune-teller's crystal ball and a geopolitician's globe.

"I was quoting de Gaulle," she said, "and not out of admiration. One of the joys of leaving government service is that you can once more afford to have friends as well as interests."

"Of course." The Russian nodded approvingly. "I will not deny that I have political motives. I represent my government and its interests and I wish only two things. The first is to recover the Ruby Surprise as quickly and quietly as possible. The second is to minimize the cost to the Russian republic."

"We aren't cheap," Cruz said. "Ask the Peruvian government what it cost them to recover the ten million bucks one of their former presidents stole from the government kitty."

"I understand your fee is fifteen percent of whatever asset you trace or recover," Novikov said. "I am willing to personally guarantee that, if you recover the egg, we will submit it to an appraiser of mutual acceptability and we will pay you fifteen percent of the value he or she establishes."

Cruz glanced at Redpath. She had her diplomatic face on. Novikov could just have offered her a handful of diamonds or a platter of cold spit. Either way, her expression wouldn't have changed.

"You will be amply rewarded," the Russian emphasized. "That is the sole way you judge your own interests and the interests of your firm in this privatized world you now inhabit, is it not?"

Gillespie and Cruz looked at Novikov, wondering if the insult was accidental or deliberate.

Cruz voted for deliberate. Then he wondered what was making the normally measured Russian so reckless.

"The ambassador didn't say we were whores," Cruz pointed out calmly. "She just said that in a free market we're free to make our own choices about clients."

"It's all right," Redpath said, smiling at Cruz. "Aleksy is merely trying, in his own singular way, to appeal to our self-interest because he believes that to be the most efficient way to achieve his goal. There was no insult intended. Is that not correct, *mon petit chou*?"

Novikov's smile was chilly. "To be sure, luv."

She glanced back at the crystal globe for a long, silent moment.

Cruz had seen the expressionless gaze before. It was a sign that the extraordinary brain behind the ambassador's striking green eyes was operating at full speed.

After a few seconds she seemed to reengage with the normal world. She looked at Novikov with a curious, dispassionate expression, as if surprised to see him still there.

"Once we recover the egg," she said distinctly, "our nomination for the appraisal will be Christie's auction house.

"Agreed," Novikov said.

"But regardless of the appraisal," Redpath added, "the fee will be not less than one million dollars. We will absorb all costs for the search. In return, our judgments are final."

"Judgments?" Novikov asked her. "What do you mean?"

"If we call off the search, it's over. If we call in police or federal authorities to make arrests, you won't object."

The Russian visibly swallowed. Then he nodded. "Agreed," he said to her, because he had no other choice. "When can you begin?"

"We already have."

"A theft such as this one is not the work of amateurs," Novikov said. "The investigation must be in good hands."

"Of course."

Novikov glanced at Cruz and added, "Two good hands."

Cruz came to his feet with deadly grace but Gillespie was already there, bending down to pick up an empty lemonade glass, blocking the way to Novikov. It looked accidental.

It wasn't.

"Your investigation will be in good hands," Redpath said. "Sergeant-Major, did you check with the pilot while you were getting refreshments?"

"Aye. Same old thing."

"*Damn* that electrical panel," Redpath muttered. "You'll have to drive Mr. Novikov and Mr. Gapan back to Los Angeles." She turned to Novikov. "But don't worry, Gillespie hates long drives so he goes at a high rate of speed. You'll be there almost as quickly as flying. Can I get in touch with you through the Hudson Museum?"

"Yes."

"Excellent. I presume you have a picture of the Ruby Surprise and the waybill for the entire shipment with you?"

"A picture, yes. I will inquire after the waybill."

As Novikov spoke, he reached into his pocket and pulled out a small envelope. Gillespie took it and handed it over to Redpath.

"Thank you," she said.

Then she stood up, signaling an end to the discussion.

Automatically Novikov stood and reached out to take the hand Redpath offered. Before he knew quite what was happening, he and Gapan were being herded by Gillespie out of Redpath's suite of offices.

As soon as the door closed behind the three men, Redpath

sat down again in her chair and stared into the transparent globe on the table.

Cruz crunched ice cubes from his glass while he waited for her to finish her analysis. Finally she looked at him with faint irritation.

"You'll ruin your teeth doing that," she said.

"Yes, Mother. You'll be thrilled to know I only do it when I'm irritated."

"At me?"

"At that slippery little bastard insulting you like Risk Limited was some overpaid rent-a-cop outfit."

She waved her hand, dismissing the insult.

"Don't trust Novikov," Cruz said.

"Any particular reason?"

"He was lying from top to bottom and side to side. If he's nothing more than a bureaucrat with culture, how the hell can he authorize a million bucks to recover an egg he hasn't even reported stolen?"

Redpath looked amused. "Better clean up. You're back on duty."

"I am? I was under the impression you promised Novikov someone with *two* good hands."

"Crap," she said succinctly. "Get off your buns of steel and get cleaned up. The pilot is going through the preflight check right now."

"Electrical panel is working again, huh?" he said dryly.

"Convenient things, electrical panels."

"You don't trust Novikov any more than I do. Why did you take the job?"

"I'm interested in what Novikov hasn't told us about that egg."

"Such as?"

"Rumors. Hints. Whispers."

"Such as?" Cruz repeated.

"It could be simple disinformation."

"So give me a rumor, hint, or whisper, and I'll decide."

"You have good instincts. I trust them. You should too."

He grimaced. "In other words, I'm flying blind."

"But not alone. Not for long. Get moving, Cruz. I'm afraid we'll have a lot of ugly competition on this one."

Without a word, he turned and went toward the door.

"Cruz?"

"Yeah?"

"Wear black."

11

Swann glanced at his watch and headed for the worktable, where Laurel was patiently, *slowly,* trying to figure out the secret of the egg. But when he reached past her to take the egg, she shoved his hand away.

"No," she said curtly. "All your poking and prying is as likely to ruin the egg as it is to open it. Leave me alone."

Moving quickly despite the emotions seething beneath her calm surface, Laurel turned on another overhead light, centering it on the egg. The different illumination suggested an approach to her. A few more moments of study made her decide that the approach might work.

She pushed back from the table.

"What?" he asked instantly.

"I might have found the way."

"Thanks, Laurie, I—"

"Don't thank me," she cut in.

"—knew I could count on you," he said over her words.

"I couldn't let you chop this up like egg salad."

As Laurel turned and went to the locked cabinet on the wall, she saw the satisfied gleam in Swann's eyes. He'd known all along that she would help him rather than see the exquisite egg destroyed.

"Do you always know the right buttons to push?" she asked coldly, spinning the combination lock.

He didn't answer.

The cupboard door popped open. She grabbed a leather satchel and looked back over her shoulder at her father. He was watching her with hooded amber eyes.

"If it helps," he said gently, "I'm not doing this just for myself."

"I told you I don't want money."

"Suit yourself. But I've got some friends who need cash as much as I do. Maybe more. They were screwed over by the system too."

The cupboard door slammed. With a vicious twist of her hand, she spun the combination lock. Then she took a deep breath and let it out slowly, calming the race of her heart.

"Laurie? Is it so awful to help me a little bit?"

"Just stay off my buttons while I do it. I need steady hands for this."

"Sorry. I didn't think you would take it so hard. I guess I've just gotten used to the whole world being as bent as I am. I never should have come back."

She wanted to be angry because it was safer that way, but the pain in her father's voice made anger impossible.

"It's all right, Dad. If I can help you, I will. God knows you've done enough for me, especially since Mom died."

The mention of Laurel's mother brought a shadow to Swann's eyes that he couldn't conceal. "You and Ariel are the best things that ever happened to me. I wanted to be as good for both of you . . ."

"We loved you," Laurel said. "I still do. In the end, that's all that matters."

"Love?"

"Yes."

Though her father didn't disagree aloud, his smile was so sad and yet so hard that she couldn't bear looking at it. So she went to the worktable, put down the leather satchel, and opened the lock that secured the satchel's flap. Inside there were several leather-covered boxes and a portable laptop computer. She ignored the computer and took out one of the boxes.

The box had two compartments. The first section was filled with sheets of paper that had been folded around loose gems. The results were small, rectangular parcels that she'd lined up like filing cards on their long edge. Half the size of her palm, the little paper wraps were the traditional way jewelers kept track of small, valuable items like loose gemstones.

The second compartment of the box held tools of all kinds. The most striking were beautifully machined picks, files, probes, and jig heads, all lined up in a special leather case.

Swann came and looked over Laurel's shoulder. He whistled appreciatively when he spotted the matched set of tools. "Maybe you did get something from me, after all. That reminds me of a kit I used to carry. Mine wasn't so fancy, though."

"You made jewelry?" she asked, surprised.

"Nope. Bombs and timer mechanisms, but the picks and probes were the same."

The casual revelation sent ice sliding down Laurel's spine. Suppressing a shudder, she chose a dental probe that had been coated with thin rubber. With a silent prayer of apology for any damage she might accidentally do, she bent over the jeweled egg.

Soon she was lost to everything but the goal of finding the egg's hidden secret. The jewels themselves she dismissed quickly, but she lingered over the settings, which could have concealed a mechanism.

None did.

Disappointed but not surprised, she turned her attention to the solid gold filigree itself. It was beautifully wrought and so cleverly soldered that she saw no break in the pattern, no variation, nothing that would point the way to opening the egg without damaging it.

Frowning, she straightened.

"Nothing, huh?" Swann asked, correctly reading her expression.

"Not yet."

"Well, there's always my way," he said, reaching past her.

"No." She blocked his hand with her body. "Give me a few more minutes. Surely you can spare that much time to save something as extraordinary as this."

He hesitated. "Okay. But only a few minutes, Laurie. Every second that thing is here increases your exposure."

Without a word she went back to working on the egg.

While Swann waited, he watched his daughter. He saw himself in the tiny frown lines gathered between her black eyebrows and in the intensity of her concentration. Not for the first time he wondered what life would have been like if he'd been more settled and the world less wild.

Time only runs one way.

"The whole purpose of the egg is the surprise, right?" Laurel mumbled to herself.

"Art was never my best subject."

She ignored him. "The last thing Fabergé would have

wanted would be to irritate the czar. Therefore, any mechanism would have to be easy to operate. Concealed, yes, but still natural for someone to find."

With her right hand, Laurel grasped the egg like it was a present she'd just unwrapped. One of her fingertips fell naturally onto an intricate filigree knot. There were other knots just like it in the pattern, but none were placed exactly where a right-handed person would grasp the egg.

One cord of the filigree was raised slightly.

"Oh, you were a clever courtier," she murmured to a long-dead craftsman. "Hide it just enough so there is a sense of victory in finding it, but don't hide it so well that your lord and master would get frustrated."

"Do you have it?" Swann asked sharply.

"I think so."

He reached for the egg.

Again she blocked his hand with her body. "Wait. It's delicate."

Gently she pressed on the raised filigree, trying to slip the gold wire first one way and then the other.

There was a soft metallic sound as a hidden lever moved. The jeweled shell split into two pieces, as if the top had been sliced off a soft-boiled egg. As the top came off, a hidden internal mechanism lifted up a red gemstone that was bigger than the ball of a man's thumb.

"My God," Laurel whispered, shaken by the size of the gem.

The stone was deep red, with large flat facets. Despite the odd cut, the gem burned with a ruby fire that was eerie. Alive.

"So that's why they call it the Ruby Surprise," Swann said.

She barely heard him. She was focused exclusively on the

stone. The color was too deep to be described as pigeon's blood, the standard by which all rubies were judged. But the gem itself seemed flawless.

"I've never seen a stone quite like it," she said. "Light pours *through* it. I guess the czar's likeness would have gone on one of the broad facets."

Swann grunted.

"But the color is a bit off the highest standard," she said. "The ruby would be hard to match with any other stones. It's dark."

"Like blood that's just starting to dry," he said.

Laurel had used the term pigeon's blood for so many years that she no longer thought what the comparison really meant. With a grimace, she looked away from the hypnotic stone.

The interior of the bottom of the egg had a design that was an intricate, asymmetrical, curved lattice made of silver and gold wires and pieces of what looked like clear crystal. If there were other jewels inside the egg, they weren't immediately obvious.

Something cheeped rhythmically, startling Laurel from her intense study.

Swann pulled up the tail of his loose shirt and reached for the beeper on his belt. The motion gave Laurel a glimpse of the gun butt in the small of his back. Black, deadly, yet oddly beautiful in its shape, like a Stealth aircraft. A practical objet d'art for a practical man.

When Swann saw the readout window of the beeper, he nodded like he'd expected to see just that number.

"Over there," she said, pointing across the room to a phone.

He went over, punched buttons, and waited while it rang.

She couldn't tell from his expression if he was pleased, angry, or indifferent to the interruption.

"It's me," he said when the call was answered. "What's up?"

He listened briefly. "What did he say?"

As Swann listened, Laurel sensed the gulf between them opening wider with every second. Gone was any hint of an affectionate father, or of a lover who still grieved for a woman seven years dead.

Now her father was what life had made him, what he'd chosen to be—a contract warrior. Hired muscle. Perhaps even an assassin.

I cut my share.

"Then squeeze his nuts harder," Swann said distinctly. "Twist 'em until they pop. He'll come around."

As he listened to the response, his eyes almost disappeared in a cold, humorless squint of a smile.

"Then twist harder," he said curtly. "I'm headed south now. I'll see you in a few hours."

After he hung up, he stared at the phone for a long moment, as if trying to decide something. Finally he looked around. When he saw his daughter, his eyes widened. He'd forgotten he wasn't alone.

"Is there anything else you need from me?" she asked. Her throat was so tight the words were hoarse.

Swann studied Laurel for a long time. Gradually his expression of dark intensity gave way to a kind of bleak gray melancholy.

"I need a few minutes alone," he said. "I—uh, I have to make a phone call. After that I'll take the egg and go. Then you forget about it. All of it. Got that?"

"The package never came. I never opened it. You never were here."

For a moment he stared at her, surprised by her succinct summary of what he wanted from her. Then he blinked, grinned, and the happy-go-lucky pirate of a father was back.

"You stick to that and everyone will be okay," he said approvingly.

"Are you in danger?" she asked bluntly.

"Run along upstairs. When you come back down in ten minutes, I'll be gone."

"You didn't answer my question."

"Don't worry about me. I can take care of myself."

Sure, Laurel thought. *That's why you're in this mess.*

"I'll leave you my pager number," he said.

He went to the dry-marker board where her next three projects were listed in different colors, with the phone numbers of various gem suppliers across the United States written in red down one side. Swann added an 800 number and beeper code to the red list.

"Don't call just to say hello," he said as he wrote.

"Have I ever?"

"I've never given you the chance before."

Swann turned around. Laurel was standing close to him, her face lined with tension.

"Keep your answering machine on, baby," he said, kissing her forehead. "I'll be in touch. And if you go anywhere, take your work valise with you. Valuable stuff always comes in handy."

"Dad, what—"

"Go upstairs," he interrupted, but his voice was gentle. "Everything is fine. You're out of it now, back to the world of cozy little moral choices."

He turned his daughter by the shoulders and pointed her toward the stairs.

Reluctantly she took a few steps, trying hard to find words that might make a difference. No words came except the words that had never made a difference in the past.

When Swann heard the upstairs door close softly, he waited a moment longer, listening. Then he moved like a ghost up the stairway. He stood very close to the door, listening with senses honed by years of living on the edge.

No sound of breath. No impatient shuffling of feet. No rub of cloth against the door.

Laurel had done just what he had asked.

You're paranoid, Swann told himself. *Good thing, too. Damn few paranoids die with a knife in their back.*

Whistling softly under his breath, he began pulling tools out of Laurel's satchel until he found what he wanted. Still whistling, he bent over the egg.

Ten minutes later Jamie Swann kept his promise and disappeared.

12

At just past four, a Cadillac limousine cruised down Hill Street past the winos and dope dealers in Pershing Square. As the city unrolled on either side, Damon Hudson stared through the limo's darkened windows. It had been years since he'd been to the downtown Los Angeles jewelry district. A lot had changed.

None of it good.

The jewelry district had once been a dark, quiet corner in the Anglo enclave called "downtown." Jews and Armenians and Syrians, all of them dealers in gold or precious stones, had rented small stalls in buildings owned by the Chandlers and the Shermans, the Strubs and the Gerkens. Now those same Middle Easterners owned the buildings and rented stalls to Vietnamese, Mexicans, and Filipinos.

Some people felt downtown Los Angeles had blossomed. Others felt it had metastasized. Hudson's vote was for the cancer simile. Financial and political power had spun off in all directions—to Century City, to the San Fernando Valley, to Orange County. In the rush to suburbia, the jewelry district had been left behind.

Without fanfare, the jewelry district had grown until it overwhelmed the heart of the old downtown. Twelve square blocks had been transformed into a vivid, vital, and sometimes shady crossroads of the Pacific Rim jewelry trade. The district was a microcosm of the new Los Angeles, a polyglot, postmodern melting pot. Hudson didn't like any part of it.

The black limousine slid around a pair of double-parked Brink's armored trucks in front of the 550 South Hill Street Building. The structure was a perfect example of the district's change, a Tower of Babel built from gem, gold, and diamond profits. Inside the building, Israeli, Dutch, and Indian diamond cutters rubbed shoulders with Japanese pearl dealers, sapphire and ruby brokers from Southeast Asia, and gold merchants from South Africa and the Middle East.

Ordinarily Hudson would have avoided the shouting and shouldering of the jewelry district. There was something wrong about a man of his stature frequenting such an obviously greedy place. He'd long since outgrown the kind of shameless hustling that went on behind the district's guarded high-rises.

But right now, he didn't have much choice about mingling with the brash new kids on the block. He needed to walk in cold on Armand Davinian. Dead cold. No warning and no chance to hide. It was the only way Hudson could hope to get an unguarded response from his former associate and onetime friend.

The limousine pulled to the curb in front of 609 South Hill, one of the older buildings in the area. Without waiting for the driver to serve him, Hudson pushed open the door, slid out, and stalked across the sidewalk. The elevator in the lobby was old. It was crowded with people and languages he didn't understand.

Hudson took the stairs, quickly climbing up three flights. At the top he was a bit out of breath. He paused to let his racing heart slow down. Davinian was old and weak, but he was dangerously shrewd. Hudson would need every ounce of mental advantage he could summon, including the psychological edge that came from superior health.

The third-floor hallway stretching in front of Hudson was dark to the point of being secretive. Small suites opened on either side. Each suite presented a large glass display window to the world. Each suite was guarded by a thick glass door whose lock operated only from inside the room.

That, at least, hadn't changed. The people who locked themselves into their gold and gem rooms had a keen understanding of human greed.

Hudson walked swiftly down the hall, not stopping until he was in front of a door discreetly labeled DAVINIAN AND SONS, DIAMONDS AND METALS TO THE TRADE. A bigger sign in one corner of the dark, virtually empty display window warned: NOT OPEN TO THE PUBLIC.

Leaning forward, Hudson stared through the glass door into the gloomy shop. Most of the display area was dark. In the back room a frail bald man sat hunched like a vulture over a workbench.

Hudson tried the door. As he expected, it was locked. He rattled the knob sharply instead of knocking.

The old man looked up. In the pitiless white light of a work lamp, his face looked cadaverous. He wore conventional steel-rimmed glasses with extra magnifying lenses mounted on pivoting stalks. Owllike, he blinked, letting his eyes adjust to the changed focal distance.

Slowly his glance came to rest on Hudson's face. For a

long moment, the old man simply stared like he didn't believe what he was seeing.

Hudson rattled the door again and kept on rattling, demanding entry.

Finally the birdlike man touched a button on the wall beside the workbench.

A buzzer sounded. Suddenly the knob turned beneath Hudson's hand. The door opened with a distinct squeal of metal on metal.

Before Davinian could change his mind, Hudson was inside. Without a glance at the astonishing array of gemstones, he crossed the display area. All he cared about was the old man who was watching him from the work area.

Behind Hudson the door locked audibly, isolating the two men from the rest of the world. A display counter joined by a locked gate prevented Hudson from getting into the work area where Davinian waited.

"Armand, what kind of madness have your people committed now?" Hudson demanded.

Davinian blinked and said nothing.

"Has all of Russia gone crazy, or are just a few of its less intelligent members stirring the pot?" Hudson continued angrily.

Slowly Davinian straightened, left his workbench, and walked to the display case that was holding Hudson at bay. He stood across the case from Hudson, watching carefully, a man expecting some kind of trick.

"You should not talk to me of craziness," Davinian said in a reedy voice. "You are the one who came here during working hours for the whole world to see. Why, for the sake of God? Our business is finished. We agreed never to meet."

"I didn't think I'd ever have to see your face again. Then

your big black dove landed on my shoulder yesterday, and I changed my mind. We need to talk. *Now*."

Davinian cocked his head. It was the gesture of an old man whose hearing had begun to fail.

"Black dove?" Davinian asked softly. "Who or what are you talking about?"

"Six feet of female. Dark. A journalist with a well-oiled snatch."

"I don't know any—"

"The hell you don't," Hudson cut in. "The knowledge behind the kind of questions she asked could only come from one source. You."

"I say again that I do not know this person."

"Bullshit. Only a handful of people in the world know enough to ask questions about parcels of diamonds that were sold at auction in Antwerp in 1937."

Davinian's eyes widened in shock.

"Or questions about French Impressionist paintings in my own collection," Hudson added savagely. "She knew about other paintings too, the ones that were sold at auction from the late 1930s on into the sixties."

"On my soul I do not—"

Hudson kept on talking. "She even asked questions about Fabergé pieces that began appearing in the West in the fifties."

Davinian leaned heavily against the counter.

"There are only a few people who know me well enough to know how embarrassing the answers to those questions would be," Hudson said. "Only one of those people is here in Los Angeles—Armand Davinian. Ready to talk now?"

With hands that showed the involuntary tremors of age, Davinian took off his glasses and rubbed the bridge of his nose.

"Why did you betray me?" Hudson asked. "Did you think I was too old to beat a spy like you until you begged for mercy?"

Automatically Davinian began polishing his glasses with the end of his dark blue necktie. The silk of the tie was frayed, showing it had been used like this for a long time.

"I am a jeweler," Davinian said firmly. "I was born in Soviet Armenia. I have maintained some contacts there. I have done business with you from time to time. I am not a spy."

"Bullshit. You're an unregistered agent of a foreign government. You acted on behalf of the Soviet Union. We both know where the diamonds came from, and the paintings, and all the rest of the stuff you sold through me."

"You were well paid."

Hudson's open hand slammed onto the display counter. The glass rattled.

"And we both know the money from every sale went right back to your bosses in the KGB," Hudson said. "Now tell me again that you aren't a spy."

Davinian spread his own gnarled hands on the glass as if to hold it in place.

"Calm yourself," the Armenian said in his dry, whispery voice. "Unlike you, I have had no contact with Moscow in some time. My associates are no longer in positions of power. Much has changed."

"Changed?" Hudson smiled sardonically. "Things never change. Not in any way that matters. There are always more pigs than there are places at the trough. So you figured to feed from my trough instead of fighting for a place at Russia's."

Davinian shook his head, silently repeating his innocence.

"How much?" Hudson demanded. "How much will it cost to buy you off?"

"Think past your anger. I cannot be the source of your troubles. If the past is revealed I have as much to lose as you."

The papery whisper of the other man's voice finally penetrated Hudson's rage, revealing the fear beneath. He'd spent a lifetime making certain that he was immune to poverty, snobbery, and bad health. For years he'd felt invulnerable.

But no longer.

Abruptly Hudson turned away, not wanting Davinian's shrewd eyes to see the fear.

A buzzer sounded. The latch on the gate popped open. A frail hand touched Hudson's arm.

"Come in the back with me," Davinian said. "Sit down, have some tea, and then tell me precisely what occurred. We will find a way past this difficulty, just as we did with other difficulties in the past."

For a moment Hudson remained stiff. Then he cursed and turned around.

Davinian was there, waiting, watching Hudson with dark eyes that even time hadn't managed to cloud.

"All right," Hudson said. "Christ, what a mess."

While Davinian brewed and poured tea, Hudson talked. Without appearing to, Davinian listened with the silent intensity of the assassin he once had been. While he listened, he sipped the potent tea. The more Davinian heard, the more he understood Hudson's fear.

Claire Toth was dangerously well informed.

"The bitch must have been reading my mail—*our* mail— for years," Hudson said. "You should have seen her rubbing against my prick and sticking her tongue in my ear while she described every deal you and I ever did."

"All of them?"

"Everything from the diamonds to the Old Masters."

"Diamonds are common and anonymous," Davinian said.

"Some of them weren't."

"She knew of those too?"

"Yes. The Romanov blues and those pinkish ones that Harry Winston bought."

"Truly?" Davinian sighed. "That is not good."

"It gets worse. She recited a list of paintings that was accurate and detailed. She knew it all. She even knew how we divided the profits, and how I invested mine."

"Ah. Now you must know I was not involved."

"What?" Hudson asked.

"I never bothered myself with the details of your business, just as you never intruded into my life."

After a moment, Hudson nodded reluctantly. "But what about those Russian pals of yours? They don't trust anyone. Not even me."

Davinian almost smiled at the irritation in the other man's voice.

"Despite all the friendship I've shown the Soviet Union over the past five decades," Hudson said, "all the trade embargoes I've fought, all the right-wing American lunatics I've antagonized, the Russians never once confided in me. And now this—Christ. I deserve better than this from those peasant bastards."

Davinian shook his head. "You would have made a fine actor. One would think you did not know that betrayal is the first rule among men."

"But I had a vision. All my life I've worked toward world peace and cooperation. I cultivated warm relations with every Soviet leader from Stalin to Gorbachev. I'll even make my peace with this idiot Yeltsin, if I must."

The sound Davinian made could have meant anything.

"Everything I've done was in the name of breaking down the barriers between peoples," Hudson said earnestly.

"And in the name of profit."

"They used me!"

"Just as you used them."

"But—"

"Please," Davinian interrupted, "do not play the naive international philanthropist with me. It is unbecoming. You were a friend of the Soviets because it profited you."

"No. I *believed*."

"Then you were a fool. I do not think you are now or have ever been a fool, Damon Hudson."

For a moment the two men looked at one another in silence.

Although they were about the same age, Davinian had always been envious of Hudson's strength and aggressive virility. Now Davinian was seeing Hudson in a different light. Hudson's body was amazingly sound, but his mind seemed to have gone soft. Davinian wondered if it was a side effect of the sexual booster shots Hudson was taking in secret.

At least Hudson thought the process was a secret.

And it was, from most people. But not from Davinian. The very places Hudson frequented in Eastern Europe—business trips, if anyone asked—were the places where Davinian had old friends.

Abruptly he understood why Hudson was so panicked at the thought of being betrayed by the Russians. Hudson was afraid of losing the source of his unnatural virility.

Even as Davinian mentally noted and filed that fact for future use, he set about soothing the other man's fears.

"I think you are giving this female more credit than she deserves," Davinian said softly. "Others have written about your international business efforts in the past and nothing has come of it."

Hudson dismissed the words with an impatient wave of his hand. "I spend millions on public relations men to make sure that nothing comes of muckraking articles."

"Your money has been well spent."

"Only because most journalists are lazy. Not one of them ever dug as deep into my personal history as Claire Toth did."

"Interesting," murmured Davinian.

"If she knows so much about me, she most assuredly knows about you as well. Have you thought of that?"

Davinian nodded. "Yes. It is an unhappy circumstance. A very unhappy one."

For more than thirty years, Davinian had been part of a large and carefully concealed network of political operatives. He was a technician, not an ideologue, but he had plied his craft exclusively on behalf of Moscow.

His primary task had been to act as a liaison with Hudson, but Davinian had undertaken other jobs as well. He monitored certain individuals in the Los Angeles Soviet émigré community, passing along information gleaned by a small but efficient network of operatives in Southern California's defense and aerospace industries.

He had also arranged the disappearance of troublemakers.

Although Hudson knew nothing of these other activities, the man was shrewd enough to guess that Davinian had secrets that were better off not revealed.

If Davinian was named as a Soviet operative in an article about Damon Hudson, an investigation would surely follow. A good counterintelligence investigator would dig until the whole network was uncovered. The men Davinian had worked for were still in place in Moscow, if not exactly in power.

Their interests were the same as Hudson's. Which meant that, for now, Davinian's and Hudson's interests were the same.

"No one on our side is betraying you," Davinian said, wondering as he spoke if it was true. "Russia would gain nothing by it, and we would lose a great deal."

"Not as much as I would," Hudson shot back.

"I will make you a promise. I will make some inquiries about the Toth woman."

"There's no time for your usual inquiries. She's coming to see me tomorrow morning."

"So soon? Why?"

"To show me the proof she intends to use in her article."

Davinian rested his hand gently on Hudson's. Part of the Armenian's mind noted the vast differences between their flesh. Davinian's skin was loose, thin, and marked with liver spots. Hudson's was thick, firm, and clear, the skin of a healthy man in his forties.

In an odd way, Davinian realized that he had an advantage over Hudson. Davinian knew he was nearing the end of his life. No matter what happened, he had little to lose. Hudson was frightened, for he believed that much could be taken from him. Davinian wondered if the other man knew his life could easily be one of the things that was taken.

But all Davinian said was, "I will have something for you before the journalist returns."

13

Over Karroo
Monday evening

Shutting out the lingering twilight, Cruz Rowan studied the dark, rumpled desert landscape below Risk Ltd.'s plane as it lifted off the runway into the gathering darkness. Not only had he wasted too much time dancing with Novikov, but it had taken much longer than expected to finally get airborne. The pilot was a fussy bastard when it came to having everything about the plane just so. One light blinking, or one dark that should be lit, and the plane was grounded.

Not that Cruz really objected. Better an overzealous pilot than a landing nobody walked away from.

As the plane climbed, the Karroo compound shrank rapidly in size. The power was strong, steady, and smoothly applied. Though sunlight was all but a memory, Cruz could just make out the dark slot canyon where he'd been digging only hours ago.

For an instant he allowed himself the luxury of real irritation. He'd been damned close to solving the mystery of the new fault. He'd sensed it in the same way that he sensed danger. It was simply the way his nervous system was organized.

He suspected that the isolated fault was the first clear surface sign of an entirely unknown subterranean system. There were even tantalizing hints that the fault represented the earth's efforts to ease the tension that had been building for centuries along the infamous San Andreas Fault.

To Cruz the thought of discovering such a network of faults was like a shot of 180-proof scotch. The network would be something new and unique under the desert sun. Such a collection of cracks in the earth's thick skin might have broader meaning. It might even be proof that chaos could really be a self-righting system.

That was what fascinated him—chaos and order and the exhilarating, dangerous zone between.

That zone was the only place in the world Cruz Rowan truly loved, both in his profession and in his avocation. That dangerous zone was always present, always elusive, always compelling, and never the same twice.

For a few minutes longer he studied the gaunt, familiar face of the desert. Then he drew a deep breath and shifted his mind to the chaos more immediately at hand. He pulled a palm-sized color photo of the Ruby Surprise from his pocket and studied it. The picture and the name of the air freight company responsible for shipping the Russian exhibit were all that Novikov had been able to contribute to the investigation.

Or all he'd been *willing* to contribute. Big difference.

As investigative leads, the photo and the name were just slightly better than nothing. All the same, Cruz's pale blue eyes studied the photo intently. From what he could see, the Fabergé egg was intricate, ornate, expensive, and had no purpose except to please the senses.

What an odd and useless thing, he thought. *Like too many women—decorative and without real function. But then again, maybe beauty is supposed to be its own reward, its own function.*

Lots of beautiful women sure seem to think so.

There were even times when Cruz agreed. There was nothing quite like waking up hard and sliding into a soft, warm woman.

I've been out in the desert too long. Next thing I know, I'll start believing that the fucking I get at the beginning is worth the fucking I get at the end.

Beneath the starboard wing, a blacktop highway snaked toward the multilane interstate that led toward Los Angeles. Cruz glanced at the narrow, twisting blacktop and smiled thinly. He hoped Novikov was enjoying being chauffeured by Gillespie. The sergeant-major had once made the drive in a few hours. Once he'd taken seven. It depended on how pissed off he was.

The more angry he was, the slower he drove.

At least Novikov was out of the way for the moment. Sometimes the client was more a problem than a help, particularly when he couldn't be trusted. Still, there were questions Cruz wouldn't mind asking Novikov. Maybe the Russian would even answer.

Maybe.

Cruz reached for the cellular phone on the bulkhead wall in front of him and punched in a number.

Gillespie answered from the Mercedes somewhere on the desert below.

"Gillie, ask your passenger if he can get a waybill number for the missing crate on the shipment from Tokyo."

The sergeant-major relayed the question. The cellular connection was hollow and silent for a time. Then Gillespie came back on.

"We'll call you in five."

"Affirmative."

Five minutes later by the clock, Gillespie called the plane and gave Cruz a ten-digit number.

"Anything else?" asked the sergeant-major.

"Not yet."

Cruz rang off and dialed Los Angeles information. Two minutes later he was talking to the firm's international traffic manager. It took a few more minutes to reach the air freight manager.

"Sam Harmon," the man said. "Make it quick."

Cruz smiled. The accent was military. Probably recently retired and not yet used to the fact that people didn't have to obey him or get court-martialed.

"Harmon? I knew a Harmon in the air force," Cruz said. "He was a loadmaster in Starlifters."

"I was a marine officer," Harmon said curtly. "Thirty years and four months."

"Combat?"

"Logistics. How the hell else you think I'd land a job like this?"

Cruz smiled to himself. A retired marine logistics officer. If anyone understood the system, he would.

"I've got a logistics problem," Cruz said, "and you're probably the only man in the world who can help me."

"Fire away."

Gotcha, Cruz thought. Nothing like being needed to get a retired man's full attention.

"I've got a client who lost a package," Cruz said casually. He didn't describe the contents of the shipment. He didn't want to panic Harmon unless he had to. "Someone told me you have a computer system or something that could help us to backtrack."

"We've got computers, bar-code scanners, locator beacons, and Global Positioning System monitors," Harmon said. "I can track any package anywhere in our system anywhere on earth. If it's in a warehouse or an airplane, I can tell you. If it's on a truck, I can let you talk to the driver who's delivering it. We're squared away around here."

Everybody believed in something. Sam Harmon believed in his system.

"Great," Cruz said enthusiastically. "Where do we start?"

"You got a waybill number?"

Cruz read the number and heard the hollow clacking of a computer keyboard. He held his breath, wondering how much information would come up on the shipment.

"Negative on that number," Harmon said quickly.

"What does that mean?"

"It's a null. The number isn't in our system."

Cruz thought for a moment. There was no reason for Novikov to lie about something that could be checked so easily.

"It's a good number," Cruz said.

"Not here it ain't. Unless it was part of a larger shipment?"

"It was."

"Why didn't you say so?"

More hollow clacking sounds came over the cellular.

"Got it on the scope," Harmon said. "It was with that bunch of art that came in on the seven forty-seven yesterday from Tokyo."

"That's the one."

"Motherfu—er, *damn,* don't tell me we lost one of them."

"That's what I'm trying to find out," Cruz said. "But relax. Even if it's AWOL, it's not the Mona Lisa."

Harmon made a noise that sounded like relief, but he was already punching the keyboard again. Fast.

"I've got the shipment on the screen," Harmon said after a few moments. "Fifty-five pieces."

"Where are they now?"

"They all passed through Customs inspection and then were logged by the scanner before they went to the Customs broker. From the broker, they were trucked directly to the museum."

Harmon's fingers rattled on over the keys, then stopped.

"That's funny," he said.

Cruz felt a little tingle. It told him he was entering the zone where neither chaos nor order ruled.

"What do you have?" he asked softly.

"I just displayed the manifest for the entire plane," Harmon said. "Sometimes a single piece will get separated from a shipment in Customs and be held up for a day or two for secondary inspection. Everything passed on that flight, though."

Cruz made an encouraging sound.

"But," Harmon said, "I'm getting this anomalous number all of a sudden."

"What kind of number?"

"It's a domestic waybill all mixed in with a bunch of overseas ones. It's not in the plane's manifest, but it shows up in the return from Customs."

"Like somebody misread a number?" Cruz asked.

"More like somebody plastered a domestic waybill over the international paperwork."

Cruz leaned back and laughed silently. This was going to be fun.

"The sorting process is pretty much mechanized," Harmon

explained. "The machine might have kicked the domestic number into a local delivery line by mistake."

Or on purpose, Cruz thought, *if the switch was performed by a clever thief.*

"Okay, we've got a number for the domestic waybill," Cruz said. "What now?"

"Wait one."

There was a machine-gun burst of keystrokes, then another. Fifteen seconds later, Harmon made a relieved sound.

"Nailed it. Package was delivered today up the coast a ways, a place called Cambria. Stand by for the number."

Cruz memorized the address as he heard it.

"Got that?" Harmon asked.

"Yeah. Did somebody sign for it or did they just leave it on the porch?" Cruz asked casually.

"Laura—no, Laurel—Cameron Swann signed for it. Sierra Whiskey Alpha November November on that last name," Harmon added, spelling it in the international radio alphabet.

"Your machine tells you all that?" Cruz said. "Hell of a system."

Harmon made a gratified sound.

"I'll put a tracer on the package right now," Harmon said. "Somebody will go out and pick it up tomorrow morning. It should be back in Malibu at the museum by tomorrow at the latest."

"My client will be thrilled," Cruz said. "Thanks a lot."

He hung up and hit the intercom that connected him with the pilot. "Set me down as close to Cambria as you can, and don't spare the fuel."

He switched back to the cellular and punched in Redpath's private number.

"Yes?" Redpath said.

"Cruz here. I've traced the egg to an address in Cambria, California. See if we have anything on it or on a Laurel Cameron Swann."

14

Cambria
Monday night

The Shrike touched down at the Paso Robles airport just after nine. Even though there was a rental car waiting for Cruz, it was almost ten-thirty when he drove into the quiet seaside village of Cambria.

He wasn't in a good mood.

All Risk Ltd.'s computer had come up with on Laurel Cameron Swann was that she was twenty-nine, unmarried, no debts, no brothers or sisters, parents divorced, mother dead, father a decorated military man, also dead. No grandparents. Some uncle or another rumored in the background, but could have been the mother's lover.

Not one thing in Laurel's record pointed to a person who had the skill or the contacts to pull off the theft of the Ruby Surprise.

The oceanfront street at the south edge of town where the package had been delivered looked as innocent as Laurel's record. Finding the residence itself was no problem. The old A-frame sat alone on a steep little bluff.

From what Cruz could see, the residence was a small well-kept property with a clean Ford Explorer in the open garage. If there were any lights on, they weren't visible from the street level. The nearest neighbor was fifty yards away. Like Cambria itself, the house was well out of the fast lanes of California living. There was a quality of serenity about the setting that made him wonder if Laurel Swann might not be every bit as innocent as she seemed.

Maybe the package went astray by mistake, Cruz thought. *Maybe this is all a false alarm.*

Then again, probably not.

When it came to human nature and coincidence, he was a skeptic to the marrow of his bones. That was why he made a quick pass to reconnoiter the sleepy town before he went back to Laurel's home.

Nearly everything in Cambria was closed or deserted or both. The only exception was a beer bar set back on one of the side streets, its sign crooked and blinking erratically. A handful of vehicles were parked around the bar. There was no reason to believe that anyone was leaving anytime soon.

Farther on, a gas station squatted at the north edge of the business district as if apologizing for the very fuel that drove the modern age. Though the station was open, there were no takers. The night manager was so old that Cruz doubted he could tell a car from a truck.

A sheriff's department substation next to the volunteer fire department was dark. Cruz guessed there was a patrol car somewhere in the area. It didn't worry him too much. Cambria wasn't the kind of town that kept beat cops alert at night.

Satisfied that there was little chance of being interrupted at an inconvenient time by edgy cops, nosy neighbors, or random pedestrians, Cruz turned onto a road that ran parallel to the beach. He parked in a small cul-de-sac a quarter mile past Laurel Swann's house, shut off the headlights, and got out of the car like a man who wanted to enjoy the smell and sound of the ocean at night.

No house lights came on around him. No doors opened, letting light out into the night. Nobody was walking the dog or putting the cat out or sneaking off to jump into a neighbor's bed.

Cruz walked beyond the streetlight's illumination and vanished into the night. Very quickly he found a path down to the narrow, rocky beach. Soon he was looking up at the modest cottage that held, innocently or not, a priceless Fabergé egg.

The surge and roll of the surf was loud. It made a perfect cover for any sounds Cruz might make in his approach. Even so, he made no unnecessary noise as he climbed up the wooden stairway that clung to the bluff. A large weathered boulder gave him cover while he studied the little house.

No water bowls for pets, no fenced run, no sign of dogs. No night-light burning outside, no alarm box, no barred windows or deadbolt locks on the doors. From all outward appearances, Laurel Swann had nothing to hide and no fear of her fellow man.

She must be as willfully naive as the town itself.

Despite the sleepy, unguarded appearance of the cottage, he waited until a cloud blocked the half-moon in the western sky. Only then did he leave his cover and cross the rocky stretch to the side of the house.

There was no sound coming from inside, no flickering glow of a television in any of the windows he could see. Laurel Swann was either asleep or out on a date. From what he'd seen of the town, Cruz decided she was probably asleep.

He circled to the back, made mental note of the license

plate on the Explorer, and waited in the dark garage. It would take a little time for his eyes to adjust to the interior darkness after the relative brightness of the moonlight.

The garage was neater than most but otherwise unremarkable. It held a washing machine and a dryer, storage cabinets on the wall, something piled where a second car could have fit, the Ford station wagon masquerading as a four-wheel drive utility truck, and a new metal trash container just inside the open garage door.

As his eyes completed their adjustment, Cruz looked more closely at the stuff piled in one half of the garage. He discovered a pair of large, refillable butane cylinders, an old scarred workbench, and a stack of boxes.

The boxes intrigued him. He pulled out a tiny pinpoint flashlight to inspect them. Each box was marked with a clear, legible hand, probably female: CASTS. MOLDS. STONE-HOLDERS. MOUNTINGS.

Jewelry maker's terms, Cruz thought.

He shut off the light and stood in the darkness, putting together what he'd seen.

A woman, a jeweler or jewelry dealer, apparently living alone. Neat without being fussy, reasonably well off, unafraid.

Something is wrong about this setup, he thought unhappily. *This isn't the home of a thief or a fence. Crooks are paranoid. Crooks have guard dogs.*

Crooks at least close their garage doors at night.

Abruptly Cruz felt uneasy, out of place, like he was the criminal. The setting was too calm, too serene. The air smelled too clean.

The cottage felt innocent.

He'd done more than his share of residential prowling over the years. As a federal agent, he'd crept around suspects' homes without a flicker of conscience. He seldom gave a thought to the privacy of others.

But tonight he was an intruder. He knew it as surely as he knew he had only nine fingers.

He had an impulse to withdraw, to leave Laurel Swann in peace.

Whatever her secrets are, I doubt that they're important enough to justify this kind of invasion.

Surprised by the intensity of his reaction, he struggled with the feeling of being in the wrong. Up until that moment, he would have said he had no such scruples. He'd spent his life in the netherworld, pursuing bank robbers and kidnappers, international terrorists, and drug merchants of all stripes. As a result, he didn't think much of humanity as a whole.

The exceptions he'd encountered—Cassandra Redpath and Ranulph Gillespie were among the select handful—had only reinforced Cruz's certainty that, as a species, *Homo sapiens* wasn't any better than it had to be.

Despite that, he couldn't shake off the feeling that the little beach house in Cambria was not part of the netherworld. It was clean and neat and open. It smelled of ocean spray. He had no right to be here.

But he was here just the same.

Slowly he turned around, giving the garage a final look. The shiny new trash can that stood beside the door drew his eye again. He'd learned a lot in the past by trash-diving. Most crooks were stupid. They thought whatever went into the trash was gone forever. Out of sight, out of mind.

Cops knew better. Out of sight and into the hands of a patient investigator.

He walked toward the can. He cursed silently when he

confirmed that it was indeed metal and already warped by a careless trash collector. Experience told him that he wouldn't be able to get the lid off quietly. He reached for the lid anyway.

Experience was right.

Grimly he struggled with the ill-fitting lid. It had been jammed on hard, but after a few scrapes and one distinct squeal, the lid came free.

At least the lady of the house should be a sound sleeper, Cruz told himself. *The sleep of the innocent. She'll never know I was here.*

Setting the lid very gently on the concrete floor of the garage, he looked into the can. He didn't have to go diving. It was right there on top.

A wad of pale wrapping paper and a shipping label.

For the first time in his life, he felt more disappointed than exhilarated to find himself in the danger zone again, where no one could be trusted.

I'm losing my edge. I really believed this Swann female was clean.

I should have let Cassandra call in Williams and gone back to chasing that fault line.

Maybe Laurel Swann has had a birthday since the last trash collection. That would explain it. A perfectly innocent present mailed from anywhere on the face of the earth except Tokyo.

Yet even as he was trying to explain to himself how his instinct about Laurel's innocence had been so wrong, he was fishing out his small flashlight to have a closer look.

The pinhole beam reflected harshly off the plastic sleeve that had been glued to the paper. He moved the light, shining it indirectly on the document inside the sleeve. It was a domestic waybill with Laurel's address on it and had been transported by an international air freight company.

He peeled a corner of the plastic off the paper. Beneath the plastic was another waybill, one that was marked FOR INTERNATIONAL SHIPMENTS ONLY.

Without reading any further, he knew the box originally had been addressed to the Damon Hudson Museum of Art in Los Angeles.

But he read further anyway, wanting to be absolutely certain that Laurel Swann wasn't as innocent as her cottage.

The international waybill was addressed to the Damon Hudson Museum of Art.

Inside Cruz, disappointment struggled with triumph. Neither won. He simply felt tired.

Then the familiar metallic *click* of a pistol being cocked sent adrenaline exploding through his body. He froze, thinking fast, knowing that any movement could bring death.

The sound had come from behind him.

Though he couldn't see the pistol, he sensed the black eye of the muzzle staring at him from the shadows. Silently cursing how badly he'd misread Laurel Swann, he braced himself for the blow of a club or a bullet.

Nothing happened.

Relief curled through him. Very slowly, he raised his hands to shoulder height, showing he wasn't armed.

No one ordered him to hold still. No one said anything at all. The garage was as silent as death.

By slow degrees he turned his head until he could see a white figure standing in the darkness of the garage. A woman. Her arms were raised in classic target-shooting posture.

From the corner of his eye, he could just make out a pinpoint of Day-Glo orange where the muzzle of the gun would be. That dot was known in the trade as a speed sight. This wasn't a fashionable purse pistol. This was a blow-your-head-off gun.

And every taut line of the woman's body told Cruz she knew just how to use it.

"It's your move, Laurel Cameron Swann," he said quietly.

15

Cambria
Monday night

The sound of her own name shocked Laurel. It had been the last thing she expected to hear from the mouth of the prowler who'd been rummaging in her garage. The voice was a surprise too. Low, almost lazy, calm. Soothing. Reassuring.

Gentle.

Suddenly Laurel knew how the wolf had caught Red Riding Hood. It was the dark, irresistible lure of his voice.

"Are you going to shoot?" he asked.

"I'm not sure," she said honestly.

The husky uncertainty of her voice made the hair stir at the base of Cruz's skull.

"But when you decide, I'll be the first to know, right?" he asked sardonically.

She fought a frightening impulse to laugh. *Velvet voice and a sense of humor too. Red Riding Hood went up against a stacked deck. At least I've got a gun. Poor old Red only had a basket of cookies.*

Laurel backed through the small door into the house,

keeping the intruder's spine in the center of her field of fire.

"Walk backward through the door," she said, "and keep your hands up."

When he obeyed, the relief she felt was so great that for a moment the gun wavered.

But only for a moment. The sight of the prowler backing toward her definitely wasn't reassuring. Her first impression was of size and overwhelming darkness. Dark hair, dark sweater, dark jacket, dark jeans, dark shoes. Dark everything.

The second impression was of catlike coordination. Not a domesticated cat. A wild one. The kind that should be kept behind one-inch steel bars.

My God, she thought in dismay. *He's as big as Dad. No, he's bigger. And quicker.*

Then the man turned his head slightly. The pale flash of his eyes was as unnerving as his size. He watched her with an intensity that was chilling.

He's waiting for me to make a mistake. Just like Dad told me would happen if I ever held a gun on a professional.

She took a hidden, steadying breath as Jamie Swann's lessons came rushing back to her. She'd agreed to let her father teach her how to shoot only if he also taught her how to avoid shooting. He'd done just that. It showed in everything she did now.

She kept her distance from the man she held at gunpoint. She never took her eyes off him. She kept the muzzle trained on the middle of his back as they made their way into the house.

"Go to your left, to the windows," she said. "No! Don't turn around!"

The man did as he was ordered.

While she groped for the wall switch on the stairway

that led to the upper floor, Laurel kept the man silhouetted against the moonlight coming through the windows.

Electric light flooded the room.

Seeing better didn't help. It simply proved that her first impression had underestimated the man. He was strong, from his wide shoulders to his muscular thighs. Being indoors in the light only emphasized his graceful, coiled way of moving.

She'd never been so clearly aware of the unfair difference between male and female physical strength.

Now he was looking around her workroom, taking in the details like a computer scanner. Then he made a half turn and looked at her.

Shimmering, ice-blue, clear, riveting in their intensity, his eyes held her as surely as her gun held him. Then he looked away from her eyes to her body.

His expression changed subtly, unmistakably.

Too late Laurel remembered that she was wearing nothing but the thin silk nightshirt she'd grabbed when she heard a noise in the garage. Static electricity made the cloth stick to her body, particularly to her breasts and hips. The prowler was noting every place the silk clung. Especially at the top of her thighs.

"Maybe you should get down on your face," she said, irritated by his frank scrutiny.

He lifted his glance, trying hard not to smile. "It's not necessary," he said gently.

"I'm not sure about that."

He looked at the muzzle of the gun. "That's a big pistol. Are you sure you know how to handle it?"

"The safety is off, the hammer is cocked, and there's a round in the chamber," she said in a clipped voice. "All I have to do is remember how to pull the trigger."

"Not how," he corrected. "When and *if*."

She fought a smile. Her father had told her the same thing, in the same way, emphasis and all.

"Your job is easier," she retorted. "All you have to remember is that you don't want to give me a reason to shoot."

"I can handle that."

She didn't doubt it.

As the probability of having to pull the trigger became less with every passing instant, she found herself noticing the weight of the pistol more. As her father had pointed out more than once, most women didn't have the shoulder muscle to hold a weight at arm's length for long. Laurel was no exception.

On the other hand, the prowler looked like he could hold a rifle at arm's length in each hand and not notice. And he was slowly turning toward her, half facing her now.

"That's far enough," she said.

He's damned good-looking, she thought distantly, *if you don't mind eyes that make ice look warm.*

But the man kept turning very, very slowly, watching the tension of Laurel's trigger finger. When she began gathering slack, he stopped moving. By then, he was three-quarters facing her.

Suddenly she was sure she knew him. Yet she knew she didn't. She wouldn't forget meeting a man like him.

"Who are you?" she demanded.

"Cruz Rowan."

The name, like the three-quarters profile, was oddly familiar.

"What are you doing in my garage?"

"I'm on an Easter egg hunt."

Adrenaline pumped through Laurel's already overloaded system. For the space of a breath all she could think was how incredibly good it would be to have Cruz Rowan on her side.

But he wasn't on her side and wishing was dangerous.

An approving smile curved the tight line of Cruz's mouth, softening the hard planes of his face.

She realized that he was appraising the clinging silk of her nightshirt again. She dropped the gun muzzle until it was aimed somewhere just below the buckle of his belt.

"Easy, Laurel," he said. "I don't want to get shot. You don't want to shoot me."

"Don't bet anything important on it."

"You're an amateur," he said gently. "If you were going to shoot me, you'd have done it by now. If you were going to call the cops, you'd have done that too."

"I'm keeping my options open. Besides, you look . . . familiar."

Cruz knew there was only one reason he would seem familiar to Laurel Swann. *Same old bullshit. Again.*

She watched a look that was both shuttered and weary come to his face. Then his expression became neutral, a mask that gave away nothing of what lay beneath.

For a moment she had an utterly irrational impulse to apologize to him and then to soothe away the brackets around his mouth with gentle touches.

You're losing it, she warned herself. *Why didn't Dad warn me that the first man I held a gun on would also be the first man who looked interesting enough to take risks for?*

Grimly she gathered her scattering thoughts.

"Take three steps to your left," she said with a totally false calm. "Turn all the way toward me."

As Cruz stepped fully into the light from the stairwell, he turned to face Laurel.

Silently she studied him. She told herself she was only

trying to identify him. She certainly wasn't memorizing him, wasn't noting the lines of past pain and present tension, wasn't looking at the clean curve of his lips and wondering how they would feel on her body, wasn't wondering if there were names for all the colors of blue crystal she could see in his eyes.

"Well?" he said neutrally.

"You're handsome enough, but you already know that. You're strong and physically confident, and you know that too. Have we met somewhere before?"

He smiled ironically. "Isn't that supposed to be my line?"

"To hell with lines. Have we met?"

"No."

"Are you certain?"

"Yes."

"How can you be?" she demanded.

"You have the most remarkable eyes of any woman I've ever seen. The rest of you is damned memorable, too. Especially in that scrap of silk."

Well, she told herself, *I asked for it. And Cruz is the man who can deliver.*

Tantalizing thought.

"All right," she said through her teeth. "We haven't met. Then why are you so familiar to me?"

"You tell me."

Deliberately Laurel studied the rest of him. Her glance went slowly from his black hair to his wide shoulders, narrow hips, and muscular legs. When she reached his black athletic shoes, she looked him over again. If the scrutiny made him uneasy, it didn't show.

For the first time she looked at his hands. They were beautifully made, with long, slender fingers—except for the index finger of his left hand, which was little more than a stub.

Cruz saw where Laurel was looking. He fought the impulse to ball his left hand into a fist.

Then her golden eyes widened in shock and he knew she'd remembered why he seemed familiar. He'd seen that sudden change come over other people when they recalled his face from the television screen or the front pages of the newspaper.

Notoriety like that was hard to live with. It had driven a wedge between Cruz and his friends, between Cruz and what little family he had left in the world, and between Cruz and himself.

But to see the shock and surprise and loathing spread across the face of the most interesting woman he'd ever met was infuriating.

Yeah, Cassandra, he thought bitterly. *Time for me to get past it, huh? What about the rest of the world? When will they get past it?*

He waited for Laurel to speak. When she didn't, he did. "I take it you read the newspapers."

The sound of his voice made her flinch. Gone was the dark velvet and gentle reassurance. Cold, brittle, sarcastic, his tone could have frozen sunlight.

"Why do you say that?" she asked.

"I've seen that look before."

The combination of bitterness and acceptance in his voice reminded Laurel of her mother every time Jamie Swann had left his family to chase an adrenaline-filled dream.

Whatever else this man has been and done, Laurel thought, *something hurt him all the way to his soul. Like my mother. But unlike my mother, he's still alive. Still hurting.*

The sound of the safety snapping on shocked Cruz even more than hearing the safety come off in the garage had. In raw disbelief he watched the gun muzzle point away from him to the floor. Slowly he lowered his hands to his sides.

"Let me get this straight," he said. "You discover that I'm the cold-blooded bastard who murdered two teenagers in front of God and a photojournalist, and you put your pistol on safe!"

She looked at the gun as if surprised to see it pointing at the floor. "It was a long time ago. And they weren't teenagers."

"It was five years. And one of them was nineteen."

Frowning, Laurel tried to understand why she'd instinctively decided that Cruz wouldn't harm her. All she could remember of the incident in front of the South African consulate in Los Angeles was that two young black men had been killed by a white FBI agent.

Then the city had gone up in flames. Rioting, looting, shooting, and editorials about how society once again had failed its black citizens.

But all she recalled clearly was the photo, which had become the symbol of all that was wrong in the world in the last quarter of the twentieth century. In the chaotic instant after the two men were shot, a news photographer had snapped a chilling portrait of the FBI marksman who had fired the fatal bullets. Most people had looked at the photo and seen a killer who was intent, cold, brutal.

Inhuman.

The photo had won a Pulitzer Prize. It was reprinted time and time again. Politicians and journalists, demagogues and social critics, each found his or her own meaning in the portrait of the federal shooter. In his black Kevlar vest and with a black watch cap covering his hair, Cruz Rowan had been the image of a mindless, brutal automaton, a government executioner with a sniper rifle and two more notches on his gun butt.

Three congressional investigations had done little to alter

the image, despite the fact that no grounds for any charges against Cruz had ever been discovered.

When Laurel looked at the sniper's face five years later in the shadows of her own workroom, Cruz still seemed dark and cold. But not inhuman. He was a hard man, probably a dangerous man, but far from brutish.

"There's more to you than met the camera's eye," she said simply.

Cruz was too stunned to speak. Then he saw her glance at his left hand again.

"Did that happen at the consulate?" she asked.

For an instant Cruz looked rather like he had in the photo.

"I'm sorry," she said instantly. "That's none of my business, is it?"

His expression softened. "I thought I'd heard all the questions and given all the answers about the consulate," he said after a moment. "No one has ever asked me that one. If we had more time, I'd answer you. But we don't."

Puzzled, Laurel looked at Cruz. He seemed less intent now, less savage, but his expression was a long way from reassuring.

That didn't keep her from asking another question.

"Are you still an FBI agent?"

"I take back what I said about you reading newspapers," he said sardonically.

"What does that mean?"

"I resigned in the middle of the third congressional hearing. That was the one called by the Congressional Black Caucus after the press got wind of my so-called 'sympathies for the South African government.' "

He spoke the last words as a single phrase, like a mindless political slogan. Yet for all its familiarity, it obviously still left a bad taste in his mouth.

"I must have missed that part," she said.

"You were one of the few people in America who did. I tossed my badge on the witness table and handed my Bureau weapon to the director, still loaded."

Laurel would have smiled, but she saw the brackets of remembered pain on either side of Cruz's mouth.

"It was on all the networks that night," he said. "Of course, they blipped my words. The truth is too harsh for politicians' tender little ears."

"So you're not government."

"No. I'm private. Just like I said. I work for a company called Risk Limited."

She felt a sudden stirring of hope. "If you're not an FBI agent, what are you doing here?"

"Like I said, I'm on an Easter egg hunt. Are you the bunny with the million-dollar egg?"

"I don't know what you're talking about," she said tightly.

His grin was wolflike. "Honey, you don't lie worth a damn."

"Then you should believe me when I say there's not one lousy Easter egg in the whole place."

His smile vanished.

"You signed for the package this afternoon," he said in a clipped voice. "The shipping label is in your trash. You should have burned it, by the way."

"I guess I'm not much of a crook," she said quietly. "I can't lie. I can't shoot you. I can't even destroy the evidence."

Laurel put the gun on the worktable and waited for whatever came next.

16

Cambria
Monday night

Without looking away from Laurel's unusual golden eyes, Cruz picked up her gun, popped a catch, and caught the fully loaded magazine as it dropped out of the butt.

She grimaced. She'd decided on an instinctive level to trust Cruz. If she'd made a mistake, she'd find out real soon.

Before he laid the magazine aside, he inspected the bright copper-headed rounds that filled it. With deft, automatic motions he worked the slide and caught a single cartridge as it arced out of the ejection port. He checked the chamber to be doubly sure it was empty and then sighted down the barrel.

"Nice piece," he said. "Model Nineteen-eleven-A Colt. The action has been loosened, tuned to a woman's hand. Good Day-Glo night sight. The magazine is loaded with jacketed rounds."

She watched him put the gun on the table next to the magazine.

"Quite a piece of iron for a lady jeweler who doesn't know how to lie," he said casually. "Your boyfriend's?"

Laurel felt a flash of irritation at the assumption that only a man would be at ease with her gun. "I don't have a boy-friend."

The instant she spoke, she recognized her mistake. Swann had warned her often how people, through indirection, could draw information about him from her.

"Whose gun, then?" Cruz asked casually. "You handle the piece well enough, but that gun was worked on by a pro-fessional who cared about you."

"I'm good with my hands," she said evenly.

He looked at the array of expensive tools laid out on the workbench. "You must be. There aren't many women who could afford a setup like this for a hobby."

"I'm so good I don't have to resort to Easter egg hunts to pay my bills."

"Did you already melt the egg down?"

She looked coldly at him and said nothing.

"I didn't think so," he said. "It wouldn't be your style."

With his left hand, he reached into his jacket pocket and produced a photo of the Ruby Surprise.

"This is worth a lot more than the sum of its bullion and gemstone weight, isn't it?" he asked gently.

She shrugged.

"You aren't the kind to destroy a priceless artifact for a handful of Russian-cut diamonds and a lump of gold," he said.

A faint chill moved over Laurel. Somehow Cruz Rowan knew more about her after a few minutes than her own fa-ther did after a lifetime.

"Do you think it's real?" Cruz asked.

His question was so offhand that she started to reply be-fore she realized what she was doing. The chill went down her spine again, redoubled.

Cruz is good at his work. Too good.

And the fact that she trusted him only made protecting her father harder.

Cruz smiled almost sadly as he watched Laurel's expressive face.

"You really shouldn't play this game," he said. "You aren't cut out for it. Just tell me where the egg is and we'll forget you ever saw it."

"I can't."

He didn't like her response, but he didn't doubt the truth of it. "Why?"

"I don't know where it is. Even if I did . . . I wouldn't."

"Funny. You don't look like a lady with a yen to see the inside of a federal prison."

Her breath came in sharply. She wanted to tell Cruz that he might be privately employed, but her father was a government contract worker. She wouldn't go to prison for helping him.

If Swann was working for the government this time. And if the government could afford to acknowledge it.

If.

"It won't happen," she said tightly.

"You keep saying it often enough, you might believe it."

She turned her back, shielding herself from his penetrating eyes and even more penetrating intelligence.

"When the freight company figures out that the egg is missing, they'll start hollering for the feds," Cruz said calmly. "Then the search warrants and arrest warrants will start raining down. Theft from international shipments. Receiving stolen property. Conspiracy. Those are just the beginning."

He left the table and went to stand behind her, staring over her shoulder at the dark ocean beyond the window.

"I can afford to be a bit more understanding," he said.

"Unlike the shipping company, I don't have any reputation to protect. Unlike the feds, I don't care about prosecuting anybody. I just want the egg back."

Laurel discovered she was holding her breath. He was standing close to her, so close that she could feel his warmth through the silk nightshirt. It sent shivers coursing through her that had nothing to do with fear.

What a hell of a time to be attracted to a man, she thought bitterly. *What a hell of a man too. Is this what happened to mother? Did she get in over her head so fast she didn't know she was in trouble until it was too late?*

"I'm a sucker for an innocent girl in trouble," he said gently. "Tell me what you know, honey. Let me help you."

Without warning she spun around. In the shadowed light of the room, Cruz's expression was both weary and intent.

He'd done this before. Too many times.

"You're good," she said, her voice husky with conflicting emotions. "You're damned good. But good doesn't get it done with me."

He didn't reply. He was surprised to find himself wanting to kiss the lovely crook with honey eyes and a voice to match.

"You're the one who's good," he said. "Dynamite, in fact. Who's the lucky guy?"

"What?"

"Who's your partner? That's what this is all about, isn't it? Protecting the son of a bitch who left you holding the bag?"

"Do you really mean what you say about recovering the egg? If I helped you get it back, would you be satisfied?"

"Yes."

"No criminal charges? No publicity?"

"I'll do everything I can," Cruz said. "After that, you're on your own. Rather, your partner is. He deserves it. A man who puts a woman like you in the line of fire isn't worth protecting."

She closed her eyes for an instant. What he'd promised wasn't enough, but it was all she was going to get.

Both of them knew it.

"At least you didn't lie to me," she said huskily.

Eyes open again, she walked past him and picked up the phone. Without glancing at the board behind her, she punched in her father's pager number. When the signal came, she entered her own callback number.

Then Laurel hung up and looked at Cruz Rowan, the man her instincts told her to trust. He looked confident. Intelligent. Strong. And as remote as the moon.

"It must be useful," she said.

"What?"

"To be able to make people trust you, even when they know they're being manipulated. God, you must think we're stupid."

Without another glance at him, she headed for the stairway.

"Where are you going?" he asked.

"To put some clothes on."

"Don't bother on my account."

"Go to hell."

"Already been, thanks."

"You must have liked it. You never really came back."

17

Los Angeles
Monday night

West Los Angeles was full of discreet hotels that catered to the international elite of the arts and business worlds. Jamie Swann belonged to neither. But years of operating in the international underworld had taught him to use the haute monde as camouflage.

He was checked into the Century Plaza as an international representative of a Swiss chemical firm, just one more traveling salesman with a big expense account. If anyone cared to investigate, his cover would hold up. He actually had been on the payroll of the company at one time. Its personnel department still believed that he worked for the firm.

Swann had ordered a suite on the north side of the building. From his window he could look out through the glare of Century City to the grounds of what had once been a wealthy Santa Monica Boulevard synagogue. Recently, Damon Hudson had acquired the land, bulldozed the house of worship, and erected in its place a monument to his own power.

When Swann's pager went off, he was examining the

walls of the museum building with a pair of high-powered binoculars, trying to trace the wiring pattern of the alarm system. Alarms were a hobby of his. He wanted to see what was the best that money could buy in the private sector.

He pulled the compact pager off his belt and squinted at the return call number in the plastic window. The light in the room was too dim for him to read the numbers. With an impatient curse he moved to the pool of light beneath the lamp on the dresser.

His daughter's number appeared in the window.

"Come on, Laurie," he muttered. "You should know better than to bother me."

Despite his irritation he went to the room phone, got an outside line, and called the number.

She answered the phone on the first ring. "Swann residence."

"What's the problem?" he asked curtly.

"There's a man downstairs. He's on an Easter egg hunt."

Swann's gut twisted. His heart beat too fast in his chest. It was the first time in a long time that he'd felt anything close to real fear.

It was for his daughter.

"Shit," he hissed. Then, "Damn it, Laurie. That wasn't supposed to happen."

"He says he won't prosecute. He just wants the egg back."

"Lots of people want that egg. You can't trust a single one of them. Did he give you a name?"

"Cruz Rowan."

"I know that name. . . ."

"He was the FBI agent who shot the terrorists in front of the South African consulate five years ago."

"Is he still a fed?"

"No."

Swann thought quickly. "Who does he work for now, or is he an independent?"

"He works for something called Risk Limited."

Swann's mind raced, making connections with a speed that had saved his life more than once. He remembered Cruz Rowan. He also remembered Risk Ltd. The firm had built an intimidating reputation in the tight, bleak little world of international spies and spy chasers, terrorists and freedom fighters.

"That outfit is bad news," Swann said bluntly. "How did Rowan get on to me?"

"He doesn't know it was you. He just knows about me. It must have been through the air freight company. He was interested in the shipping labels he found in my trash can."

Swann whistled soundlessly. The best scams were always the simple ones. His diversion scheme had been direct and nearly foolproof. A hundred bucks to a clerk and a new domestic waybill got pasted over the old international one.

Yet Cruz Rowan had traced the package almost immediately, which meant he must have been able to tap directly into the shipping company's computer tracking system.

Swann muttered an unhappy curse. His plan had been as close to perfect as they came, but it was unraveling now.

And Laurel was getting tangled up in the mess.

Rubbing his forehead, he tried to see a way out. Only the most brutally direct ones—bribery or murder—came immediately to mind.

"Where is Rowan now?" Swann asked.

"Downstairs."

"Listening in?"

"Not unless he has a way to do it without lifting the

receiver. The sound quality changes drastically when you have more than one connection open in this house."

Swann grunted. "Good. Get rid of him."

"How? I can hardly call the police, can I?" she said acidly. "He isn't leaving without the egg. But we made a deal. He gets the egg and we get off free."

"No."

"It's the best deal you're going to get from him. It's a lot better than you'll get from the feds, unless you're working for them and they're willing to back you openly."

Swann laughed. It wasn't a reassuring sound. "You've got to stop thinking like a good little civilian."

"What does that mean?"

"The law is for little old ladies who worry about burglars or for salary slaves whose flashy cars get stolen. You're in a different world now, a world where it's power against power, and law has got sweet fuck all to do with it."

There was a long silence on the line. Swann could hear his daughter's disapproval humming through the silence.

"Look, Laurie. I'm doing this for you, and for me, and for a few other sorry schmucks who thought loyalty went two ways."

"But it's not—"

"So just stay out of the way and let me do what I'm good at," he said over her objections. "I'll call you later, after this is all over."

"Wait! What am I supposed to tell Cruz?"

"Don't tell him anything. The trail ends with you. He won't be able to find me unless you lead him to me. And you won't. Promise me, Laurie."

"Don't do this to me," she said, her voice edged with desperation. "I'm not used to your world. I don't like it. I can't promise I'll do what you think I should."

"Listen and listen good," her father said harshly. "You may not like my world but you're in it now, and you can't get out by clicking your heels and wishing for Kansas. You can help me or you can pretend you're above it all and blow things straight to hell. Which will it be?"

The line hummed again.

"I'll do as well in your world as you do in mine," she said finally.

Pain shot through Swann at the emotions vibrating in his daughter's voice. Ariel had sounded like that the last time he'd said goodbye, regret and disappointment and love, all mixed together. At the time, he hadn't known which hurt most, the regret or the disappointment or the love.

He still didn't know.

Without another word he hung up.

"Goodbye, baby," he whispered to the empty room. "If it matters, I love you."

18

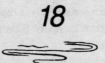

Cambria
Monday night

Moving as though underwater, Laurel pulled a loose cream-colored cotton tunic over her dark turtleneck and jeans. Socks and athletic shoes completed her outfit. As she tied the laces, she realized that her shoes were the same brand as Cruz Rowan's, and the same color. She hated the silly pastels that were forced on women, so she bought her shoes in the men's department.

With a sour smile she wondered if Cruz would notice.

Of course he will. He'd notice new fly specks in a barn the size of California.

With the same unnaturally slow movements she'd used to dress, she picked up her hairbrush and ran it through her hair until she lost count of the slow strokes. She was stalling and she knew it. She suspected Cruz knew it, too.

Finally she left her bedroom and went downstairs. She found Cruz inspecting several wax-working designs she'd left on one of the shelves beneath the window. He seemed to be fascinated by the carved shapes. Delicately, he traced one fluted flower with the middle finger of his left hand. If he was aware of her return, he didn't show it.

"Be careful," she said stiffly. "The figures haven't been cast yet, and I'm supposed to deliver the piece next week."

He put the mold down carefully. "This really isn't a hobby, is it?"

"No. Unlike some people, I use the truth on a regular basis."

He gave her a sideways glance and then returned to admiring the figures. "Did you design these?"

"Yes."

"Who sells them for you, or do you do that yourself too?"

"Several galleries around the country carry my work."

"Under the name Laurel Swann?"

She wondered if he really was interested or if he was just asking questions out of habit. In the end, it didn't matter. At least she could answer these questions without weighing every syllable.

"I work under the name Swann Cameron."

"Are you under contract?"

"I don't have the touch or the temperament for production work," she said. "I freelance a lot."

He nodded, looked more closely at the delicate curves on the mold, asked in the same casual voice, "What did your father say?"

Shocked, shaken, Laurel spun toward Cruz. "You son of a bitch. You listened in."

"I tried. I didn't want to risk someone noticing an open line, so I stood at the top of the stairs. I could hear your tone but not all of your words."

"Then how did you know I was talking to my father?"

"You said you don't have a boyfriend—"

"I don't."

"—but you were talking to someone you're comfortable with. And you're not reading him or her the riot act for getting you in trouble."

She couldn't move, couldn't speak.

"You don't have any siblings or cousins or aunts or uncles, and your mother died in front of witnesses, but your father . . ."

Cruz noted the telltale dilation of her pupils and the abrupt speeding of the pulse in her neck and knew he'd guessed correctly.

"Yeah," he said. "That's what I thought. He's listed as Missing in Action, but nobody found the remains. Is he Agency?"

She said not one word.

"The gun was the giveaway," Cruz continued calmly. "Whoever customized it and taught you how to shoot was a bit old-fashioned. U.S. Army, Vietnam era, probably. Somebody more up-to-date would have given you a small lightweight nine-millimeter."

She forced herself not to look away from his brilliant, icy eyes.

"But the most convincing piece of evidence was your own attitude," he said. "You were worried about whoever was on the other end of the line more than you were worried about yourself. And you were used to obeying him. Otherwise you'd have told him to go piss up a rope when he asked you to lie for him."

Abruptly Laurel turned her back on Cruz. "I almost wish you'd listened in. I don't like being read like headlines in a daily paper."

"You're easier than most. You're honest." He shrugged. "What can I tell you?"

"Try goodbye."

"Don't want to talk to me anymore, huh? How come?"

"Since you're so damned smart," she said between her teeth, "you tell me."

"Under normal circumstances you have every right in the world to protect your father," Cruz said. "But we're talking about high-level international theft of artworks. The law will twist you like a wet cloth to get at your father."

"Nice try, doesn't fly," she said flippantly.

"You think your daddy is working for the feds, is that it?"

"The law doesn't have anything to do with it. That's why you're here. Your client doesn't want the cops."

Surprise and rueful approval showed for a moment on Cruz's face. "You're catching on. Or did your daddy fill you in?"

"Does it matter?"

"I don't know. I do know you won't be immune forever."

"Who is?" she asked sardonically, turning toward him.

"No one. But a lot of people make the mistake of thinking they are."

He looked around the workroom again. The expression on his hard face was unreadable. Then he gave her a view of his back.

Uneasily, she waited for the next round in the undeclared war between them. She doubted it would be long in coming.

It wasn't.

"Our client isn't interested in attracting attention," Cruz said, turning swiftly back to Laurel, pinning her with his brilliant light eyes. "But he'll do what it takes to get the egg back."

She simply stared at Cruz, hoping her game face was half as good as his.

"If chewing up the thief's innocent daughter gets the egg back, then you'll get chewed like gum." Cruz hesitated before adding gently, "I'd hate to see that happen."

"Yeah. Right. You'd cry all over your Risk Limited paycheck."

His eyes narrowed.

"Dad told me all about you," she said tightly. "You're in the same business he was, so don't talk to me about how you worry for the poor bleating lambs of the world. By training and by nature, you and Dad are users and liars. People are pawns to you."

The silence stretched until both Cruz and Laurel could hear themselves breathe.

"Does your father know how much you hate him?" Cruz asked softly.

"No, because I don't."

"You could have fooled me."

"Then you're easily fooled. I love my father. I simply don't *like* him very much, especially when he's in work mode."

She stared past Cruz to the window, where darkness spread over the sea.

"I don't like being a pawn," she said, "but at least I know where I stand that way. Dad loves me as much as he can love anything, including himself."

Cruz heard the sharp edge of sadness in her words and felt a primitive male urge to comfort and defend a female who was more helpless—and more desirable—than she understood. Before he could act on the urge, an old, savage memory flashed before him.

A woman turning to face him with a gentle smile on her face and a heavy black gun in her hand. A searing pain in his own left hand as a bullet shattered the knuckle of his index finger. Then the sound of his gun firing twice, rapidly, the double tap of death.

With some women mercy was a dangerous mistake.

Laurel could be one of them.

19

Los Angeles
Monday night

Jamie Swann sat in the expensive hotel room, watching the lights of the city through the dirty fog that crept in each night from the Pacific. Finally he got up and poured himself a straight shot of vodka from the minibar. He finished the drink in two gulps and was pouring another when he heard a knock.

Shaking himself like a man emerging from a trance, he pulled his gun and went to the door.

"Who's there?" he asked.

"It's me."

He recognized the voice, holstered the gun, and opened up.

Claire Toth stood on the threshold, smiling like a woman who expects to be well and truly welcomed by a man.

"Come on in," he said, turning back to the room.

Hands on her hips, Toth stood in the doorway. "Is that the best you can do, lover?"

"We've got troubles, *lover*," he shot back.

The quality of Swann's voice told Toth that there

wouldn't be any sexual athletics for a while. She shut the door, shot the security bolts, and turned back to the handsome charmer who was the best cocksman she'd ever had. Which put him in a class all by himself. On her rise out of brutal poverty, she'd screwed more men than she could or wanted to remember. They thought they were screwing her, but she knew better.

She was the one who walked away with the money.

And in this world, money was all that mattered. Anyone who didn't think so had never been poor enough to eat cockroaches.

"What happened?" she asked.

"Somebody traced the egg as far as my daughter."

Toth looked surprised, then thoughtful. As she watched Swann walk to the bar, her expression of heavy-lidded sensuality vanished, replaced by a calculating look.

"Daddy's little girl will hold her tongue, won't she?" Toth asked.

The subtle challenge in her voice would have been missed by a less experienced man. Swann didn't miss a thing. He turned around and looked Toth in the eye.

"You can bet on it," he said flatly.

He lied very well. He'd had a lot of practice. So much that he wasn't sure where lies stopped and truth began.

If it ever did.

"Good," Toth said, her voice supple and warm once more.

For the space of two breaths she held the glance of the man whose tawny, feral eyes had fascinated her from the first time she'd seen them. Lion eyes. As sexy as they were dangerous. She didn't know which she liked better, the danger or the sex. She only knew she had to have both or neither was any good.

With Jamie Swann, she got both.

Looking him in the eye, she walked up and stood in front of him, close enough to touch him, close enough to invite his touch.

"Where's the egg?" she asked, but her tone was asking if he felt as much like a man as she felt like a woman.

"In a safe place."

"Did she get the ruby out for you?"

"I didn't ask her to." He smiled thinly. "The less Laurie knows, the better for everyone."

"Who's dogging her?"

"Cruz Rowan."

"Rowan? The fed that murdered those innocent kids?"

Swann laughed curtly. "Jesus, Claire. When did you begin believing your own bullshit? We both know the little assholes were terrorists."

He took a fast drink, draining the glass of vodka.

"Hitting the sauce pretty hard, aren't you?" she asked.

"Don't worry. It won't take the lead out of my pencil."

Her smile changed into a sultry, inviting pout. "Nothing takes your lead out for long. Even me."

He smiled almost cruelly. With a swift movement he bent down, caught her mouth beneath his own, and bit her hard enough to bring involuntary tears to her eyes—and her nipples to hard points.

"You lie like the whore you are," he said, licking the mark he'd left on her lower lip.

"And you believe me like every john that ever paid for it."

Swann threw back his head and laughed. Her savage emotional resilience was the exact opposite of his dead wife's endless capacity to be hurt. With Toth, he didn't have to hold back anything.

"You're like fucking a cat," he said. "Drawing blood only makes you hotter."

"You talk a good game, white boy. When you gonna follow through?"

"When you make me want it so bad I can't wait."

When Toth's hand went to Swann's crotch, he simply watched her through half-lowered eyelids and kept talking.

"Too bad your faked exposé of Rowan's connection to South Africa made him quit the FBI," Swann said.

"Why?" She traced Swann's erection with her fingernails, digging in just short of pain.

His breath came in sharply as he grew beneath her hand. "Rowan's working for a private outfit called Risk Limited."

Her hand went still. "Not good, lover."

"I know. I had to dodge them last year."

She caught the tongue of Swann's zipper between two scarlet fingernails. She toyed with it, watching him. His pupils had expanded and his heartbeat was visible in his neck, but he was nowhere near the limits of his control.

That's what she liked about him. He was almost as cold emotionally as she was. Almost as controlled.

Almost.

The difference was her safety margin.

"What happened?" she asked.

"We bought some electronics gear for a former ally, stuff that was on the Commerce Department's shit list. The manufacturer hired Rowan to find out who was getting embargoed goods from them."

"Did he?"

"Yeah. He blew the deal right out of the water," Swann said.

The sound of his zipper coming down was clear in the silence.

"Everyone gets unlucky," she said.

Her hand slid inside his fly.

"I wasn't unlucky," Swann said. "Rowan was too damned good. Better that he'd stayed with the FBI."

"You'd rather be running from the FBI?"

"They have to play by a few rules. The private guys don't."

For a time there was only the sound of Swann's breathing, deeper now, as Toth threaded him through his shorts and open fly.

"Is the egg close by?" she asked, squeezing him with both hands.

"Close enough."

"Where?"

When he didn't answer, she sank to her knees. Her expression was closed, unreadable, the one she'd used with Damon Hudson, the one she'd used on all men except Swann.

Until now.

"Get it," she said.

The sight and feel of his cock being sucked into Toth's red-rimmed mouth never failed to excite Swann. Even when she raked him with her sharp little teeth.

Especially then.

He could barely breathe for the sexual urgency hammering at him, but he wasn't going to let her know it. Not yet. Not until he couldn't hold back a second longer. And maybe not even then.

"I don't take orders from you," he said.

"Even when your dick is in my mouth?"

"Especially when my dick is in your mouth."

She laughed and licked him like candy. Then she gave him the sharp edge of her teeth. His breath hissed. Abruptly his strong fingers closed around her throat in both caress and warning.

She shivered wildly and made a low sound of arousal.

His smile was as cruel as his eyes. "If I put my hand up your skirt now, it would come away wet."

She didn't deny it. Swann was the only man who could truly excite her, because he was the only man she'd never wholly controlled with her sexuality. Even now, when he should have been at her mercy, his hands could choke the life from her.

And would, given a good enough reason.

Yet she was certain that she excited him more than any other woman had. Because she too could kill. Would kill.

Even him.

"If I'm ever killed," she said, "I hope you're the one who does it."

He fought the heat rising from the base of his spine and asked thickly, "Why?"

"You'd make me come while you did it."

"You'd do the same for me."

"Mmm, yes."

He laughed softly. It was as close to love as hell got.

His hands flexed, savoring the wild beat of his lover's pulse. Then he put his hands beneath Toth's arms and lifted her to her feet with an ease that belied her size.

"Already?" she asked, smiling at the swift victory.

"How about you?"

Without waiting for an answer, he dragged her short skirt up to her bikini underwear. Two fingers slid inside the damp strip of silk and sank into her until he could go no farther.

She made a low sound and clenched around his fingers, redoubling the pressure. Pleasure twisted through her.

"Yeah, babe," he said, biting her lip. "I like it when you get wet."

Without warning he released her and stepped away.

Surprised, she watched as Swann stuffed himself back into his pants.

"I'll be back in ten minutes," he said. "With the egg."

Breathing unevenly, Toth watched him leave. She bit her lip, tasted blood, and bit down harder.

Then she went to the phone, punched in a number that went directly to a cellular phone, and waited.

A rough, guttural voice at the other end of the line answered with one word. It sounded like "Yeah," but it could have been in any number of languages.

"Did she have a visitor?" Toth asked neutrally.

"Possibly. There was unusual activity. The lights came on. They are still on."

"Kill everyone there."

"When?"

"Now."

She hung up and went to the window, staring at her reflection, feeling the heat between her legs and wondering who would come and who would die.

And when.

20

Cambria
Monday night

Cruz Rowan studied the woman who had chosen to face the night rather than him. The whole posture of Laurel's body reinforced her silent decision—back straight, legs apart, head up.

She was willing to take on the unknown alone.

No surprise there, he decided. *She's probably been on her own a long time. A father like Jamie Swann wouldn't have been around much. The artist mother probably lived in her own world a lot of the time.*

With Swann for a husband, who could blame her?

"You want to help your father?" Cruz asked finally. "Okay. Tell me where the egg is."

The quality of his voice made ice slide down Laurel's spine. She looked over her shoulder and then quickly looked back at the night. She'd never seen anything quite as bleak as Cruz Rowan's eyes. Compared to them, darkness was inviting.

"I've told you," she said evenly. "I don't know where the egg is."

"Did your father take it with him?"

She shrugged.

"Where did he go?" Cruz asked.

"I don't know."

"Where would he go?"

"I can't help you."

"Can't or won't?"

"Both," she said. "Even if I could help you, it just isn't in me to betray him."

Cruz wished he didn't believe her. But he did, and that left him up shit creek without a paddle.

Puzzled by his silence, she turned around. She expected to confront all the hard planes and angles of masculine determination. What she saw was an expression of compassion and admiration that vanished almost before she could identify it.

This time it was Cruz who looked away. He turned toward the worktable because he could no longer face the woman whose spirit he had to break in pursuit of the real offender—her father.

Cruz picked up the heavy black pistol that had been lying on the table. Though he regularly practiced with a variety of arms, there was something very different about pulling the trigger on a living target. He knew he would never get used to it. In fact, there were times when he wondered if he could do it again.

Shooting people wasn't as easy as the media made it look. It sure as hell wasn't as neat.

He worked the slide of the pistol and locked it in the open position. He reversed the pistol and stared down the muzzle, turning it until the light on the worktable poured through the open receiver.

"Dirty," he said, squinting down the muzzle again. "Didn't your father teach you how to clean it?"

Numbly Laurel watched him handle the heavy pistol. It seemed utterly ordinary in his hands, like a carpenter's plane or a jewelry maker's chasing tool.

"That gun is cleaner than the day it came from the factory," she said. "Why is your client afraid to call the police?"

He lowered the gun, picked up the magazine from the table, and slapped it expertly into the handle.

"You're very quick," he said, "but you're playing a game whose rules and penalties you can't even begin to guess."

"Is that a threat?"

"No. Just the truth. I can accept your decision not to betray your father. I can even admire it, though I know you're wrong. And if you keep going the way you have, you'll be dead wrong." He shrugged. "I can't let you do that, any more than you can betray Jamie Swann."

The hair at the base of Laurel's skull rippled in primal response to Cruz's tone. He wasn't using his richly masculine voice to persuade her. There was no lilt, no shading, no dramatic pauses, no sensuous hush of darkness and velvet. The words came out flat and matter-of-fact.

"You can't stop me," she said. But her voice, unlike his, had shades of uneasiness in it.

"I could take you with me."

She glanced at the pistol in his hand. Her pistol.

"At gunpoint?" she asked acidly.

His mouth kicked up at one corner in an odd little smile. "I think I'll just throw you over my shoulder and carry you off to my desert hideaway. I've always wanted to do that to a beautiful woman."

"You're retrograde," Laurel said, but there was a shadow of laughter in her voice.

"Thank you."

"Besides, private investigators don't have desert hide-aways."

"No?"

"They have cheesy little offices with secondhand desks and the kind of old telephone you see in film noir."

He laughed out loud. "And you call *me* retrograde."

She found herself smiling, pleased that she had removed the ice and distance from his eyes.

"I'm a different kind of private eye entirely," he said. "All our phones are cellular. We have a worldwide radio system to keep in touch with our operatives."

"Pagers too?"

"Yeah. I'd like to flush the damned thing." He looked again at the heavy, old-fashioned, and still quite deadly pistol in his hands. "You might like the desert. You'd certainly enjoy Cassandra."

Laurel's expression became wary. "Wife, girlfriend, or pet iguana?"

"None of the above. She's my boss, Cassandra Redpath."

"*The* Cassandra Redpath? Ambassador, professor, historian?" Laurel asked, startled.

"You left out analyst for the CIA and the State Department."

"It wasn't mentioned on the book flaps."

Cruz looked at Laurel with an intense personal interest he could barely veil.

"Books, huh?" he asked softly. "You actually read her?"

"Actually, I devour her. Dr. Redpath is the only historian I've ever discovered who understands art as fully as she does politics. That's probably because she's a woman."

Cruz looked pained. *Another female chauvinist. Cassandra will love her.*

He slipped the slide release on the pistol and let the action snap closed. Then he set the safety, laid the gun on the worktable, and looked at Laurel expectantly.

"What?" she asked.

"Better get going. We don't have much time."

"Excuse me?"

"Go pack your things. Or do you want to travel light?"

"I'm not going anywhere."

"Sure you are," he said, smiling.

But his eyes were deadly serious again.

"No," she said.

"I don't want to be retrograde, honey, but it's either off to the desert with me—"

"That's kidnapping."

"—or I call in an operative to live in your hip pocket until this is over." Deliberately his glance lingered over the flare of her hips. "On second thought, I might volunteer for that duty myself."

"Retrograde is too nice a word. Now get out of here before I—"

"Call the cops?" he interrupted, deadpan.

Fear, anger, and frustration warred within Laurel. She was boxed. Cruz knew it as well as she did. Better. He was the man hammering down the nails.

"While you're thinking of all the ways I'm a mean, nasty, brutish son of a bitch," he said gently, "go pack."

"No."

"Suit yourself."

She'd never have guessed that a man his size could move so quickly. Before she realized what was happening, he'd grabbed her and lifted her across his chest like a child.

"Damn you," she said, struggling. "Put me down!"

"Fight me or scream and I'll knock you out cold."

Behind Cruz the door vanished with a blunt, shattering

sound. He'd heard those sounds before. Without looking he knew that a shaped charge had just blown a man-sized hole in the door between the workroom and the garage.

He dumped Laurel back onto her feet and whirled to grab the pistol on the worktable.

"Get down!" he shouted to her as he snapped off the safety and cocked the gun.

Dazed, she simply stared as two dark figures leaped into the room. Both of them carried guns. The muzzles swept the room, looking for targets.

Cruz kicked Laurel's feet out from under her and took her down to the floor, covering her body with his own. As they fell, he brought her gun up, twisting to face the men.

She would have screamed but she didn't have the breath. Cruz's forearm was barred across her back, holding her flat on the cement floor. Her face was turned toward the intruders. She heard two odd, coughing sounds followed by a pair of flat, slapping sounds, like a baseball bat hitting flesh.

Cruz jerked. The sharp, rolling thunder of two shots burst from Laurel's pistol.

One bullet struck an intruder in the shoulder, knocking him off balance and flinging him against the wall. His gun went flying as he screamed in pain.

Before that gun hit the ground, Cruz fired again.

Twice.

The second intruder clutched his wrist and screamed. His gun hit the floor and skidded. When he bent to pick up his weapon, Cruz sent two quick shots after him. Bullets whined off concrete and vanished into the darkness outside.

Suddenly the two men retreated, running raggedly from the room, leaving their guns behind.

Cruz came to his feet in a crouch, aiming the pistol with both hands, watching the empty doorway into the garage with an intensity that seemed to throw light into the darkest corner of the room.

Nothing moved outside. No sounds came but the rapidly fading steps of the retreating men.

"Are y-you—" Laurel began.

"Quiet." Though softly spoken, his command cut off her shaky question.

Silence echoed.

He waited for the space of five long breaths. Nothing happened to disturb the returning peace of the night.

Without moving his eyes from the doorway, he reached behind him with his free hand until his fingers found Laurel's arm. He squeezed once, firmly, and motioned for her to stay where she was.

Her cold fingers curled around his hand and pressed once in acknowledgment.

With the lethal grace of a hunting cat, he stalked silently toward the door. An intruder's gun lay in plain sight. A glance told him that the gun was a heavy-caliber semiautomatic pistol with a sausage-sized silencer screwed onto the muzzle.

Professional talent, professionally equipped, he thought with the cold part of his mind.

He looked more closely at the assassin's gun. Where the serial numbers should have been, there were fresh marks left by a steel file.

Thoroughly professional and squeaky clean. Pretty good, too.

Meat hunters.

They had put two of their four shots into the space between Cruz's belt buckle and his rib cage. His mind knew it, but his body was slow to get the message. Adrenaline made a fine anesthetic.

Until the crisis passed.

He bit back a sound as pain finally lanced through his system. Though he told himself to walk to the door and pick up the second gun, all he could do was sink slowly to one knee. A groan came from between his clenched teeth as he fought to stand.

He lost.

Laurel appeared suddenly beside him, bracing him. He looked at her, faintly surprised and a bit groggy. He saw her beautiful golden eyes widen with horror as they focused on two gaping holes in the fabric of his dark sweater.

"No worries," he said through clenched teeth.

"If you believe that, you have the IQ of nail polish."

She bent to see his wound. He fastened his fingers in her hair and dragged her head upright.

"No time for that. Not if you want to live."

"Me? What about you?"

"They were after you. I was just in the way."

Her eyelids flinched. She didn't want to believe him. "Will they be back?"

"I would."

She looked into Cruz's clear, savage eyes. Distantly she knew she should be terrified of him. And she would have been, but for one thing.

He'd taken the bullets meant for her.

21

Cambria
Monday night

Laurel shook her head roughly, trying to stop the savage ringing in her ears. The motion made the ringing worse, but she shook her head again anyway, trying to make something return to normal.

The world had been kicked out from under her feet.

She could still see her pistol spitting orange fire, feel concussions of sound that were like being hit with fists, hear a man's scream, guttural words, two dark figures lurching off into the night, and Cruz crouched like a hunter looking for prey.

It had happened in less time than it took Laurel to run through it in her mind. But even more stunning was the fact that someone wanted her dead. At least, that's what Cruz believed.

She still couldn't.

"Cruz?" Laurel whispered.

"Go pack your things. *Now*."

The dark, angular face of the man who had saved her life

was drawn with pain. He locked his left elbow against his side and got to his feet. Then he leaned heavily against her worktable. The big black gun was still trapped in his hand like a toy.

But it wasn't a toy.

"Move," he said through clenched teeth.

"You can't go anywhere. You're wounded."

"Banged up real good, but not wounded."

"I felt you flinch when the shots hit. I felt it!"

"So did I. Believe me."

He smiled grimly as he put the safety on the pistol and set it on the worktable. Then he tried to get out of his sweater and shirt without moving his left arm.

"What are you doing?" she asked.

"Stripping. Want to help or do you just want to stand around and tuck dollar bills in my jockstrap?"

Laurel muttered something that sounded like *retrograde macho son of a bitch* and reached for his sweater.

"Jesus, take it easy," he said, biting back a groan.

Her hands froze in the act of pulling his sweater up his chest. Close up, she couldn't see any sign of blood.

Thank God. The bullets must not have hit him after all.

But his skin was the color of salt.

"Cruz?" she asked uncertainly.

"Still here. *Wait*. Don't—move."

She heard his breath whistling in and out between clenched teeth. Then came a low sound that could have been a groan as he gave up trying to work his right arm free of the sweater sleeve.

"All right," he said, breathing hard. "Pull it off. Gently."

"I'm sorry. I didn't mean to hurt you."

"Yeah. Take it off the right arm first."

Hesitantly she began dragging the sweater off his right

arm, then over his head. When she eased the knit down over his left shoulder, he sucked in his breath hard.

"Cruz . . ."

"Just take the goddamn thing off," he said through his teeth.

She pulled the sweater free and threw it on the table. Her hands were shaking. Looking at his closed eyes, pale face, and pain-sharpened features didn't help to calm her.

"Now the shirt," he said.

"I don't want to hurt you anymore."

His eyes opened. He looked at her, saw that she meant it, and smiled crookedly.

"It's okay," he said, touching her cheek gently. "Next time I get shot, I'll be damned sure not to wear a sweater."

She wanted to shout at him for wisecracking about something so serious, but she was standing so close to him that she could see every sign of pain on his face. If he'd rather joke than moan, then she'd just have to suck it up and pretend along with him.

"Okay," she said. "No sign of blood so far. Where does it hurt the most?"

"Left side. Pull the shirttail out first. Then unbutton it."

Laurel would have gone around and tugged the cloth loose from the back, but Cruz had his hips braced on the worktable. Awkwardly she reached around him with one hand, avoiding his left side. Leaning her cheek against the right side of his chest, she grabbed a bunch of cloth. It was warm.

So was he.

"You smell good," he said.

"You don't. Sweat and cordite."

He started to laugh, then swore. "Don't make me laugh, honey."

The midnight-and-velvet voice was back again. Warily, she looked up at him as she tugged on the cloth.

Looking at him was a mistake. His eyes were like Brazilian aquamarine, clear and crystalline and brilliant, watching her. She'd seen nothing so starkly beautiful as the contrast between his silver-blue eyes and his dense black eyelashes.

She ducked her head. "It only hurts when you laugh, right?"

"Wrong. It hurts all the time."

"This shirt of yours must hang to your ankles," she muttered, pulling gingerly at the cloth.

"Use both hands."

"What about your left side?"

"Just stay away from the ribs."

Taking a deep breath, she bent over, put her arms around his lean hips, and reached up to pull gently on the shirttail. To her relief it went much quicker with both hands. Having his belt buckle cool against her cheek was doing unnerving things to her. Not to mention the vital muscular heat of him radiating into her hands, her arms, her face.

"Laurel?"

She glanced up just as the shirttail came free. What she saw made her forget to breathe. The expression on his face was a mixture of pain and humor and intelligence.

And desire. Unmistakably.

That was when she realized that his belt buckle wasn't all she had her cheek against. She straightened so fast she nearly fell.

"Easy, honey," he said soothingly. "It's just the adrenaline. Best aphrodisiac on earth."

She hoped the light from the staircase was too dim to show the scarlet on her cheeks. "Don't worry. I won't faint on you."

"Good. I'd have a hell of a time carrying you out to my car."

Rather than start an argument over where she was—or wasn't—going with him, she went to work on his shirt buttons. The fact that he watched each tremor of her fingers with interest didn't help calm her down.

"Close your eyes," she said as she fumbled over the last button.

"Why? I've seen myself without a shirt before."

She laughed almost helplessly. Then she took a breath that wanted to turn into a sob. Grimly she clamped down on her unruly emotions, pushed the final button free of its hole, and concentrated on getting Cruz out of his shirt without hurting him any more.

Slipping the dark shirt off his right shoulder wasn't difficult. Pulling it off the left one made Laurel bite her lip until she left marks. It was no easier on Cruz. Despite his effort not to, he groaned low and deep when he had to lift his left arm.

To her dismay, beneath his shirt there was yet another layer of clothing to remove, a singlet of dark cloth. It was thick but not bulky.

"That's why there's no blood," he said.

Frowning, she noticed a pair of deep furrows in the cloth over his ribs. She bent down and peered more closely, still expecting to see blood. He was right. There wasn't any.

Very carefully she touched the furrows. Just beneath the surface of one she felt a hard object the size of a marble.

"What in the world?" she asked.

Instead of answering, Cruz probed the cloth for a moment. After a heartfelt curse, he pulled out a bright, shiny slug.

"Hold out your hand," he said.

She did. The hard, smooth weight of the bullet hit the center of her palm. The metal was unpleasantly warm, like a piece of cast gold that hadn't been allowed to cool long enough before she broke the mold.

Laurel stared at the bullet and then at the singlet covering Cruz's chest.

"What are you, some kind of robot?" she asked, unnerved.

"Just your average knight in matte black armor," he said, biting back a groan.

With a grimace he peeled two Velcro tabs at one edge of the singlet. The front half of the garment lifted off his chest in a piece. Beneath it, he was naked.

"Soft body armor," he explained. "Courtesy of the British Special Air Services."

Speechless, she simply shook her head, unable to believe that he'd caught a bullet and wasn't covered in gore. Given the absence of blood, she'd assumed the worst he'd suffered was a flesh burn from a near miss.

But he'd taken at least one direct hit.

"It's a couple of steps up from Kevlar," he explained. "One of Sergeant-Major Gillespie's spookier pals developed it and let it out to us for field tests before he tries to sell it to Her Majesty's government."

With his right hand, Cruz plucked the warm slug from Laurel's palm and inspected the metal carefully.

"I can report that it works pretty good against nine-millimeter slugs at about seven feet," he said, throwing the slug up in the air and catching it deftly. "Of course, bullets lose a lot of their punch when you run them through a silencer."

She stared at the bullet, then at the body armor, and finally at the fragile human flesh that had been beneath. Two dark smudges were already forming on his rib cage, just below his left nipple.

Without the armor, either bullet would have killed Cruz.

"Retrograde m-macho son of a bitch," she said, her voice shaking.

"Talk dirty to me some more, honey. I love it."

"You really get off on catching bullets, don't you?" she said angrily. "Most fun you've ever had with your clothes on, right?"

"Beats hell out of the alternative."

Very gently he tested the larger of the two bruises with his fingertips. He winced but kept probing.

"If pain is your drug of choice," she said, watching him poke at what surely was very bruised flesh and bone, "why don't you just bang your head against the wall?"

"Tried it. No future in it." He let out a long breath. "You'll be happy to know that I've got torn cartilage and maybe a broken rib."

When he turned toward the light to examine the bruises more closely, she noticed an odd pattern on the skin around the injury.

"What's that?" she asked sharply.

He looked where her trembling finger was pointing. "It's just the pattern of the bulletproof fabric. The shock wave stamped it into my skin."

Laurel turned aside and tried to still the shaking of her hands. The realization that he would have been killed but for some high-tech body armor kept breaking over her in black waves.

She didn't want this, any of it.

And she certainly didn't want to be responsible for Cruz's death.

22

**Los Angeles
Monday night**

Claire Toth stripped back the comforter on the king-sized
bed, piled the pillows, and undressed. Room service would
arrive in half an hour with the late-night snack she'd ordered.
Jamie Swann should be back real soon with the egg. She
didn't want to waste any time after he arrived. She was already on fire.

When Swann let himself back into the hotel room, the
box holding the Ruby Surprise was under his arm. Toth lay
propped against three pillows. The top sheet was tucked art-
fully around her torso, leaving one hip and most of her full
breasts uncovered. Against the stark white of the bed linens,
her skin was the color of well-rubbed, ancient ivory.

Smiling, he closed the door and threw the security bolts
with measured movements of his hand. Then he stood and
looked at her. When her nipples hardened as though he'd
pinched them, he felt like throwing himself on her, holding
her down, and screwing her until she screamed.

"That didn't take long," Toth said.

"I didn't want you to start without me."

Her slanted, almond-shaped eyes were as black as the night, as clear, and far more intelligent. She patted the bed beside her.

"Show it to me," she said.

He put the rectangular wood carrying case on the bed and sat down. After he undid the catches, he laid the lid aside and removed the egg on its ornate pedestal.

"Come here," he said.

She sat up and leaned closer. The sheet that covered her breasts slid as far as her dark nipples, hesitated, and then slowly fell away to the nest of her lap.

He cupped his hand over the smooth, cool, pointed end of the egg like it was a woman's breast.

"Pretty, isn't it?" he asked in a low voice.

"Pretty? It's stupid. Why did they put all that work into the outside? What's inside is all that matters."

Swann laughed. He ran the back of his hand down between Toth's breasts to her belly and from there to her crotch.

"The same could be said of a woman," he said.

She laughed with him and opened her legs until there was more room between. With one hand he pulled on the thick, curly hair. With the other, he held out the beautiful egg. She touched it with her palm, then traced its jeweled length with the elegant tip of her finger, mirroring the motions he was making between her legs.

Swann wondered whether it was his hand or the power implicit in the Ruby Surprise that was making Toth's nipples gather into dark daggers.

"Show me," she whispered. "Show me how it works." Her voice was throaty and urgent, heavy with arousal.

Abruptly he didn't care whether his hand, the egg, or both were turning her on. He was going to get the benefit of it.

The thought made him hot. He'd taken women of all sizes and races, all over the world. Toth was unique. Some of it was her spectacular body. Some of it was her cunning mind. A lot of it was her prowling, challenging sexuality. The way she climaxed was incredible. He could get off just thinking about it.

So could she.

Lightly, teasingly, he rubbed one thumb over the cool surface of the egg. His other thumb was searching a much warmer surface. With slow movements, he quartered the egg, closing in on the single knot of gold that, when touched just right, would open the egg's riches to him.

She made a low sound as his thumb rubbed over her repeatedly.

"Open it, damn you," she said huskily.

"Patience.

"Fuck patience."

He laughed and teased both egg and woman, watching both, feeling Toth's increasing heat, holding her on the ragged edge of climax. Then he dragged one thumb over a solid gold knot and one thumb over a straining knot of flesh.

There was a faint click and the top half of the egg parted slowly, smoothly, almost languidly, revealing a big faceted ruby at its center.

Toth gasped and shuddered. The scent of her climax was a musk more potently sexy than anything ever packaged and sold over sterile perfume counters.

Swann admired the ruby and the woman.

"You're an inventive bastard," she said huskily. "You're the only man I've ever had who screws me as much with his mind as with his dick."

"You're the only woman I've ever had who needed both."

Languidly she rolled onto her side, keeping his hand between her thighs. She could see that he was hard and hot as a cheap pistol. She licked her lips and smiled.

"What do you figure it's worth?" he asked. "Five million? Twenty?"

She stared long and hard at the ruby, as if trying to read a message concealed deep within it.

"This pony will take us anywhere we have the hair to ride it," she said after a moment. "All we need is the bridle. Where is it?"

"It's coming. Patience."

The sound she made was distinctly impatient. She drew the nail of her index finger across the cold, polished surface of the ruby.

"When?" she demanded.

"When I'm good and ready."

With a fluid movement, she took his hand from between her legs, straightened up, and drew the top sheet across her breasts, covering the aroused nipples like a fan dancer.

"You told me you had everything you needed, *lover*," she said coldly. "You want to get off tonight, you handle it yourself."

Swann knew what Toth was doing as well as she did. But it was like knowing about gravity—it didn't change the fact that gravity worked. Down was still down and he was still hard and she was ready for more and they both knew it.

"Relax, *lover*," he said. "I don't wander around with custom-made power cables and E Bloc computer links in my luggage."

He reached over and lightly traced the outline of Toth's nipple through the cool sheet. His fingers left damp marks on the cloth.

"But I can make the damned thing work in a couple of

hours . . . when I want to. All we need is some fast, anonymous cash from Hudson and we'll be on our way."

She stared at Swann for several heartbeats. Beneath his finger, her nipple was softening rather than becoming harder.

"You think you're a cold one, don't you?" he asked.

His lips drew back in a feral smile as he used his thumb and forefinger to pinch the flaccid nipple into renewed response.

The tip of her breast remained as smooth and lifeless as silicone gel in a plastic envelope. She fixed him with an expressionless stare while he twisted and manipulated her with increasing force. What had been titillation became abuse and finally punishment but her expression didn't change.

Smiling oddly, he loosened his grip and went back to teasing. "Not into pain tonight, huh?"

She just looked at him.

"Someday you're going to run into a guy who will rape you just to watch you scream and bleed," Swann said.

"I met that kind before I went to first grade."

Swann wasn't surprised.

"Mother-daughter acts were big where I came from," she said casually. "I learned to go away to somewhere else in my mind a long, long time ago."

"You don't have to with me, remember? Any blood that gets drawn is mutual."

"I know. I just wanted to make you work a little. If it's too easy, you'll lose interest."

As she spoke, life returned to the tip of flesh between Swann's fingers. The nipple grew and filled and hardened as though by magic.

He dragged a deep breath through his teeth as his own body responded savagely. There was something perversely exhilarating about a woman who was so completely in control of herself. Toth was right—if he'd been dead certain of her response every time, he'd have been dead bored a lot of the time.

"How could I lose interest in this?" he asked, pressing his hand against her crotch again. "So long as you don't get any ideas about going back to that queen Novikov, we'll do fine."

Shifting, smiling slightly, Toth let Swann do what he liked between her legs while she thought of her next move.

Very quickly she discovered it was damned difficult not to come in Swann's hand all over again. She'd never been so hot, never so close to losing all control.

The excitement of ordering death was explosive.

She rested her hand on his thigh. Then she touched the cool, beautiful egg with her palm as her fingertips stroked rhythmically against his erection.

"Aleksy isn't really gay," she said huskily. "He likes little boys or big boys or girls or knotholes in the fence. But most of all he likes power."

"So do you," Swann said. "Political, sexual, physical. You name it. If it's power, it turns you on."

She laughed low in her throat and opened her legs wider, taunting him even as she showed her trust that he wouldn't hurt her. Not really. Not the way she'd been hurt in the past.

"You sure about that, lover?" she asked.

"Dead sure, baby. It's what I like about you. When do you see Hudson again?"

"What are you, my pimp?"

"Whatever it takes."

"It takes a lot more than it's getting," she retorted.

Swann laughed and kept teasing her without ever coming close to the knot that would open her as easily as the egg.

She knew she should punish him by going cold again. She

knew, but she couldn't make herself do it. Not tonight. There would never be a night like this again with Swann. She was going to use both of them to the fullest.

"Tomorrow morning," she said.

"Will Hudson have the money?"

"He'd better. The stuff Aleksy already had printed out is dynamite. All about the first deal between Hudson's petrochemical firm and the Soviet state fertilizer concession."

"Old news," Swann said. He twisted flesh precisely and was rewarded by a gasp. "Nobody cares anymore."

She closed her eyes and savored the skill of the man who was playing with her the way she liked it best, holding her suspended between pleasure and pain, letting her know it could go either way.

"They'll care," she said huskily. "There's a complete description of the way Hudson International supplied the critical technology for a nerve gas plant in Libya. Hudson doesn't even know the Russians found out."

"You'd better be careful when you break the news. He's old. His heart might not take the shock."

Her eyes opened like twin slices of midnight. "Not likely. He's a potent bastard."

"Did you haul his ashes for him?"

"I didn't have to. He came in his shorts while I was reciting his file."

Swann laughed and stretched her with his thumb and forefinger.

"I almost feel sorry for Hudson," Swann said. "Probably be a week before he gets it up again."

"He had it up again in five minutes," she said, shifting her hips languidly.

"Impressive."

"He's been taking Romanian sex hormone treatments for the last ten years."

"Painful, if rumors are true."

"Yeah. And like heroin, you can't just stop after a few. The longer you take the hormone, the more you need it."

"Lovely," Swann said huskily.

"I'm trying to figure out how to use it against him."

"You really get off on blackmail, don't you? Makes you a good journalist."

"Public kiss-and-tell isn't real power. Real power is letting some poor bastard like Hudson think you're about to print his secrets. He'll jump through ten thousand hoops to avoid it. The fun comes in designing the hoops especially for him."

"Is that what you did with the guy who's bothering my daughter?" Swann asked. "Make some hoops and watch him jump?"

Toth cut a narrow-eyed glance at Swann's face, wondering for the first time if he somehow suspected what she'd done.

Swann was watching his fingers. The look on his face was bluntly sexual.

Smiling, she flexed her body, reminding him of how it would be when they finally quit torturing one another. She was rewarded by a flick of his thumbnail that made her squirm hungrily.

"Cruz Rowan was a righteous, stiff-necked prick," she said, breathing quickly. "All he had to do was cooperate with Aleksy and I wouldn't have printed a word. The Soviets didn't want to destroy Rowan. They wanted to use him."

"Clever. A well-placed federal agent, a man deep in the heart of the American counterterrorist corps. Quite a coup."

"You got it, lover. Rowan would have been a hell of a lot

more valuable working on our side than the momentary propaganda benefit my article gave the Soviets."

Swann leaned forward and put the gem-studded egg between Toth's big breasts.

"Hold on to that," he said. "I'm going to need both my hands."

"What for?"

"Watch."

With a lithe movement, he knelt between her legs. His hands went beneath her, sinking into her full hips, holding her in a vise that would leave marks.

She didn't care. She knew what was coming. She was wild for it, twisting and straining up toward him, only to be held down by the clenched power of his hands.

"Not yet, baby," he said thickly, looking at her flushed, swollen flesh. "I've never had you this hot before. I'm going to see what you've been holding back."

Slowly he dragged a stubble-roughened cheek down the length of first one thigh, then the other. By the time he lowered his mouth to Toth, she was shaking uncontrollably.

It was the first time she'd experienced the dangerous sexual thrill of ordering the death of an assassin's only child one moment and surrendering her body to that same assassin in the next. It was a dark, compulsive thrill, and it could only happen once. She tried to hold back, but it was too late. Swann was right. She'd never been this out of control before.

She climaxed at the first raking touch of his teeth.

23

Cruz looked at Laurel's rigid profile and wondered how much longer he would have to wait before he could risk pushing her. If she blew up, it would take too long to settle her down again. The assassins or others just like them would be showing up at her house real soon. She couldn't be here when that happened.

He wanted to go to her, hold her, comfort her. Yet he knew that anything he offered in the way of gentleness would be thrown right back in his teeth. The aftermath of an adrenaline jag took most people that way—pure, raging, hairtrigger temper. He was used to that reaction in himself and largely controlled it.

But Laurel was new to the game.

He looked at his watch and decided. If push came to crunch, he could always knock her out, stuff her in his car, and drive.

"Help me get back in the armor," he said calmly.

She wrapped her arms around herself and shook her head.

"If that's all the thanks I get," he said dryly, "the knight business isn't what it used to be."

"Knights don't go around s-shooting people for the thanks it g-gets them."

"You're right. The image of professional knighthood has taken a hell of a beating around here in the last few minutes."

She took a ragged breath. Then another. It helped calm the frantic rush of adrenaline and the pounding of her heart. "Are you saying those creatures that sh-shot you are knights?"

"No. But your father is. At least, he used to be."

"What does that mean?"

"It's a hell of a world when a knight throws his own daughter to the dragons."

She turned to face Cruz so quickly that she nearly fell. Distantly she realized that her knees were shaking. She braced herself on the worktable and ignored the weakness in her knees.

"My father didn't throw me to any dragons," she said distinctly.

"I'm sure he didn't mean to."

"He didn't do it. Full stop. Period."

"Who else knows about you and the egg?"

"You do!"

"Oh, yeah," Cruz drawled. "Now I remember. I want you dead so I save your life. Stupid of me. But what can you expect from a retrograde macho son of a bitch?"

She wanted to scream at him. The reaction was irrational, and she knew it. Even so, controlling herself took an unbelievable effort.

"They could have been after you," she said carefully.

He heard the desperation in her voice and was divided between a desire to shake some sense into her and an even stronger need to hold her in his arms until she cried all the fear and adrenaline out of her system.

But there wasn't enough time for that, or for what would surely follow once he got his hands on her. Ripped cartilage or not, bruised bone or not, he wanted her until he could barely stand up straight.

It's just adrenaline, fool, he told himself savagely. *It will pass. She's not the kind of woman for a little medicinal screwing.*

And that was all it would be. He'd learned very painfully that it was easier to live without all women than to live with any one woman.

"They weren't after me," he said.

"How can you be so damned certain? You're the one they shot."

"No one could have followed me here," he said patiently, "because I didn't know where I was going until I was in the air over Los Angeles."

"But what about—"

"Think, Laurel," he said over her words. "Use your mind and not your emotions."

A visible shudder went through her body.

"No," she said harshly. "He would never set me up for execution."

"Did you know the egg was coming to you?"

"No."

"Did he?"

Reluctantly, she nodded.

Cruz reached out and laid his hand gently along her upper arm. Her flesh was rigid, trembling.

"Laurel," he said as gently as he could. "Somebody—your father or one of his partners—tried to kill you."

"But w-why?"

The break in her voice made Cruz even more grim. All he could do now was hope that he'd read her correctly, that honesty rather than false comfort would keep her going. If he'd guessed wrong, in less than thirty seconds he was going to have a hysterical female on his hands.

"They were trying to cut the link between you and your father," Cruz said calmly.

"Why?" she whispered.

"They didn't want someone like me to follow that link to the egg. With you dead, the trail ends here."

She took a long, shattered breath. What he said made an ugly, savage kind of sense.

"I can guarantee more assassins will be sent as soon as word of the failure gets back," he continued. "That's why you have to come with me. You don't have the training to run without leaving tracks that the hunters would follow."

Under his palm, he could feel the tension that rippled over her skin. He could also feel the elemental female softness lying beneath the tension. Not weakness. Not in this woman. Rather it was a special quality of smoothness, a sensuous yielding of flesh that told his senses she was female rather than male.

Laurel met Cruz's eyes. He noted that her pupils were still dilated, her eyes black but for small rims of gold.

"Maybe those creatures did me a favor," she said. "You no longer look at me with a weary kind of calculation, like I'm just one more piece of scum on your radar."

His dark eyebrows rose. "You see me very clearly."

"No. Just the shadows."

"That's all there is, honey."

He ran his thumb gently over the long, firm muscle in her arm. The touch was soothing rather than sensual.

Letting out a long, broken breath, she looked at him like

he was a map leading out of the hellish world she'd stumbled into without warning.

"Go pack," he said softly. "I'll take you to a safe place."

The temptation was great, but Laurel knew she would be a long time forgetting the ugly, deformed lead and the furrows and the pain on Cruz's face. And most of all his words telling her a shattering truth.

They were after you. I was just in the way.

"No," she said tightly. "Taking bullets for me isn't in your job description."

He was amused and touched by her unwillingness to put him at risk. "Page four, section two, paragraph three. 'Fair damsels are to be rescued by all good knights without regard to personal danger.' "

"No. I couldn't bear it if you were hurt again." She shook her head firmly. "I have a safe place to go. Nobody knows about it except . . ."

"Jamie Swann."

She didn't answer. Words were echoing in her head, Cruz's words.

They were trying to cut the link between you and your father. They didn't want someone like me to follow that link to the egg. With you dead, the trail ends here.

"I can't lead you to my father," she said starkly to Cruz, "so there's no point in playing the role of knight. It won't work."

He loosened his hold on her arm, but his thumb still rested with disarming familiarity along the muscle. She shifted a little, trying to withdraw. He moved just enough to maintain the gentle connection.

"Why don't we make a deal that has nothing to do with your father?" he said.

"Can we?"

"Sure." Cruz lied, because he knew it was the only way. "I need a driver to get me over the mountain and back to the airport in Paso Robles. You do it and we're even."

"That's all? Just drive you there?"

"Uh-huh." Then he added ruthlessly, "Not much to do for the guy who took two bullets for you, is it?"

The part of Laurel that was still capable of rational thought knew she was being manipulated by a man who was far too good at reading her. And he was persistent. If the first gambit didn't work, he tried another, and then another, and another, until he found a way past her defenses. Under normal circumstances she'd have held her own with him and even enjoyed the skirmish.

But there was nothing normal about tonight.

Gently, without demand, his thumb stroked the taut muscle in her upper arm. She shivered and fought against the desire to crawl into his arms and be held, simply held.

With a light tug of his good arm, he pulled her against him. She wanted to fight but now that the moment of danger was past her strength was gone. With a ragged sigh, she leaned her forehead against the right side of his chest. He stroked her hair, making no attempt to hold her any closer.

His restraint was an irresistible lure. Without realizing what she was doing, she turned her head and rested her cheek against his chest. Beneath a cushion of hair, resilient pads of muscle shifted and flexed with each soothing motion of his arm. His heart beat strongly, smoothly, reassuring her in an elemental way that he was truly alive.

After a moment she turned and looked up at him. He was watching her with a combination of weariness and shadows and warmth in his eyes that made her heart turn over.

God help me if Cruz ever decides to seduce me, she thought in dismay.

"Thank you," he said softly.

She flinched like she'd been struck. He read her with shocking clarity.

"What's the matter?" he asked.

"I don't like the way you read my mind."

"Did I?"

"I was just thinking how good—" Abruptly she realized what she was saying and switched in midsentence. "Why did you thank me?"

"For seeing me clearly and not backing away. It's taken me a long time to do that with myself. Hell, I'm still working on it."

"God," she said hoarsely. "Why couldn't you have been stupid and repulsive and old and ugly?"

"Three out of four isn't bad," he said. "Time will take care of the 'old' part."

Helplessly she laughed.

Knowing he shouldn't, unable to stop himself, he bent just enough to brush a kiss against her temple.

"Better pack," he said huskily. "Whatever you decide to do, you can't come back here for a while. Do you accept that?"

"I don't have much choice, do I?"

"Not if you want to stay alive."

She turned away, then looked over her shoulder at the man who was leaning against her worktable wearing half of a modern suit of armor. Cruz Rowan was the last male on earth who should have appealed to her all the way to the soles of her feet, but he did, and she was too honest with herself not to admit it.

"There's an ice pack in the freezer over there," she said, pointing.

"Think I need cooling off?"

"Your ribs might appreciate it."

He smiled. "Thanks, honey."

Normally Laurel disliked endearments from men. Yet when the word came with a smile like that, she liked it.

A lot.

Right. I'm losing my mind, she told herself. *But under the circumstances, I'm not sure sanity has much going for it.*

While Cruz got the ice pack, Laurel gathered up the tools that were scattered in unusual disarray across the workbench. She didn't remember making such a mess while she worked on the egg, but she must have. The evidence was in front of her.

As she put familiar tools in their familiar places in the leather box, she began to feel less like someone wading through a nightmare. Inside the satchel, the box that held all her loose gemstones wasn't positioned correctly. She settled it in the right place, pushed the box of tools in beside the other box, and shook the satchel experimentally.

Everything stayed put. She fastened the leather straps, closing the satchel, and threw the wide carrying strap over her shoulder.

When she turned back to Cruz, she was surprised to find that he'd managed to dress himself without help.

"Will it be more than a week?" she asked.

He looked up from the button he was worrying into place one-handed. "Before the egg is found?"

"Yes."

"If it is, our client will be lip deep in hot sauce. Get packing. We're on a short clock."

"I'm ready to go."

His eyes narrowed. "Just that? What about clothes?"

"I don't need more clothes to drive you over the mountain."

"Then what are you going to do?"

"I'll think of something."

He didn't doubt it. What she didn't know was that he'd thought of something already.

And he was bigger than she was.

24

Cambria
Monday night

As soon as Laurel got to the garage, she automatically headed for her car.

"No," Cruz said, leading her out of the garage. "They'll know the license plate and make of your car. We'll take my rental."

With a careless snap of his right wrist he threw the keys to Laurel. Though he gave no warning, she caught them without fumbling.

"Nice reflexes," he said.

It was the last thing he said directly to her for a long time. While she drove, he pushed her out of his mind. As far as he was concerned, she'd spent too much time in it already.

He reached into the glove compartment, pulled a tiny, battery-driven cell phone out, and turned it on. His first call was to a Risk Ltd. number.

Because his little pocket cellular didn't have a scrambler or a decoder, he had to be very careful what he said. Every word he spoke was in the clear, available to anyone with another cellular and enough curiosity to surf the channels for interesting conversations.

When the curiosity was professional, there would be a mainframe computer doing the surfing and recording all conversations that contained certain key words. It was how the CIA and the FBI routinely kept track of things.

If Cruz's message had been more complex, or if the timing had been less urgent, he'd have waited until he reached the airplane to make his calls. The cell phone on the aircraft had a first-class scrambler. But every minute he delayed was another minute Swann could use to bury himself deeper in whatever cover he was using.

"This is John Smith the Second," Cruz said when the call was picked up.

"Lousy weather," came the answer.

"Maybe where you are. I'm in the clear."

"What can we do for you?"

"I gave the guv an address," Cruz said. "I need a little cleanup there."

"Will you be helping us?"

"No."

"Will anyone else be around?"

"Not so far as I know, but it was a professional job," he said.

"How much cleanup?"

"Odds and ends of metal. Then you might hang around to help out anyone else who shows up."

"Any systems damaged?"

"Not enough to matter," he said.

"Anything else?"

"Tell your crew to wear black. The occasion could become formal without any notice."

"Black. Affirmative."

Cruz hung up, punched in another series of numbers, and began talking as soon as the phone was picked up.

"This is Red Two and I'm running barefoot, so I'm running fast. First: Juliet, Alpha, Mike, India, Echo. Second: Sierra, Whiskey, Alpha, November, November. See what the Agency has. And dig. He knows how to hide. If you try for the personal touch, wear black. He's expecting someone."

Cruz cut the connection, punched in more numbers, and repeated the message, except that he asked the second operative to check with the FBI.

Three more calls covered the legitimate government agencies that might have employed Jamie Swann. The numbers got longer as Cruz began covering international bases, reaching out to Risk Ltd. sources around the world.

Numbly Laurel drove, listening to call after call in three languages, one of which might have been Russian. She'd quickly sorted out the international radio code; Juliet, Alpha, Mike, etc., were letters spelling Jamie Swann's name.

That didn't bother her. She'd known Cruz would go after her father. What bothered her was the blunt assessment of Swann's character that marked the conclusion of each of Cruz's English conversations.

He's expecting someone. Wear black.

She wondered if modern body armor came in any other color. The more she thought about it, the more she doubted it.

Cruz hung up, shifted in the seat, grimaced, and shifted again. Then he reached inside his clothes, pulled a Velcro tab, and fished out the ice pack he had taken from Laurel's freezer. Thin, flexible, still largely frozen, the pack was obviously filled with something other than water.

"Wonder if Gillie has one of these," Cruz said under his breath. "Damn thing works."

Laurel didn't bother to look his way. She knew he wasn't

talking to her. In fact, he hardly seemed to know she was there.

She wondered how often someone had driven Cruz through the night after he'd been "banged up," and then listened in while he made thirty phone calls to thirty world-class spooks. She knew it must have happened more than once.

She'd seen other scars on his body.

The thought of him being hurt like that made something twist painfully within her. It wasn't reasonable that she should feel his past pain so clearly, but she did. And the thought of Cruz being hurt in the future made her skin go cold.

The certainty that he'd been injured saving her life was agonizing. She barely could control the impulse to run her fingers over his cheek, his eyebrows, his lips, to feel the living warmth of his breath on her hand. Then she thought of his own hand, the injury that spoke eloquently of past danger, past pain.

Does my father have scars too? she asked the night while she stared out at the black, winding road. *Is that why Mother finally divorced him? Did she get tired of waiting for him to come home dead?*

There weren't any answers for Laurel's questions. There never had been. Her mother simply had refused to talk about Jamie Swann and marriage problems. Nor had Swann spoken of Ariel in anything other than wistful terms.

For an instant Laurel took her eyes off the road to glance at the man beside her on the front seat. In the half-light of the rental car's dashboard, Cruz was a study in shades of darkness. He was bent over slightly, as if to favor his injured ribs, but the lines on his face came from intense concentration rather than pain. The intelligence in him burned with the clarity of a laser.

She knew that she was capable of such focus when she was dreaming a new design or bringing an intricate metal shape into three-dimensional life. But she'd never encountered another human being with that ability to exist utterly without self-consciousness, living in the center of each moment, no time but the endless, vivid *now*.

She wondered what Cruz was like when he let down his guard and relaxed. If he ever did. In his business, a man who was caught napping tended not to wake up again. Ever. Living on the edge instilled a kind of bone-deep wariness that made relaxation difficult.

Like her father with his wide smile and narrowed eyes.

Odd sounds came from the cellular when Cruz punched in yet another number and began speaking in Spanish.

Laurel knew enough of the language to catch the gist of the conversation.

Black on black.

25

Although it was past midnight, the galleries of the Hudson Museum were alive with frantic activity. Beneath flood-lights, work lights, and spotlights, curators and workmen moved quickly to reassemble display cases and mount paintings on stark white gallery walls. The only still point in the chaos was Damon Hudson. He stood with hands on hips, looking at the mess.

"I have half a mind to cancel the entire exhibit," Hudson said coldly.

Aleksy Novikov didn't bother to look up from his work. "A little more to the right. No, no, no. That is too much. Move it closer to the top. That is better."

Bending over slightly, he focused on a gleaming silver and gilt Fabergé table service that was being arranged in a chest-high display case by an assistant curator.

"This jumble will never be ready in time," Hudson said.

Novikov squinted and tilted his elegant head to one side as he weighed the effect of the display. He'd dealt with

Hudson and his arrogance many times over the years, both in the United States and in Russia. Novikov despised the industrialist but was too pragmatic to show it.

So the Russian ignored what he couldn't change.

"Black velvet," Novikov said to the assistant. "Surely it would not be too much trouble to find truly *black* velvet here in Los Angeles? This trash has a yellow cast to it. We need something the color of a Moscow night."

"It's Tuesday—" Hudson said.

"Barely," Novikov interrupted coolly.

"—which means that even if you get the exhibit ready for the Thursday morning preview, it won't be up to my standards. I want a world-class show, not a third-rate Third World pile of crap."

Finally Novikov looked up. His pale eyebrow arched in feigned surprise, as if he hadn't known Hudson was nearby.

"Do not be agitated," Novikov said. "The exhibits will be superb. We have an abundance of time."

Hudson looked at Novikov's theatrically perfect features and silky, flaxen hair. Hudson had a real dislike of homosexuals, but not for the usual reasons. He saw homosexuals as competitors. He saw heterosexual males in the same way.

At a gut level Hudson believed his prick ought to be the only one in use, anytime, anywhere.

"I've a good mind to throw you and your traveling show out on your ass," Hudson said. "I'm beginning to believe that all Russians are liars and cheats."

"Am I to assume that there exists a reason for your sudden chauvinistic anger?"

Hudson glared at a red velvet wall hanging that had once covered the wall of a small chapel in St. Petersburg. The hanging was now spread carefully inside a hard plastic shell that was being hoisted in place on a south-facing gallery wall.

"Your countrymen have lost all sense of loyalty," Hudson said, biting off each word.

"Why? Merely because the new Russian republic refused to settle for your first offer of reimbursement for the honor of having our exhibit?"

Hudson gave Novikov a hard look.

"Surely you know how expensive it has become to stage international exhibitions," the Russian said calmly. "You certainly have sponsored enough of them in your unrelenting drive to become the principal patron of the arts in Los Angeles."

Splotches of color suddenly showed on Hudson's pale cheeks. "Don't presume to taunt me. I'm generous when it comes to art and artists, but I've broken stronger men by far than you."

With an effort Novikov held his temper. For the past hour he'd suffered Hudson's arrogance and anger, waiting for the industrialist to slip and reveal some guilty knowledge of the Ruby Surprise. Novikov knew Hudson had served Soviet interests over the years as a way of serving his own. Potentially Hudson was in a position to have discovered the true value of the Ruby Surprise and then to have stolen it for his own purposes.

But Hudson had said nothing to suggest he'd stolen the imperial egg.

"I would not taunt anyone," Novikov said. "I am only a patriot. I do not like to hear such attacks on Mother Russia from anyone, not even from the very wealthy capitalist Damon Hudson.

The flush on Hudson's cheeks darkened. "I've been a friend of the Russian people for years. At times, this friendship has cost me a great deal, both personally and professionally. I've spent millions of dollars of my own money furthering Russian causes—including the three million dollars it cost just to get this exhibit."

Novikov measured Hudson. The older man looked to be in a fine state of rage. His eyes were glaring, his cheeks were flushed, and his thick silver eyebrows were drawn together in a fierce line. Idly Novikov wondered if baiting Hudson some more would help solve the mystery of the missing egg.

"Exemplary," Novikov murmured. "Of course, I understand that you were well compensated for your support of the Russian people."

"That support has cost me more than money can repay," Hudson said bitterly. "And what do I get for my lifelong friendship and sacrifice?"

Before Novikov could decide on an answer, Hudson spun in place, glaring in all directions, his arms thrown out in disgust.

"I get a slapdash collection of icons and altar paintings, snuffboxes and cigarette cases, a few marginal socialist realist paintings, and a handful of propaganda posters from third-rate Stalinists."

Novikov worked to keep his temper.

Hudson turned and advanced on the Russian in frank menace.

"Where is the Fabergé?" Hudson demanded.

The Russian looked closely at Hudson. If he was concealing guilty knowledge, any normal man would have avoided the subject of Fabergé. But Hudson wasn't any normal man. His question proved nothing either way, guilt or innocence.

"The Fabergé is being unpacked and placed as we speak," Novikov said. "Look around you more carefully."

"Not that crap! Where are the imperial eggs? I want them out here where I can see them. Where the press can see them and know that—"

"Why are the eggs so important?" Novikov cut in casually. "The Japanese cultural press paid them little attention. They dismissed them as garish and of secondary cultural importance."

Hudson swept away the question with a contemptuous wave of his hand. "The Japanese think an object has to be a thousand years old and have a slicing edge to be valuable. Americans are more discerning. We recognize craftsmanship and beauty, no matter what the age."

"Remarkable," Novikov said under his breath.

"Listen, you high-nosed son of a bitch, I've promised a special viewing on Wednesday for the principal art critics of the *New York Times,* the *Los Angeles Times,* and other important media."

"The American art press will come to the trough quite willingly," Novikov said smoothly. "You do not need to treat them as though they had importance."

Glowering like an Old Testament patriarch, Hudson drew himself up to full height and stood over the slight curator.

"This show is crucial to my reputation," Hudson said harshly. "Especially now, with that bitch Toth sniffing around, trying to embarrass me by dredging up old news."

Novikov barely managed to conceal his surprise at the mention of Claire Toth. She was the last subject he'd expected Hudson to bring up. But there Toth was, as the Americans said, like a turd in the buttermilk.

26

Paso Robles
Very early Tuesday

By the time Cruz finally put away the cellular and leaned back in the seat, Laurel was on the outskirts of Paso Robles. The sound he made when the seat took the weight of his torso could have been a sigh of relief or simply weariness.

"How are your ribs?" she asked.

"Still there."

"Would aspirin help? I have some in my purse."

He started to shrug, winced, and cursed under his breath.

"Unless you're allergic," she said, "aspirin can't hurt."

"Can you reach behind the passenger seat? There's a bottle of water somewhere."

Driving one-handed, she leaned to the right, fished around, and finally came up with the water bottle. Despite the awkward position, she kept the little rental car in the center of its lane, just as she'd held the lane while the narrow little road snaked through the mountains leading to California's Great Central Valley.

She handed him the water bottle and went back to driving.

"Thanks," he said.

He found the aspirin in her purse and swallowed several pills. Then he leaned back again and let the night stream by on either side of him.

"Better?" she asked quietly.

"Not as good as a double scotch, but not bad."

"Scotch, huh? I like wine, myself. And brandy, if it's been a really long day hunched over the worktable."

Cruz smiled faintly. Then he turned his head and watched Laurel while she drove, enjoying the play of dashboard lights over her face. Her eyes were catlike, almost pure gold, and her eyelashes threw ragged shadows that shifted with each movement of her head. The lighting emphasized the height of her cheekbones, the depth of the hollows beneath, and the darkness of her lips. Her hands looked almost delicate in the odd light, but she held the wheel confidently.

If she noticed his close attention, it didn't make her self-conscious. She handled the car with efficiency and skill, getting the most from it and the road without pushing either one too hard. Her eyes moved constantly but not nervously. She was simply checking gauges, mirrors, and the shape of the road speeding toward her out of the darkness.

"You drive very well," he said.

"You sound surprised."

"Most women would have thrown me all over the car coming through the mountains."

"Most men would have, too."

He laughed, winced slightly, and went back to watching her. It was a lot better than thinking about his ribs.

"Did your father teach you to drive, too?" Cruz asked.

"Too?"

"He was the one who taught you to shoot, wasn't he?"

"Yes. But the driving I did on my own. I took some courses years ago."

"Racing?"

She shook her head. "I just wanted to drive well."

"Why?"

She glanced quickly at Cruz. It was one of the rare times she'd looked away from the road while talking to him. One of the things she'd learned during the driving courses was that you can talk to someone without looking at him.

But you couldn't judge expressions that way.

Cruz looked the way he always did—intent, hard, intelligent, focused.

"I don't like to feel out of control," she said, looking back at the road.

"What if I insisted on driving now?"

"It would depend on how well you did. I don't like driving too fast for anyone's skill, including my own. That's why I went to a class that sharpened my reflexes. It also taught me how to drive until I find my own limits, the limits of the car, and the road."

"Another control freak, huh?" he said.

"Like you?"

"I prefer the term 'self-sufficient.' "

"Most control freaks do."

Saying nothing, he pointed to a left turn. She made it without asking where they were going.

"So you like self-sufficiency," he said. "Is that why you live alone?"

"Is that a roundabout way of asking why there's no man in my life?"

"Why? No. But if there is a man, is he trained for what you're up against now?"

"What if I was the one with training?"

"A male of the species, trained and competent, is a better bet in hand-to-hand combat than a female of the same training and competence, unless you're talking about falcons or hawks."

"Ever heard of an equalizer?" Laurel asked.

"What if the bad guys have one too?"

"What if they don't?"

"Are you willing to bet your life on it?" Cruz asked. "Are you willing to pit your physical strength and training in violence against mine?"

"Don't be ridiculous."

"I'm not. You are."

"I've taken care of myself since I was sixteen," she said in a flat voice.

"Not against this lot, you haven't."

He pointed to another turn. As soon as she made it, she saw the lights of a small airport ahead.

"Turn right just past that marker," he said.

The road led through an open gate and onto the taxiway of the rural airport. In the distance Laurel saw the sharp, clean outlines of a waiting executive aircraft. It was a substantial plane. Whatever Risk Ltd. did, it was profitable.

"Park by the plane," Cruz said.

She parked but left the engine running.

He didn't get out. "I want you to come with me."

"What if I don't want to go?"

His black eyelashes lowered, making his eyes little more than glittering lines drawn against the darkness of his face.

"Then," he said, "I'd figure you're too much of a damned fool to save your own life and I would act accordingly."

"Meaning?"

"You're a bright woman. You figure it out."

27

**Los Angeles
Early Tuesday**

The Russian workers had watched warily from the corner of their eyes while Novikov and Hudson wrangled their way through the exhibit. Hudson's temper hadn't improved at all.

"Fabergé is what will grab headlines," Hudson said loudly. "The imperial eggs are what will put my show—and my museum—on the front pages of every newspaper worth reading. So trot the eggs out, *sonny*, and do it now."

"As I have said to you before, the Fabergé eggs are being examined by specialists to see if there was any damage during shipment," Novikov said in a soothing voice.

Hudson didn't buy it. "Where are they being examined? I'll look at them there."

"They will be put in place when the rest of the exhibit is ready. Until then, they will be kept—how do you say it?—under lock and key."

"Show me the goddamned eggs!"

Beneath the curator's attentive, soothing expression, Novikov was cursing like a peasant. He'd prepared a story for just this awkward moment, but he'd really hoped not to have to use it.

"The eggs will be in place by this afternoon," Novikov said. His voice, like his posture, was confident.

Hudson grunted. "Every one of them?"

"Except for one," the Russian said with a dismissing wave of his hand. "It suffered some minor damage in transit."

"Which egg?"

"One of the junior curators has returned with it to Moscow, where it will be repaired and returned within forty-eight hours."

"The press viewing is in thirty hours. Which egg is missing?"

Novikov sighed and cursed the persistent industrialist. "The Ruby Surprise."

"Moscow?" Hudson shouted. "Are you telling me the egg is in fucking *Moscow*?"

Several of the Russian staff turned and openly stared at Hudson. His own staff didn't. Hudson's temper was a fact of employment. All his own workers cared about was that for once Hudson's wrath wasn't aimed at them.

"Jesus Christ," Hudson snarled. "Why wasn't I told? I promised those newspaper sluts a national scoop—the first American showing of a long-lost czarist art treasure!"

"Naturally we wanted it to be in perfect condition for your showing," Novikov said.

"So repair it in Los Angeles!" Hudson yelled an inch from Novikov's face. "Christ knows we have enough wogs on Hill Street to make a new egg, much less repair an old one."

Gapan materialized nearby, looking like a rumpled proletarian specter at a decadent artistic feast.

Hudson glowered at the second Russian, repelled by his seamed, ugly face. Hudson had heard his workers speculate that Novikov and the ugly Russian were lovers. Certainly Gapan was protective of the lithe, elegant curator.

Novikov glanced once at Gapan, then back to Hudson.

"Moscow is the only place where Fabergé's tools and workshop still exist, largely intact," Novikov said with thin patience. "If there are any marks of workmanship left on the egg, we want them to be indistinguishable from Fabergé's."

"This is outrageous! I'm calling the minister of culture about it. He'll have your balls—assuming you have any."

"Balls?" Then Novikov remembered what the slang meant. He laughed. "Ah, yes. Be assured that I have balls and use them as regularly as you do."

Gapan gave Novikov a dark glance.

"Do not embarrass yourself by calling the minister," Novikov said politely. "He is far too busy to be bothered by such a minor matter as repairs to a bit of gold filigree."

Hudson opened his mouth.

Novikov kept on talking. "There are one hundred and fifty-three Fabergé items in this show, none of which has ever been displayed in the West. Surely you are not going to be deprived of your national adulation because one piece is missing for a few hours?"

Hudson wanted to argue, but the rush of adrenaline was passing, leaving him empty. He closed his eyes for an instant, feeling more spent than he had since he began treatments in Romania.

"Take advantage of this time to rest and look again at your speech," Novikov coaxed, his voice low. "The displays will be in place before your Wednesday press showing."

Hudson looked into Novikov's unusual light eyes and felt the world slipping away. The supple tenor voice was like a caress. For an instant Hudson found himself wondering what it would be like to have sex with a man.

If Novikov was truly a man.

At a gut level, Hudson doubted it. No man was that beautiful, that . . . alluring. Certainly no man had ever been to Hudson.

Smiling like a Madonna, Novikov put his hand on the older man's sleeve.

"If you wish," the Russian said, "I will assist you in giving the journalists a tour. I can reveal to them aspects of several pieces that are more impressive artistically than the red egg."

Hudson took a deep breath. With it came the faintly exotic scent of Aleksy Novikov. Hudson shook his head as if confused. Silently he promised himself not to drink vodka again, no matter how stressed he was. He simply had no tolerance for it anymore. It undermined his sense of reality.

But then, so had Claire Toth.

Swearing beneath his breath, Hudson gathered the threads of his unraveling concentration.

"I have a huge investment in this show," he said.

"So does Russia, my friend," Novikov assured him. "It is vital in the rebuilding of good relations between peoples who have been divided too long by a foolish ideology. Is that not correct, Gapan?"

Gapan looked from Novikov to Hudson, then said something in Russian.

Hudson didn't know what the words meant, but he doubted that they were flattering. Gapan struck Hudson as the kind of man who wouldn't flatter God or Lenin, much less a capitalist.

"Ah, Gapan," Novikov said, shaking his head. "The new Russia needs friends if it is to survive. That is why you were allowed to join this goodwill tour. Friends cannot be purchased. They must be won."

Gapan looked bored.

"Ignore him," Novikov said to Hudson. "He is a—how is it said, a hangnail?—from the old days."

"Hangover," Hudson said.

"Yes, I thought so." Novikov squeezed the older man's biceps gently, approvingly. "You should rest, my friend," the Russian murmured. "We need you full of your usual vigor. This exhibit is Russia's gift to the rest of the world, a sign of our desire to join with all other peoples in harmony."

"And make money," Hudson added sourly.

"But of course." Novikov smiled. "You, of all people, must understand our cash difficulties. Surely a few hundred thousand dollars is not a great sacrifice for a man of your wealth?"

"Your government is charging me three million for the privilege of hosting this exhibition, and you know it."

"Still." Novikov shrugged gracefully. "Not a vast amount for you, yes? You, who are so very, *very* rich."

"Now that you have renounced your socialist ideals, is there no limit to Russian avarice?"

Novikov tilted his head slightly and studied the other man. "If you feel the fee charged for the exhibit was excessive, I will try to intercede with the minister," Novikov said. "Your friendship is valued."

"Is it? Then why the shakedown?"

"Pardon? What is this word, 'shakedown'?"

Silence stretched until the murmur of workers in the background seemed loud.

"I don't know whether you're part of this blackmail scheme or not," Hudson finally said. "When I make up my mind, you'll be the first to know. In the meantime, get that egg here."

With that, Hudson turned his back and headed for the front of the museum.

Novikov watched as Hudson stalked down the polished

marble corridor and out the arched thirty-foot-high ebony doors of his private monument to himself.

"Gapan," Novikov said softly.

"I am here."

"Find that bitch Toth."

28

Beyond the car's hood, the plane's engines were spinning. A dark-haired woman in a neatly tailored uniform waited at the head of the short stairway. Obviously the preflight checks were finished. All that remained was to get the passengers aboard.

And for Laurel to make up her mind how far she wanted to push Cruz.

"A jet complete with flight attendant," she said finally. "Impressive."

"And you think I'm retrograde," Cruz said. "She's the pilot."

"Touché. How are your ribs?"

"Still there."

"You really think you could carry me up those stairs kicking and screaming?"

"I'd just as soon not try."

"I'll bet. Especially after you find out that I've studied tae kwan do for seven years."

His eyebrows lifted. "A woman of many parts."

"And all of them independent."

With that, she set the brake, turned off the engine, and reached into the backseat for her leather satchel. Then she turned toward Cruz, who was watching her with eyes that glittered like ice in the moonlight.

"I thought you were in a hurry," she said.

"I am. But not if I'm going alone."

"You're not."

"You're coming with me?"

She nodded.

"Thank you," he said huskily.

As Cruz spoke, he lifted his right hand and ran his thumb over Laurel's lower lip, tracing it as lightly as a kiss. The swift intake of her breath made desire burn in him more fiercely than the pain from his ribs.

Knowing he shouldn't, unable to stop himself, he threaded his fingers deeply into her silky hair. He couldn't say whether he tugged her closer or she came to him as silently as the moonlight. All he knew was that her lips were warm and her breath tasted as sweet and clean as the night. He brushed his mouth over hers once, then again, before he forced himself to release her.

"I reserve the right to go home whenever I want," she said in a low voice.

"Fair enough," he said. *For now.*

He got out, interlaced the fingers of his right hand deeply with hers, and squeezed gently.

"I'll take care of you," he said simply.

"I know. But that's not why I'm going."

Through narrowed eyes, Cruz looked at Laurel's upturned face. Slowly, giving her time to turn away, he bent down to her mouth. This time the kiss was less gentle, more intimate, more hungry. She leaned toward him, matching his hunger, heightening it, tasting him as deeply as he was tasting her.

For Cruz it was like standing near lightning. His body hardened in a wild rush of heat. Giving a groan of need, he dragged her closer with his right arm, letting her feel what she'd done to him. She made a husky sound that could have been surprise or approval.

He expected her to retreat.

She didn't. She softened, letting her supple body fit against him, giving him back the passion he had aroused in her.

Abruptly he straightened, ending the embrace. Cursing himself for a fool every step of the way, he led Laurel to the plane. Touching her broke every rule in the professional book. Kissing her gently broke every rule in his personal book.

Finding out she wanted him as much as he wanted her was pure stupidity.

He consoled himself that at least it had taken his mind off of his ribs . . . and centered it about twelve inches lower.

"Take us home," he said to the pilot as they walked aboard. "Fast."

The door closed seamlessly behind them. No sooner had Cruz and Laurel sat down in facing seats than the pilot ran up the engines for one last check. Moments later the plane eased forward, turned, and taxied onto the runway. The take-off was swift and smooth.

During the whole process, Cruz neither spoke to nor looked at Laurel.

"Impressive," she said again.

"Taking care of people is our business."

"I haven't hired you."

"It doesn't matter," he said.

"What if I decide to go off on my own?"

"We'll burn that bridge when we get to it."

He leaned over and touched a switch, dimming the lights in the cabin.

After a few moments, Laurel realized that he wasn't setting the stage for seduction. He was watching the earth down below, where the landscape was drawn in moonlight and knife-edged shadows. His eyes worked the dark ground outside like radar.

She stared out her own porthole, wondering what he saw in the maze of shadows and silver light that so fascinated him.

"Where are we headed?" she asked after a bit.

"If you were as good a geologist as you are a gemologist, you'd recognize that ragged line down there."

"Where?"

"See the line that cuts those hills in half?"

She peered through the darkness. Moonlight was a lot more deceptive than sunlight. It took time before she could make out the line that intrigued him.

"That one?" she asked, pointing.

"Yes."

"What is it?"

"The San Andreas fault," he said. "It's the most perfect example of faulting in western America. Someday I'm going to spend a month walking it."

"Shake, rattle, and roll."

His smile flashed and he laughed despite his ribs.

"Our flight route will follow the San Andreas straight south and then out into the desert," he said. "After that, the fault branches off to the west, toward a place called Anza-Borrego, just west of the Salton Sea."

"Were you a geologist once?"

"No. But I like to track the chaos that Mother Nature throws at us just to make sure we're still awake."

For a time there was silence while Laurel watched the giant fault unreel below them. She stole small glances at Cruz, but he never looked away from the rumpled land. He focused on it with the same intensity he'd shown while he traded shots with the assassins.

Like him, she was fascinated by the earth, but in a different way. She loved the tiny blossoms of beauty and color that the earth produced, the gems and the beach agates and the mineral specimens she turned into jewelry.

Slowly she settled back into the seat. She no longer looked at the land. Instead, she watched the man who sat with his knees a few inches from her own. He looked at the earth and saw chaos and violent potential. He was trained in violence. Most of his life seemed consumed by it.

Yet he wasn't simply a windup assassin. He was intelligent, ruthless, and frighteningly perceptive. He was also capable of surprising tenderness. His combination of strength, intelligence, and gentleness was as unusual as it was beguiling.

It certainly beguiled me, she admitted to herself. *I'm on this plane as much because of Cruz as for any other reason. That doesn't speak highly of my intelligence, but that's the way it is.*

As if sensing her uneasiness, he looked up.

"Don't worry," he said. "You made the right choice. Bet on it."

"I already have."

And what she'd bet was her life.

29

Karroo
Tuesday

Laurel awoke in darkness. Disoriented, still half asleep, she couldn't remember where she was. The air in the small bedroom was still and cool. She was dressed in a light cotton shift and covered by a smooth sheet. She didn't know how long she'd slept.

There was no clock in the room. The only hint of time came from the narrow border of harsh white light that outlined a heavily curtained window. She studied the light. There was a fierce quality to it, as if it had been forced through a crystal prism and magnified to laser intensity.

Desert light.

Slowly she began to remember bits and pieces of the previous night. The cool white light of the moon had outlined a severe landscape of dry mountains and rolling dunes. She'd seen them as the jet banked and landed on Risk Ltd.'s private strip at the foot of the Santa Rosa Mountains.

Risk Ltd.

Cruz Rowan.

Her father and the Ruby Surprise.

The images came flooding back to her, and with them an urgency that brought her upright in bed with her heart pounding and gunfire echoing in her mind. She felt again the chill of the cement floor hard against her body while Cruz's weight covered her, holding her down.

Protecting her.

Then she remembered the warm, gentle pressure of his thumb on her mouth, and the hot, urgent pressure of his kiss.

With a swift motion she peeled away the sheet and surged out of bed. The tile floors of the room were smooth, clean, almost cold beneath her bare feet.

"Better than my cement workroom floor," she told herself.

But her heart was still beating too hard, too fast. Some of it was fear. Some of it wasn't.

"I wonder if Risk Limited has any way to protect foolish women from getting involved with men like Cruz Rowan," she said under her breath. "Probably not. There just aren't enough men like Cruz to make a business out of it. Too bad. I'm going to need all the help I can get. A country divided soon falls, and a woman divided soon falls in bed. Or in love."

Her own words startled Laurel.

No. Not that. No way.

No "like mother, like daughter" for me.

She went quickly to the window and yanked the heavy drapes apart. A blazing yellow-white cataract of sunlight burst into the room. Blinking rapidly, she waited for her eyes to adjust.

Finally a dry, rocky landscape condensed from the blinding light. There was little else to see. Except for the scattered buildings of the compound and a macadam runway lying like a dead black snake rigid under the weight of the sun, the desert was empty.

She was isolated, alone, a stranger in a strange land.

Her hands tightened on the drapes as she struggled to understand why she'd trusted Cruz Rowan so much that she'd come to this desolate place with him.

I was in danger.

Was I really?

Again she heard gunfire in her mind, felt the jerk of Cruz's body as he took the bullets that had been meant for her.

Right. I was in danger.

Now I'm safe.

And I have to find a way to tell Dad, a way that won't lead Cruz right to him. But how?

The question had haunted Laurel before she fell asleep. In the past, if she'd thought about it at all, she'd have assumed that a cell call couldn't be traced.

After last night, she doubted it.

In addition, she had to assume that every Risk Ltd. phone within her reach was attached directly to a tape recorder, if not a human monitor. Unhappily, she stared at the telephone on the bedside table.

"So near and yet so far," she muttered.

Abruptly an idea crystallized in her mind. It often happened that way. A problem she had worried over before falling asleep somehow would get solved while she slept. She looked at the phone's number pad, picking out what she needed.

Three, two, six, four, three, seven.

She lifted the receiver, punched in her father's cellular number, waited for the signal, entered the six digits as a callback number, and hung up quickly. The whole thing had taken less than thirty seconds.

Praying she'd done the right thing, she looked around for her clothes. She couldn't find anything beyond what she already wore, the sheer green nightgown that had been left on the turned-down bed last night. It was pretty enough, but hardly the sort of thing she'd wear in front of strangers.

She went to the closet. Except for a thin cotton robe that matched her nightgown, the space was empty. She swept the robe off its hanger and pulled the frail cloth around her shoulders. It wasn't much, but it was better than nothing. Still tying the sash, she stepped into the cool hallway, looked both ways, and headed for the lighted room she saw at one end.

A sturdy woman with glistening black hair and skin the color of a rich red brick was setting a table. The room was large, floored with terra-cotta tiles, and comfortable in the colorful yet spare way of Southwest design. The furniture was one of a kind rather than mass-produced. The Native American rugs were at least ninety years old, with not one bit of pastel pink or garish turquoise woven in.

"Good morning, Ms. Swann," the woman said cheerfully. "I'm Grace Mendoza. I work for the ambassador. Did you rest well?"

"Yes, thank you. Where are my clothes?"

"In the dryer. They should be ready by the time you've eaten breakfast—or lunch, if you prefer."

Laurel blinked. "What time is it?"

"Almost eleven. Cruz said we should let you sleep as late as possible. It sounds like you had quite a night."

"It had its moments," she said tightly. "Where is Cruz? I need to speak to him right away."

Mendoza looked at the young woman's gown and robe, and smiled. But all she said was, "I saw him head out to the gym a few minutes ago with Sergeant-Major Gillespie."

Laurel remembered how Cruz had talked her into accompanying him in the first place. He'd claimed that he was too hurt to drive.

"The gym?" she asked in disbelief.

"He works out at least once every day when he's here."

"Even when he has a broken rib?"

"Cruz heals quickly," Mendoza said, barely hiding her smile.

"Quickly?" Laurel's voice was acid. "The man is a walking medical miracle. Where's the gym? I can't wait to see a real, live miracle."

"It's in the far building under the old pepper trees," Mendoza said, pointing. "But wouldn't you like a glass of orange juice or a cup of coffee instead? Cruz will be back soon."

Laurel didn't answer. She was already striding through the heavily glazed doors, heading for the gym, eager to confront a lying son of a bitch known as Cruz Rowan.

30

Los Angeles
Tuesday 11:00 A.M.

Highland Park in West Los Angeles was almost like Gorkiy Park on a hot summer day. A bad loudspeaker made the balalaika music sound properly tinny, and the smog reminded Damon Hudson of Moscow's hazy summers. The sidewalks were crowded with dumpy women in cheap clothes. The benches in the park were jammed with dour old men who smoked and talked out of the corner of their mouth, as if afraid someone might be eavesdropping on their unimportant conversations.

Hudson hated it.

Although he'd made a civil crusade of his admiration for the Soviet Union and its people, the truth was more complex. He loved the system and despised its surly inhabitants.

Millions had died in the Great Patriotic War against Hitler. On top of their bodies were piled the millions more who died in gulags and death camps from Belarus to Siberia. But despite all those deaths and the recent political upheavals, little had changed in the Russian people themselves. Even after seventy years of Soviet reform and rule, Hudson found the Russian people to be sour, smelly, and superstitious.

He was reminded of that unhappy truth each time he came to the émigré community in West Los Angeles. That was why he avoided the whole place like a leper colony.

Today he didn't have any choice but to be among the stubborn peasants. Davinian would be more at ease in these surroundings than anywhere else. The jeweler had grown sentimental in his old age. He loved to soak up the ambience of Mother Russia the way other old men loved to soak up the summer sun.

For their last meeting Hudson wanted Davinian to be as comfortable as possible.

The jeweler was sitting quietly beneath a bloomed-out jacaranda tree. With his bald head and bony limbs, he looked like an awkward, morose bird. He wore sunglasses with round metal frames, but they weren't enough to protect eyes gone squinty with age. He looked right past Hudson without recognizing him.

"Davinian," Hudson said quietly.

"Ah, Damon," the old jeweler said, turning toward the voice. "I was not expecting you from that direction. I did not see your limousine pull up."

"I walked."

"Walked?" Davinian shook his head. "Next you will be jogging, to help you appear young again."

"Here, I brought you some iced tea from the Crimean restaurant."

As Hudson spoke, he rummaged in the paper bag he'd carried to the meeting. After a moment he held out a plastic cup that rattled with ice and liquid. When Davinian took the cup, Hudson reached into the bag and got his own drink. He sat on the bench near the old jeweler and uncapped his tea.

A sip told Hudson it was just as bad as he remembered.

"Lemon?" Davinian asked, cocking his head to one side and looking at his own drink.

"Double lemon, just like always."

"Thank you," Davinian said, saluting him with the cup. "It is already a warm day."

In silence Davinian sipped at the dark, bitter tea and watched the other old men. They sat as he did, enjoying sunlight filtered through lacy leaves and the faint wail of the balalaika.

"I love this place," he said. "It has become like the neighborhood in which I grew up. Someday I suppose I must go back to Moscow, just to see how much it has changed."

Hudson made a sound that could have been laughter. "I was there last month. It has changed far less than you might have wished." Certainly less than Hudson had liked.

"Maybe in the society you frequent. The trough has remained the same, and the biggest swine still eat first." Davinian sipped more tea and sighed. "But down at the level where the rest of us live, things are different, very different."

"Are they?"

"The generals stayed in place, but the people who were my colleagues—the colonels, the majors, and the captains—they are all gone. All of them, gone."

"Does that mean you weren't able to learn anything?" Hudson asked sharply.

Davinian shrugged his thin, slumped shoulders. "I found out a little, but very little. There is a whole generation of men, good men, capable men, men who were my comrades, after a fashion. They have been cut out of power as though they suddenly became senile."

"Spare me the sad tale. I'm not one of the ones left behind. I'm still in the game. I need all the information I can get."

Davinian drank a bit more tea, drawing out the moment. Like the other old men in the park, he had little else of interest to do that day.

"I was able to obtain some information on the woman, Toth," Davinian said finally. "It was just as you suspected. She has worked for Moscow several times, mostly in spreading stories that Moscow wanted spread."

"What kinds of stories?"

"There was no pattern. Her first notable work came when she was very young, still in college. It was during the Olympics here in Los Angeles."

"The Russians boycotted that one."

Davinian nodded his head. "The Second Directorate mailed threatening letters to some of the black African delegations. It was made to appear that the letters came from the Ku Klux Klan. It was a small effort to embarrass the organizers of the Olympics."

"Crude."

"Such methods often work." Davinian sipped. "However, the Olympic authorities intercepted the letters and diverted them. The entire stunt would have been a failure, except that someone was able to leak copies of the letters to your Miss Toth. She publicized the matter in the college newspaper and turned it into an international incident."

Expectantly Davinian looked at Hudson.

"That won't help me," Hudson said. "It's ancient history."

"More recently," Davinian said, sipping lightly, "Toth was unusually helpful in publicizing an example of grievous misconduct by an American FBI agent. It was a major news story that did much to establish her reputation as a national journalist."

"What story?"

"Surely you remember the incident? The FBI special

weapons team killed two terrorists who had taken the South African consul general hostage here in Beverly Hills. The killings came at the end of days of negotiations and threats. There were television cameras everywhere."

"Oh, that." Hudson remembered it only because he'd maintained a cordial relationship with the South African diplomat who had replaced the consul general. The diplomat had been helpful in Hudson International's acquisition of coal gasification technology from his homeland. "What does it have to do with Toth?"

"She was the conduit through which our people were able to discredit the FBI agent who actually did the killing. The media had portrayed him as something of a hero, until it was suggested that the young terrorists had tried to surrender after executing the South African consul general."

Hudson became still. "Go on."

"There was a hint, nothing more, that this agent Rowan might have meted out some informal justice, dealing more harshly with the terrorists than the courts would be expected to do. The suggestion became even stronger when the *Los Angeles Times* printed a picture of the agent attending a neo-Nazi rally."

Watching Davinian carefully, Hudson drank some of his tea. The old jeweler shifted uneasily on the bench, as though its slats were too hard. He sipped at the tea in his hand, then looked at the cup.

"Did I put in too much lemon?" Hudson asked. He held out his own tea. "Here, would you rather have mine?"

"No, thank you." Davinian drank a little more, just to be polite. There was indeed too much lemon.

"Was the neo-Nazi rally picture a fraud?" Hudson asked after a moment.

"Of course. We gave it to her."

"That's not much help for me. It's an open secret that aggressive reporters don't worry too much about whatever ax their source might want to grind."

Davinian smiled. "Ah, but Toth knew precisely where the photo came from. She also knew it was a lie. It had been taken six months before, when the FBI agent was working undercover. He was investigating the neo-Nazis, not participating in their rallies."

"Surely the FBI knew that too."

"Their investigation was still alive. They could not tell the truth without jeopardizing their work and, apparently, several of their informants. The agent was publicly pilloried and eventually resigned in disgrace."

"So?"

"So Toth won several significant journalistic prizes for her stories. That photo was her springboard to a national reputation as a slayer of conservative dragons. She has never looked back. Nor have we stopped using her."

"Then I was right," Hudson said. "Your old colleagues are behind this effort to blackmail me."

The old jeweler shook his head. "That I cannot tell you. The people I talked to are all out of power. There could be an operation of some sort involving this woman, but those men would be the last to know of it."

Hudson hissed a word between his teeth. "I have to be certain, old man. You don't take on a tiger like Toth with a wet noodle for a whip. Is that all you found out?"

"I was fortunate to find out anything. The new government has taken over the apparatus. My old contacts are either frightened or desperately bored. One of them would still be talking to me now, if I had not finally hung up."

"You can just pick up a phone and call these men in Moscow?" Hudson asked in genuine amazement.

"But of course. The American Telephone and Telegraph satellite links are every bit as efficient as any the Soviet Union ever put up."

"Dangerous. Anyone could listen in."

"I have worked with these men for decades. We need to say very little to make ourselves understood. In any case, my comrades no longer have enough power to be under surveillance by secret police."

"So that's it, huh?" Hudson asked. "Toth may or may not be getting her information straight from Moscow."

"Yes."

"Nothing to add?"

"I am sorry. I have done all I can. I am weary of the game."

"I see that," Hudson said. "I won't bother you after this. You have my promise."

31

Karroo
Tuesday 11:05 A.M.

"You're slow, white boy. Too slow, way too slow. Where's your speed? You leave it on the jet? Was that a try for me or are you scratching your arse?"

The taunting voice was British Oxford English, softened by the rhythms of Scotland and mixed with America's western tier. Gillespie was a hand taller than Cruz. His head was shaved and shiny with sweat. The sergeant-major moved with the agility and strength of a professional athlete in peak condition. He was barefoot. He was crouched in a position that looked awkward but allowed him to shift direction instantly without disturbing his center of gravity.

Cruz was dressed in a black judo smock and loose trousers. He also was barefoot, circling clockwise on a thick white workout mat, his arms loose and limber at his sides. His eyes were fixed on the tall, muscular, dark man who circled with him. The sergeant-major's skin had been browned by genes as much as by the desert sun. Like his color, his eyes, nose, and mouth were a mixture of two races.

Each man was watching the other for an opening with the intensity of a mongoose watching a cobra. They were so focused that they didn't notice Laurel standing and watching them from behind a glass partition, her cheeks flushed from the desert heat.

"You're tipping," Gillespie taunted. "You're giving yourself away."

Without warning the sergeant-major reversed and began circling in the opposite direction.

Cruz feinted.

"Bloody hell," Gillespie said in disgust. "Why don't you just wear a neon sign?"

To underline the point, he took a swift step forward, pivoted on one straight leg, and aimed a blindingly fast roundhouse kick at the left side of Cruz's chest. Cruz had anticipated the attack and was already turning to face it. He caught Gillespie's foot with both hands and quickly levered upward. The sergeant-major executed a brilliantly coordinated somersault in midair and rolled through to a standing position.

Laurel wiped her forehead and watched the men with a combination of anger and fascination. She'd never seen such powerful, lethally graceful men face one another in unarmed combat.

It was Cruz who drew her eyes most. Cruz, who had just tossed at least two hundred pounds of sergeant-major ass over teakettle. Cruz, who had saved her life. Cruz, who had kissed her as if she was the first and last woman on earth.

Cruz, who had systematically lied to her.

She'd driven him to the airport because he told her he was too banged up to drive. He'd even nicely agreed that, given her martial arts experience, he wouldn't want to try carrying her aboard the aircraft against her will.

She winced at the memory.

Her seven years of unarmed combat workouts wouldn't keep her in the ring with Cruz for seven seconds. Yet what was really infuriating was that he'd known her well enough to understand that if he dragged her kicking and screaming onto the plane, he wouldn't be able to keep her at Karroo without shackles and a jail cell.

The two men were circling again, feinting, testing each other with a muscular, sweaty pleasure only another male could appreciate. When she opened the glass door to the exercise room, neither man noticed. They were totally focused on attack and defense.

"What do you say now, old man?" Cruz asked sarcastically, mimicking Gillespie's British accent. "How much have I lost?"

"I say you're quick to compensate. Let's see how long you can keep it up, laddie boy."

"As long as I have to."

"Good," Laurel said from the doorway. "Now I can stop feeling guilty for the bullets you took."

Cruz spun toward her. A single look told him that whatever he said wouldn't be good enough to get past her anger at being deceived.

"Take it easy," he said quickly. "You don't have any idea what is—"

"Shove it," she cut in. "I know when I'm being made a fool of for your convenience. Too bad I didn't have—"

"Honey, if you'd just—"

"—as much fun playing the game as you did, but solitaire is like that. Fun for one only."

"Laurel, I didn't—"

She kept right on talking coldly over Cruz. "I'll be leaving this place Alpha Sierra Alpha Papa."

He blinked.

She turned to Gillespie. "You're right. Cruz is slow today. 'As soon as possible' isn't a difficult concept. And that's when I'll be leaving. ASAP."

"No," Cruz said flatly.

Gillespie looked from Laurel to Cruz.

"Yes," she countered, without turning back to Cruz.

"You said—" Cruz began, only to be cut off again.

"I suppose your job would be easier if I'd stayed dumb, slow, and manageable, but shit happens," she said.

Gillespie fought a smile. "And it just happened here, is that it?"

"A whole bagful," she agreed grimly. "So ring up your pilot or your chauffeur or whatever. I'm out of here."

"No," Cruz said.

So did Gillespie, more quietly. "That wouldn't be wise, Ms. Swann."

"So Cruz lied about that too," she said. "I'm a prisoner."

"You're a valued guest," Gillespie corrected.

"Wrong. Nobody values a fool. Especially the fool in question." She spun to face Cruz. "You think I'll help you find Dad."

"Laurel, honey, I—"

"Hold your breath until you turn black, *honey*. It's your best color."

She turned and strode out of the exercise room. The door closed softly behind her.

Both men would have felt better if she'd slammed it.

Laurel's strides never hesitated. She covered the distance to the main building with long, quick strides, her temper hotter than the desert day. This time she didn't pause to admire the native landscaping or the elegant, shaded walkway from the gym to the rest of the compound. Heat, anger, and humiliation at how easily she'd been fooled burned through her. The emotions flushed her cheeks like sunburn.

She'd trusted him.

And wanted him, she told herself ruthlessly. *Don't forget that. You were a world-class sucker.*

She covered the ground to the rest of the compound in record time. Mendoza was still working over the table.

Laurel ignored her.

"The ambassador would like to speak with you," Mendoza said. "She's in her study."

Laurel turned away. "I wouldn't dream of bothering her."

"It would be no bother at all. The nearest town is due east," Mendoza added, as if the younger woman had asked.

Laurel hesitated. "How far?"

"Over fifty miles."

Abruptly Laurel stopped moving. *Fifty miles.*

"If you plan on walking," Mendoza said, "wait until evening."

Laurel opened her mouth. No words came out.

"I'm a Soboba Indian," the other woman continued calmly. "My people have been trekking this country, winter and summer, for the last five centuries. None of us would try five miles of desert under high sun, much less fifty."

Taking a deep breath, Laurel fought the panic that was rising in her.

"Talk to the ambassador," Mendoza said gently. "She's very good at sorting out these kinds of things."

All Laurel said was, "Where is the laundry room?"

"Down that hall, third door on the left."

Laurel started down the hall.

"You really should see the ambassador," Mendoza called after her.

Laurel kept walking, trying not to panic.

Trapped.

No way out.

32

At the jeweler's urging, Hudson had stayed for a few more minutes, but he was growing impatient for it to begin so that he could be gone. He smiled rather grimly as he held up his plastic cup of tea in silent toast, touching it against the other man's and drinking deeply.

After a slight hesitation Davinian did the same.

Hudson studied the other man. Bright sunshine only served to accent Davinian's pallor, his frailty. He was as old and worn out as his colleagues on Dzerzhinsky Square. But unlike them, he no longer cared about the game of power.

That made Davinian almost as dangerous to Hudson as Claire Toth.

If the jeweler understood that, he didn't seem concerned. He lifted his dark glasses and rubbed his eyes. They were red and unfocused. He looked like an owl with a hangover.

"You look awful," Hudson said. "You don't take very good care of yourself."

"I do not feel well." Davinian shifted on the bench,

uncomfortable and unsure why. He sighed deeply and wondered why the sun which had felt so warm earlier felt so cool now. "I am too old for this. I have been dozing here in the sun because I missed much of my sleep talking to Russia last night."

"You don't seem worried about what Toth might do, yet you have as much to lose as I do."

Davinian shook his head. "I have given the matter some thought. It is not the end of the world. I have only a few years left, if that. I no longer care very much who finds out what I have done in the past forty or fifty years. Even if I am arrested, I would not outlive the trial to go to jail."

Hudson's mouth turned down. He was older than Davinian, but Hudson planned on living a lot longer. Living, not existing. Prison wasn't part of his plans.

Turning toward Hudson, Davinian smiled oddly. "You see," he said in his dry, papery voice, "becoming old has made me free. It is different for you. You are determined to live many, many more years, and to live them as a young man. You even have found a fountain of relative youth. My congratulations."

Hudson's mouth flattened. He should have known Davinian would find out. Just one more reason to bury the past.

"Surely," the jeweler said, "you can understand that we normal mortals are less impressed with the problems of the immortal and the near-immortal among us."

Hudson chuckled softly, but without amusement. "So your colleagues told you about my medical treatments."

The other man gave a slight shrug. "I've known for years. It was not what one might call a state secret, only a matter of idle curiosity and gossip."

Davinian glanced at Hudson, trying to see if he was offended.

Hudson didn't look up from his tea.

"Perhaps you should just give the woman, this reporter, what she wants," the jeweler said. "You have enough money to afford even the most rapacious of gold diggers."

"I don't know what she wants. I'm not even sure *she* knows what she wants. At first it sounded like money, but then it didn't. It seemed like she was making up the rules of the game as she went along."

"That does not sound like Moscow. Not even the new regime is that foolish. These new boys, they always know what they want. If Claire Toth is indecisive, she is probably playing out of school. Give her a bone and hope she will be satisfied for a time."

Hudson was quiet for a while, thinking. Finally he straightened on the bench as though gathering himself to leave. "What about you, Davinian? What am I to do with you?"

Something in Hudson's tone surprised the old jeweler. He dropped his chin a few inches and peered at Hudson over the top of his glasses. Hudson stared back, watching intently, looking for . . . something.

Davinian felt the chill sink more deeply into the pit of his stomach, into his bony hips, down his spindly legs. "What do you mean?"

"It's simple. You've gotten too old. You've lost your zest for the game of power. That's what kept us going all those years, the joy of the game. The almost sexual thrill that comes from knowing secrets and using them."

Hudson sipped his tea again and glanced at the jeweler's paper cup, which sat half empty on the bench between them.

"No more tea?" Hudson asked gently.

His smile deepened the coldness that Davinian felt. Weakness invaded him, forerunner of an endless night.

"What have you done?" the jeweler whispered in a strained voice. "I am cold. Did you—"

The words were interrupted by a sudden burst of chills. Trembling, he wrapped his arms around himself, trying to hold in the warmth that was draining from his body.

"Me?" Hudson said. "I didn't do anything. You're just old."

Davinian jerked his head so sharply that his glasses leaped, then settled crookedly on his nose.

"You're too old for the stress anymore," Hudson said. "You really should take better care of yourself. I could arrange for some treatments, just because you're my old friend."

Abruptly, the jeweler shivered in the hot sunlight and slumped against the metal arm at the end of the bench. Then he doubled over in response to the cold that was spreading through him, pushing warmth and life out of his body.

"You are a m-monster," Davinian whispered through chattering teeth. "What d-did you use? Tell me! I have a r-right to know how I will die."

Sadly Hudson shook his head. "If you continue to act so irrationally, I really will have to leave. I can't afford to be seen with senile old Armenians and homesick Russian Jews."

Davinian tried to respond to Hudson's soft taunts but couldn't. A wave of cold like the Russian winter welled up within him. His frail, dying body shook with spasms that were frightening but not painful.

Without seeming to, Hudson looked carefully around the park. No one seemed to be paying attention to the two men beneath the jacaranda tree. From their casual out-of-date clothes, they might have been old friends reminiscing quietly in the sun. He glanced over at Davinian. For a second he almost felt pity.

"Is there pain, my friend?" he asked softly. "I was told it would be painless. Consider that my parting gift to you, a death without pain. It's more than most old men get."

Unable to speak, Davinian huddled at his end of the bench. All he could do was clench his chattering teeth and glare with his failing eyes at the man who had killed him.

Like an old friend saying goodbye, Hudson reached over and touched Davinian on the shoulder. No response.

Hudson picked up the jeweler's tea, stood, and walked away. He didn't look back. There was no reason to. Davinian was part of the impotent, dead past. Hudson was firmly astride the potent, living future.

Or he would be as soon as he got a handle on Claire Toth.

33

Karroo
Tuesday, noon

Dressed finally in her own clothes, pleasantly full from a beautifully prepared omelet and fresh fruit, and nerved up on coffee that could have etched steel, Laurel walked to the heavy door of the ambassador's study. It was open just a crack, enough to show that it wasn't locked.

Laurel thought about the coming conversation and decided she should have had less food or more coffee.

Quit stalling and go on in like Ms. Mendoza told you to. What do you have to lose? Certainly not pride. Cruz took care of that already.

Hey, the good news is that I'm finally dressed.

The memory of confronting Cruz in the gym wearing little more than two flimsy layers of cotton made Laurel's cheeks burn. Without knocking she shoved the heavy door open.

The room was large, cool, and had no windows. Despite that, there was light everywhere. She closed the door behind her and looked around. All four walls were lined with beautiful display cases. Many of the cases held ancient manuscripts that were either originals or very fine copies. Ranks of freestanding bookshelves were grouped about.

She recognized English, Latin, French, German, and Russian texts. She didn't know enough to decide whether the ideographs she saw were Chinese, Japanese, Vietnamese, Korean, or all four. No matter the language, there was enough research material in Redpath's office to make a university reference librarian drool.

On one wall hung a backlighted Mercator-style world map that was also an intricate "real-time" clock. The brightest parts of the map represented the parts of the globe that were in daytime. The darker parts were in night.

On the wall opposite the clock, above an adobe brick fireplace, there was an old life-sized portrait of a bearded Highland Scots chieftain wrapped in a green and black tartan. The Highlander gazed at the world with the most penetrating green eyes Laurel had ever seen. They were vividly alive, and fierce in that life.

Ambassador Cassandra Redpath rose to her feet behind a cherrywood desk that filled one end of the room. The desk gleamed with a deep polish. The work surface held only three telephones and the large leather-bound book Redpath had been reading when Laurel walked in.

"How are you, Ms. Swann?" the ambassador asked, setting aside the book. "I understand from Cruz that you had a rather demanding evening yesterday."

As Laurel walked closer, she discovered that Cassandra Redpath's eyes were the same shade of intense green as the Highland chieftain's—and even more penetrating.

"I'm coping," Laurel said coolly, "but I feel like I've fallen down the White Rabbit's hole."

"That would make me the Queen of Hearts, then," the older woman said, smiling slightly.

"I hope not. Alice didn't have much luck with that one."

Redpath laughed and settled back into her desk chair. "I think we'll do very well together. Come here and sit down while I describe the world you've fallen into."

Laurel sensed in the ambassador the same swift intelligence and basic goodwill that had first made her trust Cruz Rowan. Under the circumstances, that wasn't an entirely comforting thought.

Cruz had lied to her.

With a final look around the room, she walked to one of the leather chairs that faced the expanse of desk. As she sat down, she glanced at the oversized leather-bound book that lay open on the desk. The language was Cyrillic. The color photographs vividly displayed a group of Fabergé creations.

"You have a remarkable collection of manuscripts," Laurel said. "I assume they're originals."

"Wherever possible. No matter how meticulous the monks or scribes tried to be, copying introduced errors. If necessary I'll have an unattainable volume photographed. But the result lacks a certain intangible power that exists in the original."

"I've seen old volumes and museum-quality manuscripts before," Laurel said, glancing around again, "but never so many in the hands of a private collector."

"I'm a scholar, not a collector."

"Even now that you're no longer an ambassador?"

"How else do you think I find the time to read?"

"Cruz said you were in charge of Risk Limited. I don't see how that would leave much time for research."

Redpath folded her hands, rested her chin on them, and watched Laurel without speaking.

Laurel felt like the ambassador was trying to read her as she would a manuscript whose language wasn't totally familiar.

"I run Risk Limited, but I do most of it right from this desk," Redpath said after a moment. "Cruz and other operators like him do nearly all the fieldwork themselves. They call in from time to time to keep me from worrying too much, but I've chosen them for their initiative, ability, and independence. They don't need me."

Laurel remembered something her father had once said and smiled slightly. "Having men like that working for you must be like trying to herd cats."

Redpath's laughter was as vivid as her eyes. "Precisely. So I don't attempt to herd them. Instead, I pursue my first love."

"Ideas," Laurel said, looking around the room again. "How they change, how they remain the same, how they never quite pass on enough of the unspeakable truth to satisfy us."

The ambassador's intelligent green eyes gleamed with appreciation. She began to understand why Cruz had brought Laurel back with him instead of putting her under guard in some nameless motel.

Or using her as bait.

"If all my operators were like Cruz," Redpath said, "I'd probably never be disturbed at all. He's very much a loner. It's his greatest weakness. It's also his greatest strength."

"Hooray for Cruz Rowan," Laurel said. "God's gift to the intelligence community."

Redpath's ginger-colored eyebrows rose. "Did Cruz treat you badly?"

"As in clouting me around or calling me babe or pinching my butt? No."

"That's a relief. For a moment I thought I'd have to find a whip and try my hand at herding cats."

Against her will, Laurel smiled.

"What did Cruz do to you?" Redpath asked.

"He led me to believe that he was seriously injured saving

my life, so I had to drive him to the plane. Then he threatened . . ."

Redpath's gaze sharpened.

Laurel's voice died. Cruz hadn't threatened her.

Not exactly.

"He said," Laurel corrected, "that if I chose not to come with him, he'd conclude I was too stupid to protect myself, and he'd be forced to take appropriate measures. But it was my choice, of course."

Her cheeks burned as she remembered her foolish certainty that she was more than a match for the injured Cruz. What was even more humiliating was that he knew her well enough to let her think she was in control of the situation.

What a joke. On me, of course. I haven't been in control since the moment Cruz walked into my house. I had a gun on him, and he looked at me like he'd never seen a woman he wanted more.

She wondered if his dreams last night had been like hers. Restless. She kept remembering how vulnerable he'd looked with his black armor shell removed, revealing his warm flesh and the brutal gouges left by bullets. She kept seeing his male grace in the gym today, a sheen of sweat highlighting his strength. She kept thinking about what it would be like to be the focus of those laser eyes, to feel those big hands caressing her, to make Cruz grimace with pleasure rather than pain. . . .

You're a fool. He's way out of your league. He's way out of any woman's league.

Yet the images of Cruz kept burning like candles in her mind.

Redpath waited, watching Laurel with the patience of a cat or a chess player.

"When I told Cruz I'd studied tae kwan do for seven years and he would have a hell of a time carrying me to the plane,"

Laurel said distinctly, "he didn't disagree. But from what I saw today, Cruz could have taken me with a lot less fuss than a cougar takes a rabbit."

Though Redpath didn't smile, the crinkling at the corners of her eyes hinted at her inner laughter.

"In short, Cruz lied to me," Laurel said. "I don't like being lied to like a child. It's humiliating."

"Cruz wasn't lying."

"He sure as hell wasn't telling all of the truth. Especially about his ribs."

"He looked quite sore this morning," Redpath said.

"Yeah, right. That's why he's frolicking in the gym with a drop-dead handsome black guy who's doing his best to kick Cruz's teeth out. Guess who I hope wins."

The warmth of the ambassador's smile surprised Laurel.

"Do you really think the sergeant-major is handsome?" Redpath asked. "I'll have to tell him. He'll be delighted."

"Surely the man has a mirror."

"Gillie is a little too—shall we say, dangerous-looking?— for most modern women."

"Some women like lapdogs."

"But you don't," Redpath said calmly. "That's why you followed Cruz."

It wasn't a question, so Laurel didn't answer.

"Let me tell you a bit more about the rabbit hole you find yourself in," the ambassador said. "That way, your choice of whether to stay or to go will come from your intelligence as well as your emotions."

"Do I really have a choice?"

Redpath gave her the kind of look she gave a difficult operative. Then she moved the heavy book from in front of her and settled back in her chair.

"Risk Limited grew out of my experiences in government,"

she said, "but it also grew out of my conviction that we've entered a new age in human civilization. The world has become a global village."

Laurel glanced at the intricate world map, where the line between daylight and darkness was slowly sweeping across the face of the earth.

"Exactly," Redpath said, following her glance. "Without getting up from this chair, I can talk simultaneously to New York, London, and Moscow and receive a fax from Hong Kong in the next room."

"Your phone bill must be the size of the national debt."

"It would be, if we didn't own the company. Our communications section put together a system of satellite relays that allows me to speak directly with my operators in the most remote spots on the face of the earth, so long as they can see the sky."

"I had a sample of it on the drive here. Very efficient. Cruz put the word out with a vengeance."

"Ah, yes. 'Wear black. He's expecting you.' "

Laurel's eyelids flinched. It still bothered her to hear her father described in terms of the violence he might commit.

"Technology has changed radically in the last several decades," Redpath said. "Unfortunately, human beings haven't. People who want to create rather than destroy are still confronted daily by the same kinds of evil, inertia, and ignorance that have plagued human endeavors throughout history."

" 'Vanity of vanities, all is vanity,' " Laurel said.

Redpath nodded. "Ecclesiastes. More wisdom and less comfort than any other philosophical treatise I've ever read."

Laurel waited.

For a moment the ambassador looked at her hands. Then she sighed and focused on her reluctant guest.

"Civilization needs men like Cruz Rowan," Redpath said.

"Men who are capable of violence *and* restraint, action *and* thought. Cruz is one of the most perceptive, tenacious investigators I've ever known. He's a gifted bodyguard. As well as sheer native intelligence, he has sharp reflexes, physical agility, strength, and stamina."

Images of Cruz burned in Laurel's mind, experience, and imagination combined. She shifted uneasily. She'd never been drawn to a man as she was to him.

It wasn't a comfortable feeling.

"In short," Redpath said, "I require a high level of physical readiness in all my operators, both male and female. Should I ever be tempted to let my emotions override my intellect in this matter, Sergeant-Major Gillespie will point it out to me with great pleasure."

Remembering what she'd seen of Gillespie, Laurel didn't doubt it. The man was formidable.

"Gillespie was one of the most effective operators in the history of the British Army's Special Air Services," Redpath said. "He trained some of the best cadres of counterterrorists in recent history. Here at Risk Limited, he is the unchallenged judge of physical readiness. If he refuses to certify an operator for duty, that operator is off the case, no matter what my feelings on the matter might be."

Belatedly, Laurel realized the trap she was being gently led into. She'd planned on using Cruz's lies as a reason to leave the compound; Redpath was on her way to proving that Laurel was wrong in her view of the situation.

"Cruz's injuries were and are real," Redpath said. "He tore cartilage between two ribs. Right now he is strapped into a corset the likes of which I haven't seen since my great-grandmother's time. Every breath is a knife in his side."

"He didn't look it."

"Several years ago, Cruz had a crash course in hiding

his feelings. It was something he learned all too well."

"After he killed the terrorists?"

"Yes."

"He told me."

"Did he? Remarkable."

Redpath looked at Laurel intently. Then the ambassador continued talking. "With torn cartilage, Cruz could handle communications and other light duty. But he was inflexible about staying on this case. He was even more inflexible about retaining his job as the primary operator. He seems to feel some responsibility for your safety. Some *personal* responsibility."

Laurel knew better than to open her mouth. If she denied that there was a real personal attraction between herself and Cruz, she'd only be pointing it out.

"As for the question of Cruz's physical state," Redpath said, "he and Gillie are settling that right now."

Laurel flinched at the thought of what Cruz must be going through. She had misread him. Again. He hadn't lied to her. He'd simply allowed her to draw whatever conclusions comforted her. If they were the wrong conclusions, she had only herself to blame.

Grimly Laurel realized that Cruz's insight into how her mind worked was going to make getting free of Risk Ltd. that much harder. The reasons she had to flee were being systematically stripped away, leaving only the reason she didn't want to discuss.

Jamie Swann.

34

~~~

The lunch crowd milled around Jimmy's on Santa Monica Boulevard. Stockbrokers and lawyers from Century City knocked elbows with talent agents and executive producers fresh from studio meetings.

Tourists tried to find Rodeo Drive.

And men of all sorts braked sharply when they caught a glimpse of the statuesque woman standing on the corner. There was a touch of the streetwalker in her—the revealing clothes, the arrogantly hip-shot stance. But a second glance, and a third, told the men that whatever she was selling, they couldn't afford to buy.

Claire Toth's cream silk clothes came from Neiman Marcus and had been fitted by a loving tailor. A few hours earlier, her scarlet leather pumps and shoulder bag had been in the window of an expensive Italian boutique on La Brea. Her necklace was also scarlet, a bold postmodern mixture of female decoration and leering cartoon faces that drew attention to her striking cleavage. With a graceful motion she smoothed the line of her eel-tight slacks and pursed her mouth, redistributing the carmine lipstick.

Standing next to her was as close as Jamie Swann would ever get to outright invisibility.

"You do get off on having men look you over, don't you?" he said sardonically.

"Yeah, babe. It's a real rush, knowing you have more control over a man's body than he does."

Swann smiled sourly.

"But best of all," she said, "is the secret game that goes along with it. The one you play. It's like screwing a man in front of his wife without her even knowing what's going on."

"Crisscross double-cross. Some fun and games."

As Swann spoke, he again chewed over Laurel's cryptic message—six numbers spelling out DANGER.

At least, Swann assumed Laurel had sent it. Anyone else who had his pager number knew better ways to pass information than a crude code taken from the telephone number pad.

DANGER.

What in hell could be worse than having Risk Ltd. on my ass? Swann asked himself. And why isn't Laurel at home to pick up my calls? Or is someone screening her calls for her?

That possibility was the reason Swann hadn't left any message on Laurel's answering machine.

Christ. How in hell am I going to make that egg work without her?

There was no answer to Swann's silent inner seething. All he had was the gut feeling that the whole game was falling apart around him.

Time to pick up the markers and try another table. But not without whatever Claire can squeeze out of the old bastard.

Running and hiding took money. Swann was broke.

Dead broke.

That made him very edgy. He was trying to conceal it by leaning casually against a spun aluminum light standard. The dark Ray•Ban sunglasses he wore concealed his eyes. His loose cotton shirt hid the pistol rammed into the waistband of his jeans at the small of his back. He looked like what he'd been from time to time—hired muscle.

From behind her own sunglasses, Toth watched Swann with a wariness she could scarcely conceal. All she'd heard from her assassins was that they had failed on their first attempt. If Swann had heard from his daughter about the attempt on her life, he hadn't said anything about it to Toth.

If he'd heard and not told her, she was dancing on a whirlpool and could be sucked under at any minute. *If* he'd heard. If not, everything was as solid as the cement sidewalk under her high-heeled sandals.

But there was no way to be certain.

She'd never lived this close to the edge. If Swann had talked to Laurel and not mentioned anything, it meant he was just waiting for the right moment to confront Toth. If Swann hadn't heard from his daughter, he soon would.

Then Swann would try to keep his promise to Toth before she could keep her promise to him.

If I'm ever killed, I hope you're the one who does it. You'd make me come while you did it.

A shiver went through her, fear and sexuality combined, each reinforcing the other. She knew she would push the savage combination too far one day.

Knowing that only added to the rush.

Toth ran her hands down her body and then over her thighs, unconsciously making certain that her lethal assets were in place.

The movement drew Swann's attention from the busy street. He watched while Toth repeated the motion, running her hands over her body the way some snipers caress the weapon of their choice while waiting for their target to show up.

"You going to screw the old man or shake him down?" Swann asked.

"Same difference. Trust me. I know what I'm doing."

Swann snorted. "You've been playing at being a spook for years. Well, babe, I've been doing the real thing since you were in diapers. Informants, agents, patsies, assets—they're all the same. They really want to be dominated, not sweet-talked."

"When did you ever try sweet-talking?" Toth asked, remembering how Swann had put his business proposition to her. Hard, blunt, heavy.

"I blew in a guy's ear once. Damn near had to kill him to get his attention after that."

Toth started to speak.

Swann cut her off. "Here he is. Let me handle it."

A long gray limousine with smoked windows slid through the afternoon traffic like a hearse and pulled up beside them at the curb. The back door popped open. Damon Hudson sat calmly in one corner of the backseat, like a pasha on a pleasure cruise aboard his magic steel carpet.

"Ah, Ms. Toth, you brought a friend," Hudson said. "How unfortunate. Our conversations will be conducted in private or they won't be conducted at all."

Swann leaned down. His swift, deadly grace pointed out all that Hudson's treatments could *not* do for him.

"Wrong, old man," Swann said coldly. "I come along for the ride or the information goes to the media before you can get this big piece of shit to the nearest freeway on-ramp."

Bill Cahill stepped out from behind the wheel and stared

over the hood of the car. His eyes were hidden by glasses that were as dark as Swann's.

"Mr. Hudson's car, pal," Cahill said. "Mr. Hudson's rules."

"Not this time," Swann said without looking away from Hudson.

Swann and Hudson locked eyes in a silence whose tension was only increased by the random street sounds around them.

"Ride up front with the driver," Toth said to Swann. "That puts us on level ground."

Ducking around Swann, she tried to get into the seat next to Hudson. Swann's casual grip held her back like she was a child rather than a big, unusually strong woman.

Hudson said something out of the corner of his mouth. Cahill slipped back behind the wheel. The electric lock on the passenger-side front door snapped to like a well-trained sentry.

After a tense moment, Swann released Toth and slid into the front seat. He slammed the door before she could get in and close her own door. As the limousine pulled back into traffic, Swann and Cahill sat side by side, eyes front.

Hudson touched a button hidden on his armrest. Silently a thick panel of smoked bulletproof glass slid out of its hiding place. Toth watched with a faint smile of amusement while the glass sealed off the passenger compartment.

Leaning forward, Hudson opened the door of a small built-in refrigerator. Someone had already unwrapped the foil and wire cage that enclosed the cork on a bottle of Cristal. Now Hudson pulled the heavy cork.

"I believe you'll like this," he said, smiling the smile of the perfect host. "Maybe your, uh, friend up front would like some too."

"He's working. Like your friend up front."

"Is he working for you?"

"Of course," she said.

Her smile revealed none of the doubts that still lanced through her at odd intervals. The double-cross had been Swann's idea. He'd approached her shortly after the Russians had. He planned on doing what the Russians had always done—use her as a cat's paw. But this time the cat had her own agenda.

All she had to do was get out from under the claws of the lion-eyed man in the front seat.

35

The ambassador was as clever an opponent as Laurel had ever faced. No matter how polite the discussion, no matter how many conversational ploys Laurel offered, Redpath never moved away from her own agenda.

"You should consider Cruz's interest a compliment," Redpath said. "He isn't a ladies' man. Of course, if you'd feel safer with another operative, I will assign one."

"I would prefer to be on my own. Period." It wasn't the first time Laurel had said the words. She doubted it would be the last.

"You're too intelligent to believe you'd be safer on your own."

Laurel didn't argue. She closed her eyes and saw again the gouges in Cruz's living flesh, felt again the jerk of his body when he was hit. Without his protection, she would have died. She was certain of it.

She just didn't like admitting it, much less living with the complications.

"I also agree with Cruz that our actions in contacting you have put you in danger," the ambassador continued. "There will be no charge for our services."

"I haven't asked for any services. And I won't."

Someone knocked on the door.

"Come in," Redpath said.

Gillespie's naked head appeared in the doorway.

Redpath nodded a bare half inch.

Laurel decided it must have been a signal, for Gillespie and Cruz padded into the library on their bare feet. She was reminded of a panther and a cougar turned loose in a museum—an amusing sight, so long as the beasts weren't hungry.

Cruz stared at Laurel with an intensity he couldn't disguise. Then he looked away like she wasn't even in the room.

Laurel felt his brief glance as clearly as a touch. She didn't look back at him, afraid that she'd somehow reveal the turmoil just beneath her control. Instead she watched Gillespie like he was indeed the dark panther he resembled.

"Ms. Swann," Redpath said, "this is Sergeant-Major Ranulph Argyle Gillespie, Twenty-second Special Air Services Regiment, Retired. He's our chief of training and discipline."

Laurel nodded and kept on not looking at Cruz.

"Gillie is also a wicked specialist in the cooking of any dish that uses habañero, poblano, or serrano chilies," Redpath said. "Otherwise, he's quite useless."

Gillespie gave the ambassador a hooded, sideways glance that was entirely masculine.

"Well," Redpath said, her eyes gleaming, "maybe not completely useless."

The sergeant-major straightened and popped a stiff

palm-out salute whose perfection was ruined only by his inability to make his bare heels click when they met.

"Mum," he said, to Laurel. "Pleased to meet you. Formally, as it were."

Laurel inclined her head an inch or two, feeling like a royal princess. Gillespie couldn't have been more imposing if he'd been wearing a bearskin hat and the uniform of the Queen's guard.

"How did the workout go?" the ambassador asked.

"I kicked his ass," Cruz said. He gave Gillespie a look that challenged him to dispute the claim.

"He kicked my ass as long as I moved at half speed," Gillespie said. "Of course, that makes him a lot better than ninety-nine out of a hundred of your average fuck-wits, begging both your pardons. But he's bloody vulnerable to his left. It won't take a good man but a minute to see."

"It's my weak side naturally," Cruz said. "If you're going to hold me to some ridiculously artificial standard of readiness—"

Redpath cut Cruz short with a gesture.

"Sergeant-Major," she said crisply, "is Cruz clearly incapacitated?"

The towering soldier's face was expressionless for a moment. Then, after a purposeful pause to show that he wasn't entirely happy, he shook his head. "He's sound enough . . . in the body."

It was less than a ringing approval and Cruz knew it. Before he could argue, Redpath was talking.

"If you have reason to change your mind," she said to Gillespie, "I'll reassign Cruz. Otherwise, he'll remain the primary operative on this case."

Gillespie nodded.

"Excellent," Redpath said.

Laurel was silently amused by the way Redpath easily handled both men, when either one of them could have broken her like a bread stick. Even as the thought came, she realized it was the key to both men; they treated Redpath with a deference that was born of true respect.

And deep affection, at least on Gillespie's part. The look he'd given Redpath when she'd teased him about being useless unless he was fighting or cooking had been the look of a man who was very confident of his appeal to a particular woman.

Redpath pulled the large Russian volume back in front of her. "I was able to borrow this book from a friend of mine who is a professor of Russian history at UCLA. It's a czarist-era catalog of the output of the Fabergé workshops in St. Petersburg and Moscow. My source assures me it's the most complete catalog on the subject in existence."

"What does it say about the Ruby Surprise?" Cruz asked.

"That it was never made."

"What?" Cruz and Laurel asked at the same time.

"There is no indication that a Fabergé workshop ever executed an imperial egg using a large gem-quality ruby as the surprise," Redpath said. "Talk of one, yes. Some rather rudimentary sketches, yes. But the plan was shelved when no suitable ruby could be found."

The room was absolutely silent for a moment.

"Do the records go all the way to the Revolution?" Cruz asked.

"Yes," Redpath said.

"Bloody hell," Cruz said.

"It's an interesting situation, isn't it?" the ambassador said cheerfully. "Full of possibilities. Why don't we all meet in a few minutes over lunch and discuss them."

It was neither a question nor an order.

Not quite.

Without looking at Laurel, Cruz turned and started for the door. She watched him move across the room, noting every motion, the light that turned his eyes to burning blue, the power implicit in his easy stride, and the faint stiffness in his left side.

Then she realized that she was staring. Hastily she got up and followed Cruz out of the room.

When the door was safely closed behind Laurel, Redpath looked up from the desk and studied the warrior who stood in his customary at-ease posture, hands clasped behind his back. Slowly she came around the desk and leaned against it so she could see into Gillespie's clear black eyes.

"Tell me the rest of it," she said.

He dropped his hands from behind his back and stretched his arms over his head. Then he smiled down at her, his military formality gone as if it had never existed.

Redpath smiled, remembering Laurel's description of Gillespie: drop-dead handsome.

"Cruz is knocked out with this girl," Gillespie said. "He almost fell on his face when she walked into the gym. She turned his brain to bean dip. That's not a good situation for an operator. It's bloody deadly."

"And it goes both ways," Redpath added.

"That it does. She was so careful not to look at Cruz when he first came in I almost laughed out loud."

"Yet she watched him leave."

"Too bloody right. Men would kill for a look like that from a woman like her."

"I don't think mayhem is what Cruz has in mind," Redpath said dryly.

"He'll be looking out for her when he should be looking out for himself or our client. It won't do, guv."

"Normally, I'd change the mixture," she agreed.

"But you won't this time. Why?"

Redpath stared thoughtfully at the tips of her fingers and then at Gillespie's hard face, as if remembering how it felt to touch him.

"Oh, I changed the mix somewhat," she said. "I made Laurel our client."

"Bloody great. I'll bodyguard her."

"No."

"Cruz?" Gillespie asked, irritated.

"Yes. He's been fighting other men's causes all his life. Maybe having something of his own will . . ." Redpath shrugged.

"Open him up a bit?"

Redpath nodded.

"Judas priest. You're a closet romantic." Gillespie gestured toward the painting of the fierce Highlander. "Your grandfather the mercenary would be disappointed to know that."

"Would he? Are you?"

Gillespie smiled. "Closet, table, floor, or a bloody trapeze, anywhere you want romance is fine with me."

Redpath's smile was as luminous as her eyes. "Ah, Gillie, the best Scots are romantic. And the black Scots are the best of all."

Gently Gillespie lifted the ambassador until she was at his eye level and asked, "What will you do when Laurel tells Cruz to go to hell?"

"Will she?"

"To protect her, Cruz will have to use her to get to Swann," Gillespie said. "You know it. I know it. Swann knows it. Cruz knows it."

Redpath nodded.

"When Laurel finds out how badly she was used," Gillespie said, "she'll cut Cruz's heart out and feed it to the ravens."

"At least Cruz will know he has a heart."

"Bloody hell. I hope we have the Ruby Surprise by then, whatever it is."

"So do I. Do you have anything on those numbers Laurel dialed yet?"

"First one was a cellular registered to someone in Manhattan whose name doesn't ring any bells in any file we have."

"Interesting. What about the second number?"

"It's not a number here or overseas. It's a code."

Redpath's eyebrows lifted. "Are you certain?"

"Yes." Gillespie smiled with unwilling approval. "Cruz has himself a real smart lady tiger. She looked at the letters above the numbers on the phone, pulled the numbers she needed to spell out DANGER, and hung up."

"Who do you think she was warning?"

"Jamie Swann."

"She doesn't trust us at all, does she?"

Gillespie laughed humorlessly. "Like I said, Cruz has caught himself a smart one. It's going to make our work bloody hard."

36

As the limousine cruised through Los Angeles, Claire Toth accepted a refill of her half-empty champagne glass. Damon Hudson topped off his own as well. Before she drank, she paused, waiting for him. Hudson took the second glass, saluted her, and touched it to his mouth. Toth lifted her glass and let the cool, bubbling wine brush against her upper lip. She lowered the glass and used the tip of her tongue to taste the liquid that clung to her mouth.

The man next to her watched each motion with an intensity that was purely sexual.

She smiled and shifted in her seat, presenting him with a fine view of her cleavage. Every bit of distraction on his part was a plus in her bargaining column. She and Hudson had been playing sexual cat and mouse since the window went up. So she licked at a bubble of champagne like there was nothing else on her mind. She could lick tulip glasses with the best of them.

"You're sure the glass partition is soundproof as well as bulletproof?" she asked.

A small smile shifted the line of Hudson's thin lips. He leaned back in the seat and inspected the tulip glass whose stem he held between thumb and forefinger.

"I have my share of enemies," Hudson said. "Every powerful man does. I take as many precautions as I can."

"So do I."

Hudson glanced at the back of Swann's head. "Is he one of them?"

She settled into the seat and stretched her elegant legs in front of her. The scarlet sandals glowed like rubies against the smooth dark skin of her feet. She wore no nylons, having no need to make her skin look tanned and supple. It already was.

"One of him is all it takes to get the job done," she said.

She turned a bit more toward Hudson and put her elbow on the armrest between them. Coolly she sipped her champagne, letting the clean, yeasty wine rest on her tongue for a moment before swallowing it.

With every breath Toth took, Hudson's eyes were drawn to the deep, alluring shadow between her breasts. Today she wore no lace camisole, only a thin bra, a nearly sheer blouse, and a necklace of leering crimson faces that threatened at any moment to stick plastic tongues into her cleavage.

"Taking Jamie out of the game won't solve your problems with me," she said easily. "Taking me out will put you in a world of hurt with the Russians. You've got more money than God, so why don't you just transfer six million American into this numbered account and say goodbye to us?"

She handed Hudson a slip of paper with the account number on it.

"Six? I thought it was three."

To Toth's surprise, his voice was amused rather than angry.

"Inflation," she said casually. "Tomorrow it will be nine."

"It takes time to gather that much cash."

"Cash?" She laughed. "Do I look stupid? Wire transfer, babe. From one of your companies here to one of your companies in Brazil and from there to a Panamanian bank. Routine stuff. You do it all the time."

Hudson made a soft sound with his lips and shook his head sadly. "Your socialist friends would be disappointed in you if they knew what was going on."

"Maybe. More likely they'd just up your ante and take a share."

"You don't care if they find out?"

"Babe, you can print it on red cloth and fly it from every flagpole in the former Soviet Union. I've got enough on my socialist friends to keep their mouths shut until hell freezes solid."

Turning away, Hudson studied the back of Swann's head. The weathered, taut skin, the easy flex of tendons, the muscular rise of deltoids, and the clearly outlined blood vessels all shouted of a man who didn't have to sell his soul to stay physically fit.

Hudson's body suffered by comparison and he knew it. But he had something Swann didn't have.

Power.

And Hudson had learned enough about Toth in the past twenty-four hours to know what she really liked and how she liked it.

Without a word, he turned back to the woman whose primal sexuality surprised him every time he saw her. While he watched, she removed several sheets of folded paper from the outer pocket of her scarlet leather bag. She held the papers out, inviting him to reach for them.

Hudson's eyes flicked from the woman to the papers, then returned to her. "Your proof against me isn't necessary. I believe you."

"Just like that?"

He laughed softly. The dry, rustling sound was like a snake sliding through dead leaves.

"Hardly," he said. "I've checked you quite thoroughly. I wonder if the editors who purchase your stories would be interested in knowing that the documents you use often come directly from the files of a hostile intelligence service."

Toth shrugged. Journalistic unemployment would be the least of her problems if she got Hudson to put millions in her Panamanian account.

"I can see a screaming headline now," he said. *"Reporter Ruined Top FBI Agent, Won Pulitzer with Fake Documents from KGB!"*

Surprisingly, she laughed. "Wrong, babe. Journalists don't write about other journalists. Impeach one, impeach all."

"An exception might be made in your case."

"All you have on me is gossip from your Russian friends. You don't have the kind of proof a reporter would demand before he took on a journalist of my reputation. But I have that kind of proof against you."

She flicked the papers in her hand.

Reluctantly Hudson shifted his glance from Toth's breasts and looked at the folded papers.

"I suppose I must," he said, sighing. "If nothing else, I'm interested in the general quality of the documents."

He set the tulip glass in a velvet-lined holder and took the two sheets of paper.

She sipped champagne.

"There are more papers, I assume," he said.

The offhand comment was a richly colored dry fly, floated by a master of the cast. He saw the instant of faint unease that showed beneath the sculpted perfection of Toth's face.

"Sure," she said.

Satisfied that there was a weak point if he chose to probe, Hudson settled back in the seat and unfolded the papers. The documents were copies, of course.

And he quickly realized that the original, wherever it was stored, was absolutely authentic. The reproduced state seals in the margins, the letterhead with its endless titles and initials that took up almost as much room as the text, the eight-digit document number, all were in place. The USSR had evolved the most stifling bureaucracy ever seen outside of China.

Most convincing to Hudson was the dull, bureaucratic prose style of the text itself. Soviet intelligence agents were masters in qualifying everything, avoiding analysis that might prove to be faulty, and never making direct statements that might later be used to hang the author of the text. Report writing was an important part of the KGB training process.

The document in Hudson's hand contained no analysis, no conclusions, just facts. It was a chronological recitation of a set of international wire transfers that began in a numbered Swiss account and ended in a numbered Panamanian account.

He knew from personal experience that the Swiss account belonged to the chief of intelligence of a small, vastly ambitious Middle Eastern country. The account holder was the younger brother of that country's president, which is to say he was blood kin, errand boy, and chief executioner all in one.

The elder brother had become an international outlaw

among civilized countries. In addition to political extortion and theft, he'd devoted millions of dollars to the creation of a chemical and bacteriological warfare capability second to none in the world.

A vital component of that capability was a germ-culturing lab in the middle of the desert. It had been state-of-the-art, containing the most recent Western technology, and it had been a month from operational status when a flight of Israeli F-16s appeared out of the sun at noon one day and turned the lab into high-tech trash.

The attack was a stunning setback to the outlaw's ambitions, for the plant had been paid for, cash up front. The most important components had been funded through the numbered Swiss account whose statement was part of the record Hudson was holding.

Hudson also recognized the numbered Panamanian account, the one that had received the outlaw's funds. The account belonged to Hudson International, which had supplied the equipment for the clandestine lab through several of its international subsidiaries. Neither the Americans nor their Israeli clients had ever penetrated the smokescreen of secret bank accounts and shell corporations that obscured the identity of the Western firms that helped build the plant.

The document in Hudson's hand would hang him in any national or international tribunal.

"There are thousands of numbered accounts in Switzerland, and thousands more in Panama," he said mildly. "Wire transfer requests are as anonymous as eggs. That's why you use them yourself."

Casually he refolded the papers and held them out to Toth.

She smiled like a cat and waved the papers away. "The second sheet, babe. Look at it."

Hudson slipped the top sheet to the bottom and looked. The second sheet was a copy of the Swiss account's signature card. The baby brother/executioner's signature was quite legible.

"Since the United States has old Pineapple Face's records from Panama," Toth said, "it won't be difficult for them to find out who owns the account that received the money."

As she spoke, she watched Hudson for signs of stress. None showed. Instead, there was something oddly like satisfaction in the line of his mouth.

"I assume there are more files such as this one?" he asked.

"Everything the Russians had on you, we have on you."

"Interesting. I assume there are other targets for this shakedown?"

Toth's dark eyes cut toward Swann. They hadn't discussed what to do if someone asked about other victims.

"Not your problem," she said, turning back to Hudson. "Either way, you're lip-deep in shit."

"That's the sort of thing he might say," Hudson said, nodding toward Swann. "I was hoping you were bright enough to take a different approach."

For the space of three slow breaths, she stared at Hudson, trying to read his mind through his cool, ageless eyes.

"How different?" she asked, her voice flat.

He picked up his crystal tulip glass but didn't drink. "I've always found that I can neutralize an enemy and turn him into an ally, if I can demonstrate that his interests and mine coincide."

"Him? His?" she asked sarcastically. "You should learn a new vocabulary, babe. In today's world, some of your enemies are going to be female."

"I don't consider you an enemy. How many other files are there?"

"I don't know."

Hudson couldn't decide whether Toth was telling the truth. Not that it mattered.

Yet.

"Are the other files as good as this one?" he asked.

"Yeah."

"Get them. Bring them to me. I'll make you the most powerful woman in the world."

"I'll have more money than I—"

"Power," he corrected with a flash of perfect teeth. "Not money. Surely you know the difference? You, who love your own sexual power so well?"

She lowered her eyelashes, shielding her black eyes. "Keep talking. You just might say something interesting."

Satisfaction uncurled in him, a thrill of heat that was partly sexual. He understood Claire Toth very well. Watching her was like looking into a gender-bending mirror.

"I can make you powerful." Hudson waved a hand at Swann. "Your muscle-bound friend cannot."

She glanced through the glass. Both Swann and Cahill were watching the traffic behind the limousine through their rearview mirrors. Swann was saying something to the driver, but neither man looked away from traffic around them.

"Don't let the muscles fool you," she said. "He's dangerous in other ways."

"Of course he is," Hudson said, amused. "Why else would you bother with him? Leave him to me."

Toth had been wondering what to do about Swann. Now she knew.

"All right," she said.

"Good. Do you know where the files are kept?"

She almost laughed aloud. "I know. But I may need some help decoding them."

"Is it difficult?"

"Does he look like a rocket scientist?" she asked, glancing toward the partition. "If he figured it out, you can."

Hudson smiled and said softly, "Get the files. Then we'll worry about decoding and translating them."

He lifted the crystal glass in his hand. Tiny bubbles still rose through the champagne.

"Agreed?" he said, question and invitation in one word.

She raised her glass, touched his to make a bright crystalline sound, and nodded. "Agreed."

They both drank. This time Hudson took the level of his glass down by half. He was still swallowing when the intercom buzzer sounded. He touched a button on the armrest, opening the channel.

"What is it?" he asked curtly.

"There's somebody behind us." Cahill's voice was thin and tinny on the intercom.

Swann spoke quickly. "Rental car. Big guy with a beard."

"He must have picked us up when we stopped for our passengers," Cahill said.

Hudson looked at Toth.

She shook her head. "He's not mine."

"Her partner spotted him," Cahill said, "so it's probably a third party."

"Lose him," Hudson said.

"In this limo?" Cahill asked. "That will be some trick."

"That's why I employ you. To do tricks for me."

Hudson snapped off the intercom.

The limo began picking up speed at a surprising rate.

37

Karroo
Tuesday afternoon

"Do you think she's going to run for it?" Gillespie asked, looking past Cruz to the desert beyond the shaded window.

"Without a hat or a canteen?" Cruz said. "Not a chance. Laurel isn't a fool."

"Not according to her own estimate."

"Shit," was Cruz's only response.

For the space of a few breaths, both men watched Laurel walk through the desert landscaping that surrounded the house. She wasn't following a path. She didn't look back over her shoulder to see if anyone had noticed her leaving. The loose tunic top she wore over her jeans shifted in the wind, blurring her outline.

"She's heading right for that ridge," Gillespie said, pointing.

"She probably wants some space around her. You and the ambassador grilled her pretty hard while we ate lunch."

Laurel hadn't touched a bite. Nor had she said much. Her

tension had eaten at Cruz. He'd wanted to pick her up, put her on his lap, and reassure her that she was all right.

Safe.

"We avoided the subject of her father," Gillespie said rather bitterly. "And she still didn't eat."

"She doesn't trust us. She doesn't completely trust her father, either. That's why she's here."

"Bullocks. She's here because you're here."

"Yeah. Right," Cruz said, but his tone said Gillespie was dead wrong.

"Wake up, laddie boy. She looks at you like she wants to spread you on a biscuit and lick up every last crumb."

"Hell of an idea," Cruz said, grinning involuntarily.

"So why don't you do something about it?"

"For instance?"

"Get off your arse, go after her with a picnic basket and a bottle of wine, and get her trust the old-fashioned way."

"Close my eyes and think of God and country, huh?"

"Whatever loads your magazine," Gillespie said impatiently. "Just get the job done. We're on a short clock."

"Does Cassandra know about this?"

"She's the one who assigned you as Ms. Swann's bodyguard."

Cruz looked skeptical.

"Listen up," Gillespie said. "Either we win Ms. Swann's trust and get a chance to set up an ambush, or we stand around sucking wind while the competition takes the high ground. By the time we find out what's really at stake, it will be too late to do anything but pray for the dead."

Saying nothing, Cruz looked out the window. Laurel was silhouetted against the burning sky. With each breath he took, she got farther away, smaller. Soon she would be consumed by the yellow violence of the sun.

"Bloody hell," Gillespie snarled. "She *has* turned your brain to bean dip. If the Ruby Surprise was never made by Fabergé, who *did* make it? *Why* did they make it? And who dies before we find out?"

"I don't know. Three times over."

"Then go after her and get some bloody answers!"

Cruz turned to face Gillespie.

"If I go after Laurel now," Cruz said, "I go all the way. I'll be hers, not yours or Cassandra's. I'll watch out for her welfare, not for anyone else's, and screw the Ruby Surprise. Still want me to go?"

The sergeant-major took a breath and let it out in a string of curses.

Cruz waited.

"The guv warned me you'd take it this way," Gillespie added after a moment.

"Is that yes or no?" Cruz asked coolly.

"Grace is packing the picnic now. Get it. Then get your sorry arse out of my sight before I use it for punting practice."

Cruz looked at the other man's dark eyes for a long moment before he nodded and turned away.

"Where are you going with her?" Gillespie asked.

"Where I always go."

"When will you be back?"

"Don't worry. I'll give you plenty of time to make calls without worrying if Laurel is listening in on the house phone or standing outside the wrong door. Or if I am."

Gillespie grunted. Laurel hadn't turned all of Cruz's brain to bean dip.

"Take the pager," Gillespie said, turning away.

"Hell. I should just have the damn thing sewn into my jockstrap."

"Sounds uncomfortable to me, but they're your balls."

"Gillie."

The tall black man stopped and turned back toward Cruz.

"Tell Cassandra that if you're planning to spring any surprises on Laurel," Cruz said, "you'll have to go through me to get to her. And I won't be pulling any punches."

Black eyes searched Cruz's face for a few moments before Gillespie nodded. "I think she already knows."

"Tell her anyway."

38

Los Angeles
Tuesday afternoon

The lobby of the Beverly Wilshire Hotel was a cosmopolitan crossroads. Three Japanese businessmen in town to check their latest studio acquisition were being greeted by a dozen studio executives, who babbled energetically in their Berlitz second language and bowed with every third syllable. Two different and apparently hostile parties of Middle Easterners were trading glares in adjacent registration lines. A retired British prime minister's entourage—press aides, personal assistants, and plainclothes policemen from London, Washington, and Los Angeles—milled around like edgy cattle, checking their own baggage and sniffing the baggage of others to make sure it didn't contain explosives.

Aleksy Novikov smiled. The mixed crowd was perfect cover for a spy in an expensive double-breasted suit. Georgi Gapan was waiting for him in a darkened corner of the bar. Despite the fact that the workday was hours from ending, the bar was busy. Gapan was uneasily rolling an empty glass between his palms. The glass looked smudged, as though he'd been fiddling with it for some time.

"Where have you been?" Gapan asked in soft Russian when Novikov approached. "I called an hour ago."

"If you have played with that drink for an hour, you had better order another. The bartender will remember you for certain."

"I—uh, I ran out of American money," Gapan admitted. "Los Angeles is a very expensive place. I spent fifty of the dollars on taxicabs alone, just to travel to and from the car rental lot."

Novikov rolled his eyes toward the ceiling and dug into his pocket. "Poor lost lamb. You should have stayed at home with the rest of the peasants."

Gapan's dark eyes narrowed, but he made no other response to the insult.

As Novikov peeled hundred-dollar bills off a roll, he waved to the bartender and ordered two more of whatever Gapan had ordered the first time. Novikov paid for the drinks with one bill and gave three more to Gapan. As soon as the bartender brought the drinks and moved on to another customer, Novikov turned on Gapan.

"Where is she?"

"Upstairs," Gapan said quickly. "Room six-twelve. I think she is alone. I saw the man she was with come down in the elevator and go to the street perhaps ten minutes ago."

Novikov sipped his drink. It was a thin, sour American vodka, straight. A peasant's drink, lacking all finesse.

"Did you identify the man?" Novikov asked.

"He is registered as J. C. Johnson," Gapan said. "Beyond that, I know nothing. He is probably forty and he dresses casually. I believe he is carrying a gun beneath his shirt."

"How about the mysterious limousine? Did you identify the occupants?"

Gapan shook his head. "It was a Cadillac, but I never saw inside. The windows, they are very dark."

"It is customary, yes," Novikov said sardonically.

"Either the driver or Toth's companion must have spotted me. They went to the parking garage of one of those infernal shopping centers."

"You lost them there."

"I am sorry." Unhappily Gapan rubbed his ragged chin fur. "I did my best. I am unused to driving. The traffic here . . . a bad dream."

With a muttered curse Novikov knocked back the rest of his drink and nodded to the bartender for another. Gapan shot his own down his throat, grimaced, and swallowed.

"So, my little policeman," Novikov murmured, "you found your subject, the alluring American journalist. Very good. You lost her. Not very good. You failed to identify the mysterious person or persons she met. Even worse. But now you have found her again. Good. How did you manage that?"

"I thought they might change hotels after they decided I was following them. I returned to the Century Plaza and waited for a bellman to collect their luggage."

"Clever," Novikov said, looking at the other man with surprise. "How did you think of that?"

"I am always the one who is left to handle the baggage when we travel," Gapan said simply.

"Ah, of course," Novikov said. *Peasant logic.* "How did you get the room number?"

Gapan took a drink of vodka. In another man Novikov would have thought it was stalling, but Gapan was too thick-witted to hide like that. Gapan belched, wiped his mouth with his hand, and hid a smile at Novikov's distaste.

"The bellman had emigrated from Russia recently," Gapan said. "I told him if he did not tell me the room number, I would have his brothers and sisters picked up."

"Unfortunately, we cannot do that anymore. The new regime pisses their pants at the thought of offending 'world opinion.' "

"The bellman did not know. He told me the room number."

"Word spreads slowly among our expatriate countrymen."

"They hear." Gapan shrugged. "They simply do not believe change is possible."

For a few minutes Novikov sipped his vodka, studying the late afternoon crowd that had begun to gather at the bar. Bright, colorful people, rich and confident and powerful. They were so unlike the denizens of Moscow, who wore the glum expressions of a people who seek oppression the way a river seeks the ocean, inevitably, relentlessly.

Peasants, Novikov thought bitterly. *Peasants who did not know when they had a good life, so they ruined life for everyone.*

He pushed the sour vodka aside and turned to Gapan.

"I am going to shorten the leash on our friend upstairs," Novikov said. "Do you know where there is a house phone?"

"Near the lobby, yes."

"Pretend to use it while you watch the front door. If the man calling himself J. C. Johnson returns, call the room. Ring once, then hang up."

Gapan nodded. "Are you going to kill her?"

"I think not. But there is always the possibility, yes?"

39

Karroo
Tuesday afternoon

Heat welled up from the floor of the low desert like steam from a hot spring, exhausting and exhilarating at the same time.

Cruz loved it. From the easy swing of Laurel's walk, she was enjoying it too. By the time he caught up to her on the ATV, he was nearly half a mile away from the compound.

She stopped and turned toward the sound of the ATV. Expressionless, she waited for him to speak.

"Want a ride?" he asked.

She blinked. Whatever she'd expected, it wasn't that. "No thanks. I'm enjoying the walk."

"Going far?"

She looked at the stony rubble of the dry riverbed she'd been following. Then she looked back toward the compound. The fringe of tamarisk trees was a dark, dusty green against the hundred shades of brown that were the desert.

"Karroo," Cruz said.

"Gesundheit."

He laughed. "Karroo is what Cassandra calls the compound."

"Karroo?"

"I think it's from Kipling."

Silently Laurel turned and looked toward the mountains that rose beyond the ridge which was her destination. The shimmering heat and intense sunlight bleached almost all color from the landscape. The Santa Rosa range loomed in gray-brown immensity, its stone faces seamed and cracked by the relentless sun. In the creases at the higher elevations, there were dark shadows that could have been ravines or vegetation.

"It's almost cool up there," Cruz said, following her glance. "There are ponderosa pines and hidden seeps where bighorn sheep drink."

"It's hard to believe there's water anywhere in this desert."

"You can thank the earthquakes. Their shock waves crack bedrock so that groundwater flows out."

"We really see the land differently," she said, turning to him.

"How so?"

The clarity of his pale blue eyes gleaming from the shadow of his hat brim made her breath catch. She forced herself to breathe normally. It wasn't easy. The land was so vast. The sense of being the only two people on earth kept sweeping over her.

"When I think of the earth, I think of gemstones and crystals, common or rare," she said slowly. "All those sparks and chips and facets of the earth's beauty waiting to be revealed."

He listened, waiting in his own way.

"You . . ." Her throat tightened in the face of his intensity, breaking her voice. "You're fascinated by earthquakes, by the primal violence that shapes the land."

He nodded. "Beauty and power, two sides of the same coin."

"Hardly. They're worlds apart."

Yet even as Laurel was denying it, she knew there was truth in what he said.

"Are they?" Cruz asked. "The gems and crystals you love are born of the greatest violence the earth knows—plate tectonics, the grinding of huge slabs of the earth's crust against one another."

"You get mountains that way, not gemstones."

"Mountains are half of the equation. The other half is when one plate rides up over another. The losing plate is drawn down, melted, and reappears as magma pools or a string of volcanoes. As the molten rock cools, crystals form. Incredible crystals. But not one of them is as beautiful as you are."

A shiver went through Laurel, heat and cold impossibly combined. She wanted to look away from Cruz. She couldn't.

"Sorry." He raked his fingers through his short dark hair and made a disgusted sound. "I shouldn't have said that."

"Why?"

He looked away from her to the high ridge. "I'm supposed to be guarding you, not frightening you. Now you'll be too nervous to go see my little canyon."

For a moment there was only silence. Then she cleared her throat. Even so, when she spoke, her voice was unusually husky. The intensity of his eyes before he turned away had made her heart turn over.

"Your, um, canyon?" she managed.

"Yes."

"Well, at least it's not your etchings."

"It could be." He turned back to her. "But only if you want it that way."

Another ripple went through Laurel. She wanted to say yes and knew that she wouldn't. She would be as honest with him about their mutual attraction as he was being with her.

"It wouldn't be worth the oxygen," she said simply. "Sex just isn't my area of expertise."

His eyes widened, then narrowed. "You don't beat around the bush, do you?"

"It saves misunderstandings."

Reaching behind his back, Cruz pulled a scrunched baseball cap out of his waistband. Before Laurel could guess what he had in mind, he reached up and tugged the cap down over her head. The rim was way too big.

"Lean forward and duck your head," he said. "I have to make the band smaller."

Automatically she bent down. He tightened the band, tucked her hair back out of the way, and settled the cap firmly on her head. His thumbs traced her cheekbones, touched the hollows beneath, and slid down to rest lightly on her neck. The sudden speeding of her pulse was as clear to him as it was to her.

"Now you're ready to go sightseeing," he said.

She took a broken breath, trying to control her response to his casual touch. The scent of soap and elemental man swept through her, filling her with a longing that shook her. She closed her eyes.

"Why you?" she whispered, her throat aching.

"What?"

"Of all the men who ever looked at me and wanted me, why are you the one I want in return?"

His breath came in sharply. His hands flexed slightly,

caressingly, savoring the soft skin and sleek tendons of her neck.

"Your brand of honesty is damned dangerous," he said. "It makes me want more than I should. More than is . . . safe."

"That's just how I feel about it," she retorted. "Not safe at all."

Slowly Cruz released Laurel. Then he blew out a hard breath and shook his head as though trying to clear it.

"Heat must be getting to me," he said. He patted the seat behind him. "I know a great place to cool off."

She looked at the seat. It would be a tight squeeze for two. "Doesn't look like a good way to cool off to me."

He smiled despite the hunger that was making him as hard as the rocks scattered over the desert. "Never an unspoken thought, huh?" he asked.

"Most people don't have your effect on my tongue."

Abruptly he remembered what it had been like to feel her tongue touching his own, sliding over it, the taste of her racing through him like fine scotch.

"I like my effect on your tongue," he said in a low voice. Then, "Damn. Now you've got me doing it. Get on, honey. It's hard for me to drive with both feet in my mouth."

Careful to touch Cruz not at all, Laurel climbed on behind him. Inches from her eyes a pale blue shirt, faded and thin from use, clung to every ridge of muscle and line of tendon on his back. Grimly she found the foot pegs, balanced herself, and tried to ignore the expanse of male shoulders stretching across her vision.

"Ready?" he asked.

She looked down the long wedge of his back to his waist, to his hips, and then to his muscular thighs. The shorts didn't cover much of him when he was sitting down.

"As ready as I'll ever be," she said under her breath.

"Hang on."

"But, your ribs . . ."

"Go below."

"What about above?"

"Too high," he said. "You'll pull yourself off balance, and me with you."

"Are you sure?"

"Want to find out the hard way?"

"I'll balance on the pegs," she said. "Just take it easy."

Cruz kicked the ATV into motion and set off at an angle to Laurel's previous trail. He drove carefully, picking his way around boulders as big as cars and climbing broken inclines with deft control.

Despite the foot pegs and the slow speed, Laurel found herself leaning uneasily to one side or the other, trying to see around the driver's broad shoulders in order to anticipate the rolling and bucking of the machine.

It worked, some of the time. The rest of the time it nearly threw her off the seat.

"That does it," he said when she barely righted herself at the last instant.

He stopped the ATV and glared over his shoulder at his passenger. Her face was flushed. Her eyes gleamed catlike in the shadow of the hat brim.

"It gets rough ahead," he said. "If you can't get hold of yourself—and me—we'll have to go back."

Reluctantly she rested her hands on top of his shoulders. With a muttered word, he set the ATV in motion again, heading up one of the many rugged alluvial fans that spread out from the base of the Santa Rosa Mountains.

The first little rise nearly finished the ride.

The ATV tilted and jolted sideways as the center of gravity shifted, almost rolling them over.

When Cruz topped the rise, he put the ATV in neutral and dragged Laurel's hands down to a point just below his waist. Then he pulled her hands together until they were overlapping and her arms were snug around his hips.

"If I can take it," he said through his teeth, "you can."

A startled sound was her only answer. She'd just felt a hard, unmistakable ridge of male flesh in his lap.

"Gimme a break," he said curtly. "It can't come as a surprise that you turn me on."

Before she could think of a retort, they were moving again. Instinctively her grip tightened. She felt the sudden tension in his back, heard the hiss of his breath through his teeth, and started to remove her hands.

Instantly one of Cruz's big hands settled over hers, clamping them in place.

"Stop wriggling," he said without turning around. "The more you move, the harder it is on me."

"We don't have to—" she began.

"Keep your arms around me," he said over her words as he kicked up the speed. "Harder, or you'll go flying at the first bump. Good. Now hang on and try to match my movements."

She obeyed because the only other choice was to dive off the rapidly moving ATV and do a face plant in the rocks. Closing her eyes, she told herself that if he could take it, she could.

Besides feeling good, sitting wrapped around him made the ride easier. With their bodies in close contact, she quickly caught on to the trick of matching his motions, leaning with the turns, shifting against the slope, and rising up on the pegs to take the bumps.

After a few minutes, she began to feel the unique freedom of good teamwork, the give-and-take and silent sharing of movement. Two bodies shifting, turning, holding balance between them like a shared gift. During a particularly rough stretch where they lifted and swayed and dipped in close unison, she laughed aloud with exhilaration.

Hearing her, he smiled recklessly. Despite the brace he wore, he felt every soft motion of her breasts against his back. He was even more violently aware of her hands linked in his lap, causing an ache that competed with the one from his ribs.

With a wolfish grin he kicked up the speed a notch more. He was rewarded by her laughter and by the closely matched movements of their bodies as the ATV hurtled over the land.

When the way finally got easier, Laurel realized that her cheek was snuggled between Cruz's shoulder blades and her breasts were pressed fully against him. Each adjustment he made to the steering caused the sleek muscles of his back to flex and slide beneath his shirt and her cheek to nuzzle against him. He caressed her with every breath he took, every movement he made, everything.

She stiffened as heat cascaded through her from nape to knees, tightening her nipples in a rush that was almost painful. Abruptly she sat up.

"Don't lose your nerve," he said. "We're not there yet."

Teeth clenched, she hung on to him, wondering how far *there* was.

And what it was.

A few moments later Cruz braked to a stop. Nearby a shovel stood up straight in a pile of stony rubble. The mouth of the slot canyon was just beyond the pile.

When Laurel got off, solid ground felt oddly uncertain to

her. She'd become so attuned to the dune ATV's motion—and to his body—that moving alone felt strange.

It was an unsettling sensation.

Cruz's eyes followed each of her steps like blue radar. Her movements were lithe and graceful, as feminine as the sway of her breasts beneath the loose tunic top. The sun was at her shoulder, a light so powerful that her breasts were silhouetted in perfect detail through the veil of cloth.

Slowly he drew a breath and let it out, trying to loosen the tension in the center of his body. He hadn't had this uncontrolled a response to a woman since he was sixteen and found out firsthand just where a girl was softest. He'd been wildly excited then.

Right now he was damned annoyed.

Part of his intense response to Laurel was simple and physical. He understood that. He could even ignore it. What he couldn't ignore was the growing suspicion that with her, he was balanced on the edge between chaos and structure, adrenaline and boredom, darkness and light. He'd never felt that kind of seething anticipation for anything but his job.

Until now.

Gradually Cruz realized that Laurel was looking at him as intently as he was looking at her. Silence stretched tightly between them while heat welled up from the desert below. A hot breeze lifted a tendril of her hair from beneath the cap he'd put on her. She caught the hair and tucked it away, but her eyes never left him.

Gillespie was right, Cruz told himself grimly. *Being close to Laurel turns my brain to bean dip.*

But all Cruz said was, "Feel up to a little walk?"

She nodded eagerly—walk, jump, skip, anything to break the spell of silence and a man's fiercely restrained desire.

"Follow me," he said, heading for the narrow slot canyon.

The canyon was dry, radiating savage waves of heat from its cracked stone walls. It was like walking into an oven, so hot that sweat evaporated before it dampened skin or clothing.

Laurel thought of the bottles strapped to the ATV. "Shouldn't we go back for water?"

"Relax. Let somebody take care of you for a change."

"That just makes it worse when the somebody goes away."

Her matter-of-fact words told Cruz more than he wanted to know about Jamie Swann, Swann's daughter, and trust. But Cruz kept his mouth shut. It wasn't time to talk about her daddy yet. Laurel still believed it was her duty to protect the son of a bitch rather than herself. Somehow Cruz had to change her mind.

And he had to do it soon.

40

Aleksy Novikov pushed away from the bar, leaving Gapan with another round of drinks to stare at. Looking like one of the hotel's wealthy guests, Novikov walked confidently across the lobby to the elevator. When he stepped off at the fifth floor, the setting sun was filtering into the hallway through sheer, very expensive curtains. The Karastan carpet on the floor was the color of cranberries.

What a country, Novikov thought, *to afford such opulence in what is merely a good hotel, not a great one.*

The stairwell at the end of the hall was more spare and businesslike than the rest of the decor. Most guests of the Beverly Wilshire never saw the stairwell, because the elevators always worked.

Novikov climbed the stairs and carefully opened the sixth-floor entry door. The hall was empty. He found room 612 and knocked softly, surprised that such a costly hotel didn't afford the basic security of a fish-eye viewer in the center of the door.

"Who's there?"

Ah, my lovely Claire de Noir.

"Valet," Novikov replied, disguising his voice to sound like a youngster.

The door opened to the end of the security chain.

Novikov's foot lashed out in a swift, precise kick. Wood splintered as one end of the security chain jerked free of the frame. A second later he was inside. With one hand he grabbed Toth by the throat, shutting off any chance for her to scream. With the other hand he slashed down on her right wrist. A gun dropped from her suddenly numb fingers.

Pushed by Novikov's foot, the door shut softly behind them.

"Hello, sweetheart," he said, doing his Bogart imitation. "Long time no see."

Toth's eyes were as dark and cold as the gun lying on the floor.

"I will not kill you unless you force me to," he added calmly. "Where is the egg? Think carefully, my beautiful black angel. I have no patience today."

Despite the hand gripping her throat, Toth took her time choosing her response. She wanted to make sure she didn't tell him any more than he already knew.

"Can't . . . breathe," she said hoarsely.

"I doubt that." But Novikov loosened his fingers somewhat.

She gasped as though starved for air.

"Talk to me," he said.

"I don't know where the egg is," she said huskily. "I'm just bait in this, like I was for you. I didn't want to help him steal it, Aleksy. You know that. He forced me to. Now I have to help him sell it. Somehow he got files that prove I worked for the Soviets, and if that gets out nobody would hire me and—"

"Shut up," Novikov murmured, flexing his fingers against her throat.

She shut up.

He thought rapidly, watching her dark eyes, unmoved by her fear or her calculation or her beauty.

"You're just trying to sell it?" he asked after a moment.

She nodded quickly.

"Who's the lucky buyer?"

"Damon Hudson," she whispered past the steely fingers gripping her throat.

"How much?"

"Six."

"Million?"

She nodded.

Novikov's fingers relaxed somewhat. It was all he could do not to laugh out loud. She hadn't figured out the true value of the Ruby Surprise, or the asking price would have been sixty million, not six.

He doubted that her partner was so stupid.

With deadly grace Novikov released Toth, scooped up her gun, and flipped on the safety. Then he pressed the security chain screws back into the wood. They wouldn't hold against much more than a tap, but if anyone should happen to get past Gapan and surprise Novikov, the lock wouldn't appear to be obviously broken.

Satisfied, he turned back to her. She had one hand around her neck and was trembling slightly. The random shivers rippled visibly through the clinging silk of her blouse. He deliberately let his attention rove over Toth's body.

Her nipples tightened as if he had stroked her.

"You are one of the only two adult females I have ever found sexually attractive," he said idly.

"I know." Her voice was husky. "Who's the other?"

"A woman twice your age, a quarter your looks, and possessing one of the finest political minds of this or any century."

"You can't screw her mind."

Novikov smiled slightly. The curve of his lips was both hard and deceptively vulnerable, that of a recently fallen angel who might still be capable of redemption.

Toth licked her lips and ran her hands over her slacks. The gesture could have been unconscious, but he doubted it.

"Poor mongrel bitch," he said softly. "You have a pathological need to attract men sexually. You feel safe only when you can control a man's cock. That is why I was chosen to run you as an agent. They knew my taste ran to boys."

"And little girls," she said, smiling maliciously. "Don't forget them."

"Sometimes," he agreed. "But you are not a little girl anymore. Did you feel frightened when you grew breasts and your father started spending nights with your little sister?"

Rage showed for a second in Toth's eyes, but she knew better than to act on it. The Russian was a man of impressive cruelty.

"Who is acting as your father now?" Novikov asked.

She'd been expecting the question and answered immediately. "Jamie Swann."

Novikov frowned. "I do not recognize the name."

"He's not one of ours."

"How did he get to you?"

"I don't know. He just showed up with a fistful of proof that I was working for you."

Novikov waited.

So did she. Silently.

"What did he want you to do?" Novikov asked.

"Like I said. Bait. I can get past all the dragons and whisper Fabergé into some very rich ears. The bids keep coming in."

"This Swann fellow . . . is he a computer man?"

She laughed. "Jamie? Babe, he would barely know where to plug it in. He's contract muscle."

"Shrewd muscle, to take the egg out from under my nose."

"I'll bet he had some help in good old Russia," she said with smiling malice. "Not everyone is sure the new government will stick. People are looking out for themselves."

"Why don't you write an opinion piece about Russian uncertainty for the *Los Angeles Times*?" Novikov said smoothly. "One thousand words of wisdom from a traitor dressed as a journalist."

"Is that a suggestion or an order?"

He smiled. He really did enjoy teasing the beautiful bitch kitty.

With outward calm she turned away and sat on the edge of the bed. Bracing her hands on the bed behind her hips, spreading her legs a bit, she leaned back. The pose had the effect of lifting her breasts, making them strain a little against the silk of her shirt.

Female breasts were a matter of sexual indifference to Novikov, but there was something undeniably stimulating about Toth's large nipples. Like a boy's penis, her nipples had a life of their own. He watched them pucker gently and begin to harden. It was an effective little trick, somewhat akin to the stunts he had seen bottomless dancers perform in sex shows all over the world.

He went to the bed and stood between Toth's thighs. Her knees closed, caressing the outside of his legs.

"I am disappointed in you," he said gently as he watched

her nipples. "You should have come to me when Swann started blackmailing you."

"My loyalty is about as strong as yours."

"It is not your loyalty I mourn, it is your lack of foresight. If you had come to me, you could have had a hand in reestablishing a power that once ruled half of the world."

"Once, but no more." Both of her knees moved subtly, rhythmically, stroking Novikov. "That's not good enough, babe. We have to live in the world as it is, not as it was."

"What was, will be again. Soon."

"Too late for me. You'll never trust me, and all because someone in Russia gave Swann my files."

"You are wrong, my dark angel. I will trust you. All you have to do is bring me the egg."

"I don't have it," she snarled.

The anger and frustration in Toth's voice were real. Novikov almost laughed.

"Get it," he said softly. "Bring it to me. All will be well. I take very, very good care of my friends."

As though to prove his words, he reached over with a long, elegant finger and gently circled one of her nipples. Her breath came in hard, either artifice or true desire.

He didn't care which. He had to make her believe that he might be seduced by her. If she believed that, she would feel confident of her ability to control him. Sexual power was the only kind she trusted.

"Do not worry about my loyalty," he said. "I do not worry about yours. Trust, like love, is much overrated. Mutual benefit is all that really holds people together. Once you realize that, life becomes much simpler. You can take your pleasures, and give your pleasures, without ever surrendering control."

Novikov slid his hands up Toth's thigh an inch at a time.

"For instance," he said softly, "we could have the pleasure of one another at just this moment and not surrender a bit of control. At least, one of us would not. Which one, dark angel?"

Smiling, she licked her lower lip and caught it between her teeth. She bit down gently, as though savoring the sensations of pleasure and pain at the same instant.

"What if I still had the gun?" she asked. "What if the barrel was in your mouth?"

"I would suck on it."

Her eyes half closed. She tipped her head back, then slowly rolled it from side to side, loosening the tension in her neck. The movement made her breasts shift invitingly.

"Poor little girl," he said, "so many enemies. So many choices. Choose me, dark angel. I will make you fly."

"I already know how to fly."

"That is what all baby birds think. They mistake their hops and flappings for real flight. Then one day they step out of the nest and know why they were born."

Toth looked into the smoky brilliance of Novikov's eyes and wondered what sexual combat would be like with him. The thought was exciting and frightening in equal parts.

"After me, you wouldn't be satisfied with boys," she said.

"You are not the first woman to suggest that," Novikov said, smiling with invitation and contempt.

She drew a quick breath that was almost like a sigh and caught her lower lip between her teeth again. This time she bit down harder.

"I'll be the last, Aleksy. You can bet your balls on it."

"It is a deal, as the Americans say. We will see who is master and who is slave . . . *after you bring me that egg.*"

His hands flexed and his thumbnails scored soft skin in promise or punishment.

The phone rang.

Novikov froze, waiting.

It didn't ring again.

41

A small palo verde tree grew from the canyon floor where the walls closed in, narrowing the passage down to a slot. A pair of dark birds called to one another, their cries pure and musical in the silence. Until that moment, Laurel hadn't realized how quiet the desert had been.

"There's water ahead," Cruz said. "That's why you're seeing birds here."

His words reminded Laurel that Cruz knew her frighteningly well. He not only knew that she would notice the birds but that she would be curious about why they were here and not back at the mouth of the canyon.

She gave him a swift glance, but he was walking along like nothing odd had happened—certainly nothing frightening. She shook her head and wondered how he'd feel if she read him like a first-grade book.

Just beyond the palo verde, a tongue of rubble blocked the canyon. Cruz scrambled up the obstacle, then held down his right hand to Laurel. She ignored it, taking the rubble in a rush that left her breathless and slightly off balance. His hand closed over her elbow, steadying her.

"I'm not a frail little flower," he said, almost roughly. "Remember?"

"Fine. I still don't want to hurt you."

His mouth flattened as he thought of Laurel and her father and what had to be done. Trust created. Trust destroyed.

And then the pain.

"Sometimes hurt can't be avoided," he said.

She knew without asking that Cruz had been hurt in the past, and by more than simple physical violence. What surprised her was that the pain in his eyes was still fresh, sharp, bleak, as if there wasn't any end to the agony. She couldn't bear what she saw in him without reaching out and trying to give him the only comfort she could. That would be stupid.

So she looked away. For the first time she looked at the rest of the canyon. The hot rocky oven had become an oasis. A pond the size of a small swimming pool shimmered at the shady base of a rock wall. Lacy palo verde bushes provided fragile shade. Their green was so startling after the sterile rock that it almost hurt her eyes.

"The oasis is too new to appear on maps," Cruz said, answering Laurel's questions as if she'd spoken them aloud. "The spring that feeds the pool only began to flow in the last decade or so."

"Water from rock," she said softly. "A miracle."

"And earthquakes. Don't forget them."

He went down the tongue of debris and knelt by the rocky pool. While he scooped up a double handful of water and drank, she slid down the slope to stand beside him.

"The water is so clear," she said, surprised.

"Most plants haven't gotten a foothold yet. Back here the canyon is too narrow to pick up dust from the desert winds and there's nothing to eat. I've never seen tracks of anything but ravens by the water."

One edge of the pool was in sunlight. Ripples caused by Cruz's hands glittered brightly in the light. He scooped up water and splashed it over his face. Great drops clung to his shirt and expanded darkly. Smaller drops gleamed in the black hair that showed in the opening of his shirt.

"Does it taste as good as it looks?" she asked.

"Better."

She made both hands into a bowl and scooped. After the first sip she drank eagerly, recklessly. Water ran down her arms and neck.

"Ah," she sighed. "Unbelievable."

The shiver of pure sensual pleasure that went through her made desire coil hotly in Cruz. He watched with naked hunger as thin streams of silver water drenched her lips and skin and blouse. She wasn't wearing a bra. The cotton of her tunic clung wetly to her skin, outlining the tops of her breasts.

"Drink your fill," he said in a low voice. "Then we can go in and cool off."

She gave him a wary, sideways look. "Are we talking skinny-dipping?"

"Swim in your clothes," he said, smiling. "I'm going to. Five minutes after we get out, they'll be dry again, and we'll be hot again."

While he spoke, he took off his shoes, socks, and shirt. There was a ripping sound as he peeled open the Velcro fastenings of the brace that had been binding his ribs. He breathed in tentatively, then with less caution. It hurt, but so did a lot of things.

Cruz saw that Laurel was watching him. The look on her face told him she liked what she saw. Then she looked at his bruised ribs and made a low sound.

"Finished drinking?" he asked, wanting to distract her.

"Yes."

He waded to the center of the pool. The water was barely cooler than his body and no deeper than his waist. He settled onto a knee-high, flat-topped boulder and closed his eyes with pleasure as the water rose to just below his shoulders.

Gentle splashing sounds told him that Laurel was on her way in. He watched through his lowered eyelashes as she shed her jeans. The tunic top came to midthigh. She gave a subdued gasp as water rose to her hips.

"It's not really cold," he said.

"No. Just surprising. Like warm milk."

Through slitted eyes, he watched her walk out until the water was just below her breasts. Then she lowered herself into the pool until only her head was above water. A sweep of her hand removed the baseball cap and sent it sailing to the rocks beyond the pool. Her hair fell free. The ends of it touched the water, then curled coolly against her neck.

There were no rocks high enough for her to sit on and still lift her head above water. Kneeling, she kept her balance by gentle motions of her hands. Then she tilted back her head and let silky fingers of water caress her scalp. A low sound of pleasure threaded from her throat. She kicked back and floated, sculling slowly with her hands to stay in place.

"When you get tired of swimming, you can sit here," Cruz said after a time.

His tone was unusually deep, a dark velvet that caressed as surely as a touch. Unwillingly she smiled.

"I haven't heard that voice since you were trying to get me to trust you back at my house," she said.

"It didn't work."

"Are you sure?"

She stood up and slowly walked toward him. The tunic

clung to her like a wet shadow. He watched her with silver-blue eyes that traced the curves of her body like hands.

"On second thought," he said, "maybe you better go back to floating around beyond my reach."

There was the thickness of desire in his voice. It acted on her like another kind of caress.

"I probably should," she agreed, "but this feels . . . right."

His arm swept out and pulled her onto his lap before either of them could think better of it.

"How much of me do you want?" he said. "Tell me now, while I can still hear you."

"Whatever you want to give me."

He searched the golden eyes that were watching him, luminous with trust and desire. "Are you certain?"

"I'm certain I've never felt like this before, ready to take risks."

A shudder that was more than desire went through his body. He started unbuttoning her tunic, then stopped, looking at her with burning blue eyes, silently asking again.

"Don't worry," she said, touching the sharp peaks of his upper lip with her fingertip. "I won't change my mind. I'm not that kind of tease."

Slowly Cruz bent down and kissed Laurel's lips, tracing the curve of her smile with the tip of his tongue, probing gently, asking for more of her softness. With a broken breath, she gave her mouth to him.

The taste of him swept through her. The heat and textures of his kiss made her breath shorten. He was taking her so delicately, so gently. It both excited her and made her hungry for a kiss that was less restrained, more wild.

Her hands kneaded the resilient muscles of his shoulders and back, testing his strength. He made a low sound and pulled her closer. Only then did she realize that her tunic was completely undone. The tips of her breasts hardened in a rush as they pressed against masculine hair and muscle. She moved slowly against him, increasing the sensuous pressure.

Instantly his kiss changed, becoming hard and deep and urgent, a mating of mouths that was almost violent. She was with him every bit of the way, demanding and giving equally, inciting him even more.

Finally he managed to end the kiss. Breath hissed out from between his clenched teeth as he fought for self-control.

"Is it your ribs?" she asked anxiously.

He shook his head without looking away from her eyes. They were golden, smoldering, as hot as her kiss had been.

"It's you," he said hungrily, watching her. "I wanted to take all day with you. I wanted to peel off your clothes and look at you before I tasted you, pleasured you."

The tremor of response that went through Laurel at his words did nothing to reduce his hunger.

"I'm not fighting you," she said.

"Maybe you should." He smiled ruefully, stroking her cheek with his fingertips. "You're so damned responsive you make it hard for me to go slow."

"Responsive?" She laughed.

Then she realized that he meant it.

"You look shocked," he said dryly.

"I am. Men usually accuse me of the opposite."

It was Cruz's turn to be shocked.

She turned her face into his hand, kissing the palm that had been caressing her cheek. "But then, those men never made heat splinter through me just by walking into the room."

She ran the tip of her tongue up his index finger.

He waited for her to draw back from the old injury. Instead, she kissed it softly before she ran her tongue back down to the base of the middle finger, probing the sensitive skin between.

"Those men," she said in a low voice, "didn't make my breath shorten every time they looked at me with eyes hot enough to melt stone."

"Laurel."

It was all he could say. The fingers of his right hand brushed the cool wet tips of her hair before he drew the back of his fingers down her neck, her collarbone, across the curve of her breasts.

"Those men—" her voice broke. She drew a quick, sharp breath as his fingertips traced the dark circle of one nipple. "They didn't make me feel like you do."

"How do I make you feel?"

"Female. Violently female."

He smiled. "You are."

She started to shake her head. He caught the tip of her breast between his fingers and squeezed rhythmically. Shivering, she arched her back. From deep in her throat came a sound of approval and pleasure that made him want to strip off every bit of clothing and take her with a savage thrust of his body.

"And you make me feel rather violently male," he admitted.

"You are."

He smiled oddly. "Not for a long time. And never like this. I was beginning to think I'd lost it."

Reluctantly he released her hard-tipped, creamy breast and lifted her off his lap.

"Stand up, honey," he said. "If I don't get into my pockets now, I never will."

Puzzled, she did as he asked. He stood and thrust a hand into the pocket of his desert shorts. The movement pulled the wet cloth even more tightly across his fully aroused flesh. He watched her eyes widen as she looked at him.

"Don't worry," he said. "I won't hurt you. I'll make sure you're as ready as I am before I take you."

"I don't think I've ever been that ready," she said, her voice torn between anxiety and sheer female approval.

He laughed despite the pain in his ribs and the even hotter ache of arousal. He dragged his hand out of his pocket and dropped a small foil packet on her palm.

"Keep track of this," he said.

"You're a better Boy Scout than I am a Girl Scout. I wasn't prepared."

"I'm a bodyguard, remember?" He unzipped his shorts. "My job is to protect you in every way I can."

"Is making love to the client part of the job description?"

His hands hesitated at his waist as he remembered Gillespie's order. "Is that what you think?" he asked, his voice toneless.

"I think you wanted me the first time you saw me. I know I wanted you. That's never happened to me. It still . . . surprises me."

For a moment he closed his eyes and fought for self-control. Her honesty was as exciting to him as her kiss had been.

"It's never happened to me like this either," he said. "Gillespie saw it. He wanted to take me off the case."

"But he didn't."

"No. He decided to use it, instead."

"What did *you* decide?"

Cruz looked at her with smoldering blue eyes. "I decided to guard you like I've never guarded anything, ever—come hell, high water, or Sergeant-Major Ranulph Gillespie."

The intensity of Cruz's voice left Laurel as shaken as his naked hunger for her had.

"Why?" she asked starkly.

"You make me feel alive again. I can't walk away from that, honey. I'm yours for the duration, however long that may be. If you still want me . . . ?"

Her hand clenched around the bright foil packet. The proof that he cared enough to protect her when she was too foolish to protect herself went through her like lightning, shaking her. She closed her eyes.

Cruz was making her tremble with a look, a smile, a hunger that was both physical and something less tangible, something that drew her as surely as the flame draws the moth.

"I still want you," Laurel whispered. "More than ever."

Water swirled and splashed. When she opened her eyes Cruz was naked. Waiting.

Awkwardly she began to peel the long tunic top off one arm. Before she was done, he was there, kissing her, taking the tunic from her hands, her body. Long fingers slid over her breasts, into the water, and down her stomach, spearing inside the bikini pants that were all that remained of her clothing. His mouth followed his hands, licking and biting and kissing all the way down until her pants were gone and he was kneeling in front of her.

"Brace yourself on my shoulders."

She smiled to hear the dark velvet voice again, brushing over her, making her shiver with anticipation.

Water swirled and he vanished. She felt the sweet sting of his teeth on her belly and then the wild heat of his mouth between her legs. She made a hoarse sound as her knees buckled. He held her suspended between his hands and his consuming mouth, burning her despite the water surrounding them.

Then water seethed and boiled and the world turned dizzily around her. When it was still again, Cruz was sitting on the knee-high rock and she was astride his lap, facing him. She tried to say his name, but all that came from her lips was a broken sound. His mouth found hers and his tongue thrust deeply inside. In wild silence they tasted one another, each straining to be closer and then closer still.

His left arm curled tightly around Laurel's hips. His right hand slid down her body until he held her in the palm of his hand. He rubbed slowly, savoring the silky textures of her desire. Then he slid one finger deeply into her.

She went still, then trembled and pressed closer, rocking against him, her nails digging heedlessly into his strong shoulders. He kissed her hard, was kissed even harder in return, hunger spiraling up to the edge of control.

Swiftly he redoubled his presence inside her, testing her, caressing her, stretching her, preparing her. She moaned and shook as if the pool had turned suddenly cold. Her mouth tugged at his in the same rhythm as his caresses. A heat greater than that of the water clung to his fingers and his palm.

With the last of his self-control, Cruz pulled his mouth from hers. Laurel looked at him with dazed golden eyes. His hand moved again, deeply, and again he felt her hot response.

"You," he said, dragging at air, "are burning me alive."

She started to answer, but his hand stroked again, pleasure burst again, and she trembled, clinging to him.

"Now or never," he said. "Put it on me, honey."

"You'll have to stop—"

The words ended in a ragged sound as he caressed her again.

"I don't want to stop," he said. "I love the sounds you make, the way you feel deep inside. God, you're soft. All silk and cream."

She fumbled with the thin, slippery foil packet. The fact that her hands were shaking didn't make her job any easier. Finally she managed. Then she got revenge by sweetly torturing him, taking unnecessary time and fussing and stroking before everything was fully in place.

"You enjoyed that, didn't you?" he asked, smiling a bit grimly.

"Yes," she said, biting his lower lip recklessly. "Every last bit of it."

"How about this?"

She tried to answer, but couldn't. He was pressing into her, filling her, merging their bodies until they were so deeply joined that neither knew whose mouth kissed and whose hands caressed, whose arms held and whose voice cried out. There was only one body, one rhythm, one voice.

Then there was pleasure, swift and fierce and final, ecstasy burning them alive.

42

Karroo
Wednesday morning

The sheer inner curtains at the Karroo compound softened the intense desert sun, making the bedroom glow. But it wasn't the subdued radiance that awakened Laurel.

It was the feel of warm breath caressing her neck and lips nibbling softly on her nape.

Yesterday came back to her in a flood of images and sensual memories. Even before she rolled over and opened her eyes, heat shivered through her. Fingers teased her breast in the instant before a warm tongue licked one taut nipple.

"Mmm," rumbled a deep voice. "You do tempt me, honey. And I was trying to be such a good little flower of manhood and let you sleep until noon."

"Two out of four isn't bad," she said, her voice husky with sleep and rising desire.

"Which two?"

"You're not little, and you're not a flower. But you've got the good and the manhood parts down real well."

He laughed, kissed the dark peak he had been teasing, and forced himself to release her.

"Don't stop now," she murmured. "You were just getting to the interesting part."

"After yesterday, I thought you might need some time off for good behavior."

She looked at him. He was smiling but quite serious.

"Why?" she asked.

"Are you sore?"

"No."

"You sure? I wasn't as gentle as I wanted to be, not until the last time. And then I shouldn't have taken you at all."

"Why not?"

"You aren't used to having a lover."

She flushed. "Was my lack of finesse that obvious?"

For an instant he didn't understand. Then he laughed and allowed his fingers to curl into her feminine warmth. One fingertip sought and found the heat that had haunted his dreams.

"I wasn't talking about technique," he said, sliding just a bit into her, tracing her layered softness. "I was talking about this. You're tight, honey."

Heat cascaded through her in a shimmering wave. An instant later it spilled between them. He swore very softly, more reverence than true cursing.

"That was the only bad part about the pool," he said, his voice velvet with desire. "I couldn't feel your response this clearly."

"I could feel yours. I loved every bit of it."

She shivered as heat and memories coursed through her. Her legs moved restlessly. "Cruz? I'm not sore. Truly."

He hesitated, then reached past her into the drawer of the bedside table. Moments later, he settled between her legs.

"We'll take it slow and easy," he promised.

"Next time."

Despite the tempting movements of Laurel's body, he took her so slowly that she thought she would die of wanting him . . . and when the mutual possession was finally complete, she was certain she would die of the pleasure. Like dawn, ecstasy expanded inside her until she surrendered her body to the tender, ravishing heat.

It was the same for him, ecstasy tender and fierce, giving him completely to her until he was too spent to lift his head. Groaning, he forced himself to roll aside. Then he gathered her close and held her until they both could breathe again without having each breath shatter over bursts of pleasure.

Laurel kissed the scratchy line of Cruz's unshaved jaw, sighed, and rubbed her cheek against the dark, resilient pelt of hair that curled over his chest. Slowly she ran her fingertips over his cheeks and shoulders, lips and chest, hands and torso. Nearly everywhere she touched there was an old scar or the slight irregularity of a bone that had healed after being bruised or broken.

Then there were the fresh marks left by two bullets. She kissed him and rested her fingertips very gently just beneath the bruises on his ribs.

"So many scars," she whispered.

"You should see Gillie's body. On second thought, forget it. You'd never look my way again. 'Drop-dead handsome,' I believe you called him? God, he'll never stop strutting now."

Smiling, she nuzzled against Cruz's chest. "You're every bit as handsome as he is."

Cruz snorted. "Open your eyes, honey. I look like the south end of a northbound aardvark."

"That explains it."

"What?"

"Why lady aardvarks walk two steps behind their men."

Chuckling, smiling, Cruz looked into the amber eyes that were watching him with open pleasure.

"I can't remember when I've laughed so much," he said.

"With your job, it's no wonder. You use yourself too hard."

"If I wasn't doing this, I'd be doing something else that was physically demanding," he said, stroking her dark, tangled hair. "It's just the way I am. Hell, a professional athlete has a shorter career span than I do."

"What do they do when their playing days are over?"

"Is that what happened to your father?"

Laurel stiffened.

It was the first direct mention of Jamie Swann since she'd arrived at Risk Ltd.

Cruz's hand never paused, stroking her hair, silently reminding her just how close they had become. She let out a breath she hadn't known she was holding and relaxed against him again.

But not quite as much.

She knew the dream was over. Reality had returned with a vengeance. Now the choices she faced were even more cruel.

Her father or her lover.

"I guess so," Laurel said. "I know he's getting old and he's frightened of getting old. He even apologizes for wearing reading glasses."

"It happens to everyone who doesn't die first."

She winced. "Cold comfort."

"He's an adult. What does he expect? A vodka-and-cocaine tit to suck on for sweet excitement everlasting?"

"What is Dad supposed to do?" she asked sharply. "Shuffle off to the old folks' home with a smile and an apology for having been born in the first place?"

"He might try yoga or lawn bowling, or swimming or bird-watching, or fishing or growing orchids or hiking or breeding dogs or the senior triathlon or bridge or billiards," Cruz said impatiently. "Hell, he might even go back to school or fall in love or—"

"He might get a life, is that it?" she cut in.

"It's that or get dead."

"You really don't like my father. Why? Because you think he's working for himself rather than for his country?"

"The son of a bitch used you," Cruz said in a soft, deadly voice. "He set you up with that egg and then got in the wind, leaving you to face two assassins alone."

"He didn't know that they—"

"Bullshit, honey," Cruz interrupted impatiently. "He's a pro. He had to know what could go wrong, and where, and who would pay the piper—you."

"I don't believe that."

"You don't *want* to believe it."

"Do you know what you're asking?"

"I'm asking you to trust me," Cruz said.

"No," she said, pushing away from his powerful arms. "You're asking me to betray my father."

"Use your head, not your heart. You're in danger."

"Not from Dad."

"Just from your daddy's nasty playmates."

"Not anymore," she retorted. "I'm out of the game. He took the egg. It's over."

"Wrong. It's just beginning."

"What does that mean?" she asked bitterly. "Do you know something you're not telling me?"

"You don't want to know what I know."

"I'm not a child."

"You're all woman in my arms, but in your mind you're

still Daddy's little girl. Well, little girl, let me tell you about your dear old daddy."

Laurel stiffened and tried to get out of bed. Cruz held her where she was with an offhanded ease that reminded her of just how strong he was.

"There are fat files on Jamie Swann in the archives of both the Central Intelligence Agency and the Federal Bureau of Investigation," Cruz said.

"I know."

"Have you seen them?"

"No."

"I have. Your daddy is a legend among field agents at the CIA. He's been in on the most dangerous covert operations for the past twenty-five years. He's been decorated three times for bravery and twice for exemplary initiative."

"Sounds like a career to be proud of."

Cruz smiled. It wasn't comforting. "To be that good, your father needed the skills of a professional assassin, the inventiveness of a gifted practical joker, and the scruples of a mink. As a result, Jamie Swann is brave, tough, smart, and has total contempt for any authority but his own."

"Is that why you're worried?"

"No. I'm worried because sometime in the past few years your daddy went sour."

Laurel became very still except for her heartbeat, which doubled. This was what she'd feared.

This was what she didn't want to hear.

"Maybe the world changed and he couldn't," Cruz said. "Maybe he just grew old. Maybe it was inevitable that a man of his temperament would jump the fence, crossing over from gifted field operative to gifted criminal."

"No!"

"Yes," Cruz said flatly. "I know a lot of men like your

father. Even the spit-and-polish FBI has its cowboys, its rogue warriors, its corner cutters, its black-bag experts. They're damned valuable when the time comes to get down and dirty. But all too often their virtues are exactly the same as their vices."

"Dad wouldn't—"

"He did," Cruz cut in ruthlessly. "In the past few years he's been involved in at least three illegal schemes to divert heavy arms or combat aircraft to Third World nations. Enemies, Laurel. We went to war with one of them and damn near burned down the Gulf."

"But—"

"No," he interrupted again. "You asked about your father. I'm telling you, and I've got the files to back up everything I say."

The chill in her increased as she looked at Cruz. His words were relentless, as hard as the pale, crystalline blue of his eyes.

"Swann is suspected of delivering high explosives to a South American terrorist organization," Cruz said. "He's known to have supplied chemical precursors for nerve gas to the government of a small nation in Asia."

She made a low sound.

Cruz's eyelids flinched in a sympathy she didn't see, for her own eyes had closed, shutting him out.

"The nerve gas didn't involve a direct violation of law," he said. "And Swann redeemed himself to some extent by destroying the cache of gas."

"Why?" she asked raggedly.

Cruz didn't know if Laurel was asking him about her father's motives in destroying the gas or simply asking why Swann had gone rogue.

"Swann destroyed the gas when he learned that it was

going to be used to wipe out stone-age tribes who stood in the way of exploiting the hardwood forests. But he found out too late for one clan. The youngest victim was four hours old. Swann killed the man who'd released the gas, but it didn't bring back the dead."

Laurel tried to breathe, to force air past the sickness rising in her throat.

"Don't get me wrong," Cruz said, seeing her stark pallor. "Your dad didn't mean for any innocents to die. He just didn't check his buyers well enough. It's a common problem when you go rogue. You have to deal with the biggest chunks floating in the global cesspools. Heard enough, or do you want me to go on?"

Numbly she shook her head. She'd heard enough.

Letting out a breath that hissed through his teeth, Cruz released his hold on her. He wanted very much to gather her closer in his arms and hold her, but he was afraid he would have to fight her to do it. He didn't want that for either of them.

He didn't want any of this, but it was his to do just the same.

"Something went wrong in one of those cesspools," he said, trying to make his voice gentle, failing. "Now your dad is on the run, and all the hounds of hell are baying at his heels."

Slowly she opened her eyes. They were huge with pain and horror and tears that hurt too much to shed. With a bitter inner rage at what he knew must happen, Cruz did what he'd avoided doing for too long.

He pushed her right into a corner.

"Your dad needs our help as much as you do," Cruz said. "If they catch him, he's dead meat."

"I—" Her voice broke. "I warned him."

"Yeah. Three, two, six, four, three, seven. DANGER."

"You knew?"

"Hell, yes, of course we knew. But Swann already knew his ass was on the line. That's why he dropped the egg on you."

"I'm his daughter. He's entitled to look to me for help."

Cruz bit off a vicious curse. His temper had never been more uncertain, and never had he needed it to be so steady.

"You don't invite innocents into a game played only by assassins," he said finally.

"Good for our side," she said in a strained voice. "I'm out of the game now. No harm, no foul, isn't that what they say?"

"But you're not out of the game. Your home telephone has a message on it from your father."

"How did you—" she began.

"Christ," Cruz snarled. "We've got hackers who can get into Department of Defense computers. Your answering machine spilled its guts to us in four seconds flat. Then we erased it so that no one else could do the same thing."

With unnatural calm Laurel asked, "What was the message?"

"'Hi, baby. Let's get together at our special place. Soon. Oh, and bring your leather valise. We might take a little trip.'"

The words sank into her like razors made of ice, chilling her even as they made her bleed. Her father had never asked for her company. Not even once.

Ever.

"Don't you get it yet?" Cruz asked. "Your father is using you."

"And I suppose you aren't?"

Even as he started to deny it, Gillespie's cynical order echoed in his mind: *Get her trust the old-fashioned way.*

Cruz lost the battle with his temper. "At least I made you scream with pleasure. Your father only made you scream with fear."

With that, Cruz snapped back the sheet and shot out of bed, heading for the bathroom, calling himself every kind of fool there was. He slammed the door. He did the same thing to the door on the opposite side of the bathroom, the one that led to his own bedroom. A vicious twist on the shower faucet started the water.

Laurel lay in bed and listened to the drumming of water against tile until she could breathe without feeling like she was breathing fire.

I can't choose between them.

I simply can't. Choosing Cruz means believing my father is so selfish—or so desperate—that he's willing to risk my life for retirement pay. But choosing Dad means believing that Cruz seduced me in cold blood, using me to get to my father.

Dad might be that desperate.

Cruz isn't that cold.

She would never forget when he'd told her that he wasn't as gentle as he wanted to be, not until the last time they made love. Those weren't the words of a man who only wants to use a woman to get to someone else. And there were other words.

My job is to protect you in every way I can.

A chill went over Laurel as she realized that Cruz's job also meant protecting her from her own father.

No, she denied instantly. *Dad wouldn't put me in danger. That's why he took the egg.*

But then why did he tell me to take the "valuable stuff" with me, and to check for phone messages?

"He was worried about me," she said quietly, as if hearing

the words spoken aloud would make them true. "He wanted to keep in touch."

The fierce drumming of the water stopped. She tensed, expecting Cruz to reappear. When he didn't, she knew that he'd gone to his own room to dress.

Slowly she got out of bed and walked to the closet. She picked up her leather valise, opened it, and pulled out the box that held the "valuable stuff." Swiftly she went through the small packets. An inch from the end of the second row was exactly what she had prayed she wouldn't find.

For a long time she simply stood and looked at the evidence that damned her father more thoroughly than anything in the government files.

43

Malibu
Wednesday morning

The crashing, rhythmic thunder of surf met Claire Toth as she stepped from the back of Hudson's limousine. Thickened by smog and salt air, the sunlight was a rich orange. Stretching lazily to conceal her unease, she looked out at the cold blue Pacific.

Huge rollers generated by a storm thousands of miles away turned over and exploded on the deserted beach. The combers moved with an inevitable, overwhelming power that fascinated her even as it chilled her. Unlike men, the ocean would never be controlled by a desirable woman.

"Nice beach," she said to the driver. "What happened to the tourists?"

"Mr. Hudson doesn't have any of them," Bill Cahill said. "They mess up his sand."

At the moment Cahill wasn't a happy employee. He was a security expert and a bodyguard, not a chauffeur and errand boy. Yet for the past two days, Hudson had been running him around like a minimum-wage jerk.

"How much sand is his?" she asked.

"A quarter mile in either direction."

"One-half mile of Malibu beach frontage. Land so valuable it's sold by the inch. Thousands of dollars a *foot*." She shook off a feeling of unreality. "How often does he come here?"

"Often enough. He keeps his women here," Cahill said, baiting Toth. "This is only one of his love nests."

She laughed and licked her lips. "He's really a randy old bastard, isn't he?"

"A regular he-goat. He keeps a stable of trained whores like other rich men keep a string of top polo ponies."

Black eyes flashed in a sideways glance at Cahill. She guessed he was about fifty, relatively fit, but fully aware of the cold breath of old age on the back of his neck.

"Jealous?" she asked in a throaty voice.

Cahill gave her a long, cool look from top to bottom and back again. "Not since I saw what he goes through to keep it up. This way, Ms. Toth."

The beach house was cold, hard-edged, and austere. There was a formal Japanese rock garden in the front yard. Massive wooden doors bound in brass opened into the house.

Wood, tile, stone, filtered light . . . Toth felt like she was entering a secular cathedral. The huge doors closed softly behind her, shutting out the inhuman power of the sea. The air inside the house was cool and still.

"Down there," Cahill said, pointing. "Just follow the noise. He's expecting you."

The "noise" was some kind of New Age music that came from a room at the far end of a long tiled hallway.

Without another glance at her chauffeur, Toth set off toward the source of the music. Eventually she came to a solarium where Hudson lay nude, facedown, on a massage table made of chrome and butter-soft leather. A sturdy woman with straight black hair pulled back in a bun was methodically working on the knotted muscles at the base of Hudson's neck.

A wheeled chrome stand that would have been at home in a hospital was posted next to the table like a sentry. A bag of clear yellow fluid hung from the arm of the stand. A transparent plastic tube ran directly from the bag to a catheter in the back of Hudson's right leg.

"Come in," he said, without lifting his head. "Forgive my informality, but the past few days have been rather trying. The next few promise to be even more so. A little revitalizing seemed in order."

Uneasily Toth walked into the room. The late-afternoon sun made the damp beach air inside the solarium unpleasantly warm. She looked with distaste at the sack of fluid and the tube bleeding stuff into the needle in Hudson's thigh. Needles brought back too many memories of poverty and rape and drugs.

"You, uh, do this often?" Toth asked, looking at the catheter that was expertly cut into a vein in Hudson's leg.

"Once a month," he said, his voice somewhat muffled by his position. "It's possible to take the treatment more often without risk, but with repetition it eventually loses effectiveness. I try to stay on a fairly strict regimen."

"What's in the bag?" she asked. "It looks like piss."

He lifted his head and gave her a glance of almost fatherly tolerance. "It has some long and unpronounceable Romanian name. There's no equivalent word in English, since no one has yet synthesized the material here."

"What is it, monkey glands?"

"My dear child," he said, laughing. "Do you believe everything you read in print?"

She laughed in return, feeling at ease with him. There had been desire and approval in his eyes when he looked at her.

"I just believe the interesting stuff," she said.

"Such as eternal youth?"

"I'm too young for that to matter."

It was a lie, but she was accustomed to lying. Like sex, it was something she did very well.

"Someday you'll look in the mirror and your tits will be halfway to your navel," Hudson said, "and your magnificent ass will be halfway to your knees."

She smiled and ran her hands over the ass in question.

"Then you'll go under some smiling surgeon's knife," he continued. "He'll nip and tuck and cut and stitch, and when he's done you'll have scars, and your tits and ass will still sag again."

Hudson lowered his head to the table, but still he watched Toth, telling her what life would be like in the future.

She didn't like hearing it.

"A few years later you'll be back under the knife," he said calmly, "and then again and again, until you lose track. But by then your skin is thin and spotted and you've had so many lifts your navel has a goatee. You don't get eternal youth under some glad-hander's scalpel. You just get scars hidden in the wrinkles."

A shudder ran over Toth. Like the sea, old age was one of the few things that frightened her without exciting her sexually. There was no winning with old age. You simply got older and uglier and then you died.

"Is that what happened to you, old man?" she asked savagely. "Scars and wrinkles?"

He smiled. "Come closer and see for yourself."

"No thanks. I've seen naked pricks before."

She looked away and wondered how the hell she'd gotten herself into a place that was too much like the hospital she'd sworn never to enter again.

Hudson watched Toth's unease grow the longer she stared at the muscular nurse massaging fluids and resilience into Hudson's body. He knew exactly what Toth was feeling. He'd counted on it. It was the healthy young animal's reaction to seeing someone apparently at the mercy of tubes and needles.

But no one stayed healthy and young forever.

"I hadn't thought you a coward." Hiding his smile, he turned his face away from her. "My mistake."

Toth walked until she was within reach of the man on the table. The masseuse kept kneading Hudson like nothing and no one else was in the room.

He turned toward Toth. "Go ahead," he said, watching her with shrewd, ancient eyes. "Touch me. I'm real."

She fought her revulsion and moved closer to Hudson because she knew he was right. Someday she would lose the only weapon she had to gain power. Someday men would look at her and see an old woman rather than a red-hot piece of ass.

When that day came, she'd be better off dead.

Slowly she stroked Hudson's side from his shoulder to his knee. He had a remarkable body, very firm and supple, with the muscular definition of a fit man in his forties.

And the sexual stamina of a teenager. She'd discovered that for herself on his airplane, while she stroked his crotch and whispered blackmail in his ear.

Again she stroked him from shoulder to knee, probing lightly for anything weak or brittle. All she found was muscle and sinew and health.

"What you're admiring is the result of a combination of

anabolic steroids and something called prednisteran," he said.

"What does it do?" she asked, fascinated despite her horror of all things medical.

"It's a compound that suppresses the human growth hormone, which also controls the aging process. The Romanians stumbled across it while trying to develop wonder drugs in sports medicine. They wanted something to retard the maturation of their young female gymnasts. What they found was the Fountain of Youth."

"Except for the white hair, huh?" Toth said, ruffling his hair with her fingertips.

"The hair is my choice. I bleach it. It gives me an edge with all the people who think that gray hair means you're a stupid old fool."

"How long did it take?" she asked.

"For the treatments to become effective?"

"Yeah."

"It happened very quickly. It's an unusual sensation to watch your own body grow younger. Having wet dreams again was particularly amusing."

She laughed and released his hair.

The masseuse plunged her fingers into the muscle tissue of Hudson's shoulders again. She'd showed no expression as they talked. It was like she didn't hear or see Toth.

"Who's the woman?" Toth asked. "One of your uglier whores?"

Toth thought she detected a flicker of emotion in the woman's dead, flat eyes, but it vanished almost instantly.

"She's a member of the Romanian secret service," he said. "Her permanent assignment is to administer the medication and to monitor the results to make sure I'm not overstimulating my system. Don't worry, she doesn't understand English."

"So you figure you can go on riding this bubble for, what, another twenty years?" Toth asked.

"Easily. I'll be the most amazing hundred-year-old man this world has ever seen. I expect to be vigorous and potent long enough to bury my firstborn and only son."

"You sound like you're looking forward to burying him."

"My son is a worthless little putz. He has a death wish he feeds with drugs and alcohol."

The Romanian nurse noticed that the bag of fluid was empty. With practiced skill she removed the tube and the catheter and cleaned the entry site with alcohol. Then she gently massaged the muscles of Hudson's leg and thigh.

For a time he was quiet. Then he grunted irritably and rose up on his elbows. The nurse nodded quickly to show she understood his complaint. She went back to work on the leg with more force.

"The prednisteran can be quite corrosive if it isn't moved around in the circulatory system," Hudson explained. "It's the only real drawback to the treatments."

"That's it? A little burning?"

"A minor price to pay for physical, sexual, and mental longevity, wouldn't you say?"

"Yeah, babe. Amen."

Toth ran her hand over Hudson's body again, like he was an animal she was thinking of buying and wanted to be certain of his health.

"Would you like to try some?" he asked, turning his head toward her. "The first treatment is often the most pleasant and exhilarating experience imaginable."

She lifted her hand. "Sounds addictive."

"So is life."

44

Karroo
Wednesday morning

Laurel forced herself to shower and dress, trying not to think how desperate her father must be, trying not to be hurt that he'd used her.

Was still using her.

Suddenly she picked up her leather valise and walked barefoot out into the hall, heading for the great room that was the focus of life at Karroo.

Cruz was already there. The light cotton shirt he wore was open to the waist, revealing his bound ribs. A pair of lightweight drawstring trousers fit him as if made for him by loving hands. The window was open, allowing the rising desert wind to fill the silence with a cry that was distant, wounded, ghostly.

For a moment Laurel was afraid she'd keen in bitter harmony with the wind.

If Cruz knew she'd entered the room, he didn't show it. He lay motionless on a leather couch, listening to the wind and watching the light spread out across the desert. His face was hard, remote. Beside him, on a table in front of the couch, was his pistol and a cleaning kit. The weapon was spotless, silent, lethal.

Like its owner.

Cruz turned his head. His eyes were hooded, unreadable. They went over Laurel like hands. When he saw the valise, his eyes narrowed dangerously.

"Leaving without saying goodbye?" he asked softly.

She knew him too well to be fooled by the softness of his voice. He was furious. She looked out to the desert, preferring its stark, unforgiving lines to what she saw in his eyes.

His pain and rage and distance were too much like her own.

"We're adults," she said. "Let's not make more of it than it was."

"Is that how you really feel?"

"There are more important things in the world right now than how I really feel." She looked at the gun lying close to his hand and said bitterly, "You have a job to do and I have a life to live. Let's just get on with it."

He came off the couch in a single lithe movement and stalked toward her. She held her ground, but she couldn't meet his eyes. When he was so close to her that she could feel the heat of his body, he stopped. Slowly he reached out to touch her cheek.

At the last instant, she forced herself to turn away.

"Laurel," he said huskily. "Honey, I'm sorry."

She simply shook her head, not trusting her voice.

"Am I intruding?" Cassandra Redpath asked.

The ambassador was standing in the doorway, looking delicate and far too shrewd.

"Yes," Cruz said quickly, sharply.

"No." Laurel's answer was equally quick, but her voice was raw with suppressed emotion.

"Shit," he said beneath his breath.

Laurel still hadn't met his eyes.

"We were just comparing bags of tricks," she said, forcing her lips into a grim smile. "Cruz has quite a few in his. I'm less inventive. All I have is a handful of pretty stones."

With that she turned and went to an overstuffed chair. She was afraid if she sat down on the couch, he would sit close to her. Too close. Forcing her to choose between her father and her lover when the only possible choice was neither.

She wouldn't trust either man.

Wouldn't love either man.

Wouldn't choose either man.

"Do come in, Ambassador," Cruz said coldly. "Join our little tea party. And don't forget the strychnine."

"Charming," Redpath said. Her voice said the opposite.

He turned and looked at his boss for the first time. Adrenaline shot through him, bringing him to full alert in an instant. "What happened?"

"Addison had some company up in Cambria."

The mention of her hometown brought Laurel to the edge of her chair. "Who's Addison?"

"One of our best operatives," Redpath said. "Cruz called him in from San Francisco to watch your house after the two of you left."

Laurel looked shocked. "Why?"

"I figured the assassins would come back," he said without looking away from Redpath. "How many?"

"At least three."

The leather valise settled with a thump on the table next to Laurel, as if she was too numb to hold its weight any longer.

"Very competent, too," Redpath continued. "It took Addison two hours to spot them."

"What—" Laurel cleared her throat. "What were they doing?"

"Lying back in the bushes, waiting for you to return," Redpath said calmly.

Laurel opened her mouth. No words came from her pale lips.

"Early this morning," Redpath said, "when it became clear that you weren't coming back, they broke in and searched the place."

Cruz's fingers flexed, hungry to have something to squeeze. Jamie Swann's neck came immediately to mind.

"They made a mess," Redpath said. "Whatever they were looking for, they didn't find."

"How do you know?" Cruz asked.

"They turned every room, every cupboard, every drawer upside down and inside out. If they'd found what they wanted, they would have left some part of the house untouched."

Laurel made an unhappy sound. She had a sick certainty that she knew what the men had been looking for.

"What did Addison do?" Cruz asked, angry at the thought of Laurel's home being trashed.

"Nothing," Redpath said.

"Why the hell not?"

"Those were my orders. Addison is following the men now, discreetly, to see if he can identify them or their contacts."

"And?" Cruz asked.

Redpath shrugged. "So far he has just about as much information as you did. They are male and ruthless. Thoroughly professional. The sergeant-major is taking a scout around Karroo right now, just to make sure we don't have visitors."

"Say the word and I'll neutralize them myself." Cruz's voice was rich with the promise of violence.

Laurel's nails dug into the leather valise until her fingers were white.

"I'll keep it in mind," Redpath said dryly.

"Who are they?" Cruz asked. "Does Addison know?"

"Possibly police."

Cruz grunted.

"Ranulph didn't think so either," Redpath said. "It's possible they're private and civilian, like us. But I think, and Addison agrees, that the men are probably Jamie Swann's confederates."

"Then they haven't given up," Laurel said.

"You really thought they would?" Cruz asked. "They were sent to murder you."

"How can the egg be worth those kinds of risks?" Laurel demanded. "From what the ambassador said, it could very well be a counterfeit Fabergé."

"Laurel," Cruz said through his teeth, "people will murder for a sack of shit or the sheer bloody hell of it. Money is just an excuse."

Blindly, she began unbuckling the valise.

"There is always the chance," Redpath said calmly, "that the egg's real value is greater than its apparent one."

"Is that what Novikov says?" Cruz asked sharply.

"Aleksy has little useful to say. He's been on the phone every two hours, but he's still playing the innocent victim."

"I could have a go at twisting him by his short hairs, provided he doesn't shave down there."

"You and the sergeant-major had the same impulse," Redpath said. "Both of you are too fond of force."

"We're not fond of it," Cruz shot back. "We use it because it works better than saying pretty please."

Laurel made a sharp, involuntary sound as one of the satchel's buckles raked her hand.

He spun toward the sound and toward the woman who had been the lover of his dreams last night, a woman who so disliked him and his job this morning that she wouldn't even meet his eyes.

"Does violence bother you so much, even when it's your best chance for survival?" he asked roughly. "I'd have thought a woman who drives fast and carries a blow-your-head-off gun would understand the value of applied force."

"That's not—" she began.

"Like it or die ignoring it, we don't live in a nice world," he said, talking over her, "and I'm damn tired of being savaged by holier-than-thou types who don't have the guts to protect themselves from the results of their own stupid choices."

Silence stretched while Laurel stared at the open valise and at her clenched hands. Her face went pale, then flushed.

"Cruz," Redpath said, "you have a uniquely male gift for saying the wrong thing at the wrong time."

"No," Laurel said in a raw voice, "let him have his say. God knows he's spent too much of his life doing jobs that other people were too squeamish or too frightened to do. God only knows what Cruz has paid for it. And what my father has paid."

The room was silent for a long time except for the thin keening of the desert wind around Karroo's stone walls.

Finally Laurel turned and looked at Cruz. The darkness in her eyes reminded him of what it had been like for him until she'd come and taught him to laugh.

And all he'd taught her in return was pain.

"Laurel," he whispered, walking to her. "Honey, I didn't want to hurt you."

She stood, one hand clenched by her side, watching

him. "Not your problem. It's way past time I grew a harder shell."

He lifted his hand and touched her cheek.

"No." She flinched away. "Not while I'm betraying him."

Before Cruz could move, she turned to Redpath.

"I know where my father wants to meet me," Laurel said. "I'll take you there."

"No," Cruz said instantly. "Too dangerous. Just tell me where and wait here."

"No." Laurel's voice was soft, utterly certain.

Looking at him, she said no more. She didn't have to. Anyone with eyes could see she wasn't going to be budged from her position.

"Cassandra," Cruz said urgently, "tell her how dangerous it will be."

"Don't bother," Laurel said, without looking away from him. "I was with you in Cambria, remember?"

"You damn near died there, remember?" he shot back.

"I remember. You saved my life."

"But you're still going to stick your neck out again."

"Yes."

"Why?"

"To see him again." She swallowed. "I have to know whether he's desperate or simply . . . corrupt."

"You can't be certain he'll even be there. Hell, it could just be a trap."

"He'll be there."

"What makes you so certain?" Cruz asked savagely. "He knows it could be a trap too. What makes you think he'd walk across the street to see you, much less put himself in danger?"

"I have something he wants very much. I just found it in my valise."

She held out her hand. On her palm a huge red crystal glowed like it was plugged into some cosmic power source.

"What is it?" Redpath asked.

"The stone from the Ruby Surprise."

45

Malibu
Wednesday morning

Silently Claire Toth prowled around the hot, muggy solarium, inspecting the equipment and studying the medical instruments that had been laid out. She'd made the same lap around the room many times. Nothing changed. Not even the pace of her lithe walk.

Damon Hudson watched her with hidden amusement. He'd already anticipated her initial reaction. It was hard for a person in the rich bloom of health to understand the attraction of everlasting vigor.

But give her a few years.

Let her feel the first crawling certainty of her own vulnerability to age and ugliness. Then she would be on her knees in front of him, begging for whatever crumbs he wanted to share with her.

"Why did you call me?" he asked softly. "Do you have the egg?"

"I'm still working on it. What about the money?"

"I'm still working on it," he said, mocking her.

Toth picked up a bottle of medicine and frowned at the foreign words on the label.

"Better hurry," she said. "You're not the only one in the bidding anymore. The former owner caught up with me."

He straightened around and sat up on the table. He dismissed the masseuse with a single look. She didn't want to go. He jerked his head toward the door. The woman stalked away, her shoulders straight and square, looking like a soldier on the parade ground.

"I thought she didn't understand English," Toth said acidly.

"I'm a careful man."

He swung his legs around on the table, stood up, and reached for a white robe on a chair. He was unself-conscious about his nakedness. Even in relaxation, his prick was surprisingly full and proud. To Toth, it was a more convincing proof of the success of his disgusting medical regimen than anything he'd said.

"Aleksy Novikov is after you?" Hudson asked, tying the robe around his lean hips. "He's not much of a threat."

"He's the one who put this little shakedown together. Didn't you know?"

"I wondered," Hudson said with cool satisfaction. "Now I know."

He picked up a crystal tumbler from the tray on the table. A matching crystal carafe held mineral water. He filled the glass and picked it up.

"The only side effect of the drugs is thirst," he said absently. "They make you dry as hell for a day or two."

When he finished drinking, he set the heavy tumbler down and turned to his beautiful enemy. She was still holding the medicine bottle as if unable to make herself put it down.

"It's remarkable material," he said. "It works on anyone,

at any age. You'd remain as youthful and alluring as you are right now, suffering none of the indignity of advancing age and ill health."

Again she tried to read the label of the bottle in her hand. It was still gibberish.

"All that from one elixir?" she said cynically. "Who are you trying to con, babe? If doctors had managed to pull that off, I'd have heard about it by now. So would everyone else in the world over thirty."

Hudson poured himself another glass of water and held it to the sunlight, admiring its clarity.

"The people who created that concoction weren't interested in money or notoriety," he said. "They had more substantial plans, more far-reaching ideas, more meaningful desires. Sadly, history caught up with them before they could implement their vision."

"What happened?"

"The usual. Execution at the hands of their inferiors."

"Shit happens," she said. "Does that mean your supply of youth juice dried up?"

"One of Hudson International's newest labs is being built to synthesize the material."

"How long until you get something?"

"I haven't found the right person to run the program. When I do, the development will be fast. In the meantime, I have more than enough for myself."

"Lucky you."

"Luck had nothing to do with it."

He drank a second glass of water before he turned to Toth again.

"I have enough material to grant the gift of extended life to at least one other person," he said, "should I choose to do so."

She wanted to look away from his cold, level gaze but found herself fascinated. There was something strangely compelling about seeing ancient eyes set in the face of a man who had the prick of a teenage athlete.

"How long has it been since a man made love to you for an entire night?" he asked.

"Since the last time somebody rubbed cocaine on his dick."

"I don't need cocaine. And you don't need to worry about any of the diseases that come from sexual contact with drug users or common street studs."

She laughed curtly. "That's what they all say, babe."

"Each of my contacts submits to regular and exhaustive blood screenings. My sperm count is high, with good motility and viability."

"Great, old man. Next time I feel the urge for an all-nighter, I'll give you a call."

"What I had in mind couldn't be accomplished in one night," he said calmly. "It would require much more of your time."

She wanted to say something flippant, but looking at his eyes froze the words in her throat.

"I find you sexually stimulating," he said, "but that's true of a great many women. Unlike them, you have more to offer me than your undoubtedly gifted snatch."

Again Toth tried to look away. Again she couldn't. Fear and excitement were coiling inside her, pushing her toward Hudson.

"You've used your position, and your Russian contacts, to build a solid power base," he continued matter-of-factly. "Considering where you came from, your achievement is remarkable."

"I worked my ass off for it."

"Many people work their asses off. Very few manage anything more than getting drunk and paying taxes."

A tremor of fear went through her. She'd said the same thing herself, many times, but never to Hudson. He must have researched her very thoroughly.

"Much of what you've done seems instinctive rather than intellectual," he said, "but I sense in your makeup and turn of mind a great natural talent for manipulating people. You're utterly cold."

"That's not the kind of thing a girl likes to hear," she said, baring her teeth in a hard smile. "Not sexy and feminine at all."

"I hope you don't believe that crap. The most powerful women in history have been the ones who used *all* their talents, not just the ones their society allowed good little girls to have."

Silently Hudson walked toward Toth with a peculiarly flowing grace that made her wonder what it would be like to have sex with a snake. When he took her by both shoulders, the heat and strength in his hands surprised her.

"What you need is a mentor," he said, "someone who can show you how to rise to the next level of power—the power to change events at the global level. When you have that, you'll finally be safe. *And not until then.*"

For a long, electric moment, she watched him watching her.

"What do you want from me?" she asked finally.

"I want you to marry me, subject to certain stipulated but generous terms. Then I want a child by you. A son, to be precise."

Her mouth opened. No words came out.

"If you flunk your blood tests," he continued, "conception

will be via artificial means. If the fetus is infected or of the wrong sex, it will be aborted and we'll begin again."

"You're serious."

"Of course. At the first possible moment, our son will be put on the medical regimen that has so greatly benefited me," Hudson said. "He'll be the most intelligent and vigorous man of his generation. With my careful tutelage, with my financial empire as a base, with your primal allure and native cunning, our son stands an excellent chance of becoming one of the most powerful men in history."

"You're nuts."

He laughed. "Too easy, darling. You can do better."

"How about this, *darling*? I'm black."

"Delightfully so. You're also Asian and Caucasian. Slightly more the last than either of the others, if my researchers are to be believed."

"Mixed bloods aren't welcome at the top," she said. "Trust me on that one."

"I do. Now you trust me. The coming decades will see an amalgamation of races, of cultures, of languages, and of nationalities. It's happening as we speak, an unstoppable social, political, and sexual juggernaut." He smiled. "Anything that inevitable will rather quickly come to be seen as a positive good."

"Not in my lifetime."

"Not in your *present* lifetime," he agreed. "But if you marry me, my wedding gift to you will be a much longer life span than the one you can expect now. Our son will live a great deal longer. He'll be able to benefit from mixed parentage in ways that you and I can't even imagine."

Toth wrapped her arms around herself and shuddered. She licked her lips, but not in sexual enticement. Her lips were dry with fear and a kind of queasy anticipation she'd never felt before.

She thought she knew it all, had done it all, had nothing left to look forward to but greater and greater risks for less and less kick until the day she miscalculated and died.

Hudson's offer changed everything.

"You're one hell of a salesman," she said huskily. "You're smart enough not to paw me or start sniveling about love."

His laugh was like his eyes, ancient and cold. "Those of us with intelligence discard such emotional baggage shortly after we outgrow diapers. Let the fools have their love. We'll control them, just as we'll control the rest of the world."

Toth felt herself respond to his searing candor in a way she'd never done with any man. He was utterly, beautifully, incredibly ruthless. He would use her. She knew it.

But he wouldn't break her.

Instead, he would teach her—father, mentor, and lover in one.

If she stayed with him, she would always be on the bubble, never quite certain that she was in control. She would be frightened and excited by turns. In short, she would be fully alive in the only way that mattered to her.

"I don't suppose the egg has anything to do with this sudden interest in getting me pregnant?" she asked.

"Of course the egg has something to do with it. Without the egg, you'd be of considerably less interest to me."

"How much less?"

"The egg is crucial to the future that the two of us can build. It's the critical component in an international network of agents and useful fools."

Watching Toth's eyes, Hudson dug his fingers into the soft flesh of her upper arms. He gauged her threshold with unerring precision, stopping just short of true pain. Then his little finger moved, gently caressing the inside of one arm.

Her breath caught as desire flooded her. He understood her body as well as she did. Better. Pain and pleasure in exquisite coupling, each feeding the other.

"Think of the egg as the dowry you bring me," he said.

"I—I may need help."

"Physical or intellectual?"

"Physical. Very physical."

"Use Bill Cahill."

"Is he discreet?"

"Of course," Hudson said.

"Enough that you would trust him to bury a body?"

"It wouldn't be his first. Who are you going to kill—Novikov?"

"No. Just a street stud I picked up a while ago. Nobody important at all."

46

Los Angeles
Wednesday evening

All around the rental car, Los Angeles spread out in a sea of light lapping against the shore of night. Laurel drove as well in the tricky twilight as she did in full sun. If Cruz hadn't been so furious with her, he'd have complimented her on her skill.

When he finally spoke, his voice was rough with barely leashed emotions. "How much longer?"

A quick glance at him was all Laurel needed. In the odd light, his eyes gleamed coldly. He was still angry. Furious, actually.

She looked away, concentrating on the traffic around her. "Just a few more minutes."

"Then tell me where we're going."

She hesitated.

"There's no time for us to set up an ambush now," Cruz said coldly. "Too bleeding bad I can't say the same for the other side, but that's the way you wanted it, right? Your father's safety and to hell with everyone else."

Silence was Laurel's only answer. She was tired of trying to explain what she didn't fully understand herself. All she knew was that she couldn't live with herself if she set up a trap for her father.

Deep inside, she believed that what her father had done, he'd done from desperation rather than greed and calculation.

Cruz didn't believe it.

Arguing with him again wouldn't change how either one of them felt. They'd been arguing since Karroo. It wouldn't end until they reached their destination.

If then.

He was furious that she wouldn't help Risk Ltd. set up a nice, sanitary ambush for her father. Gillespie had been like black ice on the subject, cold enough to burn. Only Redpath had understood. She hadn't agreed with Laurel, but she'd understood.

As Cruz shifted impatiently, light glinted off the pocket cell phone in his hands. The line was open. It would stay that way until he gave Risk Ltd. a destination.

The car's turn signal blinked. After she completed the turn, he spoke into the phone. "Up Doheny, heading directly toward the Hollywood Hills."

"Has she told you where you're going yet?" Gillespie asked curtly.

"You've heard everything I've heard."

"Balls. Laddie boy, you did a piss-poor job of getting her trust."

"Tell me something I don't know."

"Let me talk to her."

Cruz turned to Laurel and said sardonically, "The sergeant-major would like to whisper sweet nothings in your ear."

"No thanks."

He put the phone to his mouth. "She said—"

"I heard," Gillespie interrupted.

After that it was silent in the car except for Cruz's terse recital of streets and directions. The car turned again, heading up Benedict Canyon Road.

Finally Laurel turned off into a cool little coastal glen. The street was lined with new custom homes in the modernist style, all hard white stucco and smoked glass and self-conscious angles. Each house perched on a recently scalped building site that was as tiny as it was overpriced.

At the top of the street there was a house from another era, a different way of life. The floodlights that came on at dusk were for aesthetic pleasure rather than for security, although they served the second purpose very well. The house itself had a distinctive understated style. Landscaping enhanced the lines of the home and of the land itself. The house made the rest of the neighborhood look tacky and transient.

She started to turn into the driveway.

"Park on the street," Cruz ordered.

"But—"

"Just do it."

Tight-lipped, she brought the car to a stop along the curb. She reached for the key to shut off the engine.

"Leave it running."

She dropped her hand to her lap.

Quickly he read off the address and passed it on to the waiting sergeant-major.

"Got it," Gillespie said.

"Don't forget," Laurel said clearly. "No one but Cruz around, or else I won't call Dad."

Gillespie's answer was the sound of the connection breaking.

"What makes you think he isn't here already," Cruz asked, "waiting for you to call his pager?"

"He always parks right there, under the sycamore," she said, pointing to the driveway.

"Always? How long has he been coming here?"

"This was Mother's house before it was mine."

"I thought your parents were divorced."

"They were. It didn't really take, any more than the marriage did. Even though Mom didn't buy the house until after they were divorced, Dad always had a set of keys."

Cruz scanned the immediate area for any movement. Nothing caught his eye. The house was cantilevered into a shelf of bedrock at the head of the little canyon. Sycamores with giant leaves and smooth, weathered bark shaded a side deck.

"Your 'special place,' huh?" he asked, remembering Swann's message to his daughter.

"Yes, very special. In my memories."

"But you don't live here."

"I can't. The city is too close."

Cruz felt the same way about cities, but all he said was, "Turn the car around so that you're heading out. Leave the engine on."

While she maneuvered the car, he reached into the backseat and grabbed a black aluminum briefcase. He opened it, pulled out his pistol, checked its load with a few swift, expert motions, and put the weapon in a holster at the small of his back. He clipped extra magazines to a holder on his belt.

From the corner of her eye, Laurel watched him. Black shoes, black jeans, charcoal shirt, slate windbreaker, black gun, black body armor underneath it all. He was a study in shades of darkness, a dangerous man hunting dangerous prey.

Wear black. He's expecting you.

She suppressed an instinctive shiver. She'd done all she could to avoid this moment, but it had come just the same.

Her father and her lover hunting each other.

"Don't look at me like that," Cruz said curtly. "I won't shoot the son of a bitch on sight. That's a better guarantee than you can give me about my chances with him. But that doesn't bother you all that much, does it? You think I used you to get to him. You'd probably pull the trigger on me yourself."

"Don't," she said, her voice raw. "Oh, God, don't. Do you think this is easy for me, waiting for one of you to be hurt or killed, knowing that whatever happens is my fault?"

"Like bloody hell it's your fault. You didn't make your daddy's choices for him. Neither did I."

"That's no reason for me to betray him."

"You're not betraying anyone but us. We have something damned rare. You're throwing it away for a man who never cared about you enough to stick around."

"No! That's not it at all!"

Cruz didn't answer.

"My God, Cruz. Can't you see? You're incredibly quick, you're powerful, you're damned deadly. I saw you in action in Cambria. My father won't have a chance against you."

"Bullshit. He's—"

"In Cambria, you didn't kill when you could have," she said, talking over his words. "I trust you not to kill my father on sight. That's the only reason I agreed to help. What Dad did is wrong, but he doesn't deserve to die for it."

Unable to believe what he was hearing, Cruz stared at Laurel. What he saw told him she believed every word she'd just said to him.

"You're the one who's blind," he said flatly. "Your father

isn't some fumbling thug who couldn't find his ass with both hands. He's a highly trained sniper, a man-hunter, an assassin, a predator in ways I've never been and never could be. He won't shoot to injure. He'll shoot to kill."

"You're so quick," she said hoarsely. "I've seen you. *Quick*."

"Too bad you haven't seen your sweet daddy in action. A lot of men died wondering what the hell hit them."

With a savage jerk of his hand, Cruz unhooked his seat belt and reached for the door handle.

"Cruz!" she whispered, her throat aching, her hands reaching blindly for him. "Not like this. If anything goes wrong, I won't be able to live with it. *I love you*."

He turned back, saw the flash of tears and her trembling lips.

"You don't have to lie to me, honey. I promised I wouldn't kill your father on sight. I meant it. That's why I'm here instead of Gillespie."

Abruptly Cruz did what he'd told himself he wouldn't do. He leaned over and kissed Laurel until she tasted of desire as well as tears. Then he kissed her like she was a fragile dream shimmering on the brink of becoming real.

"Whatever happens," he said, breathing kisses over her face, "it's not your fault. Believe me, Laurel. You're the only innocent one in the whole lot."

He opened the door and slid out of the car. The cell phone lay on the seat. The phone's high-tech black plastic gleamed more warmly than his eyes.

"Wait for me here," he said in a low tone.

"But—"

"No buts," he cut in coldly. "Give me your word."

Shocked, she stared at him, wondering where the gentle lover of a few seconds ago had gone.

"Listen to me," he said in the same low, deadly voice. "What I feel goes against everything I've ever been taught about clients and professional detachment. But we're stuck with each other, because you refused to let Gillespie come in my place and I let you get away with it."

She waited, her nerves strung so tightly she was rigid.

"It's not too late for me to change my mind," Cruz said. "If I tell you to do something, it's not a game. Don't argue or ask why. Just do it. If you can't promise that, I'm off the case as of right now."

The impulse to argue, to ask why, to want more information almost overcame Laurel. A look at his eyes told her that her first question would be the last.

Cruz would walk out and call in Gillespie and never look back.

She took a deep, shuddering breath and slowly nodded. "What do you want me to do?"

"If you see anyone coming," he said, "punch the send button on the cellular and drive out of here as fast as you can. Gillespie will tell you what to do after that."

"What about you?"

"The sound of you laying rubber on your way down the street will be all the warning I need. Got it?"

All she could do was nod. If she opened her mouth, she would scream with all that couldn't be said, couldn't be done. Couldn't be.

Ever.

47

Los Angeles
Wednesday night

Cruz shut the car door very softly and looked around. No curtains moved in any of the houses that showed lights. No doors opened. No dogs barked.

With the ease of a man fully at home in the night, he stepped into the pools of darkness that gathered in the driveway between the floodlights. There was only the faintest of clicks as he drew his gun, cocked it, and flipped the safety off. His soft shoes made no noise at all.

When he came to the spot where Laurel had told him Swann habitually parked, Cruz reached down with his left hand and ran his finger across a black smudge on the concrete. His fingertip came away dark. He rubbed against his thumb, felt a slippery texture, and sniffed his fingertip.

Engine oil.

Fresh enough to still be fluid.

A day old, maybe, but not much more. The searing California sun turned a few drops of oil into sticky tar very quickly.

With swift efficiency, he went around the exterior of the

house, looking for any signs that someone else had done a quick reconnoiter recently. All he found were a few marks that could have been footprints in the margin of one of the flower beds around the patio.

He'd like to believe that meant Swann had been here, but Cruz knew better. A few footprints didn't prove anything. The grounds were obviously tended by at least one gardener, and gardeners had feet.

For several minutes Cruz stood motionless, concealed in the darkness and hibiscus bushes, listening to the natural background sounds. A languid breeze stirred through the sycamores. A mockingbird called. As though in answer, the sweet, desolate cry of a mourning dove curled through the darkness.

Quietly he stepped over the flower bed and onto the flagstone patio. The house keys Laurel reluctantly had surrendered to him back at Karroo were in his left hand. The second key was for the back door.

He turned aside from the patio and moved soundlessly over a small walkway leading to the back door of the house. With barely a whisper of steel on steel, the key turned in the lock. Standing to one side, he pushed the door open with his fingertips and waited.

No sound.

No movement.

After another minute he glided inside, put his back to a wall, and listened. At each hallway and room entrance he stopped in the same way, listened, and then moved on, until he finally made a complete circuit of the house. Only then did he uncock the gun, flick the safety on, turn on lights in the house, and go outside to tell Laurel it was safe.

As soon as she saw him, she turned off the engine and ran

to him, holding him for a long, fierce minute. He gave her a strong one-armed hug, but his eyes never stopped checking out his surroundings and his gun hand never was far from the small of his back.

Gently Cruz put Laurel from him. He reached into the backseat of the car to pull out her leather valise and his aluminum weapon case.

"Come on," he said. "I want to get you inside. Here. Carry the stuff. Unchivalrous and all that, but I need my hands free."

"I thought it was safe." Her voice wasn't nearly as steady as his.

"Swann isn't here now, but he's been here."

"How can you tell?"

"Fresh crankcase oil under the sycamore."

"Maybe it was somebody else," she said.

"In a private driveway on a dead-end street? Not something I'd bet my life on."

Silently Laurel walked ahead of Cruz to the house. He followed her inside, shut and locked the door, and took his weapon case from her.

"Does anyone else have a key besides your father?" he asked. "A cleaning service or security service or something like that?"

"No." She followed Cruz through the kitchen into the living room.

"Then your father was here."

"Crankcase oil on the kitchen floor?" she asked flippantly, but her eyes were a tarnished gold.

"The air is fresh," he said, "like somebody opened the place up. This morning's paper is on the kitchen table. You don't have a security system, do you?"

"No." She turned away from him, unable to bear the distance in his eyes, in his voice, in his gestures. "I don't stay here that much. Cities make me edgy."

"Laurel."

She turned back to Cruz and saw him waiting, the telephone in his hand.

With a silent prayer that she was doing the right thing, she took the phone and punched in the number of Jamie Swann's pager, then left the house phone as her callback number.

"How long does it take?" Cruz asked after she hung up.

"He usually calls within an hour."

"If he doesn't, how long does it take?"

"The record is ten days. Mom was already buried when he finally called that time."

Cruz made a low sound. "No wonder you don't trust men."

"I trust you."

"You think I'm a better killer than your old man," Cruz retorted. "Hell of a character reference."

"That's not what I said."

"Yeah. Sure."

"What's really on your mind?" Laurel asked tightly.

"The ways I resemble Jamie Swann."

"You don't."

"The hell I don't. He and I are both beyond the pale. We already know the most dangerous lessons a cop ever learns."

"What are you talking about?"

"How easy it is to break the law and skate off free," he said. "You learn it by living in the gutter world where lies are the only truth, where violence is the quickest way to peace, and where morals are as murky and fluid as the Mississippi."

"Are you saying that you're the same as my father?"

"I'm saying I could be."

"No."

"So quick. So confident. Ever think what might happen if you're wrong?"

"Why are you pushing me?" she asked.

"Am I?"

"Yes," she shot back. "You know the difference between paradox and immorality as well as I do. You know the difference between lying in behalf of discovering truth and lying merely for your own gain. It's the difference between honesty and crime."

For a long moment Cruz looked into Laurel's unflinching amber eyes.

"You have more faith in me than I do," he said finally.

"As you pointed out once, I see you very clearly."

He closed his eyes, but still he saw only her. He tried to speak. No words came but the ones he should not say.

"Cruz?"

Hearing his name on her lips sent a ripple of emotion through him. "I'm going to check around the house."

Though Laurel said nothing, he could see that his abruptness had hurt her.

"If I stay close to you right now," he said, "I'll kiss you until both of us forget where we are, who we are, what we are. And that would be the dumbest thing I've ever done."

"Cruz," she whispered, reaching for him.

"No," he said, stepping back. "It can't happen again, honey. I'm the wrong man in the wrong place at the wrong time. To protect you, I'll likely have to do things that will make you hate me. Don't make my job any harder on me than it already is."

For a long moment, Laurel looked at Cruz. Stranger, lover, bodyguard.

Hunter.

The hair at the nape of her neck stirred. She'd made her choice and this was the result. Cruz was sliding away from her, his complex shades of darkness becoming a single overwhelming night. He wouldn't flinch from what he had to do to protect her. Nothing would deflect him—not danger, not her body, not anything within her control.

She closed her eyes and shivered, wrapping her arms around herself. "No matter what happens, I'll never hate you."

There was no answer.

She opened her eyes. She was alone.

Cruz had stepped into the night, becoming just one more shade of darkness.

48

Los Angeles
Wednesday night

Wearily Laurel went to the leather valise she'd brought from Cambria. She took out calipers, a delicate mechanical scale, the ruby, and her little portable computer. Curled into an overstuffed chair, she set up the scale on a nearby table and carefully weighed the stone.

The uncertain light in the room made it difficult to read the tiny scale. She pulled the chain on the table lamp. The shade was made of prisms of clear crystal. The instant the light came on, rainbows cascaded over the table, her hand, the chair.

Color shimmered over everything.

For once, she didn't notice the lamp's silent display. She had all she could do just to force herself to think about something besides Cruz and her father, trust and violence.

Unseen, Cruz stood just beyond the doorway, watching with an intensity that ached. He'd never seen anything quite so beautiful as Laurel immersed in her work while rainbows danced all around. It took every bit of his considerable discipline not to go to her, to touch her, to hold on to what he felt was slipping from his grasp forever.

Her words haunted him.

I love you.

He'd never been in love. He wasn't even sure he knew what love was, how it felt, or how long it lasted. He'd always been too driven by his work to experience other intense emotions. And too deeply addicted to adrenaline, the drug of choice among cops and combat soldiers.

Yet somehow Laurel had reached down into his shadowed soul, seen him without flinching, touched him, awakened in him a range of feelings whose intensity both baffled and compelled him. Protectiveness, tenderness, passion, even awe. She was more vulnerable and at the same time stronger than any woman he'd ever known.

How could that son of a bitch put her at risk? Cruz asked silently. *I could go a lifetime and never find her equal. And because of Swann, I'm going to lose her.*

If I'm lucky, all I'll do is send her beloved daddy to jail for the rest of his natural life. If I'm not lucky, I'll have to kill the father to protect the daughter.

Then Laurel won't even want to remember what she once said to me.

The certainty of losing Laurel haunted Cruz as much as her words of love. Before her, he had been alone but not at all lonely.

After her . . .

He pushed the thought from his mind. Thinking about losing her would only get in the way of doing what had to be done. He'd rather have Laurel alive and free and hating him than dead and buried because he'd flinched when he should have fired.

As silently as he'd come to the room, he stepped back out

and left her alone, sitting in a blaze of rainbows. He roamed the house, analyzing it yet again, using a bodyguard's eye.

The house itself was easy enough to defend. It had clean lines and uncluttered design, which meant there were adequate fields of fire from room to room. The driveway was too open to invite an ambush. The front door was too well lighted to encourage stealth.

That was the good news.

The bad news was the chaparral-covered hillside in the rear. The brush would conceal approaching intruders right up to the backyard.

Repeatedly Cruz checked the perimeter of the grounds, standing silently, motionless, listening, thinking of what he would do if it was his job to get to the house unseen.

Too bloody easy.

I could get ten men and a dancing elephant onto the patio before anyone had a clue. But I don't think Swann will come with company. If nothing else, Laurel's DANGER *message should make him wary of his buddies.*

Cruz went back into the house. He was becoming more and more certain that the vague marks he'd seen in the flower bed around the patio had been left by Jamie Swann. He must have made the same circuits Cruz had, thought the same thoughts, reached the same conclusions.

Come through the hills.

Come without warning.

Come alone because you can't turn your back on anyone.

Swann, don't make me kill you, Cruz thought bleakly. *Even though you deserve to die for risking Laurel's life over a cold piece of stone, I don't want to be your executioner.*

Cruz didn't mean to end up back inside the house, looking at Laurel from beyond the doorway. He didn't mean to, but he found himself there just the same.

This time she sensed his presence. The computer screen was dark. The ruby was resting in the palm of her hand, gathering rainbows like a magnet gathering iron filings.

Slowly she pulled out a sheet of paper from the valise and folded the ruby neatly inside, just like all the other loose stones she kept. She tucked the paper parcel into the box with her other gems and set the valise aside.

Cruz watched her with a shadowed face and eyes that burned. He crossed the big room to the French doors that led out onto the patio. They were locked. He flipped the delicate lever and opened the doors.

Cool air that smelled of foliage and dew spilled into the room. A faint breath of evening breeze stripped a few leaves from a tall eucalyptus in the backyard. When the leaves scattered across the patio, they made a dry rustling sound, like footsteps brushing lightly over the flagstones.

When Cruz turned back to the room, Laurel was only a step away from him. She watched him with eyes the color of gold. Her lips trembled. So did her hands. Just a little. Just enough for a man with sharp eyes to see.

Cruz had very sharp eyes.

"Could you bend your rules long enough to hold me?" she asked hesitantly. "Just that. Just for a moment. I feel . . . so alone."

He didn't remember reaching for her. All he knew was that the warmth of her body against his chest was a stark contrast to the cold gun resting in its loop holster at the small of his back. His left arm wrapped around her, holding her close.

His right hand closed around the butt of his gun as more leaves skidded and whispered out beyond the patio, where the chaparral grew close.

"I should have done so many things differently," she said,

looking up at him. "The choices I made took more away from me than I thought they would. They took you."

He didn't answer. He simply released her.

"Time to check in with Karroo," he said neutrally. "Stay out of the light, okay?"

A faint sound came from the backyard. It could have been a cat prowling.

It could have been a cat-footed man.

"Cruz?" she said urgently.

He looked at her and waited.

"When Dad calls," she said, "don't push him too hard. Threats just make him more stubborn."

Cruz bent and gave Laurel a swift, fierce kiss. Then he breathed her name over her lips, regret and caress in one. She held him like she would die if he let her go.

"I know what kind of man your father is," Cruz said, gently pulling free. "I know better than you do."

For the space of a long breath, she searched his face for some sign of the emotions she'd shared with him. No matter how deeply she looked, she found only shades of darkness and new brackets of pain around his mouth.

He turned and went to the kitchen. She heard his voice as he connected with Karroo.

"Yes, I'll wait for her," he said curtly. "But not forever."

Laurel found herself heading for the kitchen, wanting simply to look at Cruz. Abruptly she turned aside, heading for the French doors instead.

It's too late for us, she told herself silently. *I made my bed, now I'll have to lie in it the same way I made it. Alone.*

She yanked the chain on the prism lamp, turning it off. The rainbows vanished. The room was dark but for a corner lamp and the concealed lights around the patio.

A breeze sighed through the open patio doors. Fighting tears, she walked outside, wishing she could simply evaporate into the darkness as the rainbows had.

A hand clamped over Laurel's mouth. A hard arm came around her, pinning her against a man's body.

49

Los Angeles
Wednesday night

"Don't scream, Laurie. It's just me."

The relief of hearing her father's voice was so great that she went limp for a moment.

Swann turned his daughter toward him and tipped her chin up with his left hand.

She stared at her father. His face was partially hidden in shadows, his features cold and hard. He carried a cocked pistol at belt level. Its muzzle was pointed past her, at the house.

At Cruz.

"Dad?" she whispered, suddenly uncertain, almost afraid.

"Who the hell did you expect? Santa Claus?"

She simply shook her head. His voice was low, carrying no farther than her ears, yet deadly for all its softness. She'd never seen her father like this. Cruel, dangerous, bluntly predatory.

For the first time, she understood why Cruz was so wary of Jamie Swann.

For the first time, she was truly afraid for Cruz's life.

Cold horror bled through Laurel's soul as she realized what she'd done, restraining Cruz when her father had no restraints.

Silently Swann searched his daughter's eyes. Whatever he was looking for wasn't there.

"That bastard has really gotten to you, hasn't he?" Swann asked in the same low, deadly voice.

"What?"

"That easy-moving gorilla who was all over you a minute ago. You damn near crawled into his pants."

She was too stunned to say anything.

Carefully Swann edged into the light, keeping an eye on the French doors like he expected a squad of armed men to burst out of the house at any moment.

"Who is he?" Swann demanded, heading toward the house. "Is he armed?"

Without stopping to think, Laurel stepped squarely in front of her father's pistol.

"Cruz Rowan isn't your enemy," she said in a low voice. "Please, Dad. Slow down and listen to me. It isn't what you think."

Swann looked at his daughter like she was a stranger threatening him. For a horrible moment, she thought he was going to keep his pistol on her.

Finally, slowly, he lowered the gun.

"Jesus," Swann said, looking at Laurel like he'd never seen her before. "I thought you were smarter than that."

"Smarter than what? Smarter than to get in your way?"

The words shocked Swann. "You really bought that lovey-dovey crap, didn't you? Rowan's a user. He's using you to get to me. It's the oldest trick in the book. Hell, I've done it a hundred times. Grow up, baby."

She felt a flush of anger and anguish, but her voice stayed

level. "I'm all grown up. I'm older than you know. But then, you haven't been around me often enough to know much about me, have you?"

It was the second time Laurel had shocked her father. This time, the pain that followed the shock was also visible to her. He looked like she'd hit him.

Instantly she regretted her words. She tried again, knowing only that somehow she must reach into this cruel hunter and find the father who loved her.

"Cruz isn't after you."

"Yeah? Then why the hell is he hanging around you?"

"To keep me alive," she shot back.

"What?"

"Just after I called you from Cambria, two men broke into the house. They tried to kill me."

Swann opened his mouth. No sound came out, but the stark horror on his face said more than words.

"Cruz was wearing body armor," she said. "That's why we're both alive. He knocked me to the floor, covered me with his body, and took the bullets meant for me. Then he drove the assassins away before they could do any more damage."

Emotions washed across Swann's face. Disbelief first, then comprehension, then a rage that consumed everything.

"That lying bitch," he said through clenched teeth. "She's dead."

"Who?"

Instead of answering, he drew a deep breath, trying to reel in his temper. It took more than one breath to get the job done. Gently he touched Laurel's cheek. His hand wasn't quite steady.

"I didn't know about this, Laurie," he said in a low voice. "So help me God, I didn't know."

"I never thought you did. Who was it? What's happening, Dad? Who wants me dead?"

"Never mind. I'll take care of it."

"How?"

Swann's face was dark and set. Rage gave his eyes a feral sheen. "That's a question you should know better than to ask. I sure as hell know better than to answer."

"I have to ask anyway," she said flatly. "The only way you can fix this mess is to turn the egg over to Cruz. He'll see that it gets returned to the Russians."

Slowly Swann's expression became less wild, but no less dark. He shook his head.

Laurel's eyelids flinched in pain. He wasn't going to listen to her.

"It's not that easy," he said. "Not that easy at all. The egg is only part of it. Even if I gave it back, there would still be hell to pay."

"From the police? Cruz said the Russians don't want any official notice at all. They just want the Ruby Surprise back."

"Yeah, I'll bet they do."

Swann's smile didn't make her feel better about what her father might do next.

"But Rowan is right," Swann added. "The local cops won't be a problem. If the Russians are smart—and they are—they won't bother the feds with it either."

He fixed Laurel with eyes the color of her own, yet so different, a dark mirror of a shadowed life.

"Did you bring your work stuff with you?" he asked.

"Yes."

"Get me the satchel and go back into the house. Two minutes later I'll be gone."

"It would be easier just to bring the stone, wouldn't it?" she asked coolly.

Swann's mouth flattened. "Shit, Laurie. You weren't supposed to find it."

"A lot of things weren't supposed to happen. But they did anyway."

"Who else knows about the stone?"

"Cruz and his boss, Cassandra Redpath."

"Have they figured out what it is?"

Laurel stared at her father. "It's a ruby. But there's something odd about it."

Unhappily Swann studied his daughter, trying to read her expression, to know what she knew without having to question her. The problem with questions was that they often revealed as much as the answers.

"Odd?" he said. "How so?"

"I can't tell without running some more tests, but the stone probably is synthetic."

"Not likely. They couldn't make rubies back before the Revolution."

"I could be wrong. The specific gravity is a hair off, but my scale could be off too."

"It must be," Swann said quickly, certainly.

"On the other hand, the stone is too clear, too perfect, too uniform. I've never seen anything like it in a natural gem."

"Baby, leave it alone." Swann's voice was soft, but there was an unmistakable threat in it.

"That's the problem, Dad. I'm not your baby anymore."

"You're Cruz's baby, is that it? He has your loyalty now and to hell with your old man?"

"If it weren't for Cruz, I'd be dead. If it weren't for you, I'd never have been born. I'd say the honors are about even when it comes to my loyalty." Her voice roughened. "I love both of you, and both of you are tearing me apart."

There was a long silence. Then Swann blew out a slow

breath. "Mother of God. What a cocked-up mess this is."

"What's going on? What's gone wrong? I have a right to know. I damn near died because of it."

"The more you know, the more dangerous it is for you. Leave it be. I never should have involved you. That son of a bitch Rowan never should have dragged you in deeper. Where's the stone?"

Automatically Laurel glanced toward the house. Cruz was still nowhere in sight, but it wouldn't be like that for long. His conversations with Karroo rarely ran longer than five or six minutes.

"Can you get the stone without Rowan knowing it?" Swann asked.

"Don't ask me to do that."

"Get it, Laurel. It's the only way you'll be clear of this mess."

"No."

"You can't get it, or you won't?"

"I won't," she said starkly. "I don't understand what's going on, but as of now I'm out of the game. If you won't cooperate with Cruz and Risk Limited, I won't help you."

Swann looked at his daughter for a long time. Slowly his disbelief turned to anger.

"Well, I'll be damned," he said finally. "You really believe you're in love with the bastard. He must be a hell of a cocksman."

Swann started to brush past Laurel, heading for the house. His pistol was ready and there was a cold intent in his eyes.

Laurel grabbed her father's arm. The muscles beneath were like metal cable, drawn tight by rage and adrenaline.

"No," she said harshly. "If you take another step, I'll scream. You might be able to catch Cruz unaware, but if he knows you're coming you won't have a chance in hell. He's good, Dad. Very good. And I don't mean just in bed."

Slowly Swann let the hunting readiness drain out of his system. Laurel had blunted his attack as surely as if she'd drawn a gun on him. When he realized that, he looked at his daughter with new eyes.

"You'd really do it," he said, more of a statement than a question.

"Yes."

He knew the answer before she spoke. It was written in her body language, a keyed-up readiness that was very like his own. Slowly he shook his head in reluctant appreciation of his own offspring.

"You're a real handful when you set your mind on something," Swann said. "Wish your mother had had that kind of cold steel in her soul."

"Would you really have wanted her that way?"

"Not when we first met. I was too young to appreciate a strong woman. Hope the bastard you chose is worth the grief he'll give you, Laurie. I sure as hell wasn't."

"Cruz is the first one I've ever met who makes the risk look worth taking."

Smiling sadly, Swann touched his daughter's hair.

"Okay, if that's the way it is, that's the way it will be. I'll straighten out what I can for you."

"Let Cruz—"

"No," Swann cut in. "Too late, baby. Too many debts to pay. But no matter how desperate I am, I promise not to drag you down into my slimy little world again."

She stood on tiptoe and kissed her father's cheek just above the edge of his beard. He touched her cheek with his lips and then stepped back, turning away from her, walking soundlessly toward the waiting night.

"No matter what, I love you," Laurel called after him in a low voice. "Just like Mother loved you. Your name was the last word she said."

Swann's voice drifted back out of the darkness. "I loved her as much as I could love anything except you. So I'm going to do for you what I did for her—get the hell out of your life."

A man-sized shadow moved against darkness, merged with the brush, and vanished.

Cruz stepped out of the shadows at the far side of the house.

Laurel stared at him in shock. "You were here all the time."

"Some of the time."

"You could have stopped him!"

"He didn't have the egg. Not in his hands. Not in the car parked down the block. It's a bloody shame there isn't someone from Risk Limited here to follow him."

"No one is keeping you here."

"I'm your bodyguard." Cruz stared up the brushy hillside as if tracking Swann's retreat. "When did you decide the ruby was synthetic?"

Laurel stared at him. She swallowed hard, trying to settle her nerves and at the same time understand where his question was going.

"Tonight," she said slowly. "I thought Dad might have been taken in by a counterfeit and all of this was for nothing."

Staring into the brush, Cruz waited and listened, making sure that Swann wasn't out there somewhere, waiting and listening, circling back to the stone he must have.

There were no sounds but those of the night itself.

Cruz reached into his pocket and pulled out the blood-red stone Swann had wanted so badly.

"Your father wasn't taken in by a counterfeit," Cruz said softly. "He already knew."

"I left the ruby in the valise," she said in a clipped voice. "You didn't trust me not to give the stone to my father, did you?"

"I didn't trust the methods your father might use to persuade you."

"He would never hurt me, not like that."

"I know that. Now."

What Cruz didn't say was that he'd stood in the shadows with a pistol pointed at Jamie Swann's head until it became clear that Laurel was in no physical danger. Then Cruz had done a fast reconnoiter until he found Swann's car.

"Oh, God, what a mess." She wrapped her arms around herself, shivering in the aftermath of adrenaline. "None of it makes sense. Why would anyone kill for a fake ruby?"

Cruz stared at the stone in his hand. Night had drained the ruby of color, leaving only its oddly cut facets to gleam coldly in the uncertain light.

"If the ruby is phony, and if Aleksy Novikov knows it," Cruz said, "this might be one of the most valuable pieces of crystal in the world. If we can get it to talk. If your father was telling the truth. Big ifs."

"What do *you* think?" she asked painfully.

"Go inside, honey. It's their move now."

50

Los Angeles
Wednesday night

Jamie Swann tried to keep a lid on the rage that was seething through him, but he wasn't entirely successful. Only one person knew that he'd sent the egg to his daughter. Only one person knew that Risk Ltd. had been in touch with his daughter. Only one person would have a motive for sending assassins after his daughter.

Swann's long, hard fingers clenched around the steering wheel. He wished it was Claire Toth's elegant neck.

The lying, double-crossing bitch, he raged silently. *She was having sex with me at the very moment she thought my kid was being murdered.*

And, God, she was enjoying it. It really got her off like nothing else ever has.

Swann blew out a harsh breath, trying to calm himself. It was nearly impossible. He'd known psychotics in his line of work, but Toth was beyond even that pale. She was in a bizarre category by herself.

But not for long. Soon Toth would be like a lot of other people Swann had known.

Stone-cold dead.

Until tonight, he'd never enjoyed the prospect of killing. It simply was part of the job, like lying and cheating and living on the slimy edge of what passed for civilization.

Tonight was different.

Tonight he was looking forward to killing someone.

Swann parked his car a block from the Beverly Wilshire. He entered the hotel through a side door. There was some kind of convention banquet that night. The hotel's public places were crowded with fancy ladies wearing cocktail dresses and lavish jewelry, and fat men wearing tuxedos and lavish toupees.

On the surface, none of the people looked worth a second glance from Swann. Even so, he spent ten minutes watching people flow back and forth through the lobby. Nobody looked like a threat. More important, nobody looked like he was working hard to avoid looking like a threat.

Satisfied, Swann casually checked that his loose, light-weight jacket still covered the butt of his gun. He headed for the elevator, walking like a man who knew just where he was going. The elevator stopped on every floor, losing people, gaining people. None of the hallways were empty.

He decided to go straight to Toth's floor rather than get off below or above and take the stairwell. There were too many people milling around for anyone to remember him.

Toth's room was at the end of a long, quiet hall. It was the last room before the emergency stairway. Outside the door, Swann paused for a moment, listening. The door was thick, but he could make out two voices. One female. One male.

Swann had heard Damon Hudson speak only a few words

in the limousine, but the resonances coming through the door were right for Hudson's age and voice. So was the situation.

It would be like Toth to plot a double-cross while Swann was in the front seat of the limousine and she was in the backseat with Hudson. It would be a rare triple. She'd betray her partner. She'd betray Hudson. Then she'd get Hudson to betray himself by being seduced by his blackmailer.

Quietly Swann slid the key into the door lock. Before he could turn the key, he felt the cold steel circle of a gun barrel press against the warm skin behind his ear.

Instinctively he froze, all rage forgotten.

For the first time since he'd left Laurel, Swann started thinking clearly. None of the thoughts comforted him. He'd lost control of the game at a time when losing and dying were the same thing.

Grimly Swann hoped that Cruz Rowan was better at protecting Laurel than her father had been.

"Finish what you were doing," a man's voice said from behind Swann. "Open the door and walk on in."

From the corner of his eye, Swann saw a white shirt, muted red tie, and a dark suit coat. Bill Cahill.

"Nice clothes," Swann said softly. "How did I miss you?"

"Never mind, asshole. Just go on in."

"You don't want to cause the kind of trouble that would come if you shot me."

"Don't worry. It'd be no trouble at all."

The muzzle bored into Swann's skull. He hesitated, weighing his chances. They weren't bad. His captor was standing too close. Every time he prodded Swann with the gun, it put the gun within Swann's reach.

Sooner or later Cahill would get truly careless. Then

Swann would take the gun and teach Cahill the kind of lesson he'd be lucky to survive.

But first there was Claire Toth.

Swann turned the key and pushed the hotel room door open. Toth and Damon Hudson were sitting together on a couch facing the door. The Ruby Surprise was on the table in front of them.

When Swann and Cahill came in like Siamese twins, Hudson and Toth looked up. Their expressions were only mildly interested.

"Smooth as silk," Cahill said. "He was so interested in sticking his ear to the door that he didn't hear me come out of the stairwell."

Hudson's shrug said he didn't care about the details.

Cahill prodded Swann with the cold muzzle of the gun. "Hit the wall. Both hands. Spread your feet. Stay that way."

Swann braced his hands against the brocade wallpaper and let Cahill frisk him. It didn't take him long to find the gun.

"Lobby surveillance cameras, right?" Swann said to Cahill as he removed the gun. "You've got a buddy in hotel security."

Cahill chuckled, more relaxed now that Swann was disarmed. "We were on the Bureau's bank robbery squad in Dallas twenty-two years ago. We still help each other out from time to time. Thought you'd never get tired of looking at the ladies in the lobby."

"Come in and sit, Mr. Swann," Hudson said in his odd, papery voice. "I was hoping you would show up soon. Ms. Toth doesn't seem to know how to make the egg open."

Swann looked at Toth. And smiled.

A silvery chill of excitement and fear rippled down Toth's spine. She'd always wondered what death would look like.

Now she knew. It was waiting for her in Jamie Swann's feral eyes.

She would have sold what remained of her soul for the chance to have sex with him one last time.

Swann's smile told her that he knew what she was thinking.

With the muzzle of his gun, Cahill shoved Swann toward a chair. Swann responded slowly, watching and waiting for the right opening. Cahill was acting like a man who had forgotten everything he'd learned in the FBI about guns and prisoners.

Swann was looking forward to the instant when he would feed Cahill his own gun. But first, Swann had to make that beautiful pit viper believe that all he wanted was out of the game. It had to be done carefully or she wouldn't believe him.

"Party's over," Cahill said. "Sit down and act civilized."

Swann sat down on a wingback chair, keeping his weight forward and his legs coiled under him, ready to spring.

"Lean back. Relax," said Cahill. "I used to eat guys like you a dozen at a time."

Swann let his weight lean back slightly in the chair, but he kept his legs coiled. Then he began easing his weight forward again, moving just a bit at a time.

Either Cahill didn't notice or he didn't care. He holstered his weapon and pulled out a leather-wrapped billy club.

"Nice bit of work, lover," Swann said to Toth. "Double or die, right?"

"Nothing that dangerous," she said. "Mr. Hudson has made us a very generous counteroffer."

"I'll bet he has."

She smiled, licked her lips, and bit the bottom one, watching Swann the whole time. "But first he needs proof that the egg is what we say it is. You can do that, can't you?"

Swann stared at her with open contempt. "Sure, babe. No problem."

"Good," Hudson said. "Please demonstrate."

"Fuck you, fool."

Hudson glanced at Cahill. The security man slapped Swann with the billy club. The blow wasn't hard enough to break the skin, but it rocked Swann's head back.

"Is that the best you can do?" Swann asked.

Cahill cradled the billy club in his palm, weighing the weapon and watching Swann with indifferent eyes.

"You don't want to see my best," Cahill said matter-of-factly. "Make the egg do its trick or you'll be spitting teeth for a week."

Swann laughed. "Bet you were the terror of kindergarten."

Cahill looked at Hudson.

"You can knock out every one of my teeth," Swann said, "and you still won't have what you want."

"Tough guy, huh?" Cahill said. "Think pain won't make you talk?"

"You could wire my pecker to a phone and call room service all day long," Swann said, "and it still wouldn't get the job done."

Toth started to speak.

Hudson cut her off with a sharp motion of his hand. He stared at Swann. "What, precisely, is the problem?"

"It will cost you a hundred grand to find out," Swann said.

"Don't be stupid," Hudson said. "You're hardly in a position to bargain."

"Think again, old man. Yeah, I've just been cut out of the deal. Yeah, there isn't much I can do about it without screwing myself as much as you."

Hudson nodded.

"So I'll just take a hundred grand and go away," Swann said. "Under the circumstances, that's not a lot. It's less than the bribes you'd have to pay to hush up a killing in the Beverly Wilshire Hotel."

Hudson looked at Toth.

She shrugged.

"All right," Hudson said. "Ms. Toth can pay you from the money I brought with me today. Now, why can't you make the egg work?"

"Missing pieces," Swann said succinctly. "All you've got is a very fancy skeleton."

It was the truth, which only made the words more effective.

"What?" Hudson cut a hard glance at Toth. "She said you'd bring everything we needed."

"She lied." Swann smiled thinly. "Get used to it. If the bitch is breathing, she's lying."

Toth watched Swann. Her hungry black eyes looked back on being his lover and forward to being his executioner.

"Was she lying about the E Bloc computer?" Hudson said.

"Damned if I know," Swann said. "What did she say?"

"That we needed one."

"You do."

They also needed the original ruby, but Swann wasn't going to mention it. If Toth hadn't discovered the substitution yet, he wasn't going to tell her unless it gave him an advantage.

"Is there a way around the necessity for a computer?" Hudson asked.

"Maybe a cable link and a hacker could get the job done." Swann shrugged. "Ask Novikov. It's his toy."

"Under the circumstances," Hudson said, "I don't think he'd want to help."

"Yeah, well, some people just don't have any sense of humor, do they?"

Hudson eyed his prisoner carefully, suspecting that there was more to Swann than he'd seen yet.

"Is lack of a computer the only problem?" Hudson asked.

Swann just looked at him.

Cahill moved, turning his body slightly as though preparing to strike again.

The movement caught Swann's eye. He glanced at the security man.

"At ease," Swann said, lying as convincingly as he'd told the truth. "Your boss has the whole thing, or he will as soon as he gets the computer link."

For a moment there was only silence. Then Hudson looked at Toth.

"Now you're catching on," Swann mocked. "She's the one who can answer your questions. She's in this with Novikov up to her tits."

Hudson watched Toth, waiting for confirmation.

She studied Swann's face for a long time, uneasy without knowing why.

"Oh, for Christ's sake," Swann said curtly to her. "Get me the hundred grand and I'll get the hell out of everyone's life. I'm sick of this game."

Toth came around the table slowly. With feline grace she knelt in front of Swann.

"Poor babe," she murmured. "You really aren't as hard as I thought, are you?"

"I used to be. I'm getting old."

Tenderly she touched the slight bruise that was beginning to puff up on Swann's cheekbone.

"You were the best," she said in a voice only he could hear. "The only one who never had to beat me to make me come."

"My mistake. Get me the go-away money and I'll be gone."

She searched Swann's eyes, looking for a lie. All she saw was the same animal hatred she'd seen when he first walked into the room. She didn't doubt the truth of his hatred.

Slowly she stood up. She looked at Hudson and nodded very slightly.

"Now, Bill," Hudson said distinctly.

Cahill hit Swann just once. The blow landed at the base of Swann's skull. Cahill cocked his arm again, ready to strike, but Swann was already sprawled facedown on the carpet.

"That's enough," Hudson said. "We don't want him marked up."

"Why not? Let me work him over a little more, then dump him somewhere. He won't be back, believe me."

"That's not necessary," Hudson said. "Go get the limousine and bring it around to the lobby exit. We won't be long."

51

Los Angeles
Wednesday night

Jamie Swann groaned and rolled his head slowly from side to side as if dodging blows only he could see.

With a combination of fear and fascination, Toth watched. Already he was trying to roll over and pull himself up by the arm of the chair.

"Jesus, he's a strong bastard," she said under her breath. Then, to Hudson, "Hurry up."

"Help me get him into the chair."

Together, Hudson and Toth guided, dragged, and pushed the barely conscious Swann back into the chair. He mumbled and pawed at the side of his head like a wounded bear.

"Quick, get a glass," Hudson said.

She hurried across the room to the small refrigerated bar and grabbed a glass from the shelf above it.

"Whiskey," Hudson said. "Fill it."

"He drinks vodka."

"Whatever. Just get it!"

She rummaged through the narrow shelf in the refrigerator bar and came up with two small bottles of vodka. With vicious motions she snapped the seals on the caps and poured. Vodka gurgled into the tumbler. The two bottles filled the glass more than halfway. She hurried across the room to Hudson.

Without a word he took the tumbler. Turning his back on Swann, Hudson dropped two small tablets into the clear liquid. They dissolved instantly. He swirled the liquid around several times before he handed the glass back to Toth.

"Give it to him," Hudson said.

Black eyes widened as Toth realized she was going to be the one to kill Swann. And she would be doing it in front of a witness whose word in court would be even more powerful than her own.

"Don't lose your nerve now," Hudson said softly. "It will appear entirely innocent. A man has a stiff drink. A heart attack follows. He falls, bruising his cheek and the back of his skull. He dies. How sad. How ordinary."

She stared for a moment at the glass, then down at the groggy, helpless man slumped in the chair.

"Oh, babe," she murmured. "My poor babe."

She knelt beside the chair and tried to straighten Swann's head with one hand while holding the glass to his lips with the other.

"Poor, poor babe," she said softly. "I'm sorry they did that to you. I didn't know it would happen. Here, drink this, you'll feel better. Then I'll get your money and you can go."

Swann tried to push the glass away with his hand, but he was too weak, too disoriented.

Gently she covered the big hand that was warding off the tumbler. "Come on, babe, this will make you feel so much better. It's vodka. It will clear your head. Otherwise you won't be able to walk out of here with your money."

She tipped the glass until a little of the liquid ran between Swann's lips. He tasted the familiar astringency of vodka and swallowed reflexively. She tipped more into his mouth and he swallowed again.

The alcohol had a bracing effect. Swann's eyes slowly focused on the opposite wall. He shook his injured head and brushed the glass away with his free hand.

"Swee' Jeeshush," he groaned, slurring like a drunk.

Painfully he fought to control his body. He didn't know what had gone wrong. He only knew that something had.

He focused on Toth's intent face.

"Bitch. Shoulda done you when I had the chance."

The words were sloppy but coherent.

"Yeah," she agreed, smiling gently, brushing her lips over his bruised cheek. "Here, lover. Drink some more. It's making you feel better, isn't it?"

As she spoke, she brushed her long fingers through Swann's hair at the base of his neck, examining the small swelling where he had been struck.

"I'm really sorry they hurt you that way," she said in a husky tone. "They weren't supposed to."

Disoriented, Swann heard only the soft words and felt only the gentle touch on his battered head. He straightened up in the chair and took the tumbler she was pressing into his hand. He stared at the glass for a moment, trying to remember where it had come from.

He couldn't.

Automatically he tossed back a swallow of vodka. The gesture sent blood pounding through his head and he groaned again.

"Bitch," he said.

"Aw, babe, don't be like that," she said. "I only did what you would have done in my place."

Narrow-eyed, Swann stared past Toth, noticing Hudson for the first time. Swann frowned, trying to remember who Hudson was and why he was there. Fragments of memory came back.

Hudson and Toth and double-cross.

"Don' trust her, old man," Swann said, speaking carefully, wanting Hudson to understand every word. "She'll cut off your nuts and feed 'em to you like pistachios."

"Not as long as she has an interest in keeping me alive," Hudson said. "That's the secret to a happy relationship. You should have learned it."

Hudson laughed.

The dry sound was that of leaves skipping across a patio. Swann had heard it before. Recently. He knew it was connected with something important.

He just couldn't remember what.

Slowly Swann moved his head and stared fixedly at Toth. Her expression was a mixture of pity and fear and dark excitement. Distantly he realized that his head was clearing, but there was a deep chill in his belly that was slowly radiating outward, consuming his once-powerful body.

"What have you done to me?" he whispered.

"Nothing, babe," she said gently. "Just finish your drink and I'll get your money."

Swann didn't lift the glass to his lips.

She glanced uneasily at the tumbler in his hand. Less than half of it was gone. She tried to guide the glass back to his lips.

Swann batted her hands away and stared unsteadily at the glass. As the chill in his gut deepened to ice, he understood.

He flung the glass aside, sending liquid in a cold arc as he tried to grab her. His big hands were like claws reaching for her throat, but they fell far short. His nerves and muscles had already begun shutting down.

She fell backward and scuttled away like a frightened crab. "Jesus," she said to Hudson. "Do something!"

"It's already done," Hudson said quietly.

"He didn't drink it all."

"Obviously he had enough. Look at him."

Swann reared up on unsteady legs, then collapsed backward into the chair. As rapidly as his body was succumbing, his brain was clearing.

"What the hell was it?" Swann asked.

"A Soviet concoction," Hudson said, walking back to sit on the couch. "It will look like a heart attack, particularly for a big, beefy man like yourself. But you should have drunk it all. Death would have been painless that way. I doubt that it will be now."

Swann leaned to one side in the chair, fighting not to fall over.

"Well, I'll be damned," he whispered, looking at Hudson. "When I saw you here, I stopped worrying about being killed right away. I didn't think you would get your hands dirty."

"I'm a pragmatist," Hudson said. "I always have been. I'd kill a dozen men like you for this."

As he spoke, Hudson's hand grasped the egg. His thumb pressed. The egg opened, revealing a gleaming, extraordinary lattice of silver and gold.

Above it, the ruby burned like a blood-red flame.

Swann made a strangled sound that could have been either a death rattle or a demon's laughter. "The whore and the pragmatist." He gasped brokenly. "Jesus, what a pair of zeros you are. You just busted out of the game and you don't even know it."

"What are you talking about?" Hudson demanded.

Swann ignored him, looking only at Toth.

"The ruby," Swann said, gasping for enough air to tell her how badly she'd lost the game. "I switched it. You've got a dud, *lover*. Empty. *Blank*."

His body jerked with a combination of pain and horrible laughter.

Hudson picked up the egg and stared desperately at the glowing ruby. He carried it to a lamp where the light was better and inspected the stone.

"Well?" she demanded. "Is it a ruby?"

"I can't say. I know someone who can."

But Hudson had a growing, gnawing certainty that Swann had done exactly as he'd said. For a man in partnership with Claire Toth, having a double-cross up his sleeve would be simple common sense.

Swiftly Hudson crossed the room to where Swann was slumped in the chair. Hudson's fingers speared into Swann's hair, clenched, and yanked his head upright.

"There is an antidote," Hudson said distinctly. "Tell me where you put the real ruby and you'll live."

"Fuck you, fool." Swann jerked to one side in a spasm of pain. His eyes fastened on Toth. "See you in hell, babe. Bet on it."

Hudson whirled and advanced on Toth.

"Where would he have hidden it?" Hudson demanded. "Who did he trust?"

"No one. Trusting people is dumb, and Jamie was only dumb about his daughter."

"What do you mean?"

"He sent the egg to her."

"Where is she?" Hudson asked savagely.

"Now? I don't know. She has a house in Cambria. But she's not there now."

"Where is she?"

"I'm working on it," Toth said curtly. "She and her mother had a house down here, somewhere in Los Angeles. Jamie used to hide out there a lot."

"No."

Swann's hoarse cry was involuntary. His voice was strangled, almost unintelligible, but his anguish was unmistakable. He lunged forward, but his legs wouldn't support him. He crashed to the floor.

"We'll start with the daughter," Hudson said. "Bill Cahill has useful contacts with the local police. He'll find the house." He pulled Toth toward the door. "Hurry. Novikov might be ahead of us."

"What about Jamie?" she asked.

"He'll be dead by the time Bill brings the limousine around."

52

**Los Angeles
Wednesday night**

In the taut silence of the house, the ringing of the telephone was like a gunshot. Cruz grabbed the phone before Laurel did.

"Hello," he said curtly.

At first the connection was hollow, silent. Then he heard faint sounds, like labored breathing.

"Hello," Cruz said again.

No response came but more hoarse breathing. He wondered if it was some wacko looking for a cheap sexual thrill.

"Who is it?" Laurel asked, coming up behind him.

He shook his head. "*Hello.*"

Still nothing.

He was about to hang up when he heard a strangled gasp. There was no pleasure in that sound, just anguish and urgency.

"I can't understand you," Cruz said.

A sound came that was almost understandable, like a single letter, the letter "L," spoken in a man's deep voice.

Cruz shot Laurel a quick glance. She was watching him anxiously. The fear and violence of the last few days had etched lines of tension and pain around her full mouth, thinning it. He had a cold certainty that nothing had improved with this call.

"I still can't understand you," he said into the telephone. "Are you in trouble? Do you need help?"

An almost exultant sound, half grunt, half groan.

Contact.

It took no sixth sense for Cruz to guess who was trying so desperately to talk to him. Only one deep-voiced man would be calling this number if he was in extreme trouble, and the man on the line was clearly at the end of his strength.

"Easy, Jamie," Cruz said.

Laurel came alert at her father's name. She moved closer to Cruz but didn't reach for the phone.

"You got through to us," Cruz said. "This is Cruz Rowan. Laurel is safe with me. What's wrong, Jamie? Are you hurt?"

"Poi . . . pois . . ."

Swann's words were choked off, like someone was tightening a noose around his neck and then relaxing it.

"Try it again, slower," Cruz said, pulling his cell phone out of his pocket as he spoke. "Hang in there, man. We'll get to you."

The confidence in Cruz's voice seemed to help Swann. He drew a deep, gasping breath.

Cruz hit redial. Risk Ltd. answered instantly. He turned aside and spoke into the cell phone in a low tone without removing the house phone's receiver from his other ear.

"This is John Smith the Second. I'm in the clear. Did you get a trace set up on the phone at my present location?"

"Affirmative."

"Activate it."

"Affirmative," came the crisp response.

"Poisoned," Swann said in Cruz's other ear.

Swann's voice had cleared, as if making connection with Cruz had calmed him.

"Do you know what kind?" Cruz asked.

"No matter," Swann gasped. "Dying. Dead. They went to get—" The explosion of words exhausted him.

Cruz heard him panting, trying to catch his breath. "Slow down," Cruz said firmly, calmly. "Where are you?"

"—to get Laurel."

The message exploded from Swann's chest in a harsh groan. No more sounds followed. He'd done what he had to do. His battle was over. Laurel was as safe as he could make her.

Cruz heard a heavy crashing sound and knew that Swann had collapsed. The telephone at the other end of the line banged and jangled against something solid, floor or furniture.

Then there was no sound but the open line.

"Jamie," Cruz said urgently. Then, very loudly, "Jamie Swann. Talk to me. Where are you?"

Nothing answered but a faint groan, the sound of a man in deep pain, a man near death.

Cruz lowered the receiver and looked into Laurel's anxious golden eyes. He wished there was a way to spare her, but there wasn't.

"Your father has been poisoned," Cruz said. "He's in rough shape. If he doesn't have something to hang on to, we'll lose him. We may lose him anyway."

She grabbed the receiver. "Dad! Dad! Talk to me! It's Laurel, Dad. Can you hear me?"

Cruz watched intently.

Silently she shook her head.

"Try to get him to talk," Cruz said. "I've got someone tracing the call now."

"Dad. *Dad.* I know you can hear me. Give me some signal that you're still there."

At the other end of the connection, Jamie Swann heard his daughter's voice through a gray fog that was tinged with red blood, his own blood racing through his body like the wave from a broken dam.

Faint yet distinct, compelling, Laurel's voice was a fixed point in Swann's disintegrating universe.

"Laurie?"

The name was slurred but unmistakable.

She felt a stab of fear mixed with hope. Swann's voice was weak, so desperately thin and faint.

"Yes, Dad. I'm here," she said loudly. "You have to help us. You have to tell us where you are."

She listened in horrified pity to the rambling, incoherent noises that poured out of her father's mouth. For an instant she was back at her mother's deathbed, listening to the last breaths of a proud woman still furious at having to quit life so soon.

But there was a difference this time. Swann seemed more conscious, more aware of the process, more able to fight against it. His strangled sounds were distinctly defiant, as if he'd managed to focus what remained of his will and energy.

"Beh . . . Behhh . . ."

The sounds were agonizing to Laurel. She pressed the receiver against her ear so hard that both her hand and head ached.

"Again, Dad. Please. Talk to me. I love you. Let me help."

"Behhh . . . Hiiil . . .

"Beverly Hills?" Laurel guessed.

The sound that came back could have meant anything.

"Beverly Hills?" she repeated loudly. "Is that where you are?"

Swann made a sound that would have been horrifying in other circumstances, but Laurel understood it. She turned and spoke urgently to Cruz.

"Beverly Hills," she said.

"It's a big town. Narrow it down."

"Where in Beverly Hills, Dad?" Laurel asked loudly. "Talk to me. Help me."

Cruz was speaking in a low yet distinct voice into the cellular. "Swann is in Beverly Hills."

"Affirmative. Still tracing."

"Dad. *Dad!*"

Cruz closed his eyes and balled his left hand into a fist. The agony in Laurel's voice was like a whip laid across his conscience. He couldn't stop remembering how she'd looked when he stepped out of the shadows after her father left.

Even worse, Cruz remembered exactly what Laurel had said.

You were here. You could have stopped him!

And Cruz's own answer, correct for getting the job done . . . savage in the context of a girl's fear for her father.

He didn't have the egg. Not in his hands. Not in the car parked down the block.

If Swann died, Cruz knew who Laurel would blame. No surprise there. Cruz would be blaming himself too.

"Come on, come on," Cruz snarled into the cellular. "We don't pay that son of a bitch at the phone company a thousand a month for nothing. Tell him a man's life is at stake."

In the background, in ragged counterpoint to Cruz's words, Laurel cried her hope and fear and love into the telephone, trying to touch her father in the only way she could.

Cruz wanted to wrap her in his arms and hold her, tell her

that everything was all right, he would take care of her. But everything wasn't all right. He shouldn't even hold her, because taking care of her meant being more ruthless and murderous than the people who were stalking her.

Gently he touched her on the shoulder.

If she noticed the silent encouragement, she didn't respond. She didn't even look at him. Everything she had was being poured into the phone.

For Cruz, listening to her was like opening a vein and feeling blood pump away, taking light and warmth with it.

Abruptly he turned and went to his black aluminum briefcase. Although the pistol was still in its loop at the small of his back, he felt uneasy. He had a better weapon in the briefcase. He pulled out the Uzi and checked it over with swift efficiency. Satisfied, he pulled a slim, pencil-beam flashlight from the case.

Flashlight in one hand, Uzi in the other, Cruz glided from room to room, snapping off lights as he went, leaving everything in darkness but the exterior grounds of the house. When the house was secure, he spoke into the cellular with clipped urgency, directing the search for Swann while checking the front yard of the house for intruders.

Nothing had changed since his last check.

Cruz went on to his next observation post, a window that gave him a view of the street and part of the driveway.

Nothing moved.

Turning swiftly, he strode to the rear of the house. In the background Laurel's voice rose and fell in a litany whose only meaning was to hold her father to life. Distantly Cruz wondered what it would be like to be loved like that, no holds barred, nothing held back, just an emotion as complex, powerful, and unquenchable as the sun.

At the end, when all else had been stripped away, it had

been love that ruled Swann, love that had driven him to give Laurel a chance to live. Swann had seen men die close up. He'd killed. He must have known how close to death he was himself, yet he'd used the last of his strength to warn his daughter rather than calling to get help for himself.

I salute you, Jamie Swann, Cruz thought. *I hope when my time comes I have half your guts.*

It was still outside the house, nothing moving, not even the wind. All the security lights in the yard were working. All lights in the house were off.

"Anything yet?" Cruz growled into the cellular.

"Still tracing."

"Shit!"

He went to stand by Laurel. In the vague illumination of the exterior floodlights, her skin was ghostly and her eyes were black.

"Dad, you have to help me," she said hoarsely. "Where exactly are you?"

Her hand wrapped around Cruz's wrist. Against her icy fingers, his skin burned with life. The sheer animal heat of him went through her in a shock wave, heightening each one of her senses.

The noises her father was making were ghastly. She listened as if they were beautiful, vibrating with the intensity of her concentration.

" 'Hotel'?" she asked suddenly. "Are you trying to say 'hotel'?"

A rasping, gurgling noise was Swann's answer.

She'd learned that sound meant agreement. "Which hotel, Dad? There are so many."

Hoarse, erratic breathing was Swann's only reply.

Frantically Laurel searched her memory for the names

of hotels in the area. Only one came. "The Beverly Hills Hotel?"

A harsh grunt came. Negative.

Cruz leaned forward and spoke loudly into the phone. "The Beverly Wilshire?"

The sound of agreement was faint but understandable.

"It's the Beverly Wilshire," she said to Cruz. "What room, Dad?"

The rasping, strangling breathing seemed fainter.

"Beverly Wilshire hotel," Cruz said into his cell phone. "I'm calling in the police." He rang off and punched the emergency number into his cellular. As soon as someone picked up, he said, "Get me the duty commander."

His tone was clipped, aggressive, confident. The person on the other end responded automatically. In ten seconds Cruz was talking to the police lieutenant who was in charge of emergency services.

"Dad, help is coming," Laurel said into the phone. "Hang on. We'll be with you soon."

She repeated the message again and again.

There was no answer.

"Hurry," she said hoarsely to Cruz. "He's not talking anymore."

"It's poison, maybe something very exotic," Cruz said into the cell phone. "Roll paramedics. Get a link immediately with UCLA Medical Center's emergency room."

With half of her attention, Laurel listened to Cruz explain the situation and request aid. She prayed no one would argue or demand more explanations.

"I have a few contacts in FBI Forensics who may have some ideas," Cruz said, "but they'll need physiological data and symptoms to work with."

She watched Cruz with haunted eyes. Tears flowed silently down her cheeks. She didn't even feel them.

"Yes, I'll handle that and get back to you," Cruz said. "It takes too much time to explain."

He rang off and began punching in more numbers, a special sequence that would put him through to Cassandra Redpath's personal phone.

"Are they—" began Laurel.

"They're rolling right now."

Redpath picked up on the first ring.

"This is Cruz. I'm in the clear. Laurel is safe. Swann is down but not out. Medics are on the way."

"What do you need?" Redpath asked.

"Forensics," he said succinctly. "We need the best database on poisons in the world and we need it now."

"You'll have it. Any way to narrow the possibilities?"

"Given the players, start with exotic synthetics, Soviet style. Ricin, maybe. Something that would mimic a heart attack."

"Hold."

He turned to Laurel. "Keep talking to him, honey. Take the flashlight and read the phone book to him if you have to. *Keep him with us.*"

53

Los Angeles
Wednesday night

Laurel talked into the phone without stopping, drawing from her well of favorite childhood memories, sharing them with her father like shiny agates plucked from a beach where storm waves raged.

Hearing her tore at Cruz until he could barely breathe.

"Repeat," he said to Redpath.

"Three chemists. One of them used to do a lot of work for Langley."

"Call in a favor. We're on a terminally short clock at this end."

"Understood."

While Laurel's voice rose and fell in vivid memory, Cruz gave Redpath the phone number of the Beverly Hills police lieutenant he'd talked to.

"If your chemist has any bright ideas," Cruz said, "the lieutenant has a direct radio link to the paramedics in the hotel."

"Anything else?" Redpath asked.

"How are you at prayer?"

"Better than you might think."

"Then go down on your knees. There's too much riding on this to let pride get in the way."

Cruz broke the connection, pocketed the phone, and reached around to the small of his back for his pistol. He pulled it out and put it on the table next to the telephone Laurel was using.

"It's cocked and ready to go," Cruz said in a soft voice. "The safety is on. If you see anyone but me, shoot."

She shifted the telephone receiver to her left ear. She didn't pick up the gun. She just put her hand on it, ready to lift it at the first sign of trouble.

"I'm going to check the yard," he murmured. "I'll come back in through the kitchen and I'll make a lot of noise. Got it?"

Without breaking the flow of her words, she nodded. "Dad, Dad, listen to my voice, hold on to it. You did what you had to do. You warned me. Now let us help you. Stay with me, Dad. Help is coming."

No answer came but the faint, ragged sound of Swann's breathing.

It was the only answer Laurel needed. It told her that he was still alive.

For what seemed like an eternity she kept repeating her childhood memories, her hope, and her love. In between phrases, she listened to the sounds at the other end of the line.

They were fainter, farther apart, fading.

"Daddy, don't leave me."

Suddenly she heard a muffled crash, followed by the harsh sound of voices. Then came the clipped, near-code words of paramedics hard at work. The voices were quickly replaced by a woman speaking into the phone.

"This is the fire department. We have the patient now. Who am I talking to?"

"His daughter. Is he still alive?"

"Yes," the paramedic said. "We're taking him to the UCLA emergency room."

There was a curt order, an urgent request for aid.

The woman hung up, leaving Laurel alone. She fought off a rising sense of panic and fear. Her eyes filled with tears as bitter as poison.

"Laurel. I'm coming in."

The soft, low voice was Cruz's. It carried no farther than her ears.

"Dad is—"

"Quiet," Cruz cut in.

Fear washed coolly over her. She'd heard that tone of voice from him only once before, when assassins had fled out into the night and he'd waited, listening for them to return.

"All right," he said when he was within inches of her. "Your father?"

"Still alive when the paramedics came."

She tried to pitch her voice as softly as his. It was nearly impossible. Her throat was raw from tension and fear and talking to a father who was dying.

Cruz started to speak, then hesitated, looking at her in a way he hadn't before.

"What's wrong?" she asked.

"You didn't pull the trigger on me back in Cambria. Will you pull the trigger on someone to save your own life?"

"Dad asked me the same thing when he gave me the gun."

"What did you tell him?"

"Yes."

"Still feel that way?" Cruz pressed.

She thought of her father, dying. "Yes."

"Then pick up the pistol and come with me. Quietly."

He led her to the front room of the house.

"Take a peek," he said. "But don't touch the shutters. Don't even brush against them."

Carefully she leaned forward and looked through the crack. She saw nothing but her own tears. It was the first time she'd been aware of them. Impatiently she brushed them aside and leaned forward again. All she saw was an unhappy neighbor across the street.

The man was dressed in shirtsleeves and slacks. A dog leash dangled from his left hand. The dog was nowhere in sight. The man seemed to be studying the front of Laurel's house like he was expecting the dog to be rooting around in the plants. He looked in all the bushes and shadows and halfway into either neighbor's yard. Every so often he whistled, low and careful, a man who didn't want to disturb anyone but still had to find his dog.

"Come on, Charley. Where are you? Come to papa, you little black bastard. I've got a juicy bone for you. Here, Charley. Here, Charley. Mama is going to put both of us in the doghouse if you don't come back. Here, Charley. Here, boy."

Laurel stepped back from the window. "All I see is a man looking for his dog. Is that a problem?"

"What you see is a professional at work."

"What do you mean?"

"It's called the 'Lost-Dog Cover.' It's a classic surveillance technique. They teach it at the FBI Academy and probably at every other school like it around the world."

"Is he from the FBI?" she asked.

"He looks faintly familiar, but that's one of the reasons I left the FBI. We all began to look alike."

Laurel smiled and took a quick breath that could have been a laugh or a sob.

"I suppose he could be FBI," Cruz said. "But I'd just as soon not make any serious mistakes. Assume a shooting posture."

Puzzled, she did as he asked. In the faint light from the front yard, her motions were smooth, assured. The pistol didn't waver in her grip.

He let out a soft, relieved breath. "You inherited your daddy's nerve. Thank God."

Cruz bent over, opened the black aluminum briefcase that had never been far from him, and reached inside. He pulled out the Uzi, checked it with swift efficiency, and began shrugging out of his jacket.

Silently she watched while he took some kind of harness from the case, jerked it on, and used it to support the vicious-looking weapon. He put his lightweight jacket back on, leaving it open.

"What is that?" she whispered, pointing at the weapon.

"Illegal." He reached back into the case and brought out a little two-shot derringer. "Know how to use one of these?"

"What do you have in there, an arsenal?"

"I'll tell Gillie that you approved."

She looked at the little weapon in Cruz's hand and said tightly, "Dad told me how to use one of them."

"Yeah? What did he say?"

She took a quick, unhappy breath. "He said, 'Screw it into the guy's ear and pull the trigger.'"

"That's a good method." Cruz took his pistol from her, giving her the derringer instead. "It's loaded and the safety is on. Show me you know how to take it off."

She took the derringer. After a bit of fumbling, she worked the safety.

"Okay. You're good to go," he said. "Shove the purse pistol underneath your tunic."

Awkwardly Laurel put the derringer muzzle first into the waistband of her jeans and pulled the tunic top over it.

Before taking off the safety, he checked over his own pistol with unconscious, automatic motions.

For the first time Laurel noticed that Cruz's pistol had a Day-Glo dot on its sight, just as hers did. It was the kind of pistol he'd called a blow-your-head-off gun.

He handled it as easily as a ballpoint pen.

"Come on," Cruz said.

"What are we going to do?"

"If that guy is FBI, no problem."

"If he isn't?"

"Don't drink anything he offers you. Let's go."

Without hesitation Laurel followed Cruz into the darkness.

54

From the cover of landscaping just inside the gate, Cruz watched the Lost Dog pantomime. Empty leash in hand, the man stalked once more up the dead-end street past the old house and called to the chaparral beyond.

He was good. Anyone watching would expect man's best friend to appear at any moment with long tongue and wagging tail.

Silently Cruz admired the act. The man's eyes were always looking, never still, probing the landscaping to locate the house's entrances, plotting a good tactical approach, assessing dangers; and all the while he was calling to a dog that didn't exist.

With every step the man made, every motion, every turn, the muzzle of Cruz's pistol tracked the actor's head like radar. Cruz's finger was on the trigger. All the slack was gone. The smallest pressure would make the gun fire.

Laurel stepped up to the gate. As she'd been instructed, she stayed to the left side, leaving a clear field of fire for Cruz.

"Oh, good, you're still here," she said to the man in a normal tone of voice. "I was afraid I'd missed you. Your dog is in my backyard."

The man's jaw dropped. "Er, I don't think so."

"Is it small?"

"Ah . . ."

"Black?"

"Um . . ."

"Answers to Charley?"

"Er . . ."

"You *have* lost a dog, haven't you?" she asked suspiciously.

"Oh, yeah. Sure."

She opened the gate with quick, jerky motions that could have been impatience.

"Well, come and get the damned thing," she said in a clipped voice. "He's digging up my pansies."

Automatically the man stepped toward the open gate, ducking to avoid a bit of hanging greenery.

"Keep your hands in sight," Cruz said from the side.

The man jerked upright.

Laurel turned and ran.

Cruz was concealed in greenery made black by night, but the deadly glint of the pistol and the Day-Glo sight was unmistakable. The man went completely still.

"Laurel?" Cruz asked softly.

"Ready."

Her voice came from farther up the path. She was hidden in shadows, well beyond the reach of any lunge the man could make.

"Walk through the gate," Cruz said in a low, flat voice. "Close it behind you. Do it slowly. Don't trip. Don't stumble.

Don't hesitate. Smooth and easy or dead on arrival. Your choice."

The man moved slowly, carefully, up the walk.

"Call to your dog again," Cruz ordered softly.

"What the—"

"Do it."

"Charley. Is that you, boy?"

The man's voice sounded strained, but not enough to alert any backup that might be waiting for him somewhere on the quiet residential street.

The instant they were out of sight of the street, Cruz emerged from cover. He was beyond the man's reach, but the man was never beyond reach of Cruz's gun.

"Move," Cruz said. "Your backup can't see you. They can't help you."

"You're making a—"

"Shut up."

The man swallowed and didn't say a word.

"We're coming in," Cruz called in a low voice.

"I'll be just inside." Her voice was soft, confident.

When they reached the flagstone patio, Cruz spoke curtly to his prisoner. "On your face. Feet spread. Hands on the top of your head."

"Hey, who the hell do—"

"Facedown. *Now.*"

Reluctantly the man did as he was ordered.

Cruz jammed the muzzle of the pistol just beneath the shelf of the man's skull at the back of his head. Then Cruz frisked him with an efficiency that didn't include modesty. He missed none of the ordinary hiding places and probed some unusual ones as well.

"Nine-millimeter," Cruz said, taking the man's gun from

its holster and putting it into the back of his own waistband. "Billy club. Pocketknife. Pager. Wallet."

The man said nothing.

One-handed, Cruz flipped open the wallet. The driver's license was in a plastic window.

"Name," Cruz said.

"Fuck you."

Cruz leaned on the pistol muzzle. Hard. "Try again. Name."

"William R. Cahill," the man said between his teeth.

"All right, Billy-Bob. Who are you working for?"

"The FBI."

"Where's your shield?"

"I left it at home."

"If you were still working for the Bureau, the director would have your balls for that. But I don't think you're still federal. You're somebody's private gun."

Cahill muttered something beneath his breath.

Swiftly Cruz straightened and stepped back beyond Cahill's reach.

"Get up slowly," Cruz said. "Walk through that back door. Don't get cute, or the woman will blow you right out of your wing-tip shoes and enjoy doing it. She's real pissed off right now, after what you did to her daddy and all."

"All I did was hit him a couple of times," Cahill said as he got to his feet.

"No problem, then. She'll only shoot you a couple of times. Start walking."

"How'd you get on to me?" Cahill asked.

"I learned the Lost Dog surveillance trick at Quantico too," Cruz said dryly.

Cahill stopped and stared over his shoulder at Cruz.

"You? You're with the Bureau?" Cahill asked. "Wait a

minute. I know you, don't I? You're Cruz Rowan. You were with HRT."

Confident he'd just uttered a special password by mentioning the Hostage Rescue Team, Cahill began to lower his hands.

"Up," Cruz said curtly. "On top of your head."

"But I'm—" Cahill began indignantly.

"Go inside."

With a muttered curse, Cahill walked into the house.

Laurel was nowhere in sight.

"Sit on the kitchen floor," Cruz said. "Cross your legs and keep your hands on your head."

"Look, this isn't necessary."

"Fine, I'll just shoot you."

Cahill sat, crossed his legs, and kept his hands on his head.

"Laurel, come on back," Cruz said.

She walked in from the living room, circled Cahill widely, and stood next to Cruz. Not once did she get in his field of fire.

"Good job, honey," Cruz said. "There's a nine-millimeter in the small of my back. Get it. Keep Cahill covered."

"Is that an Uzi?" Cahill asked, peering into the shadows beneath Cruz's open jacket.

Cruz didn't answer. He felt the weight of Cahill's weapon being removed from his belt. Then he heard the familiar sound of the safety coming off.

"That gun is a long hard pull the first time you fire," Cruz said to her. "The second time it's quicker."

"Like Dad's."

"Wouldn't surprise me."

Cahill's expression said that having a gun held on him by Laurel was more nerve-racking than being under the gun of a highly trained professional. Nothing upset a pro like an amateur gun handler.

Cruz smiled. He'd counted on just that reaction.

"If he moves," Cruz said to Laurel, "shoot him. Don't warn him, don't shout for me. Just shoot and keep shooting until he stops moving."

Grimly she nodded.

Cruz swiftly did a circuit of his lookout points. The street was quiet. No one called for a missing dog or for the dog's missing owner. No cars cruised by slowly with lights out.

Christ, Cruz said silently to himself. *Where the hell is Gillie? He's had enough time to get here and build a bloody security perimeter around the whole place.*

Cruz looked out again.

Nothing had changed.

Silently cursing whatever was holding Gillespie up, Cruz went back to the kitchen.

"I'll take it from here," he said to Laurel.

With a hidden breath of relief, she lowered the pistol.

Cahill hadn't moved.

"We're a little jumpy here," Cruz said to Cahill, "so don't get cute. Who are you working for?"

"I was with the Bureau for twenty years. Then I punched out. Now I work for Damon Hudson of Hudson International."

"Doing what?"

"Security."

"Why were you doing a recon on this house for Hudson?"

"I—uh, I'm trying to get a line on a piece of art that was stolen."

Cruz's expression didn't change one bit. "From Hudson's museum?"

"Not exactly," Cahill said. "It was stolen from the Russian exhibition that's supposed to open day after tomorrow."

"Nice of Hudson to turn his resources over to the Russians in their time of need," Cruz said blandly.

"Yeah. Mr. Hudson is a real nice guy."

"Why were you looking around here? This isn't exactly an art gallery."

"Jamie Swann stole the piece," Cahill said, glancing at Laurel. "Ms. Toth said it wasn't in Cambria, so we figured it was here."

"Toth?" Cruz asked sharply. "Claire Toth?"

"Yeah. Swann's partner. At least she was. Now she's in bed with Hudson. She's a real piece of work, that one. Never seen an ass like that."

For a few moments Cruz said nothing. He shouldn't have been surprised to find Claire Toth crossing his path again, but he was.

"Swann's partner, huh?" Cruz said. "That poor son of a bitch. It would be like getting in bed with a cross between a chainsaw and a public toilet."

"For that ass it might be worth it."

"No ass is worth it," Cruz said. "Especially hers."

Listening, Laurel had to suppress a shiver. The casual loathing in Cruz's voice was worse than any insult put into words.

"What is this piece of art that's gone missing?" Cruz asked casually. "The *Mona Lisa*?"

"It's some kind of diamond-studded Easter egg with a big ruby inside," Cahill said. "Fabergé."

That came as no surprise to Cruz and Laurel, but they were careful not to show it.

"Who came with you tonight?" Cruz asked.

"Nobody."

"Wrong answer. And you've been so good about telling the truth up to now. I had real hope for you. Who came with you?"

Silently Cahill reviewed his options. None of them were particularly promising, and Cruz knew it as well as Cahill did.

"I thought you meant backup," Cahill said after a moment. "I don't have any."

"Dumb, Billy-Bob. Really dumb. I saw a car at the head of the street."

Cahill laughed curtly. "That's just Hudson. He really wants the egg back. If you know anything about it, he'll make it worth your while."

"He'll have to stand in line. What about you?"

"What do you mean?"

"Is Hudson making it worth your while to take a first-degree murder rap for him?"

Laurel's breath came in sharply.

Cahill didn't notice. The shock on his face was as clear as the hands on his head. "What the hell are you talking about?"

"Jamie Swann."

"I swear to Christ, all I did was tap him with the billy."

"Then you fed him poison."

Cahill's skin went pale. Sweat appeared on his forehead and upper lip. "No. I didn't do anything like that. Okay, so I've skated over the edge a time or two in helping Hudson, but nothing like that."

Watching Cahill, Cruz was inclined to believe it. But he wasn't inclined to let Cahill know it. Scared men were more cooperative.

"If you didn't do it," Cruz said carelessly, "who did?"

Cahill opened his mouth, then shut it.

Cruz waited.

"How the hell do I know you're telling the truth?" Cahill asked after a moment.

"Call the UCLA Medical Center. They got Swann about twenty minutes ago. He was dead."

Laurel made a small sound but said nothing. She'd promised Cruz that she would be quiet and follow his lead. But hearing him speak so confidently of her father's death was like being hit by a fist.

"Jesus, Joseph, and Mary," Cahill whispered. "They must have done it when I went out to get the limo."

"That's what you say. What do you think Hudson will say?"

Fear and anger warred for control of Bill Cahill's mind. He was lip-deep in a cesspool that had no bottom and he was sinking fast. He knew it.

Even worse, Cruz knew it.

"Whose version of the truth do you think Toth will support?" Cruz asked, smiling thinly. "Who's the billionaire in this trio, and who's the great body, and who's the perfect fall guy?"

There was silence while Cahill sat cross-legged on the cold floor, hands on his head, calculating his chances of surviving an alliance of Hudson and Toth against him. It didn't take much thinking, because there weren't any chances worth measuring.

"What do you want me to do?" Cahill said wearily.

55

Cruz waited long enough before responding to make Cahill swallow hard and sweat harder.

"Is there a phone in the limo?" Cruz asked.

Cahill nodded.

"Get up slowly," Cruz said. "Call Hudson. Tell him you have Laurel and me tied up, but we won't tell you where the ruby is."

Cahill wished it was true. But it wasn't. So he got up very slowly, careful not to make any move that would get him shot.

He had no doubt that Cruz would shoot.

"Tell Hudson there was a message from Novikov on our answering machine," Cruz said, watching intently. "He congratulated us on recovering the ruby, and told us he'll be by the house to pick it up in an hour. That gives you less than an hour to tear the place apart and find the ruby. You need Hudson and Toth's help."

"What if they won't come?"

"Then I'll do it the hard way. Either way it will get done."

Cahill didn't doubt it. Years ago Cruz had proven once and for all time, in front of millions of witnesses, that he was a ruthless man.

"Where's the phone?" Cahill asked.

"On the wall behind you. And remember—Hudson isn't worth dying for."

"Shit," Cahill said, disgusted, "he isn't even worth working for."

While the prisoner stood and punched in the limousine's cellular number, Cruz signaled Laurel to come to his side.

"Mr. Hudson?" Cahill said. "I'm inside and in control of the situation."

He paused to listen.

"No, Rowan didn't give me any problem," Cahill said, shooting a sideways glance at Cruz. "Most men are reasonable when they're looking into the muzzle of a gun."

Pause.

"The ruby? Uh, well, that's a problem. There was a message from Novikov on Ms. Swann's answering machine. He's coming by within the hour to pick it up."

Hudson's response made Cahill's mouth curve into a nasty smile.

"Yeah, I thought you'd feel that way," Cahill said. "But neither Ms. Swann nor Rowan is talking about where they hid it. If you and Ms. Toth want to help me, I figure we have three times as good a chance as if I was tearing the place apart on my own."

Cahill listened.

"Sorry, Mr. Hudson, no can do," Cahill said. "You want Ms. Swann slapped around, you take care of it yourself."

A few moments later, Cahill hung up the phone and turned to face Cruz. "They're on the way."

"Laurel," Cruz said, "watch the walk through the front shutters. Remember, don't—"

"Move them at all. I remember."

As soon as she was out of the room, Cruz looked at Cahill.

"I'd like to trust you," Cruz said, "but I'm paranoid about Laurel's safety. So turn around and put your hands behind your back, wrists together."

"Hell."

Cahill turned around and put his hands behind his back, wrists together. An instant later, Cruz slapped on tight plastic restraints.

"Straddle this and sit," Cruz said, turning a kitchen chair toward the other man.

Cahill straddled and sat.

Cruz turned and started for the back door.

"What, no gag?" Cahill asked sarcastically.

"If you want to sing out a warning and bring a murder-one charge down on your head, I'm not going to stop you. If you want to get up and walk out of the kitchen and get shot, I'm not going to stop that either."

Hoping with each step to hear Gillespie's special signal floating up from the underbrush, Cruz went out the back door and down the walk to the driveway. What he heard was Hudson and Toth coming up the path from the street. They walked right up to the front door and knocked.

Cruz took the steps behind them like a big ghost.

"Open it up, Laurel," he said.

Hudson and Toth made startled sounds and spun around. The Uzi's blunt promise of violence stared back at them.

"One at a time," Cruz said. "Hudson, you go first."

"Now see here—" Hudson began.

"Shut up. Get inside. You first."

Hudson looked for a long moment at Cruz, then turned and went into the house.

"Now you," Cruz said to Toth.

"Jesus, is that you, Rowan?"

"Yeah. Walk."

"Damn. Nobody has a voice like you, babe. Makes me hot just listening to you."

"Get inside."

Once inside, Cruz frisked Hudson thoroughly. He wasn't armed.

When Cruz turned to Toth, she smiled and put her hands behind her head. The action parted her stylish silk jacket and thrust her breasts against the thin silk of her blouse.

"I'm ready if you are," she said in a throaty voice.

Shocked, Laurel watched from the back of the room. Toth moved sinuously beneath Cruz's hands, turning a routine pat-down into frank sexual foreplay.

"A little lower, babe," Toth said, smiling. "Ah, that's it. Now harder. *Harder.*"

Cruz schooled his face to show nothing as his hands went over Toth's spectacular body. He didn't back off until he was certain she wasn't carrying any weapon she hadn't been born with.

"That wasn't bad, babe," Toth said huskily. "Want me to do the same for you?"

Cruz turned to Hudson. The older man was standing still, watching, thinking very hard.

"Do you have the ruby?" Hudson asked bluntly.

"Do you have the egg?" Cruz asked.

"Yes."

"We have the ruby."

"I was going to pay Ms. Toth three million for the ruby. I'll pay you four."

"Why?"

"I want my exhibit to be a success."

"Yeah. Right. Why didn't I think of that?" Cruz turned to Toth. "What about you?"

"Jamie blackmailed me into helping him steal the egg."

"Is that why you killed him?"

"What are you talking about?" she asked, her black eyes wary.

"Poison."

"Not me, babe. Uh-uh. Jamie was the best I ever had. That man could go all night and be the first one up in the morning. Studs like that are hard to find."

Cruz grunted and turned to Hudson.

"What about you?" Cruz asked. "Did you poison him?"

"Has he been poisoned?" Hudson asked calmly.

"Yes or no."

"Five million."

Cruz ignored him.

"Six," Hudson said.

The temptation to backhand Hudson was so great that it shocked Cruz. It told him how furious he was.

On the other hand, knocking Hudson out would limit the number of people Cruz had to watch. If all three got smart and jumped Laurel at the same time, he wouldn't be able to shoot for fear of hitting her.

Christ, Gillie. Where are you?

"Laurel," Cruz said, his voice harsh.

She jumped as if he'd flicked her with a whip.

"Go watch the back door," Cruz said. "I'm expecting the sergeant-major, so don't shoot until you know who it is."

When she walked out of the room, Cruz breathed a silent sigh of relief.

"Sit on the floor," Cruz told Hudson and Toth.

"Listen, young man—" Hudson began.

"Sit down or get knocked down."

Hudson sat.

Toth was already sitting. She was a much better judge of male anger than Hudson was.

"Listen up, gang," Cruz said. "You're all nominated for grand theft and first-degree murder. But all of you don't have to hang. One of you can get off absolutely free. All you have to do is give me the egg and tell me who poisoned Jamie Swann."

"Don't listen to him," Hudson said quickly. "He doesn't have any evidence or he wouldn't be doing this."

"What about you two?" Cruz asked, looking from Toth to Cahill. "You don't have billions to buy your way out. All you have is the egg and the knowledge of who killed Jamie Swann."

"I didn't do it," Cahill said. "I'll swear to that in any court in the land."

"He's lying," Toth said. "He was the one who knocked poor Jamie senseless. If Jamie is dead, it's his fault, not mine."

"What about the egg?" Cruz asked Toth. "Where is it?"

"Last I knew, Jamie had it."

Cruz made a disgusted sound. "What about you, Cahill? Can you give me the egg?"

"I—" Cahill began.

"Cruz!" Laurel called from the kitchen.

"Not now, honey."

"She really does not have a choice," Novikov said.

56

Los Angeles
Wednesday night

Cruz spun and brought Novikov under his gun.

Pushing Laurel ahead of him, the Russian walked into the room. In one hand was an automatic pistol. In the other was a fistful of Laurel's black hair. The muzzle of the pistol was jammed up beneath her jaw. It was a very professional hold.

"Let her go," Cruz said.

"Drop your gun," was Novikov's answer.

"No. You'd kill us anyway." Cruz looked at Laurel. "Take a deep breath, honey. You look like you're going to faint," he said, stressing the last word slightly. "You okay?"

As she looked into the pale, crystalline blue of Cruz's eyes, her breath stopped. The focused intensity of him was almost tangible.

Faint.

Abruptly her knees buckled and she went down toward the floor like a stone. The movement dragged Novikov off balance. Her foot hooked around one of his ankles and finished the job.

Fighting for balance, Novikov flung up his arms. The gun muzzle jerked away from her jaw.

Cruz fired even as he lunged forward. The bullet shattered Novikov's right wrist and sent the gun spinning away. Before it landed, Cruz's foot lashed out, connecting with Novikov's jaw.

The Russian hit the floor and didn't move.

Cruz didn't bother to check on him. He knew precisely what his kick had done.

He spun around to cover Hudson, Toth, and Cahill. No one had moved. Hudson and Toth looked stunned. Cahill looked very wary.

"Laurel?" Cruz asked, not looking away from the three captives. "Are you all right?"

"I'm—okay."

Laurel forced herself to take a deep breath, then another. It had been very easy to fake a fainting spell. She'd been close to the edge anyway.

"Can you stand up?" Cruz asked.

"Y-yes." Her voice trembled, but she stood up without help.

"Get Novikov's gun and stand with your back to mine," Cruz said. "Novikov's bodyguard is still out there somewhere."

Laurel picked up the Russian's gun and looked over at the boneless sprawl of his body. Quickly she looked away. She took up a position with her back to Cruz and forced herself to focus on the pistol Novikov had used.

The safety was off. The gun was cocked.

"Nine-millimeter," she said. "Just like yours."

"Is it good to go?"

"Yes, the— *Cruz, there's somebody by the front door.*"

There was a startled grunt, a thump, and a crash from the front of the house. Then an odd four-note whistle came through the darkness.

"Don't shoot," Cruz said. "It's Gillespie. Come on in, Sergeant-Major. It's about goddamn time you got here."

A moment later Gillespie walked into the room. He had an automatic pistol in one big hand and Gapan's limp body thrown over his shoulder.

"Found him lying back in the shadows," Gillespie said, dumping the bodyguard onto the floor.

"Probably waiting for me to get the ruby and the egg together," Cruz said.

"It would be the smart thing to do," Gillespie agreed. "Ms. Swann, if you like, I'll take over now."

Laurel looked up, way up, into Gillespie's beautifully sculpted features.

"Thank you," she said, lowering her weary arms and flicking the safety on in the same motion. "I wasn't cut out for this."

"Could have fooled me," Gillespie said, smiling.

Cruz smiled too, but the muzzle of his gun never wavered.

"Who's the black beauty?" Toth asked, looking Gillespie over from head to toe and back.

"Shut up," Cruz said. "The next person who talks without permission gets what Novikov did."

Silence.

Gillespie went and stood behind the three conscious prisoners. Each of them was within reach of his big hands.

"We're ready for you, Ambassador," Gillespie said.

Ambassador Redpath walked into the room and stood beside the sergeant-major. She carried a sleek, deadly-looking pistol, muzzle down, along the side of her leg. She glanced around the room, frowned at Novikov's body, and turned to Cruz.

"Is Aleksy dead?" she asked.

"Doubt it. I try not to kill clients before they pay the bill."

Redpath smiled slightly. "The egg?"

"Hudson and Toth say Swann has it. They're lying. One of them has it stashed somewhere."

"What about him?" she asked, gesturing to Cahill.

"He says he doesn't have it. I believe him."

"The ruby?" Redpath asked.

"I have it."

"Excellent," she murmured.

Redpath put the safety on her weapon, looked at the three prisoners, and smiled like a shark. "Let the negotiations begin."

57

Karroo
Four weeks later
Thursday afternoon

With shuttered eyes, Laurel Swann looked around Cassandra Redpath's office. Nothing had changed since she'd last been to Karroo. The office was still filled with rare intellectual treasures. The desert sun was still hot. And she was still trying to understand why she'd been drawn to Cruz Rowan as she had never been drawn to any man.

Too bad it hadn't been mutual.

But life was an unpredictable bitch. If Laurel had learned nothing else in the past month, she'd learned that.

"Ms. Swann," Redpath said, rising graciously from behind her desk. "It was good of you to come all the way here."

Laurel's smile was bittersweet. "Your invitation was irresistible, Ambassador. I've been curious to know how it all turned out."

What she didn't say was that she hungered to see Cruz Rowan again, if only for a moment. She wanted to know if the shadows in his eyes were the same as hers. She wanted to know if he dreamed of water hidden within a rocky canyon. She wanted to know if he'd discovered the agonizing difference between alone and lonely.

She doubted that he had, but she had to be certain.

If she was certain, maybe she would stop seeing his face, stop hearing his voice, stop remembering what it had been like to be with a man who expanded her possibilities as a woman rather than limiting them. She already had part of an answer to her questions. She didn't like it, but she accepted it because there wasn't any way to hide from it.

Cruz hadn't been on the plane that picked Laurel up.

He hadn't been waiting at the private strip to take her to the compound.

If he was anywhere in Karroo, he hadn't bothered to walk a few yards and say hello.

Which meant he hadn't missed her. Not really. Not the way she'd missed him, like having part of her body cut away.

Maybe he's out saving some other woman's life, Laurel thought, *then giving that life back to her and leaving without a word, taking her heart with him and not giving a damn.*

"Please sit down," Redpath said softly. "You look . . . different."

Laurel shrugged at the diplomatic tact. She knew that she looked different. Older. More wary. Colder.

More like her father.

"No surprise there," Laurel said. "One way or another, it's been a hell of a month."

"For all of us," Redpath muttered under her breath.

"I beg your pardon?"

"No matter. Do sit down, Laurel. I have the feeling you're going to vanish without notice."

Laurel's smile was like her eyes. Distant. But she sat down.

"You don't look a bit different," she said to Redpath. "Obviously you've found your stable center in the whirlpool of life."

"That stable point isn't mine alone."

"I didn't think it was. How is the sergeant-major? Still drop-dead handsome?"

"Oh, yes." Redpath smiled. "Would you care for something to drink?"

"No, thank you. When your invitation came, I wondered if I should accept it. Now I know. It was a mistake. The sooner I leave Karroo, the better off I'll be."

"Why?"

"Don't pretend ignorance," Laurel said evenly. "I've seen you in action. So tell me, Ambassador, what happened after Cruz drove me to the emergency room to check on Dad?"

And left me there, Laurel added silently, bitterly. *Not a word. Not a glance. Not even a wave.*

"I thought Cruz might have kept you informed."

"He might have. He didn't. I kept hoping to see something in the newspapers, but all I found were bits and pieces."

"Such as?" Redpath asked, curious.

"Oh, such as a story buried way back in the *Los Angeles Times* about two Russian visitors named Aleksy Novikov and Georgi Gapan being mugged in big bad Hollywood. One broken wrist and two mild concussions."

"They were fortunate," Redpath said blandly. "City streets have become quite dangerous these days."

"Then there was the card in front of the Ruby Surprise's empty case at the Hudson Museum exhibit."

"I didn't attend."

"Then you wouldn't know that the egg was damaged in

shipment from Tokyo," Laurel said dryly. "During the repair, it was discovered that the piece was probably a fraud rather than a Fabergé and therefore was withdrawn from the show."

"Sad. One wonders what the world is coming to."

"This one wonders in particular what happened to Damon Hudson and that . . . creature."

"Claire Toth?"

Laurel nodded curtly.

"I'm afraid Mr. Hudson's health has taken a dramatic turn for the worse," Redpath said. "It's to be expected in a man of his age, I suppose."

"His age? He looked the same age as my father."

"Unfortunately, he was taking some illegal, highly experimental rejuvenation treatments. They worked rather spectacularly for a time. Then he developed an allergy to the drugs."

"When?"

"About a month ago."

"Really," Laurel said. "Remarkable."

Redpath made a murmuring sound of agreement that was suspiciously close to a purr. "The doctors are fascinated by Hudson's withdrawal symptoms. His body is quite literally aging before their eyes, like a match being consumed by an invisible flame. They expect the process to go to completion rather soon."

"Completion?"

"Death."

Laurel took a deep breath and let it out softly. "I see. And the creature that poisoned my father?"

"Ah, yes, the spectacular Ms. Toth." Redpath glanced at the complex, worldwide clock which was one of the few modern features of her office. "As we speak, Ms. Toth is crossing the terminator into darkness."

Laurel looked at the glowing line separating night from

day on the clock. The line was sweeping slowly, majestically, from east to west across Europe.

"I don't understand," Laurel said.

"Some unforgiving soul sent a complete dossier of Ms. Toth's activities as an unregistered agent of a foreign government—"

"A spy?"

"In a word, yes. Every major newspaper in the world received the dossier. It was translated where appropriate, of course. Excellent translations, if I do say so myself."

Laurel looked around the office with its racks and rows and display cases of books in every major language on earth. She didn't doubt that every treacherous nuance of Toth's career had survived all the various translations.

"That 'unforgiving soul' has my gratitude," Laurel said. "Too bad the murderous bitch wasn't taking those rejuvenation treatments."

"Perhaps. Perhaps not. The older you get, the more you realize there are worse things than death."

"For instance?"

"Eating ice cubes in a Siberian gulag for the rest of your miserable life."

Laurel turned swiftly to the map. The glowing, golden-orange line of the terminator had moved on, leaving Siberia in the blue-black zone of night.

"How did you get Toth on the plane?" Laurel asked.

"Aleksy took care of that little matter for us. It was your father's idea."

"Dad? I didn't know that. But then"—she smiled thinly—"I know very little about my father."

"He knew Ms. Toth better than any man. He knew exactly what she would hate the most."

"He was more generous to her than I would have been. I would have put her on death row for what she did to him."

"Actually, Jamie was planning to kill her for what she'd done to you," Redpath said. "But I pointed out the limitations of that approach. The publicity, for one. A jail cell, for another. He finally agreed."

"You talked Dad out of something? I'm impressed. How did you do it?"

"I simply asked him to design a particular, personalized hell for Ms. Toth. He did. Mr. Gapan located it and sent her there."

Laurel was almost afraid to ask, but curiosity got the better of her. "What is Ms. Toth's personal and private hell?"

"A life sentence in a gulag where the ground never thaws, the cells are heated by burning manure mixed with straw, and the other inmates are homosexual males or pederasts. Every single one of them."

Silence followed Redpath's words.

Then Laurel let out a long sigh. "May she have a long, wretched life."

"Amen," the ambassador said quietly. "How is your father, by the way?"

"Much better. They expect a nearly full recovery. He'll never be as strong as he was, but he'll be able to lead a normal life."

"Excellent. Is he considering my offer of employment?"

"He didn't say anything about it." Laurel closed her eyes for a moment. *How like him. Always another secret up his sleeve.*

"That's what I appreciate about your father. A man of many secrets, all of them worth keeping."

"I'll take your word for it." Laurel's voice was clipped,

her eyes restless as they measured the room. "Was Gapan in on this from the start? Is that why he helped you?"

"Is that what your father said?"

"No. It's what you said. My father designed Toth's hell. Gapan helped you by finding it."

Redpath's eyelids half lowered, concealing the fierce intelligence in her green eyes.

"I've had plenty of time to think about the Ruby Surprise," Laurel said. "Someone had to be helping Dad on the Russian side. Someone who—"

"Why?" Redpath interrupted swiftly.

"What?"

"Why do you say that your father had a Russian partner?"

"The second ruby."

Redpath waited, silently pressing Laurel to continue.

"The ruby that Dad substituted in the egg when he made me leave my workshop in Cambria. The ruby that fooled the lethal Ms. Toth. The ruby that looked, felt, measured, and weighed exactly the same as the first one."

Redpath's eyelids lowered a fraction more. The green that remained was intense, almost incandescent. "How do you know that?"

"Easy. Dad isn't stupid. He wouldn't substitute trash that could be discovered by anyone with eyes, calipers, and a scale."

Saying nothing, Redpath waited again.

Laurel could have kept silent, but she didn't care anymore. All that mattered was getting out of Karroo as soon as possible.

"It follows that the substitution was planned in advance, by someone with access to the Ruby Surprise," Laurel said. "That means either Gapan or Novikov. Given Novikov's actions, I suspect that Gapan is the one who hired Dad to steal the egg in such a way as not to lead back to Gapan and his supporters in the government."

"Impressive," Redpath said, looking at Laurel directly.

Laurel shrugged. "I had a lot of time to think about it."

What she didn't say was that it had been easier to play with the pieces of the puzzle called the Ruby Surprise than with the jagged pieces of a closer, much more personal puzzle called Cruz Rowan.

"Is there more?" Redpath asked.

"Sure. The tricky part was in figuring out what the ruby really was."

Stillness gathered around Redpath.

"Shall I go on?" Laurel offered coolly.

"Please do," the ambassador said.

And meant it.

"Despite what Cruz said about people killing people for no reason at all," Laurel said, "governments are motivated, and power is their goal. In modern societies, information is power. That's what espionage is all about."

Laurel waited, searching Redpath's face for some sign of agreement or disagreement. There was nothing in the ambassador's expression but intense interest.

"So I thought about that for a while longer," Laurel said. "Then I remembered some articles I'd read years ago, about lasers and synthetic gems and the possibility of information storage in crystal lattices. Information retrieved by a beam of focused light, just like in your garden-variety CD player."

Again Laurel paused, searching for some sign that Redpath agreed or disagreed with the speculations.

There was no sign of anything either way.

"But instead of a very, very thin film used for information storage, like on a CD," Laurel said, "a ruby has three dimensions. It's one of Mother Nature's very own crystal lattices.

The amount of material that could be stored is staggering, like carrying the Library of Congress around in your hip pocket. If the information happened to be state secrets—military, technical, espionage, that sort of thing—you'd have something worth killing for. Wouldn't you, Ambassador?"

"Indeed you would."

Laurel waited.

Redpath had had a lifetime of practice at outwaiting, and outwitting, negotiators.

"If your group was out of power at the moment, but not necessarily out of the fight," Laurel said, "control of such files might be particularly valuable."

Redpath made a neutral noise.

"So . . ." Laurel hesitated, then shrugged. "So I decided that the Russian old guard probably swiped the files and tried to turn them into money and/or influence. The new guard wanted them back but didn't have enough power to just walk in and take them."

Redpath managed to look interested and uninterested at the same time. It was the diplomatic version of a poker face.

"In fact," Laurel said, "I'll bet the new guard didn't even know what the Ruby Surprise really was before the egg was fabricated and sent out of the country with the rest of 'The Splendors of Russia' exhibit."

"And what is the Ruby Surprise, really?" Redpath asked softly.

"The most beautiful information storage and retrieval system ever made by man."

A long silence followed Laurel's words.

"I begin to think I hired the wrong Swann," Redpath said finally. "Did your father teach you this kind of analysis?"

"No. It's rather like designing a piece of jewelry. One

central gem and a host of fascinating possibilities. You study it. Live with it. Dream with it. Then, one day, patterns emerge and it all falls into place."

"Is that why you turned away from Cruz? The pattern displeased you?"

"Is that what he said?"

"Cruz has said nothing at all."

"What a coincidence," Laurel said sardonically. "That's what he said to me at the emergency room. Not one damn thing. I was talking to the doctor about Dad, I looked around to ask Cruz a question, and all I saw were strangers. Cruz was gone."

"Perhaps he thought you'd blame him for what happened to your father."

"Not likely. Cruz knew I loved him. I suppose he was trying to be kind. A clean, quick cut and all that."

"I think you're missing the pattern."

"I don't." Laurel stood up. "Goodbye, Ambassador. Thanks for satisfying my curiosity."

"Won't you at least stay for dinner?"

"No. Being here reminds me that I can't compete with the bitch goddess adrenaline for a man's loyalty, much less his love." Swiftly Laurel turned away.

And slammed right into Cruz Rowan.

She made a shocked sound as he grabbed her, setting her back on her feet.

"Perhaps now you'll believe me," Redpath said acidly to Cruz, "rather than digging your grave in that damned slot canyon."

With a crisp, almost military stride the ambassador walked around her desk.

"If either of you tries to leave the office in the next thirty minutes," Redpath said, "the sergeant-major will throw you bodily back in here. With great relish, I might add. Gillie is as heartily sick of Cruz's noble mulishness as I am. Now, children, *negotiate*."

The door shut quite forcefully behind her.

58

Karroo
Thursday afternoon

Cruz's eyes never left Laurel's face. She was too pale, her mouth was too drawn, her pulse beat visibly in her temple, and her eyes—her eyes looked like his, too many memories cutting at her until she bled.

"Laurel, I never meant to hurt you. That's the last thing I wanted. That's why I left you."

She closed her eyes, shutting him out.

But nothing she did could shut out the feel of his hands on her arms, the strength of him, the warmth.

"Let go of me," she said hoarsely.

"No."

Her eyes opened, shocked.

Cruz's smile was so sad it made her heart turn over.

"I can't," he said simply. "I tried, God knows I tried. I thought it would be best for you."

"Why?"

"I don't know what love is. I've never loved a woman. I didn't even know if I could. I still don't know. All I do know is I keep seeing you out of the corner of my eye, hearing your voice behind me, and my heart hammers and I turn around and you aren't there and . . ."

His voice frayed into silence. His fingers were wrapped too tightly around her arms but he couldn't let go.

She didn't care. She was looking in his brilliant, shadowed eyes and seeing herself.

"I turn around and you aren't there," he said huskily, "and I discover all over again how much I miss you. I thought I'd get used to it. But each time is like the first time, except that it hurts more. Is it that way for you?"

"Yes," she whispered.

"I can't look at water without remembering the canyon pool and feeling you like fire in my body. I can't lick my lips without tasting you. I can't close my eyes without seeing you give yourself to me. I can't breathe without hearing your breath close to me, broken with passion, calling my name. Is it that way for you?"

"Yes."

"The nights are the worst," Cruz said raggedly. "Just as I fall asleep, I feel the warm weight of your body curled next to mine, feel the softness of your breath against my skin, feel a kind of peace that I found only with you. Then I wake up."

He closed his eyes and fought for control.

She breathed his name and lifted trembling hands to his face. Her fingers traced his eyebrows, his nose, his mouth, the strong line of his jaw, the glistening darkness of his eyelashes.

A tremor went through his strong body.

"Laurel?"

"Yes," she said huskily. "It's that way for me too. As painful as it is beautiful. It's called love."

His eyes opened, brilliant with emotion. He started to

speak, couldn't, and simply pulled her close, burying his face in her hair, holding on to her like she was life itself.

She held on to him the same way.

After half an hour by the clock, the sergeant-major walked away from the office door, whistling softly. He found Cassandra Redpath sitting beneath the ramada's lacy shade, looking out over the desert.

"Well?" she asked.

"There will be four for dinner, mum."

Ready for more heart-stopping suspense from
New York Times **bestselling author**
ELIZABETH LOWELL?

**Turn the page for a sample
of her latest masterwork,**

THE WRONG HOSTAGE
A William Morrow Hardcover

Grace Silva, one of the most respected judges on the federal bench believes in the rule of law.

Joe Faroe has been through the political meat grinder. It cost him his career, his freedom, and a woman who still haunts him. Since then, Faroe has worked outside the rules as a kidnap specialist for St. Kilda Consulting.

When Grace comes to him, Faroe is out of the business. Retired. He's through trying to save a world that doesn't want to be saved. Past and present collide, and Faroe finds himself sucked back into the shadows, tracking a violent killer who holds the life of Grace's son in his bloody hands . . .

North of Ensenada, Mexico
August
Saturday morning

Lane Franklin told himself that he shouldn't freak out.

Most fifteen-year-olds would be high-fiving all over the place if they got to spend the summer in Ensenada. Beaches, bims, beer. Life didn't get any better.

Not that All Saints School was exactly in Ensenada's fast lane. Despite the sultry summer heat, no girls wearing butt-floss bikinis were shaking it on the school's beautiful, very private beach. But his cottage was first class and the soccer field was awesome, and with the window open he could hear the surf that broke on the western edge of the campus.

With its scattered four-bedroom cottages, apartments for teachers, dorms for less wealthy students, and a small library/recreation center, All Saints looked like a high-end resort.

It wasn't.

It was a church school where spoiled kids learned how to take orders, how to sit up straight, how to study, and how to be respectful.

Booorrrring.

I had it coming. What I did was a crime.

Even if it didn't seem like it at the time.

Just a little finger time with his nifty new computer and his F's turned into B's in the school's central computer. Too bad he got caught, and way too bad that his father suddenly decided he'd hang around long enough to see Lane registered in a more structured international boarding school.

At least they hadn't caught him when he'd hacked into a military computer, or that bank, and five or six other sacred cows. Once he got inside, he hadn't done anything except enjoy getting away with it.

Then he'd had the bright idea of changing his grades so his mother wouldn't be upset at a row of D's and F's.

Everything's okay.

I've done six months. I can do two more.

So what if his roommates had all moved out three weeks ago. He liked the silence and he didn't have to hide his computer.

So what if the school had enrolled some thugs to play soccer a few weeks ago. So what if the guys looked more like twenty-six than sixteen. So what if they targeted him every time he was on the field. He was quicker and a whole lot smarter than they were.

Lane looked at his watch. Soccer practice would begin in a few hours. Until then he'd do homework. Afterward he'd play games on the computer his mother had smuggled past the school's tight-assed headmaster a few weeks ago.

He still didn't know why they said he couldn't have access to a computer. He hadn't done anything wrong, but suddenly he didn't have phone privileges and couldn't use the library computer. All he could do was write letters.

Like snail mail isn't really lame.

At least Lane didn't have to worry about anyone discovering the forbidden computer. Each student cleaned his own quarters and his own clothes and some even did dishes for the whole school.

It would have been awesome to have an Internet connection, but short of breaking into the school offices . . .

Don't even think about it.

Don't give Dad another chance to push Mom into keeping me here. I haven't had a single black mark in four months.

After his roommates left, he didn't have friends to talk to, but that was okay. He was used to being alone. When he'd first come to All Saints, the only Spanish he'd known had gotten him black marks for saying it aloud. Some of the kids spoke English, some spoke Chinese or Japanese or French, but most spoke Spanish with various geographical accents he was beginning to be able to separate. He'd always been good with languages, but they bored him.

Now that he had a good reason to learn one, he was a whole lot more fluent than anyone guessed. But none of what he overheard made him feel better.

The last three weeks had really sucked. His telephone didn't work. When he asked for someone to fix it, nothing happened. When he asked one of his teachers if he could use hers to call home, she backed away like he'd suggested sex on the desk.

That was the day the two badasses swaggered onto the soccer field and stared at him, silently telling him that he was number one on their hit list.

Something had happened three weeks ago.

Lane didn't know what it was, he didn't know what had caused it. All he knew was that he'd gone from being a student to something else.

Something that felt like a prisoner.

So what? I've held my own with those two pendejos *for twenty-one days. I'm nailing my classes. My room is always clean and neat. The teachers like me.*

Or they did until three weeks ago.

When Mom comes to visit, I'll just casually ask her if Dad has changed his mind and maybe I could come home for a week. Or a few days.

Even one day.

Just a few hours.

Because once I'm across that border, I'm never coming back. I'll live on the streets if I have to.

Lane listened to the relentless surf and told himself that the waves weren't whispering, *prisoner ... prisoner ... prisoner ...*

But even that hissing chant was better than remembering the voices of the two thugs as they tripped him, elbowed him, kicked him: *You're ours*, pato. *You're dead meat. We're going to sneak into your room, cut off your balls, and make you eat them.*

Lane shut out the sound of the surf and the voices in his memory.

I'm not a prisoner.

I'm not scared.

Southern California
La Jolla
Saturday morning

The phone rang four times before Judge Grace Silva pulled her head out of the legal documents she was reviewing.

Maybe it's Ted.

Finally.

It had been years since she'd cared about her husband—newly ex-husband—in any way but as the father of her child. And if there was a persistent personal sadness that she'd failed in marriage, well, she'd just have to live with it. She'd worked hard to make the divorce and all the legalities entailed as civilized and adult as possible.

For Lane.

But she was real tired of getting calls at all times of the day and night asking for Theodore Franklin. Just because he'd kept his legal address as the beach home they'd once shared didn't mean he actually lived with her.

"Hello," Grace said.

"Ah, *señora*," said a man's voice. "This is Carlos Calderón. I would like to speak to your husband."

Grace didn't bother to point out that Franklin was her ex. If Calderón wasn't close enough to Ted to know about the divorce, she had no reason to announce it.

"Ted isn't here," she said briskly. *And he hasn't been here in three weeks, which you damn well should know because you or one of your employees has called every day.* "Have you tried his Wilshire office, his cell phone, and his Malibu condo?" *Or his bimbo mistress?*

"*Sí*, yes, many times."

"Is it something I can help you with?"

Grace expected the same answer she'd gotten for the past three weeks—a polite thanks but no thanks.

Instead Calderón sighed and said, "Judge Silva, I am afraid you must come to Ensenada immediately."

Her hand tightened on the phone. As a judge, she was accustomed to giving rather than taking orders. "Excuse me?"

"It is your son, Lane."

"What's wrong?" she asked quickly. "Is he in trouble? He's been so good for the—"

"It is not something to be discussed over the telephone. I will see you in two hours."

"What's wrong?" she demanded.

"Good-bye, Judge Silva."

"Wait," she said. "Give me four hours. I don't know what traffic will be like at the border."

"Three hours."

The phone went dead.